LOST ANGEL OF
PARIS

LOST ANGEL OF PARIS

Dr Dmis

Contents

CHAPTER 1

Distant Shores

The sky is grey, with fast-moving clouds and squalls of driving sleet and rain stinging the faces and hands of anyone foolish enough to be outside. For the small French port of Saint-Suliac, life has been held at a near standstill as a terrible storm has gripped it under siege for days. Fishing boats and merchant schooners alike have been held out at sea, forced to ride out the storm as best they can for fear of being beached or smashed on the rocks as they try to enter the safety of its estuary where La Rance river meets the Channel.

The port is famed for its tidal mills and winding streets that zigzag between the blue granite houses, but on a day like today, the roads and mills are empty, and only the foolhardy or desperate dare venture out in such conditions.

In the last café still open, a young lady sits at the counter with her head on her hands and a forlorn look on her face. She has only a few customers brave enough to venture out in this awful weather. But she knows them all well and will not close up shop until they have had their fill of food and drink. For once they have gone, she will be all alone for another night.

She is saddened by the storm as it reminds her of a past event that robbed her of a man that could have been 'The One'. Now looking down at the black coffee in front of her, she begins to stir it with a small narrow silver spoon. Creating a dark, ripped vortex as she stares into its depths.

Her mind goes back to a time when she would smile more, as a young man from the village had caught her eye as well as her heart. He would leave her flowers that she would find in places her uncles would not see. Like the spout of the water pump or in a delivery of fruit and vegetables. How he managed to do it, she did not know, but it went on for some weeks and it had made her feel very special.

However, despite all his best efforts, whenever he asked her on a date, she would politely find an excuse not to go with him. For she carries a secret. A deep and formidable secret. So dangerous that, should it be known by the wrong kind of person, it could cost her her freedom. If not her life.

As with many men, the constant refusals to associate with him took its toll, and one night he took to a bar to drown his disappointment as yet another attempt to take her out for the evening had been kindly deferred.

The more he drank, the more his will and resolve weakened until after a few hours he was quite intoxicated.

Little did he know that that night, he was the one being hunted. For a known working girl – with little on offer by way of sailors and travellers due to the lack of ships in the port – had been watching him. Watching and waiting for the right moment to make her move and earn a few coins.

With the timing about right, she got up and made her way to the bar beside him to strike up a conversation. Soon she was sharing a drink with the young man, listening to his bold words as she smiled and laughed at all he had to say. It did not take her long to guide him to a quieter table where she began stroking his arm and thigh while dropping suggestive comments. Expert in her ways, she became just too tempting, and he willingly followed this girl to her lair for a cheap night of pleasure.

The following day he woke, still in a daze and heavily hungover. He looked around at the unfamiliar surroundings, then down at the woman asleep on his chest. The sight of her brought back flashing memories of the night before and his heart sank as he recognised this well-known woman. Realising what a terrible mistake he had made, he immediately jumped up to leave, waking her in the process. The argument that ensued made the woman bitter and jealous, as he talked only of the woman he betrayed and not of his night with her. His swift exit without any thought for her emotions left her feeling cheap and worthless. More so as for the first time in her life, she liked this young man and his innocent ways more than a woman in her line of work should.

As with the saying of 'a woman scorned', she did not take it lightly that he upped and left in such a hurry without even paying his dues or showing her the right affection. She wasted no time in heading for the café and confronting the man's sweetheart. She let her know what he had done and where her man had been the night before.

Later that day, the young man arrived at the café. Riddled with guilt and ashamed of his actions, he held flowers as a gift and tried to explain what happened and begged her forgiveness. But the magic and passion that once filled her heart had already gone. She was done with him. It was over. For the young man the shame and guilt hit hard, along with the looks of disdain from the people who lived in the village. For now, he was just a notch on a known woman's belt.

The loss of the one he'd had his heart set on became too much to bear – more so as she would not even look at him. While her uncles would tear him apart should he try to approach the café again to make amends.

With nothing but rejection from her and the breaking of his heart every time he saw her from a distance, he decided it was best to leave the village and start afresh, signing up to crew the first ship that would take him away from the port.

It was not but a month later that reports filtered through from the sailors arriving in port that the ship he was on had gone down in rough seas with all hands lost. The news devastated her, for it could have been something special. She was saddened by all this loss and unhappiness without ever having the chance of being happy and sharing time with the young man in the first place.

She made a promise to herself on that very spot that if a man ever came into her life again, a good man who would stand up for her and show her respect and provide the attention she so desperately desired, she would not let him go again so easy. She'd throw caution to the wind and take a chance, hoping that the dark side of her past would not catch up with her.

Despite the deep love and protection of her uncles, she would take life by the horns and fight to get the happiness she so craved and felt entitled to. No looking back, no digging and asking about their pasts, just living from that moment forward.

Who knew, perhaps if they were strong enough to take on her uncles and still be standing, they may even accept him. And maybe he would stay with her for the rest of her life.

The young lady hears her name being called out; it wakes her from her daydream about the past. As she sits up and looks around the room, she notices the husband of the old couple by the fire waving his glass in the air. With a smile and a nod, she picks up a bottle and goes to fill their glasses, then pokes at the fire and adds another log to its embers. 'That should keep you warm,' she comments in French as the couple thank her for her kindness.

* * *

A mile out from the port in the grip of the storm, a small schooner chances a slight break in the weather to try to get to shore. It has been stuck outside the sea wall and coastal defences for three days and is far away from its destination some distance up the coast. It had adjusted course in anticipation of holding up in the sheltered port of Saint-Suliac until the storm had blown over, only to be unable to enter the narrow entrance due to the ferocity of the weather. Until now, it has just about been able to hold its own, battling against the huge waves and deep plummeting swells. But its resistance is starting to wear thin as the ship's exhausted crew has been working around the clock just to keep her upright and afloat and are near breaking point. While all the passengers that have been stuck below deck are sick to the gills and desperate for the safety of land, even if it is not their intended destination. The stench from people being sick runs throughout the cabins below deck, making all the passengers feel worse and unable to take much more.

Supplies of fresh water and food are now running low, and the crew's strength is down to its last reserves as the storm continues to rage in anger. At times she has been so violent that the ship has been thrown around like a rag doll. One minute up, the next down, pitching forwards then backwards as its crew try to keep her facing the waves to keep stable. Even the hardiest of the men are becoming seasick from the intensity of the ship's motion and the waves crashing against the hull and deck. While the spray of saltwater stings the eyes and rips into the faces of all those unfortunate to be assigned to the main deck.

Ropes have been tied around the periphery of the boat in an attempt to catch any fallen comrades that may slip and otherwise be washed into the sea and lost to Davy Jones's locker. For there is a real fear for life aboard this stricken vessel that not all will survive the encounter.

In a last-ditch attempt to get to safety, they have been cutting and turning against the wind and tide for hours, to get above the entrance to the estuary. Now, at last, the ship is in its best position to run to safety inside the sea walls that protect the small harbour.

The ship, La Paradis, turns across the gale-force winds one last time in preparation of her final bid for safety. Using just one medium square-cut sail on the front mast, she holds position across the wind to get past the breakwaters. It's a risk using only one sail, but the advantage is that her speed can be cut faster once she is inside the inner walls of the harbour, where there is not much room for a ship of her size to manoeuvre or slow down.

This is a one-shot deal, but with the wooden ship now at breaking point and every plank in her build creaking and flexing under the pressure of the storm, they have no choice. The relentless crashing of waves against the sides of her hull has started to break her at the seals and she is taking on water faster than the men below can remove it with the bilge pumps.

Under the captain's orders, the crew position themselves in readiness to take their chances and turn the rudder. For once committed, there is no going back. This will have to be completed at the first attempt as failure would see the ship smashed against the rocks, resulting in death to most, if not all on board. The captain spins the wheel to steer the boat into the wind and as it hits the breakwater, the ship turns and judders violently. Twisting and repositioning as the swell pushes her up while trying to rotate the hull side on to the driving wind. The crew yell and scream instructions to each other over the deafening noise of the storm and ride the waves sidewards for a while as they try to straighten her up. Listing heavily to port under the pressure of the wind, they hold high on the crest of the tallest wave before being slammed down on the other side. The ship jars back and rotates ninety degrees in a matter of seconds. Three of them now hold fast on the wheel as they try to turn the ship back on course using the huge rudder to offset the tow of the waves and driving wind. The hull and mast creak and groan heavily as they push the ship to the limits of her abilities and a little beyond. The sound of splintering wood can be heard as the vessel reaches her limits and begins to buckle under the strain.

With one last heave from the crew, the ship starts to right herself and straightens back up to face in the right direction. 'Hold it for a little longer,' shouts the captain to his struggling crew. 'Hold it, hold it, hold it, now turn hard to starboard.' He watches every part of the ship, and what landmarks he can see on land to get his bearings and best position the vessel as it lunges forward towards the port entrance.

'Faster, men. Put your backs into it and cut down that sail,' he yells as his crew fight to reduce speed as fast as possible. Two of the crewmen are hitting the sail ropes with axes at the same time and both ropes are severed with the second strike, allowing the sail to come crashing to the ground while still trailing part of the cut rope.

'Hard to port,' the captain yells as the three men struggle at the wheel. 'Hard to port,' he yells again to his men as he joins them in a frantic attempt to turn the ship. 'Pull, men, pull. Or we will ram the quayside,' he bellows out to his crew. The four of them begin to make some ground and the wheel turns faster and faster. As the ship turns, it starts to lose some of its momentum and the captain leaves the wheel to look over the side. 'Drop the starboard anchor,' he shouts. Within seconds, the anchor rope is running out at speed until it hits the seabed, then the pace of the rope pulling through the spool slows slightly.

'Lock off the anchor rope and hold, men.' Instantly, wooden pegs are pushed into slots in the spool and the deck of the ship, allowing a brass ratchet to be released and grip the metal cog round the outside of the spool. The rope stops running out as it locks up tight to the spindle. For a few moments the anchor drags the seabed before bouncing over small boulders and debris. Finally, it grips on to the bedrock, digging in hard and pulling the bow of the ship down heavily before inertia takes over and pulls the stern of the ship around.

A small rowboat that has been washed away from its moorings feels the full force of the starboard side of the schooner as it is smashes into pieces on impact. It pushes against the side of the ship and causes drag, helping to reduce the velocity of the vessel as she continues to turn until reaching a full one-hundred-and-eighty-degree rotation.

The anchor's mighty coconut-matt rope creaks under the constant and growing pressure, pulling the ship down deeper, and allowing water to wash across the front of the bow.

The rope being wet helps it to take more of the stretch and force being exerted, but even that cannot stop the inevitable. The woven strands start to snap and unwind, each time allowing just a little more give in the rope until finally the ship starts to lift back up from the depths and the pressure on the rope slackens off. La Paradis has taken the worst that the sea has to offer and survived the encounter. The crew cheers. Some smile and laugh with their shipmates while others look to the heavens as if to thank God for their salvation. A few just drop to their knees with exhaustion, relieved the ordeal is finally over.

The passengers and all on board have been saved by the skill and daring of the captain, who executed an audacious move that will not be found in any textbook of good seamanship. He has adapted to the conditions and improvised to save his vessel and all hands aboard her. Now, in the calmer waters of the sheltered port, he can relax a little and take time to reflect on his achievement. Taking off his cap, he wipes his brow and allows himself a small grin as he comments quietly to himself, 'You've still got it, me boy. Oh yes, that's one for the logbook alright.'

The crew are still celebrating such a challenging move that may well have saved their lives. They catch their breath as they look round at each other, then at their captain, who stands proud at the wheel of his ship. He is a hero to many who stand before him, for he did not falter in his duty and kept his crew together in their time of need.

He clears his throat, then speaks to his men. 'Now then, lads, let's clear away that broken sail and get us alongside the dock.' He turns to look at one of his crew. 'Bosun's mate, cut that anchor line, for I fear it will be wedged too tight in the rocks to get it out tonight. Tie a marker barrel to the line and we will retrieve it once the storm has subsided. Now the rest of you get moving – there is still a lot to do to get us safely moored up.' The captain organises his men to make safe the ship and clear away the debris as best they can in such formidable weather.

It takes the best part of another hour to free the ship from its anchor line, then skilfully turn and position her on the side of the jetty as far away from rough water as the depth of port and draught of the ship will allow. They tie up her mooring lines and lower what is left of a storm-damaged gantry to the solid ground. Even then, a few planks have to be nailed down, and side ropes replaced to hold the footbridge together. A crew member runs down the bridge and, using a small piece of rope, ties the end of it to a hooking point on the jetty to hold its position and steady its movement.

The captain stands proud on his ship by the top of the footbridge as his relieved and worse-for-wear passengers disembark the storm-battered schooner. One by one, the people walk past him and down the bridge, most too weak or sick to even look up let alone thank the man for saving their lives.

As they step onto land for the first time in a while, several start to walk towards the village while others try to find a place out of the rain to sit and rest up. Most cannot yet progress in a straight line as their balance is still with the motion of the ship. Some are more affected than others as they move as if intoxicated by alcohol, staggering and weaving in different directions. For most this feeling will go away in an hour or so. For others it may take a few days. One thing they all have in common is that they are lucky to be alive.

As the last person reaches the gantry, he stops, drops his shoulder sack and bag then turns to the captain to shake his hand. 'That be some fine seamanship by you, Captain. If it was not for that move to get us into port, they would be picking us up from the beaches come tomorrow. For I think this ship of yours was at breaking point and taking on too much water to last another night in that storm.'

The captain nods. 'You may well be right, but I feel this old girl has plenty of life left in her old bones yet. Though I dare say she be needing a fair bit of repair work for the next few days or more.' He looks at the heavily tattooed man. 'You do not seem any worse for wear, considering the storm we have just been through. Unlike them there people up yonder, some of which can barely stand up let alone walk a straight line.'

The man gives a wry smile. 'I've been through worse in some tropical storms, though none were as bad as going around Cape Horn off the coast of Africa. We hit a mean patch there that shook the gold fillings out of your teeth if you had them.'

The captain takes a pipe out of his waistcoat pocket and taps it on the handrail, then pulls out his watch fob, opens a small penknife and scrapes out the tobacco residue. Tapping it again to clear out the debris, he then blows and draws on it to ensure air flows through it correctly. Now in good working order, he refills it with fresh tobacco from a pouch. 'Aye, that be some mean water out there if a storm be brewing. Whaler is thee?' he asks. 'For that is a long way out for a common sailor to be.'

'Was thrown on me, you could say. Killed enough of those big beasties and seen more than my share of friends lost to them. Just feel I've done my time for now and need to do a bit of looking on land for a while.'

The captain lights his pipe and draws a few puffs to get it going. 'I will be here for a week or two, unloading the spoilt cargo and repairing the storm damage to the hull and sails. If your looking-time finishes and I am still here, I could always use another experienced hand on the decks. Cargo and passengers only, no whaling involved, I swear down. For I think the owners want to send us to the islands next run, taking out a new governor and his family to some island area run by the East India Trade Company. I intend to return from it full of spices and rum to sell, make a little extra for me and the crew. Your knowledge of the area and understanding of weather changes could be of use to me, not to mention advice in case we run into pirates or native savages.'

'The islands, you say?' The man thinks for a while. 'I may take you up on that offer if you are still here on my return.'

The captain holds out his hand. 'Well, good luck to you. I hope you find what you are looking for and, with chance on my side, I will see you again before we leave. By the way, if I do see you again, what name do you go by, as it would be more courteous to call you by name should we meet.'

The man looks him in the eyes as he shakes his hand. 'My name is James, and with luck we will see each other again, if not here, on the sea somewhere.'

James picks up his shoulder bag and sack and walks down the gantry. He has only one thing on his mind for now, and that is how to get to Paris. The ship being blown off course has left him with a distance of around two hundred miles to his destination. And now, after finding out that there may be a way back to the islands in a few weeks, he needs to find some way of getting there fast.

As he steps onto firm land for the first time in a month, he looks round to take in his surroundings. The rain is falling at a greater intensity as a huge lightning bolt shoots across the sky above, closely followed by an enormous crack of thunder. He decides it is better to take refuge in the village, with luck find an open bar or café and shelter for the night. With very little of the

French language known to him, James will need to rely on his wits and ability to adapt to what befalls him to get through the coming weeks. For it will be a challenge to get where he is going and even harder communicating with people to find out about his sisters. Especially as he is English and relations between the two countries are somewhat frosty in current times. However, this will not deter him from trying, for he is on a personal quest and getting to Paris and what he finds there will determine his next course of action.

James makes his way through the port, looking for signs of activity. Most of the shops and taverns are closed, but on the edge of a side street, he can see light glowing through the windows of a building. Above the doorway is a sign depicting three bottles of wine and a glass. It looks like some kind of small local bar and as he tries the door, it opens. On entering the room, everybody inside stops speaking and looks at him. This is nothing new to James. His visible neck and facial tattoos stand out like a sore thumb and his thick physical build even when clothed is an intimidating sight to people who do not know him.

He nods at a few people who are still staring at him and then walks up to the counter. Placing his bags on the floor, he wraps a string round the top of them and loops it to his wrist – a trick picked up on his travels to ensure it is harder for anyone sly of hand to steal his belongings. He sits down on a wooden stool and looks at what is on offer. There are hundreds of bottles of wine stacked horizontally in front of him and to the sides. Above and to the right, legs of cured pork and dry-cured sausages the length and thickness of a man's forearm hang from the ceiling in rows. The smell of pipe tobacco fills the air and a fire in the background crackles as a French maiden throws two new logs on top of the fading embers.

She is aware of James and once finished with the fire, she walks back to the counter to serve him. As she approaches, she speaks to him in French and continues talking as she rounds the counter, then stops in front of him as if waiting for an answer.

Not wanting to seem ignorant, he points at the bottles of wine behind her. She turns, looks at what he is pointing at then looks back and speaks some more. With James not replying, she puts one hand over the other and raises and lowers the top hand. James cottons on and moves his hands wide apart to indicate a large drink. The girl takes a bottle from the rack, uncorks it and pours some into a glass, then places both the bottle and glass in front of him.

He then points at the hanging meats, and the girl starts to talk in French again.

James shrugs, as frustration gets the better of him. 'I'm sorry, I do not understand you.'

The girl stares at him for a minute, then in a heavy French accent, she speaks. 'It is about time you spoke; I was beginning to think you were ze mute.'

James lets out a sigh of relief. 'You speak English.'

She laughs. 'But of course, we speak many languages in the cafés around our ports. Including English, as none of you ever seem to be able to speak our language.'

The relief is evident on James's face. 'Well, while you are understanding me, I would like some food and a room for the night. Also, I need directions to Paris. Even better would be transport to get there, if it is available.'

'Ha, I will get you some food first. The others are not so easy with a storm here. I have fish or coq au vin. How do you say it in English, um, chicken stew!'

'Chicken stew would be good. I'll be damned if I want anything from the sea, especially after what I have just been through to get to land.'

The girl laughs again. 'I will be back shortly with your food.'

James watches as she opens two more bottles of wine and walks around the bar. She puts a bottle down on two different tables and talks briefly to each couple before walking off into an adjacent room. A few minutes later she appears carrying a chunk of French stick, a bowl of stew and a spoon. As she reaches James, she places the items down in front of him. 'Be careful, ze stew is 'ot and will need to cool a little.'

James takes a spoonful of the stew and puts it into his mouth.

Sure enough it is hot, and he grabs for the wine and drinks heavily then coughs and splutters as the hot food goes down his throat.

'I told you ze food is 'ot. You have been out in the cold weather. So 'ot food will seem even more so as your body is colder!'

'That you did, and I was a fool not to listen to you,' he comments, drinking some more wine.

'You like the wine! Is it good to you, yes?'

'Well, to be honest the tannins are rough, and it is not a great taste, but it is better than no wine at all.'

'Oh! You know a little about wine then, yes?'

James looks at her and smiles. 'Enough to know a good wine from a bad one, yes! You see, I once lived a more privileged lifestyle in England. The tattoos and tribal markings you see on me now are from a new life started far from here.' He pauses for a minute as he thinks, then sighs before continuing. 'But that was a very long time ago. Since then, many things have changed for me.'

She picks up another bottle of wine that has already been opened, takes out the cork and pours him a fresh glass, again leaving the glass and bottle on the table.

'Most of ze sailors who come in here know nothing about wine. They just want to get drunk, so we serve them that, um, shit, but as you may know a bit about wine, try this – it is much better!'

James takes the glass, salutes the girl and takes a drink. 'Now that IS a better wine, a lot smoother and no bitter aftertaste.'

She smiles at him. 'Zat is from my uncle's vineyards some way from here in the Rhone valley. He is well known for his good wine. It is the talk of the region where it is produced.'

James ponders her words for a moment. 'So why does he have a café this far away?'

'Because it is a port, silly. From here he can send his wine anywhere he chooses, to get a better price, and you English pay well for good wine in your country.'

James laughs. 'Your uncle seems a wise man. I would like to meet him and talk about wine with him.'

'Alas, zat will not be possible. With the storm here he left days ago with his brothers to oversee the vines and ensure the grapes are being checked. They are his life, so I am afraid you only have me. But you are lucky, as 'e does not speak English very well and likes you even less.'

James smiles at her. 'Then I would say that I have got the better end of the deal as your company is well appreciated.'

'Ah you are too kind, sir.' She laughs, flicks at his shoulder with her hand, then turns to assist another person requiring her attention, leaving James to finish his stew in peace.

The food has cooled a little but is still very hot and he takes his time with his meal, dunking pieces of the bread in the juice to help cool each mouthful. As he eats, he watches the young girl as she moves from table to table with a smile and presence about her that makes everyone she meets feel good and smile back.

For the first time in years, he realises how much he has missed the company of an educated woman, someone who has the ability to question and has an opinion of their own to talk about. His tribal wife on the islands is a far more beautiful woman, but it was easy for him as he was white and from another part of the world. To her and the tribe he lived with, James was revered, as he was a focal point of the village due to his differences. A trophy to show off to other tribes, because of the colour of his skin and being from another land. He had knowledge of things they had never seen and could improve their standard of life, as they had not seen things like pistols, matches, written languages, ink and basic engineering and had no understanding of wounds and infections as well as how to survive them better.

He had stories from faraway lands, knowledge of making a still to produce alcohol. Even evaporating salt from seawater to preserve fish instead of just drying or smoking was a new idea that gave another method for preserving food.

On the other hand, tribal families support each other and have strong family bonds, helping each other without prejudice or payment in coin. They have no understanding of greed and corruption, no need for gold or great wealth. They live by their own means and make their way in life without the need to put on others. Protecting their tribe and way of life fiercely against all who would try and take it from them.

James is one of the few in this world who has seen and lived life from two completely different cultures. He has experienced the finer things in society as well as living with nothing but the bare basics needed to survive in a village community. Now, for the first time, he is emotionally torn between what he had and what he has now, living with a more simple and humble people. His mind is swiftly taken away from his thoughts as the girl arrives back at the bar and taps him on the shoulder.

'I have spoken to all ze people here about a room for the night and I am afraid I could find no place for you. But I did have more luck with getting you to Paris. We have a man – Monsieur Dupont over there.' She points to a man at a table with two others. 'He will be organising supplies from the village to go to Paris three to four days from now, once ze storm has cleared. He would be prepared to let you travel with him and his men. Even give you some basic French words to learn and speak, if you will drive an extra wagon for them.'

James looks round to view the man. He is wearing a flat burgundy cap and has a small brown scarf wrapped around his neck. As he notices James looking at him, he raises his glass. James returns the gesture by raising his own in return, then he turns back to face the girl.

'Thank you for asking around. I appreciate it greatly.' He pauses for a second. 'I have just realised that I do not even know your name.'

'Why it is Emma, Emma Christelle.'

'Well, Emma, thank you for asking around. My name is James, and travelling with them would have been good; however, I would still need to find a place to stay for three or four days. Without that, it will be best to move on and see if I can find a place to stay along the way, for time is against me.'

Emma sighs. 'What is so important that you must go to Paris so quickly? You have only just survived a terrible storm! Is it a woman?'

James looks at her. He has no wish to lie. 'No, it is not a woman.

It is potentially three women, if luck be on my side.'

Her eyes roll up at him and she steps back, a little shocked at his reply. 'Sacré bleu, three women! You are indeed a busy man, monsieur.' Emma turns to look away and steps to one side in an attempt to hide her expression. She has no reason to be upset, she barely knows the man, but for some reason his words have struck a chord with her.

'No, it is not what you think. I am going to Paris to try and find my three lost sisters. They may have been sent there many years ago.'

Emma slowly turns around. 'Three sisters! Why would they have been sent to Paris?'

James looks at her with a saddened expression. 'It is a long story, and I travel there more in hope of finding them still alive than the reality that they are no more.'

'What do you mean still al—'

The front door crashes open and slams against the inner wall of the building, while the accompanying wind and driving rain pull a cold chill into the café. Two of the crew from the ship James was travelling on enter the room. They are dripping wet and shake the water off their coats and hats all over people on the tables close to them.

As the people stand up, letting out words in French to highlight their dissatisfaction at the men's behaviour, they just stare back for a moment, then start to swear and curse back at them in English. After a brief war of words with the patrons, one of the men turns to the other. 'See, I told you I would find us a tavern open somewhere in this port; I's can smell 'em out a mile away.'

He grins, showing his yellow and black teeth to all that look up at him. The other man looks round at the disgruntled people and offers himself for a fight with all who have got up from their tables.

With no desire to fight or continue the confrontation, the customers start to place payment on the tables, put on their coats and begin leaving the café.

Emma speaks up. 'Gentlemen, this is a café, not a tavern. If you would like some wine or food, I can serve you 'ere. But we will not be open long as it is late, and I will be closing soon.'

She can tell immediately that these men are not going to be a very pleasant experience. It is not the first time she has had this type of customer, but it is the first time without her uncles around to keep her safe and maintain order in the café.

The last of the customers in the café have now stood up. Leaving their money on the table, they say their goodbyes to Emma and begin filing out of the door. Most are elderly and they do not want any part of the aggravation that is potentially coming. They know that, without Emma's uncles around to maintain order, this could be a serious problem.

'Cowards, the fucking lot of 'em,' shouts one of the sailors while the other looks across at Emma.

'Lookie lookie, what have we got here then?' he says as he walks up to the counter. 'Two tankards of ale while I look at the view,' he says, staring at her. 'And they said on the ship that we would not like a French tavern. Well, all I can say is I like what I see afore me here.'

Emma is nervous but politely speaks up. 'We do not serve ale here. We serve only wine and coffee.'

The man grins at her. 'Then two wines it is then.'

Emma reaches behind her as she dares not look away from them. She fumbles at the bottles and grabs one, steps forward and places two glasses on the counter, filling them up with wine, then steps back against the far shelf.

One of the men grabs the glass and knocks back its contents, then violently spits it back out over the counter. 'What the hell is this?' He looks at Emma. 'You be trying to poison me, girl.'

'No, no, it is red wine,' she replies swiftly.

The other man has not looked away from her in all this time. 'Be damned with the drink. I want to have fun with this one. Froggy or not, she is the first woman I have seen in weeks, and I wanna piece of 'er.'

Emma starts to tremble. Fear has now gripped her tightly. She feels very vulnerable and alone as she looks back at the two men moving towards her. This would usually be the time that her uncles would deal with the situation, if not sooner. But with them away at the château, Emma is on her own and must fend for herself.

James is a little further down the counter, finishing his food while looking straight ahead. The two men don't even notice him until he slides his finished bowl forward on the counter. Both men instantly turn and look in his direction. 'Time you were going, froggy. We have things to do 'ere and you're not invited.'

One of the men makes a grab for Emma, but she leans back and is just out of reach of his grubby fingertips.

'Come 'ere, my lovely,' he yells at her.

James finally speaks. He does not turn around, nor does he raise his voice. He just talks calmly. 'If I were you, I would leave and find another place to go before something bad happens.'

'Cor blimey, this froggy speaks English,' yells one of the men.

The other pulls a ten-inch knife from his waist belt, holds it out in front of him and wriggles it around as he speaks. 'You better leave before I cut you up.'

James unwraps the string from his wrist to his bag and slowly stands up. His stool falls backwards to the ground as he turns to face his opponents, then looks across to the window before looking back at the two men. At the same time, he shrugs off his overcoat, which falls off his shoulders and lands in a heap on the ground behind him.

His enormous, bare muscular torso and arms are covered in tattoos of whales, mythical sea monsters and other fearsome creatures. Between all the tattoos of animals are tribal symbols and patterns that cover most of his body. Across many are the tell-tale scars and healed wounds from fighting whales and other events in his life. He flexes out his chest, reaches down to his side and unclips a two-and-a-half-foot weapon from his belt. The handle is made from the hilt of a sword and the blade made from a zigzag pattern of a broken harpoon tip. As he raises the weapon, he looks at the two men and points it in their direction.

Their jaws drop down. The man with the knife lowers it and speaks. 'Fuck me, it's him from the ship.'

The other one continues to stare at him. 'Look at the size of him. He be a monster.'

James is enraged at how they have treated Emma. He steps towards the closest man and places his blade under his chin. 'I've killed things bigger than this building in my time. Now which one of you shall I work on first? Who wants me to split open his guts and lay them out for you to look at.'

Emma and James watch as the man with the weapon under his chin soils himself. The amber liquid stains around his groin area, growing larger and larger before running down his leg to a puddle around his boot.

Emma steps forward and folds her arms. The fear she once had is gone and her confidence is restored. 'Ergh, that's nasty.'

The man is now shaking intensely and drops his knife on the floor. 'Please, please. We did not mean any offence. Don't kill us, please,' he cries, quivering in his boots.

The other man starts to whimper, pure fear and dread in his eyes as he looks at the enormous man in front of him.

James thinks for a moment. 'If you were to apologise to the nice lady, perhaps honour could be satisfied without bloodshed. What do you think, Emma?'

Before Emma has a chance to speak, the catch on the café door lifts and the door slowly opens. A man steps inside, takes off his hat and looks up at James and then Emma. 'Brrrahh, that is some mean weather out there tonight.'

It is the captain from the ship, La Paradis. He stares at his two crewmen for a few seconds, looks down at the front of the man who has pissed himself and tuts. 'My, my, that's just nasty,' he comments as he turns to Emma. 'My good lady, one of your patrons came to me and said that you might be having a problem with some of my crew. I came straight here and have been observing from the window for the past few minutes and I wholeheartedly agree that there is indeed a problem here to be addressed. If you would be so kind as to return these men to me, I would be grateful to the sum of this pouch of coin.'

Emma looks at him. 'Do you not think you are asking the wrong person? It is James who has the man on the end of his thing.'

'That may well be the case. However, James saw me standing at the window some time ago. He is a gentleman of honour. On your say so, he will either kill these men or release them to me. If you would be so kind as to hand them over, I promise they will be punished in accordance with the crime.'

Emma looks at James. 'Is this true? You would kill these men if I so wished it?'

James just stares back at her.

'I see, so their fate is in my hands.' She turns to face the two men. 'You are disgusting pigs, but I do not want your blood on my floor as it is difficult to clean up the stains.' She looks back at the captain. 'You can have them. Just take them away. Zey are not worth my time.'

James lowers his weapon as the captain flicks his hand at the window. The door opens swiftly, and his first mate and a group of the crew enter and escort the two men outside.

The captain steps to the bar and places the pouch of coins on the countertop before looking back at Emma. 'This issue never happened if anyone asks. I do not want a bad relationship with this port.' As he turns and walks past James, he pats him on the shoulder and then speaks again. 'Thank you, my friend, I am short of crew as it is.' He puts his cap back on his head and leaves, closing the door quietly behind him.

The café falls silent, empty of all people but James and Emma. Only the sound of the intensifying rain can be heard as a constant drone on the slate roof of the café. The fire is now at a warming amber glow, giving additional light to the room, and there is a warm, comfortable silence between the two of them before Emma looks up at James and speaks.

'Would you have really killed those two men for what they wanted to do to me?' James looks at her but says nothing. He clips his weapon back on his belt, then picks up his overcoat and puts it on. He places a silver coin on the counter and reaches down for his bags.

Turning to leave, he says, 'Thank you for your time and the food. I will be leaving you now.'

Emma steps forward. 'I do not wish you to go, not in such bad weather. I can offer what I have 'ere for tonight and if you choose to go in the morning, then that is your choice. Or for a couple of nights you can remain here and then go to Paris with the supply wagons when they leave.'

James looks at her. 'I am a man you only met an hour ago. What would people say if I stayed here with you on your own?'

She looks blankly at the fire and pauses for a second. 'It is not just for you that I ask, for those men would have done not nice things to me. Now your ship has got into port, others will be in here tomorrow. More men who might be like them, and without my uncles I am a little afraid. But if I close the café, there are old people who come here every day for food. They have nobody and will go 'ungry.' Emma picks up the pouch of coins. 'You can 'ave this to stay a few days as payment for your time, for I will not touch it as it makes me feel sick to think what it is for.'

As she turns to James, he can see from the reflection of the fire on her cheeks that she has tears running down her face. He drops his bag back on the floor, takes the pouch from her hand and throws it back on the counter. 'Use it to buy the food you cook for the elderly.' Instinctively, he puts his arms round her to give her a comforting hug and she willingly takes his embrace and holds him tightly.

'I will stay for a few days, but I do need to go to Paris with the wagons. I must try to find my sisters, or at least find out what happened to them.'

They hold their embrace for several minutes, something James has not done with a woman in a long time, and it is as comforting to him as it is to her. Emma slowly releases him from her grasp, then walks over to the door and slides the bolts across.

James watches as she moves to the fireplace and sweeps all the embers and ash to the back wall of the hearth and moves a fireguard around the front. She looks back at James and smiles before turning down then out all the oil lights one by one. The last one she picks up by its handle and walks back towards him. 'This way, James,' she comments as she walks past him and into a large storage room.

At the back is another room with a medium-sized bed pushed up against the far wall. She puts the oil light down on a dresser top and turns to him. 'I hope you will find this comfortable.' She then turns and leaves, walking back into the darkness of the next room.

James is tired. It's been a long, exhausting few days in the storm. He places his overcoat on the chair, takes off his boots and unclips his belt with the sword, knife and money pouch attached and hangs them off the back of the chair. Then finally he removes his trousers and places them on top of his boots. Lifting up the sheets, he climbs into the bed and settles down into position. As he reaches to turn down the oil light, the ghostly white shadow of a figure can be seen coming from the storeroom. It gets closer and James can make out that it is Emma in a full-length nightgown. She walks over to the oil lamp and blows it out. He feels the sheets rise and Emma slip into the bed beside him. 'This is ze only bed 'ere. It is where I sleep, so we will have to share.'

She turns to face him and puts her arms around his shoulders, encouraging him to put his arms around her. 'I hope you do not mind.' James is surprised at her actions, but the smell of her body and the touch of her hands are quite intoxicating.

'Oh, I think I can live with this,' he says with a half-smile.

'You said that you were going to Paris to find your sisters and that you did not know if zey were alive! How did this come to be?'

'It's a long story.'

'Well, I am here in your arms, and we have all night. I would like to know what would drive a man to cross terrible seas in such a storm and risk walking to Paris through this bad weather to find them.'

James starts to talk to Emma about the murder of his father, mother and youngest siblings by his brother, the new Lord Fitzgerald. He speaks of the loss of all his other brothers out at sea on the whaling ships and the revenge he took out on the captains of those vessels. He explains how he left the whaler he was serving on and what he had done to survive over the years on the islands. The nightmares he suffered, the shaman's words and what the tribal elders had told him he must do to free himself of these evil spirits. He talks about his long journey that ended back in England and the information given to him from his two remaining friends that may lead to where they supposedly sent his sisters.

James even explains that he knows where his brother is now and what he is doing to another village community in England. Stating that, depending on the outcome of his sisters' fates, he will decide what course of action he takes against his brother.

For nearly two hours, Emma listens to every word. For in her mind she is painting a picture of the man in her arms – his loyalty, sense of honour, decency and ability to show compassion and help a stranger. He also has the strength and conviction to stand up and be counted when it is needed and is not afraid to deal out punishment to fit the crime. Perhaps he is even strong enough to handle the secrets Emma carries deep within. She ponders the thought for a while, for it would be a big leap of faith to trust in him.

Finally, she plucks up the courage to speak about her past. 'You do know that the rouge district of Paris is a very bad place and not for the faint of heart.'

James shakes his head. 'I know very little of the place, just that my sisters may have been sent there, and that is all I need to know. As for the danger I may encounter, fear not for me, little one. Fear for them who stand in my way, for I have long since passed from God's good graces and will hold back nothing to find them.'

'Life there is not an easy one to survive. I know as my mother was trapped in its dark and seedy world before I was born. I did not know 'er myself, but it was said she was once a beautiful woman and a great singer. She moved around all the palaces of Europe and performed in ze most famous of buildings for royalty and people of state. Zat is before being taken and being forced to do as the woman who runs La Fleur Blanche demanded.

'I know not who my father was from ze encounter, but I think it was someone important because as his daughter, many men wanted to get their hands on me after my mother's death. If it was not for my mother's brothers rescuing me when she fell ill and died, I too would have been stuck in that world.'

Emma strokes her fingers through James's hair, follows the lines of his tattoo around his nose and down the side of his face with her finger, staring into his eyes. 'I think you are a good man, and if they are alive, you will find zem.' She kisses him gently and passionately on the lips, then, using his lower arm as a pillow, she tucks her back into his chest and pulls his other arm around her, holding his hand with hers upon her chest.

James is left looking at the top of her head. He smiles to himself as he is comfortable with her warm body tucked up into his. *What a woman*, he thinks, as she falls asleep in his arms. He kisses her gently on the back of the head before he too succumbs to his exhaustion and drops off to sleep.

* * *

James wakes to the sun's rays creeping across the floorboards. He feels the bed around him for Emma, but the sheets are cold, and she has long since gone. Sitting up, he stretches out his arms and rolls his neck around to the left and right. The room is well lit, and he walks over to the window to the view outside. The wind is still pushing hard on the tops of the surrounding trees. Looking up, it seems there is only a small area of clear sky peeking through. All around, the dark clouds loom with a presence of more rain and storms to come.

He turns back to the chair to collect his trousers, but they are not there. They have been replaced with another pair of clean trousers of similar size and colour, along with a thick, dark-blue-and-white jumper. Pulling on the trousers, he pulls at the waist to check out the fit and nods to himself. *How do women always seem to get it right first time?* he wonders before clipping his belt back on.

Moving into the store area, James cannot believe how full it is. From floor to ceiling, it is full of crates of wine and brandy bottles, various-sized barrels and dozens of legs of cured pork hanging from the rafters. At the front, closest to the door are wooden boxes filled with fresh fruit and vegetables, along with a rack holding several rabbits and game birds.

To the left is another room that he had not noticed last night.

From inside it, there is a fine sweet smell in the air from meat being flame cooked. Peering inside, he can see Emma turning pieces of what looks like rabbit over an open fire. He watches quietly from the doorway as she turns each piece on the metal grating. As they reach the colour she wants, they are lifted and thrown into a huge black pot. She replaces each piece of rabbit with thick slices of sausage and diced pieces of pork leg. Again, she turns them over and over until she is happy with the colour, then tosses them into the pot. Once all are done, she pulls down on a lever that lifts the grate, then slides the large pot across over the open flame and pours in two bottles of red wine and a large bowl of diced vegetables.

James is curious to see what else is in the pot and approaches quietly behind her. 'Do you like to watch a woman work?' she says without turning round. Placing down the bowl, she looks up at him with a huge smile, then slowly moves towards him and kisses him softly on both cheeks.

'What was that for?'

'That was for not taking advantage of me last night.'

He holds her by her waist with both hands. 'What makes you think I would allow you to take advantage of me in that way? You might not be my type of woman.'

Her eyes widen and her mouth opens. 'Mon cheri, if I was to want you, you would 'ave no choice but to do my bidding.' Instinctively and without thought he leans forward and kisses her gently on the lips. Emma responds and they hold each other in a passionate embrace for several minutes before she steps back. Her beautiful brown eyes dazzle James and her smile burns deep into his eyes and right down to his very soul.

'I told you that you would 'ave no choice if I wanted it. Now make yourself useful and clean out the fire and start a new one. I have bread to make and a café to open in less than an hour.'

'Yes, master,' he comments with a smile on his face. 'But if I am not mistaken, did I not just make the first move?' he asks as he turns away wearing a cheeky grin.

She shakes her head and sighs heavily. 'Oh James, you only think you made ze first move. I had already planned it and set the seed in your 'ead. For you are just a man and a good woman knows how to handle any man she chooses.'

He turns to look at Emma with a puzzled expression as she continues to speak. 'The clothes, they fit you nice, yes?' She looks down at his bottom then back up at him with a wicked grin on her face and a wink in her eye.

James just stares at her, a little taken aback by how she has played him. 'I thought it was the men who did that kind of thing,' he says as he walks into the café and starts to work on cleaning out the fireplace.

With the fire built up and scraps of paper now lit and taking hold of the kindling, James starts to straighten up the tables and chairs. He clears away the plates and glasses left by the patrons yesterday and puts any money left on the tables in a glass on the counter. As he works, the smell of freshly baked bread fills the room, just like he remembers from years ago at home with his family when they would all eat breakfast together. There was always the fresh smell of bread in the early morning, coming from the kitchen and filling the halls with its enticing aroma.

By the time Emma enters the café, James has cleared, washed up and positioned everything in the room as if she had done it herself. She looks round to find fault in his work but cannot. 'Your mother must have taught you well.'

Moving over to the fire, she places another log in the hearth before going behind the bar and opening a dozen bottles of wine to allow them to oxygenate to improve the taste.

'Thank you,' she says as she steps up and kisses James passionately before continuing to wipe over the surface of the bar. 'I will open now. If you would not mind just taking a seat and watching over me, I would be grateful. I am worried about who will come in today as more ships have made it into port and that means more sailors.'

'Emma, I am all yours for three days. You can ask of me anything you want, as I am in your debt for all that you have done for me. However, I must ask, what have you done with my trousers?'

Her face turns serious. 'They were disgusting and stinking out ze 'ole place. I have them in a bucket of water outside, but I do not think they can be saved. For I have scrubbed them twice and now I wait to see if zey get up and walk away on their own.'

James starts to laugh as she unlocks the café door then returns to the counter and sits down facing him. She takes his hand and runs her fingertips around his palm and along the tribal tattoos that lead around his wrist. 'I am not sure what it is about you, James. Only once have I felt this way before about someone, but even zat was not as intense as this, yet I have known you for only a day.'

He smiles. 'How do you think I feel? You have me at your beck and call for the next few days, to do what you ask of me without question.'

'Ha, I did not think of that. I will 'ave to come up with some imaginative ways to make you regret your agreement. Ze first being when we close today and you take a bath, for you stink of old mops.'

James's expression changes to a more serious one. 'Why I only had a bath…' He thinks for a bit. 'Maybe six or seven weeks ago.'

'Ah, zat is wrong. I do not think I have enough soap to clean you. Perhaps I can soak you in a bucket next to your trousers for a day.'

'I take offence to that! My trousers and I have been together a long time and I'm very fond of them.'

Emma gives him what can only be described as a death stare. 'You English are disgusting. It is either a bath or you sleep on ze floor. The choice is yours.'

Before James gets a chance to speak again, the door opens, and the first customers of the day walk into the café. It is an elderly couple with the man helping his wife to the table nearest the fire. Emma is straight up and greets them with a smile and conversation as she takes their coats. Soon, more and more people arrive and Emma steps up another gear.

He watches in awe as she talks and serves all who enter her café with such care and compassion, delivering plates of stew, cheese with fruit, cured meats, coffee and wine by the bottle or glass constantly throughout the day. James does anything Emma asks of him, stoking and building up the fire; collecting more wood; filling bottles of wine and brandy from the barrels in the storeroom ready to serve; washing up and clearing down some of the tables. But compared to what Emma does, it is an insignificant amount of work. The people who come to the café, particularly the elderly, adore her, and the more James watches her, the more he feels the same way. She is the life and soul of the place, with a presence that is infectious and a smile that lights up the room and all that enter it.

It is around five o'clock in the afternoon when Emma turns to look at James. 'We are done for the day.' She walks over to the last few people and lets them know that it is closing time, serving them their last drinks before returning to the counter and taking a seat by James.

He looks at her. 'Why do you close so early today? It is only late afternoon.'

With a smile on her face, she answers him. 'It is Saturday, silly, and we are a café, not a tavern.'

James does not get the significance, but before he gets to say anything, the last people stand up from their table, put on their coats and thank Emma as they leave the building. She locks the door on both catches behind them, then goes to their table and collects the plates and glasses and takes them out to the sink for cleaning. Moments later, she walks back into the room and up to James. He turns round on the bar stool to face her as she climbs on him and straddles his waist. He instinctively holds her to support her while she puts her right arm around his shoulder and starts to stroke his neck.

'As I said, it is Saturday. We close early today and are closed all day Sunday as it is God's day of rest.' With her left hand she strokes her fingers through his hair while she gently kisses him on the lips. 'We finally 'ave some time to ourselves,' she comments while continuing the gentle kisses on his lips and neck. James also responds by kissing around her neck and nibbling on her ear lobe before moving back to kiss her on the lips more passionately. Emma unfastens his belt, and it falls to the ground with a clatter as the metal weapons hit the stone slab flooring. He responds by sliding his hands up and over her pert breasts and gently massages them through her clothes. This encourages Emma and she starts to undress him, first sliding his jumper up over his head. Then she nibbles his neck and slides her fingers through the hairs on his chest before kissing his nipples. Her hand slowly slips down to his trousers and starts to undo the buttons that hold them up.

James lowers his hands and takes hold of the hem of her dress and eases it slowly up, while Emma's are moving above his shoulders, allowing him to slide the dress upwards and over her head. It falls to the ground while she flicks her long hair back over her shoulder to allow him to see her large firm breasts. Her nipples are now swollen and erect and he wastes no time in feeling them with his fingers and kissing and caressing them with his lips and teeth.

She moans softly as James continues to explore and excite her. As her breathing quickens, so do her groans of pleasure, getting louder and louder as she leans back, allowing James more access to her body and encouraging him on. He takes full advantage, holding both her pert breasts and massaging them gently, kissing and nibbling each one in turn. She stands up, pulling James forward so his trousers drop down to the ground. He flicks off his boots and then his trousers. Lowering her hand to his groin, Emma feels his ever-swelling penis and gently strokes it backwards and forwards.

Both are starting to breathe heavily as their passion becomes more intense. Emma kisses her way down from his neck, moving to his chest, then his stomach as she moves lower and lower. James is holding her shoulders and trying to control his breathing, for this girl is turning him on like nothing he has ever known. What's worse is that Emma is watching him struggle to keep control as she works on his lower body.

To her slight disappointment, James starts to lift her back up towards his chest area, just before she gets him to climax. For she knows he was close and only a matter of moments away. Soon they are passionately kissing again, James holding her round the waist as they continue to feel and touch every part of each other's bodies.

Finally, and without warning, he picks her up and walks her

backwards to the nearest table. He lays her gently on her back while still kissing her passionately. Slowly, he lifts up her legs and positions himself before inserting his penis into her moist vagina. She lets out a deep moan as he slowly thrusts his manhood deeper and deeper before he retracts and starts a rhythmic thrusting motion. Again and again, he thrusts deeply into her, causing Emma to respond by moaning with each stroke and thrust of his loins and the pleasure it brings her. Gripping him tightly, she bites into his neck and drags her fingertips down his back. He pushes deeper and deeper, his rhythmic lunges bringing Emma closer and closer to climaxing. For the next five or six minutes, he is rocking her backwards and forwards on the table with their combined mass slowly moving the table across the floor. She grips his shoulders tightly and tucks her head into his neck, kissing and caressing as best she can.

The pace quickens. Emma's body is now quivering. It starts to spasm and her eyes roll as she builds up to an intense orgasm. James is also about to climax, thrusting harder and faster, his breathing heavier and louder with the effort. Her nails dig tightly into his back and her teeth nip into his neck before she yells out. It instantly triggers James, and he also yells, ejaculating into her quivering body. One, two, three times she feels him shoot inside her, if not more. She grips him tight with her legs as he lies on her trembling body. They are both sweating and breathing heavily from the effort they have put in. James has slowed his rhythm to a near standstill but is still inside her, held tight by Emma's grasp of his body and refusal to let go just yet.

Emma moves her head back from James's neck and gently kisses him again. James responds and slowly rolls over onto his back, bringing Emma up on top of him. She repositions herself, bringing her knees up onto the table, still with his semi-hard penis inside her. She leans back and pushes her firm sweat-covered breasts out, encouraging James to rub her plump brown nipples with his thumbs.

She moves her pelvis backwards and forwards, sliding up and down on his penis, the speed slowly increasing. As he becomes firmer, she continues at a steady pace and James goes from firm to hard. Soon he is as stiff as before, his hands gripping Emma's hips as he pulls and pushes with her rhythmic thrusts. He moves his left hand from her hip and rubs her clitoris as she grinds on him. Emma picks up the pace, getting more excited with each thrust, her body trembling as she begins to build up for another orgasm.

Faster and faster she goes, as her hips thrust backwards and forwards on his groin. She moans, becoming lightheaded and near to bursting with another orgasm, but she will not stop or slow, pushing on to ensure James climaxes as well. Again and again, she thrusts until finally he lets out a yell and comes inside her again. She feels his sperm shoot into her body two more times, as her body trembles uncontrollably and again spasms and orgasms. She slows her pelvic thrusts before stopping and collapsing down onto his chest. Her head is spinning, and emotions run wild with her body's reactions. She doesn't know whether to laugh, cry or do both at the same time. She grips him tightly across the shoulders and back of his neck as her body trembles, afraid to let go as she may fall off him.

James puts his huge arms round her and holds her close, gently stroking her back. It takes a few minutes to calm her body down. As he tries to slowly roll her off, she holds firm, looking down at him with passion and desire still in her eyes.

'Who says that we are finished?' She smiles that cheeky grin that he loves so much and gives him a few short pelvic thrusts along his again semi-limp penis. James looks at her with a shocked expression. 'I've fought many bull whales to the death and not one of them has left me with less energy than you.' He leans forward and stands up with her still wrapped around his groin and her arms holding tight to his shoulders, keeping her in position as she speaks again.

'I swore to myself that when I made love to a man, I would give him everything. Is it too much to ask the same of you in return?'

He smiles and chuckles at her. 'I did not say I was finished. I am just moving you to a more comfortable location before we continue.'

Emma raises an eyebrow as James smiles back. 'Bed, my dear, bed. That table damn near broke my back.' They both smile as he lifts her up and carries her through the storeroom to the bed at the back. They are still giggling as he lowers her gently down on the bed while she remains wrapped around him with both her arms and legs.

Some four hours later, James and Emma come staggering out of the bedroom, still naked. They are starving and exhausted. As they reach the bar, Emma grabs one of the open bottles of wine and pours them both a glass. The fire has long since burned itself out, but the wall lamps still have oil and light the café enough to see around the room.

'Take a seat, my dear, and I will be back with some food shortly.' James sits on the nearest stool and sips at the wine as Emma moves out into the back room. He strikes a match and lights the lantern on the counter to add more light to the area. Within minutes, she arrives back with bread, cheese and a selection of sliced meats. Barely a word is spoken as they break off pieces of food. Some they eat themselves and others they feed to each other. They just smile and stare at one another as they eat, laughing if one of them drops a piece of food or does something silly.

This was not what James was expecting when he started his quest to find his sisters. Not that he is unhappy with how events have unfolded. It has just made things a little more complex for him, as the more he is around Emma, the stronger his feelings grow for her. Just a smile, a look, or the way her eyes move makes him feel good and want to be around her more. He cannot believe how she does not see his size, features and tattoos as scary or consider him a person to be avoided. Her fun nature and strong womanly beliefs along with her fantastic body and lust for life captivate him above anything he has known before.

As for Emma, the past few days have given her something she has never had in her life but craved desperately. Adventure, passion, and a person she wants to spend time with outside of her family. A man who is willing to put his life on the line for her without any reservation. His tattoos and scars show a person who has lived and been to the ends of the world and that excites her greatly. Also, he allows her to get on with what she is doing, does not interfere or get in the way, but is always there when she needs him. This is only the second man she has ever liked, but the first she has been this passionate about and desired so much. She has no doubt in her mind that he is a man worth fighting for. From the time she first saw him, she has been drawn to his presence and sexuality and she could not have been taken any closer to the edge of ecstasy than the last several hours.

Emma has not even thought about the fact that they could have just possibly sown the seed that may have her carrying this man's child for the next nine months. After clearing up the mess they made in the café, they head back off to bed. Not that there is much sleeping going on. Lust and desire drives them both on until eventually they run out of energy and fall asleep curled up in each other's arms.

When they finally do wake, it is Sunday afternoon. The storm has subsided, and the weather is now much improved with the sun shining and the temperature pushing the twenties. They spend the rest of the evening having a bath together, talking and laughing over anything and everything. Once dressed they venture out for a walk together. Arm in arm, they head along a path on the cliffs that overlook the bay and port below. Between them they work out that six more large boats have come in overnight and have moored up. Heavily battered and storm-damaged, they will be there some time for repairs before they can be underway again.

Also, judging by the gaps in the line of local fishing vessels, some of the smaller boats that fish along the local coastline for crabs and sardines have already headed out for the first fishing trips in over a week. With some of the larger boats now having their crews moving about on board, it will not be long before the main fleet is out in the deeper water fishing for larger species like cod, turbot and haddock. It will be on their return with hulls full of fish that the village workforce will return to the salting sheds and smokehouses to start full production, processing and preserving seafood again. In the distance, they can see the tidal mills have already started up, no doubt trying to make up for the lost time caused by the storm.

As they slowly walk back to the village, they are approached by two elderly men who speak to them in French. James cannot understand what they are talking about, but the mood with Emma changes as she becomes quieter and more distant with every word they speak. Within minutes the men say their goodbyes, leaving Emma and James to continue back to the café. Emma is still affectionate and playful with James, but he can tell there is something playing on her mind, as the whole way back she seems preoccupied. Later that evening, while they are sat at the bar drinking wine and eating slices of cheese and cured meats, Emma brings up the earlier meeting.

'Those two men that approached us when we were walking were Pierre and Henrey. They were letting me know that they are leaving for Paris at six tomorrow morning with the convoy of wagons. If you still want to go, you are to be there by five to help finish preparing the wagons for the journey.'

James nods. 'I thought there was something on your mind. You have been so quiet since they spoke to you.'

She looks up at him. 'You do not understand how dangerous Paris is where you need to go. People die or go missing there all ze time, and you, not knowing any French, you will not last a day in zat place.'

She reaches over and takes his hand. 'I don't want to lose you like I lost my mother. Zat place has ze worst kind of people. If your sisters were taken there all them years ago, the chances of them being alive would be slim to none.'

James walks out into the storeroom, watched closely by Emma. He returns moments later with something in his hand. He sits back down and places a piece of material on the table in front of her. Unfolding the cloth reveals a broken picture frame, inside which is a drawing of three girls all wearing the same type of frilly dresses.

'This is all I have of my past. Everything else is gone. These are my sisters. The youngest is Anna Marie. She was but seven when I left. She cried the whole time as she watched me board that whaling ship and set sail out of port. In the middle is Elizabeth, the strong one, only eleven when I last watched her from the stern of the ship. Finally, Harriet, or Hattie as I called her. She was the quiet one of the three. She did not say much, but she held them all together. At just fifteen years old, she was wise beyond her years. My bastard brother allegedly sent them to Paris to be sold into slavery in the seedy underworld of the brothels when they were nothing more than just children. That is, if they were not disposed of on the ship as they were sent over.' Tears begin to flow down his cheeks.

'They would have looked to their brothers to protect them, but we had all been sent to sea and were being murdered one by one in different parts of the world, under the instructions of our older brother. Only when we were all out the way did that fiend send our sisters to their fate.' He fights back the tears as he tries to continue his words.

'I know what happened to all my brothers. I have spoken with the captains of the ships they were sent away on. Made sure they will never forget the part they played in my brothers' murders by leaving a reminder with each and every one of them. Something they will remember every day they live on. If I travel to Paris, just maybe I can find out what really happened to my sisters all those years ago. If I am more fortunate, perhaps against all the odds, one or more may still be alive, for some were very young when they were sent.'

He looks at Emma and notices that she is also crying and wipes the tears from her eyes with his finger. 'Before I met you, I swore an oath that if I did not find them, I would take out their vengeance on the man who caused all this suffering and kill our brother. Even if it cost my life to do so. My feelings have not changed on this matter as he has done such unspeakable wrongs to people who could not defend themselves, just so he could live his lavish and lazy lifestyle without looking over his shoulder.'

'What would you do if you found one or all three alive? Would it temper your anger?' she asks in a quiet voice.

He pauses for a moment to think. 'Perhaps I could just ruin or cripple him and leave what is left alive to reflect on what he has done to others. Watch him as he falls from grace and becomes what he most fears – poor and destitute.'

'I like that idea better,' she says, picking up the portrait of the three girls and staring at it. 'You say they were taken to Paris. How long ago would that have been?'

James scratches the top of his head and thinks for a moment. 'Around seven or eight years ago. I am not sure of the exact date as I had already set sail. He had waited until all his brothers were at sea before he put the next part of his plan into action. As sending our sisters away with us present would have caused an uproar and we would have reacted violently.'

'That is several years after my uncles took me away from Paris, but I expect it would have still been the same people running the scene. With your family being so prominent and rich, they would have been involved in their transaction, as these girls would have demanded a top price for high society entertainment. As terrible as I make it sound, it may be a better thing for them as they would have potentially been reserved for a higher class of clientele over a longer period of time.'

She thinks on the matter for a while. The plans running through her mind would put her at great risk, but she has a man in front of her in need of help. She knows that her life would not be worth anything should he not return to her. So many demons are pulling at her conscience: fear of what may happen to James, the worry of what he might find when he gets there, the chances of never seeing him again. Finally, after several minutes of complete silence between them, she speaks.

'If you are to leave so early tomorrow, perhaps you should retire and rest, as I am sure you will not get much time to sleep once you start your journey. Ze men you travel with will push for long hours on the roads before stopping to rest.'

James chuckles to himself. 'I am beginning to see that you are as wise as you are beautiful, my dear. I also know that you would prefer me not to go, but this is something that would never let go of me. I pray you understand that I could not with good conscience live my life without knowing what happened to my three younger sisters. It is not my way.'

She passionately kisses him on the lips. 'I do not like it, but I do understand, so get some rest while I clear up and get my duties done.'

James kisses her back. 'Thank you for understanding. It would have been harder for me to go if you opposed me. But even then, I would still have gone as I need to find out if they are alive or not.'

Emma nods and grimaces as James makes his way out the back. She watches him like a hawk until he closes the door to the store and her bedroom. Then she springs into action, clearing the counter of their meal and empty glasses. Within minutes she is using a knife to cut up a large cotton sheet into eight pieces, then pulling down a large cured sausage and a leg of smoked pork from the ceiling. She divides each into eight large chunks, then heads to the storeroom. Moments later she is back with a wheel of cheese and a selection of jars of pickled vegetables. The cheese wheel is cut into eight evenly sized wedges and one by one she fills each of the sheets with a piece of all the foods she has collected. Once all eight are done, she collects them up and staggers out into the street.

It is a good thirty minutes before she returns through the door and grabs a small piece of slate. She writes a note on the board with a piece of chalk and hangs it on the outside of the café door before stepping back inside and locking it. Taking a deep breath to calm herself, she throws her apron onto the counter and heads off to join James out the back. She creeps into the room, shedding her clothes and boots before she reaches the bed.

Lifting the sheets, she snuggles into her man, tucking her back into his warm chest. Just as she thinks she has got in without waking him, his huge muscular arm comes over her side and encloses her. His hand cups her breast as he says, 'I don't seem to sleep without my toys to play with.'

'Huh!' Emma jabs him in the ribs with her elbow. 'Get to sleep.' She holds the hand that is still cupping her breast and stares forlornly into the darkness, her mind running through events that have yet to unfold.

CHAPTER 2

A Trip to Paris

It's a little after four o'clock in the morning when James begins to stir. His hand moves about the bed, feeling for Emma, but just like the previous morning, she is already up and away. The oil lamp is lit and set at a low light, something Emma must have done when she got up.

'Emma!' he calls, but there is no response. Putting on his clothes and boots, he walks through to the café with the lantern to look for her.

His first thoughts are to find her and say goodbye before he leaves for Paris, but she is nowhere to be seen. After looking around without success and noticing the fire is not even lit, James concludes she must be upset that he is going to the capital and has gone for a walk so she does not have to say goodbye. This saddens him as he does not want to leave without reassuring her that he will be back. Taking a seat at the bar, he waits for around five minutes in the hope of her return, but eventually the realisation that she will not be coming back sinks in. It is painful for him to accept, but it does prompt him to write a small note and leave it on the counter for her to read.

It is still dark as he steps outside, but being a port and people starting early, the streetlamps are always lit until first light. Closing the door behind him, James does not look back, just takes a deep breath of the salty sea air and looks round in the vain hope of seeing Emma's face somewhere nearby. With no such luck, he heads off to the pre-arranged meeting point by the warehouse on the side of the dock wall.

It takes him around ten minutes to reach his destination. On arrival, he can see a line of six wagons, each with two horses strapped in full harnesses ready to go. Looking inside the back of the first wagon, James can see it is filled to the brim with barrels of wine and brandy, and salted and cured fish, all topped off with thick rolls of cloth in all colours and patterns – some wrapped in brown paper, but most bound in muslin.

He continues down the line of wagons, looking at each load as he goes. To his amazement, they are filled with all manner of different trade goods, including spices, silks and furs, many of which would not have been produced here but have come from faraway countries. Being originally from a trading port himself, he can see the advantages of taking these kinds of goods to the capital, as they would be worth triple – if not more – than what they would get selling around the local area.

All the wagons are filled with as much as can be safely loaded and carried on such a journey. Reaching the last wagon, he sees a group of men checking the horses and wheels to ensure they are in good working order, greased and ready to travel. They all greet James, speaking in French, and shake his hand. Most of them are in their fifties or older with grey beards or moustaches. From their clothing, he can tell they were all once soldiers or ex-sailors that do not take to the sea anymore. All seem pleasant enough, but apart from *bonjour*, he has no idea what they are all talking about. One of them points to the front of this last wagon and James mounts the somewhat aged and heavily timbered cart and takes hold of the reins.

'Hey,' one of them yells at James. As he looks up, the man throws him a thick red cushion. 'Sit, yes, it be long way,' the man hollers out to him. James nods in acknowledgement and tucks the cushion under his bottom.

He watches as all the men take to wagons in front of him, one to each vehicle, and mount up ready to go. Without any more words, the lead driver flicks the reins and moves off, with the rest of them following in order. The convoy of wagons slowly heads through the roughly stoned roads leading away from the port. The echo of horseshoes and metal-rimmed wheels hitting the stone cobbles deflects off the lines of tightly packed houses and stone walls, making it sound like an army is on the move.

This early, only a few people are around to brave the cold chill in the air, usually local fishermen heading to their boats to catch the early tides to the fishing and crab grounds. Without exception, every person they meet waves or greets the men on the wagons with a few choice words and laughter as they pass. It does not take long before the convoy has left the port and its stone roads and joined the quieter dirt tracks that lead them into the countryside.

Just as James's cart leaves the last of the stone slabs, it lunges from side to side and some of the produce slips and moves around. He looks back into the contents of his wagon but can see nothing out of place, so continues on without checking further.

Moving at a constant but slow pace, they put in a good six hours before stopping to stretch out their legs and aching limbs. James locks the brake on the right wheel before dismounting and heading off behind a large tree to relieve himself. 'Aah, that's better,' he comments to himself as he does his trousers back up then joins the other men. One of them is cutting thick slices of a cured salami of some description with a large, hooked knife. It is the same man who threw James the cushion at the start of the journey. He passes each man a chunk in turn. 'Eat, it is good, I make myself,' he bellows at James.

'Thank you,' he replies before taking a bite and chewing the cured meat. The first thing that hits him is just how much garlic is in it, then the heat starts to come through.

'By God that is hot,' James says as the rest of the men laugh at his attempts to swallow the burning fire in his mouth. One of them passes him a bottle of wine, which he grabs and drinks deeply before coughing and choking.

'Is good, yes?' the man repeats, patting him on the back as he passes. James is red-faced and sweating profusely, his whole mouth has gone numb with the heat, and his throat feels like it is on fire. He looks at the man who gave him the offering from hell and cannot believe he is chewing away on a chunk of this fire stick without any problem. He passes back what is left of the bottle. Out of the corner of his eye, he sees two of the men discreetly throw the salami into the hedge behind them. One of them looks back at James and shakes his head.

Moments later another slice of the fiery inferno is offered to all present. Strangely, everyone seems to be full and there are no takers for another piece of what must be the hottest, most unpleasant garlic-cured sausage in the world.

One of the men pulls a folding table from the back of his wagon, opens it up and sets it on the ground. Upon it he places a large wheel of cheese and a long stick of bread. He starts to cut chunks off each item and passes them around. As he reaches James and gives him his share of the food, he points to each man present. 'Pierre, Thomas, Phillip.' He raises his arm at the one who gave out the hot salami. 'Henrey,' he says, and on hearing his name, Henrey raises his knife with a piece of meat on it in acknowledgement before taking another bite.

The man shakes his head in disgust at what Henrey is eating before pointing at himself. 'Jack.'

James looks back at them all then points to himself. 'James.'

Henrey walks over to James. 'We know who you are. You are the one who has stolen our little Emma's heart. Know now that she is the life of our village and is very precious to us all, so best you do not hurt her.'

James looks at him, relieved that at least one of the men speaks English. 'I do not doubt you there. She is indeed a fine woman.'

'Yes, you say that now, but when her uncles return from the vineyards, you will find out how special she really is.' He turns and speaks in French to the others, who all laugh at his words.

Thomas walks over to James and pats him on the shoulder. 'You are a very brave man, yes!' he says with a smile.

James is slowly starting to get to know the characters of the men he is travelling with. The language barrier between them will be challenging at times, but for now it is working out fine – though it seems like at some stage he will have an eventful meeting with Emma's uncles.

They rest for about half an hour before mounting up. The convoy travels on all sorts of tracks and roads, through fields, woods and rocky hilltop passes. They stop for the night just before dark to start a fire and to feed the horses and check their feet over. All the animals are tethered to a long rope between two trees evenly spaced, each one with its own feed and small net of hay. The group of men sits around the campfire eating stew served from a pot simmering over the flames.

Pierre walks around each of the wagons, checking all the stock is still intact and has not become loose or moved around. Going through the final wagon, something catches his eye. He goes in to investigate and there is movement. 'Sacré bleu,' he yells before wrestling with what he has found. The men leave the fire and gather around as Pierre manhandles a stowaway out of the back of the wagon. Standing them up, he pulls down their hood to reveal who it is.

'Emma!' yells James. 'What the he—'

Before he finishes, Emma has a few choice words of her own, tearing into Pierre before kicking him in the shin. 'Aaahhhh,' he hollers and hops away, as Emma rips into him with both barrels, verbally taking him apart for how he has handled her.

The kick to the shins makes the men laugh, but it is short lived as they start to realise the situation she has put them all in. Henrey takes her by the arm and drags her away for a heated conversation. James goes to intervene, but as he steps forward, Pierre puts his arm out in front of his chest. 'No, this he must do alone.'

James looks at him. He knows if he chose to, he could smash his way through them all without even breaking a sweat. But Pierre is not doing this for the sake of conflict. He is trying to help. James nods and stands down and the group of men watches as Emma and Henrey have a battle of words in a heated debate. Several finger points in James's direction make it absolutely clear that he is the focal point of the argument. Fifteen minutes pass and still the pair are at each other, arms flailing, words being shouted out louder and louder between moments of silence. James and the others settle down by the fire and continue to eat their stew and watch the debate from a distance.

Thomas taps James on the shoulder. He takes his gaze away from Henrey and Emma to look at him. 'Er, Henrey, uumm, he be like father to Emma for long time, since she was little, yes!'

James nods. 'Yes, I understand.'

Thomas continues speaking. 'Emma, she come from a very bad people, and, um, we, we be going to where bad people be.' James starts to get concerned; he is coming to realise that there is far more to Emma's background than he was aware of. And that her smuggling herself aboard one of the wagons has the potential to cause problems for all of them – though at this moment, he does not understand why.

Emma and Henrey eventually return to the fire. While Henrey walks over to speak to the other men, Emma heads straight up to James and hugs him. 'I'm sorry, but I could not let you go to Paris alone without someone who could speak French to 'elp you. It will be so dangerous for you, and I could not bear ze thought of not seeing you again.'

James looks into her sad, tear-filled eyes. There is no way he can be angry with her for trying to help, but what is the risk for Emma that everyone is concerned about? Before he has a chance to speak to her, Henrey calls out, 'James, come here, my boy. I would like to speak to you.'

He walks over with Emma attached to his arm.

'Please sit. We all talk for a bit, yes?' Some of the men stand up to leave. 'No! All sit. This story should have been told long ago, but before I start, I must ask you, James. Is it true about your sisters being in Paris and what your brother has done?' James looks at Emma, then back to Henrey. 'I ask because these men here are my friends, friends my whole life, and if Emma helps you, we must all help you, and you must trust us.'

James pauses for a moment before answering. 'Yes, it is true.'

Henrey nods. 'Then you must tell us all what has happened. And you, Emma, you must translate into French all his words for the others to hear, yes?'

It is not easy for James to talk about his past to a group of men he barely knows, but with Emma being as brave as she has been, and now holding his arm tightly while staring into his eyes, he takes a deep breath. He starts to talk about the murder of his father, mother, younger siblings and the people who were hanged for the crimes his brother organised. How he and his other brothers were all sent to sea, and the rumours of where his sisters may possibly have been sent.

Emma translates word for word, including what he did to the captains who murdered his brothers on their voyages. He spoke of the crew and captain of the ship who would not end his life, but in a way allowed him to start a new life by letting him leave on his own terms. The men listen intently and there is a lot of head shaking and amazement about how far a man is willing to go to better his own life at the cost of his family and own personal honour. To all these Frenchmen who have sailed together, fought side by side in battles with the enemy, and lived through good times and bad, their family and friends are always first and foremost in all that they do. Far above wealth and greed, these men would give everything they have to help each other without reservation. James ends his story with his chance meeting with Emma and how he feels about her. The men go quiet, a deep silence that makes James feel very uneasy. It is like they know something is going to happen, just not when.

Finally, Henrey speaks. 'It is indeed a terrible thing that has befallen you, James. I would say it was a true tragedy and if I were to hear this story without you ever meeting Emma, it would just have been a bad luck story of an English family – an enemy of this country for many years – so I would not care. But here we sit with Emma risking her life for you after meeting just a few days ago. I do not know why she would do this, but I will now tell you a little about our Emma and why she means so much to us all.' He takes a drink before continuing. 'Do you know what she has done for you, James?'

James shakes his head slowly and turns to look at Emma.

'While you slept last night, she made parcels of food for many of the elderly in our village and delivered them to their houses as they rely on the café for food. I know this because my mother is one of them. She then closed the café so she could sneak aboard these wagons and help YOU – a man she met only days ago – to look for your sisters in a place that has been hunting for Emma her whole life. I have known her since she was but a baby and love her as if she was my own daughter. Like you, she has had a terrible past that haunts us all to this day.'

He wipes his face with a handkerchief before placing it back in his pocket.

'Now I will tell you the story of Emma, so you know what she risks by helping you in Paris and why I so strongly oppose her going. To understand the story, you must first understand the darker side of Paris and the power it controls. You see, the rich and powerful run Paris, not the government or king. And the rich want fun and entertainment. They do not care about common people. No! They want everything good for themselves at the cost of all others, for they mean nothing to them. This creates opportunities for more ruthless people who are prepared to go that extra length to make it happen. Blackmail, extortion, abductions and murder are all just tools to provide for the wealthy, who are willing to pay but not be involved in its execution.

'At this very moment in Paris, there are over one hundred and sixty state-run brothels that provide services to all. Yes! One hundred and sixty. But of these there are a few that are far more discreet, a society within a society, places that are playhouses for the very rich and powerful.

'Le Chabanais at Louvre, Le Sphinx, and the top of the group, La Fleur Blanche at Six Rue Des Moulins. Their clientele list is for kings, princes, aristocracy and heads of state from around the world. A boiling pot of wealth and influence with no limits to anything that may be desired. All these places are run by women known as "madams" to conform with state law. The most famous of them all is Madam Kelly. She is the true power of Paris, for she has the ears of the rich and the influence to do anything she wants. That woman has the best to offer for those wealthy and powerful enough to afford her.

'Her establishment is by far the finest in Paris. She can supply anything you could ever desire if you have the coin or favours to pay for it. Every room in her hotel is a world of its own. Every taste imaginable is catered for. All you have to do is ask and it will be yours. Men, women, boys, girls, animals, groups. A party at one of her rooms could cost tens of thousands, if not more, depending on the clientele's requirements. This is where your dreams are made if you are prepared to pay the price. I have heard that some royal families prefer to live there all year round at the expense of their own countries, such is the service they provide.

'She also has a special treat for those at the highest level of society. Madam Kelly's canaries. Wherever she goes she will always have two beautiful women dressed in the smallest trimmings of yellow silk and yellow feathers. They are beautiful beyond belief, with voices that could sing a lullaby to the devil and make him beg for more. Pure as fresh snow and guaranteed to be untouched by any man, they walk in front of her with the finest diamond-encrusted threads attached from her hand to their necks. These women cannot be bought for any price. They are only available or offered in return for favours. Perhaps a change in the law, the release of a corrupt politician or to influence decisions of state. Once an accepted offer is placed on one of her birds, the thread is broken, and they are released. To become the property of the user, who can decide to keep them or return them once they have finished with their service. If they are returned, they work in the best rooms of the hotel, but to my knowledge none have ever been handed back, such is their exquisiteness and desire to their new owners.

'This is where the story takes a darker side, for in Paris at the Royal Opera House was a singer whose beauty and voice were the finest in the land. She graced and sang at many palaces and royal buildings across Europe, even on one occasion at the Vatican for the pope, such was her demand. All in high society adored her and she became a focal point of many a man's dream, wishing to be her suitor. Spurning the advances of so many nobles and diplomats in society seemed to make her even more desirable to those with power and influence. She caught the eye of one man in particular, who wanted her more than anything else in the world. It was not long before Madam Kelly was made an offer by this interested party, an offer so good that she could not resist the temptation to make it happen.

'A month later, the singer was back performing at the Royal Opera House in Paris, singing like a lark to a sell-out audience. At the end of the show, she left the stage to the usual encore of people standing, clapping and cheering. They all waited for her to do her usual return for one or two more songs and delight her admirers that little bit more.

'It is hard for me to explain in the right words, but for the singer Juliet du Grande, the stage was her life. She loved to sing and perform and lived every word of what she spoke, a born entertainer whose only desire was to make everyone happy. She had no understanding of the world outside, of politics, money or power, but she could carry a word in the air like an angel calling to God. But on that fateful day she did not return to the stage. The people continued to cheer and call for her return but to no avail. The stage organisers were expecting her return, so checked her dressing room and found only knocked-over furniture and a broken mirror. They searched for her in the hallways, then the entire building, without success. Within a day, half the population of Paris was looking for Juliet. Even the King of France put out a plea to his people and the monarchy of Europe to find their national treasure wherever she may be and return her safely.

'But alas, even with an entire nation searching for her, she could not be found. Weeks, months, a year passes with no sign of the "Lost Angel of Paris", as she had become known to all. That is until one day she appeared on a jewel-encrusted lead in front of Madam Kelly. But she was not singing. Her presence and smile that would light up the room had gone. The look in her eyes that once sparkled and dazzled all who looked upon her was blank and broken. In the year that she had been missing, Juliet du Grande had spent only the one night with the man who had requested her abduction. Then she was passed back to Madam

Kelly the following day due to the immense publicity and scandal it had caused.

'Later we found out that she had been beaten senseless, her whole body bruised and battered from the ordeal. In that one day, it was said she fought him for every second of every minute of their time together, refusing to yield one inch to his advances, biting, kicking and scratching until her strength finally gave out. Violated and abused by her oppressor, few thought she would survive the night and HE dared not let her die with him or be seen so badly beaten as the country would rip itself apart looking for vengeance on those responsible. So, she was returned and hidden away from the world by Madam Kelly.

'Months later, she was found to be pregnant, an ideal situation for Madam Kelly as she had the means to blackmail this powerful man, should the need ever be required. Three months after the birth of the child, Madam Kelly showed off her first canary, thinking it would be good publicity and promoted her as the woman who could provide anything you could possibly desire.

'But what Madam Kelly had done backfired in a catastrophic way and public outrage filled the land again. She was forced to call in every favour ever owed and promise many more to survive the backlash that followed. Politically and publicly, she was ridiculed. Business and service profits dropped through the floor as people demanded she stand trial for her crimes and release Juliet du Grande from her captivity. It took all the wealth she had ever made to save her skin as well as many payments of bribes to survive the scandal, for she may have had the canary on a lead, but she did not sing or light up the room like she once had.

'For months they tried to force her to smile, sing and perform for the masses, but she refused to cooperate in any way. Now she was back in the public eye, they dared not beat, mark or damage this national treasure as they would not survive the night, such would be the French people's response. Even holding on to her precious daughter as a prisoner and using her as leverage made no difference. For again they could not risk being seen to harm a royal child as the father would level Paris, or worse, let the public know she existed. Madam Kelly had never been so vulnerable, juggling the demands of the baby, her father and Juliet du Grande. She fought everybody to stay alive and free, calling in favours from every influential person she had control over.

'As for Juliet du Grande, the next year was plagued with illness and discomfort. Some say she just lost the will to live and gave up, while others believe the man who took her broke our angel's spirit and her soul died. Within weeks the "Lost Angel of Paris" became gravely ill. For those that had never lost faith in getting her out of her cage, this was a blow too far. One day a group of men stormed the hotel, killed several of the protectors and took vengeance on the establishment, burning part of it to the ground.

'Madam Kelly survived the attack but suffered severe cuts and lacerations in the fight that ensued and now must cover up her body to hide the scars. She and her armies of the underworld spent years looking for the men who did in a day what the whole of France and its government could not do in over a year. To this day, she still searches for the men who rescued Juliet du Grande and her daughter and left her terribly disfigured.'

Henrey looks up at James. 'The men who stormed that place of ill repute, killed the enforcers and scarred Madam Kelly were Juliet's brothers and close friends. When they finished working on Madam Kelly and her entourage, they went looking for their sister and her daughter. Room to room they went until they finally found them in a suite named the Bird Cage. There, curled up in a ball on a large, yellow, egg-shaped bed, she lay. Barely six stone she weighed when they picked her up and carried her from that place. They rushed her to their family physician but were too late to save their precious sister. She died in her older brother Bernard's arms within hours of being freed, saying only, "Keep her safe, my brothers, keep her safe."

'Juliet was buried in secret, on the slopes of their family vineyard where she played as a child with her brothers. It was too much of a risk to bury her in a church or give her a marker with her name on it. So, they had the whole field consecrated by the local priests in an effort to make it as holy as possible. I have often sat on that hillside with Bernard and his brothers, Gaston, François and Sebastian, as he weeps for his sister. He still blames himself for not getting to her sooner, even though I know he did all he could. It is ironic really because Juliet means "forever young", and this beautiful woman will always be that. She never had the chance to grow old with her brothers.

'The person who carried her daughter out of that building that day was me, and the child I carried is that beautiful woman beside you, Emma. The men you see around you are some of the ones that helped free them and have kept her safe all these years.'

James is utterly speechless, while Emma just sits beside him holding his arm, staring into the fire. Tears have been running down her cheeks since Henrey started speaking about her mother, but she has made no sound. James looks at her, sees that she has been crying and moves his arm around her shoulders to comfort her. 'My dear, I am so sorry to hear of such a tragic event. Words do not cover such loss and I know not how to respond to such a terrible tragedy.'

Henrey continues, 'Speaking earlier with Emma, she was quick to remind me that she is a full-grown woman now, able to make her own decisions on what she does and who she helps. I can understand where she is coming from, but it does not mean that I agree with what she says. Our argument was over Emma explaining that maybe, just maybe, if she can help you find at least one of your sisters, she may find peace from such events that have troubled her life as well as yours. She is desperate not to lose you to the same kind of people who killed her mother, as you have become someone special to her.

'I personally think perhaps it was fate that the two of you with such tragic lives should meet and fall for each other. Maybe with time this union will make you both whole again. Learn to live, go forward in life and forget the pain of your past. What I do know for certain is what she risks for you by coming back to Paris and the fate that awaits her if she is found. For I have heard it mentioned many times on my travels to and from the city delivering produce. In the words of Madam Kelly, who is still aggrieved by that day, they will clip off the arms of the baby canary so she cannot feed herself. She will then be at their mercy, entertaining men for food and water for the rest of her life.'

James is horrified. The story of Emma's life is one to match his own tragedies, if not worse. He had no idea what she was prepared to do for him. Emma, on the other hand, does not even flinch as she speaks. 'I have heard these words so many times now that it has become part of my being. Anyway, I have made up my mind to help James, and zat is zat.'

Henrey shakes his head and sighs deeply. 'I know you understand loss and pain, James. And the act of vengeance is not unknown to you as you have done it yourself to avenge your brothers. So, understand this. If anything should befall my baby Emma in Paris, I will spend my last breath hunting you down. And when I find you, I will kill you. If I fail, my sons will find you and finish what I started. And so on. But I fear even then I will be too late and not get the chance. Because when Bernard and his brothers return from their vineyard and find Emma missing from the café, he will ask around for her. And when he hears from the locals that she has found a man who is heading to Paris, he will put two and two together and wear out horses to get to you. When he does, I doubt that even a man as big and as powerful as yourself will stop the wrath heading your way.'

James rubs Emma's shoulder. He turns to her to speak, but she is faster to the words. 'I will not leave. If you send me away, I will only come back harder. Please understand, I feel zat this is something I must do.'

With a deep exhalation, James looks down at the floor, for he is beginning to feel he is trapped between a rock and a hard place. 'Seems like whatever I do now, I will lose this one. But the risk you take is far more than I am worth. It has been but a few days since we first met and there is a lot about me you do not know.'

Emma is looking into the fire while still leaning against James. She watches the flames dance and flicker in the cool of the night in a trance-like state, clearly trying to think of the right words to say to him.

'It would seem that my whole life up until now has been one of hiding from the world through fear of being found by the people who broke my mother. I know they only want me as leverage against my father, or to use me as an example to keep others under their control. However, I also want to know who he is. I want to see what kind of man would request my mother's kidnapping. The person who would choke the spirit from her, just for a few hours of forced pleasure and amusement. Then abandon her to suffer in misery for over a year at the hands of Madam Kelly, just to hide his own crime and guilt.

'My mother's only desire was to perform on the great stage for all the people who adored her, share her talents with all who wanted to hear her sing. She did not deserve to be treated like an animal in a cage.'

She pauses for a moment, still staring into the fire as she thinks. 'In a way, I am proud of my mother. With all that they did to her, she fought back the only way she could. She never sang, smiled or performed again, resisting all that was forced upon her, while suffering alone. Yet she never gave in to the fear and pressure that she must have been under. Her refusal to cooperate and her sheer will to fight them was way more difficult than what I do now. For we are many and she was but one person on her own, cut off from the world and all she knew, with nobody around to 'elp.'

Emma looks at James. 'You arriving here when you did is not just chance; it was fate. The spark for me and you to take back our lives. I think that together we can right more than a few wrongs. I just 'ope I am strong enough to see it through. For I have a feeling that the people with the power to abduct my mother would move in the same circles as those zat would take your sisters and profit from them.'

* * *

Back at the French port of Saint-Suliac, under the glow of the oil lamps that light the narrow lanes, two men on horseback can be seen making their way into the village. The rhythmic tapping of the iron horseshoes echoes out as they head towards the livery yard. On arrival, they both dismount. One takes the horses into the livery and starts to strip off the saddles and bridles and attends to their needs. The other heads to the house on the opposite side of the road, unlocking the front door and entering the building.

It's been two and a half weeks since these men were last here, with the return journey taking three days hard riding. Striking a match, the man enters the hallway, removes the glass top from a lamp and lights the wick while pumping a lever on the side to induce pressure. Slowly, the wick catches a stronger flame, and the light begins to build. Shaking out the well-burned match, he replaces the glass housing, picks up the lamp and moves into the next room.

He kneels down at the fireplace, rotates the fireguard, pushing it up against the edge of the stone wall, and shuffles the prepared fire about to ensure the kindling is in the correct position before striking another match. As the fire starts to take hold and the kindling sticks burn, the fireguard is replaced in front and the man stands back up.

As he heads into the kitchen, he collects a bottle of wine, two glasses and a wooden corkscrew with a handle in the shape of a serpent. From a draw he takes a small knife, then moves to the pantry and lifts down a cured leg of pork wrapped in muslin that was hanging from an oak beam.

He places all the items on the table in the front room then sits down. 'Aaahhh,' he comments as he relaxes back into the chair, resting for a minute before leaning forward, pulling off his boots and rubbing his aching toes.

Grabbing a hanging brass poker, he approaches the fireplace and pokes at the collapsed kindling in the fire before best positioning several small logs on top. Then he picks up the bottle of wine, peels the wax layer off the top of the bottle, twists in the corkscrew and pulls out the cork, smelling it before pouring the wine into two glasses and pushing the cork back into the bottle.

His attention moves to the leg of cured pork. Carefully he unwraps the muslin and slices several long, thin layers of meat.

Just as he sits back down, the catch on the front door clicks and opens. 'Is that you, Sebastian?' he calls out in French.

'Who else would it be? A beautiful woman?' Sebastian laughs. 'The horses are bedded down for the night. I will give them a proper rub down tomorrow and get that shoe on your old nag looked at by the farrier.'

Sebastian pulls his boots off in the hallway and slots them over a couple of pegs, hangs his coat up on the rack and walks through to join his brother by the fireplace. Taking a seat, he turns to look at what is on offer and grabs a slice of the pork in one hand and a glass of wine in the other. He takes a bite of the meat, chews and swallows it and then washes it down with a few gulps of wine.

Bernard stares at him, shaking his head. 'You animal. You did not even let that wine breathe for five minutes before you chucked it down. And that nag, as you call it, is a Hanoverian and is the result of fine breeding over generations, unlike that mule you call a horse.'

'Brother, first of all you are too tight to open a good bottle of wine worthy of letting it breathe. Even though we produce thousands of good ones ourselves. And secondly, that nag of yours might have all the breeding, but my God it is so slow! I would have been here hours ago if it was not for that look-good, go-slow snail of yours. Anyway, to more important things… Shall we go and see Emma tonight, or go in the morning when the others arrive with the wagon?'

Bernard smiles and shakes his head. 'There is no way you can be my younger brother, Sebastian. I think I will have words with our mother when I go back to the château and ask if she was having an affair with the village drunk nine months before you were born.'

Sebastian is busy ramming another slice of pork into his mouth and finishing the glass of wine at the same time. He grabs the bottle, pulls the cork out with his teeth and pours himself another glass before topping up Bernard's to the brim.

'Father would be turning in his grave if he could hear you talk about his favourite son this way.'

Bernard tries to lift his wine glass to his lips without spilling it. Just as it reaches his lips, Sebastian bangs the table with his fist. Bernard holds steady and drinks deeply from the glass before looking back at his brother.

'The thing about knowing a simple animal like you, my brother, is that I can anticipate when you are going to do something stupid. As for Emma, she would have closed up by now and gone to bed. We will see her in the morning and surprise her with the gifts we have brought back from the estate.'

The two brothers talk for a little while longer, each one flinging insults at the other. Backwards and forwards goes the banter, as they have done so all their lives. But as the fire warms up the room, and the chairs become more comfortable, it is not long before they both fall asleep where they sit.

* * *

At dawn the following day, Bernard and Sebastian leave the house early and head towards the café. They stop several times on the way, speaking to friends and villagers about the storm, how the port coped with the bad weather and the ships that were stuck outside its walls in the vicious seas for days. All had eventually managed to get into the safety of the harbour, but at a high cost to the conditions of their ships. Many people from the village are about this morning, taking advantage of the additional work available repairing the damaged vessels that are now moored up.

Everyone exploits these types of opportunities when so many ships are awaiting attention or supplies. Even the local merchants are working deals with the ships' captains to purchase goods they have been transporting across Europe. Much of what they have been carrying is cheaper due to the damage caused by the storm, or water that has got into the storage holds and soiled the merchandise.

The villagers ask the brothers about the vineyards on the estate, how the grapes look this year and if the storm affected the crops in any way – as wine is a large part of their trade, and picking and crushing the grapes is a big part of the seasonal income for most of the older people who live around the port come harvest time.

They arrive at the café a little after eight in the morning to a chalk sign hanging on the front door. Bernard reads it out aloud to Sebastian. 'Sorry, we are closed for the next few days, Emma.'

The men look at each other before entering the building.

'Emma? Emma, are you here?' calls Sebastian. He goes through the storeroom to check if Emma is in bed, but she is nowhere to be found.

Bernard notices the letter on the counter that James had left for Emma. 'Sebastian,' he yells. Sebastian is quick to arrive at the counter and takes the letter.

'It is addressed to Emma, but it is written in English,' he says, trying to work out the words.

Bernard thinks for a moment. 'Take it to Henrey. He will tell us what it says. I will ask around with the old ones. They are here every day and may know what is going on.'

Both men leave the café in different directions. Bernard heads off to see Chloe and Antoinette, elderly sisters who live in two small adjoining cottages overlooking the port and its boats. At a fast walk, he is at the cottages in around ten minutes, his mind full of worry for Emma, who is priceless to him and his brothers. He bangs on the door of the first cottage and receives no reply. He tries again and still no reply. He moves to the next cottage and raps on the door. This time he can hear movement, and after what seems like an eternity of waiting but is in reality only twenty or thirty seconds, the door opens, and Antoinette stands before him.

'Sorry to bother you so early, Antoinette, but do you know where Emma is?'

She looks at him with a puzzled expression. 'I thought she had gone to see you.'

Bernard looks at her in shock. 'To see me?'

'Yes, she came round the day before yesterday with two big parcels of food for me and my sister. Said she would not be around for a few days as she had to catch up with the supply wagons. Then she went. I presumed she was going to meet you and your brothers as you returned, to show off that man of hers.'

'What man?'

'Yes, James is his name. Came off one of the ships that came in from the storm. Big strong man, not too pretty but seems very handy in a fight. Helped her when she had a problem with some sailors who were pushing her around, even assisted her in the café. They did seem so very happy together, walking round the village on Sunday.'

Bernard looks at her in confusion. 'Emma met a man! They were walking around the village together. I must go. Thank you for your time and information, Antoinette.'

He leaves her in the doorway and heads straight back to the café with more questions than answers in his head. He storms straight through the front door and round to the back of the bar, grabbing a glass as he goes. Then, picking up a bottle of brandy off the shelf, he pours a large glassful then pauses. Staring at the liquid, he realises it is not going to help and slowly pours its contents back in the bottle then replaces the stopper.

Taking a seat by the bar, he waits for his brother to return, hoping he has more information on the matter.

All he can do is think about his beloved Emma, where she might be and if she is safe. He wonders who this James is, what he is doing with Emma and why she did not wait for him to return as instructed. Doubt begins to set in as he thinks they should never have left her behind when they went to the château. Perhaps they have got too confident over the years and let slip their vigilance on the dangers that constantly surround Emma. What would his sister think of him if something were to happen to the daughter she entrusted to him and her three other brothers?

It's nearly twenty minutes before he hears a horse trotting up to the café. To start with, he does not think much of it, but when it stops outside and a rider dismounts, he walks to the window and looks out.

The door swings open with force, pushing him sideways as his brother storms into the room.

'Henrey was not there, but his family was. It would seem he

is taking several wagons to Paris with a group of the old guard. The local merchants have hired them to transport their goods to our warehouse for a better price in the big city. Oh, and this letter was from a man named James to our Emma. It says he is sorry he missed her in the morning, but he must leave now to drive one of the wagons to Paris and then try and find his sisters. He says that he will see her on his return once he has exhausted every option of finding them.'

Sebastian takes a few deep breaths before continuing. 'I also checked with the old man Pascal on my way back and he said that Emma dropped off a parcel of food to him and a few others the night before the wagons left for Paris. I've got my horse and I'm going to catch up to Henrey and question this man James and see if he knows where Emma is. Your horse is having all its shoes replaced at present as they are all twisted and worn. The farrier has all its hooves stripped and trimmed and is burning the first shoe in place as we speak. They will be about another hour sizing the others before it is all done.'

Sebastian turns to leave.

'Wait, let me think,' Bernard calls out.

Sebastian pauses, tapping his leg with a riding crop as he waits for Bernard to finish putting the pieces together.

All of a sudden, Bernard looks at Sebastian, an expression of dread written all over his face.

'Oh God, I know where she is and what she is planning to do. That blasted girl is on her way to Paris to help this Englishman find his sisters.'

Sebastian stops tapping his leg and shakes his head. 'No, she is not that stupid.'

'Think, Sebastian. She always wanted to go to Paris and find out who her father was and avenge her mother as much as we always wanted to avenge our sister. Yes, she has planned this very carefully, brother. Think! She has supplied all the elders with enough food until we would return, knowing they would be cared for by us. Our Emma is a very clever and headstrong woman. I think she is hidden somewhere in that group of wagons full of trade goods. This man James is English, so I doubt he speaks French, and she speaks both languages well.'

'I will kill that English pig.'

Bernard thinks for a bit more. 'No, Sebastian, he does not know she is there. If he did, he would not have written the letter. What's more, if he knew who she was or what she was planning, I do not think he would have allowed her to go. That would be why he could not find her in the morning as she was already hidden in the cargo. I would bet that at some point along that journey, she will reveal herself or be found out and will offer to translate for this man James in exchange for his help to find out about her father. This man may need to answer for his intentions with our Emma, but at the moment, he may well be the only person who could protect her, for she has had to sneak round him in the same way she has with us.'

Sebastian is quick to respond. 'What about Henrey and the others with him?'

'Henrey would die for his baby Emma. And the others, as we learned that day, would do the same to support him and protect her. But there is a difference this time; Emma is going on the offensive. No doubt the "I'm a grown woman and can make my own decisions" bit will come out, and Henrey will blindly support her no matter what she does.'

Bernard looks at his brother. 'You are not going to like this,' he says, 'but you must trust me. I need to borrow your horse and get to them as fast as I can. I have done the route they take many times and know the shortcuts a horse can handle. You need to wait for my horse to be shod then use it and ride to our brothers with the stock wagon. Divert them to Paris and meet me at our storage warehouse as soon as you can get there. I will speak with this man James and if he is anything but honest with me or puts her in harm's way, make no mistake, I will kill him myself.'

Sebastian does not hesitate. He passes Bernard his riding crop as his brother continues to speak. 'As much as I do not like what Emma has done, this was always going to happen at some stage in her life. I just hope I get there in time, and whatever happens next, we all live through it.'

Sebastian hugs his brother, who nods but says nothing more, just exits the café and mounts Sebastian's horse. With a kick to the horse's sides, he trots off down the road without looking back, his mind now focused on the best way to intercept the wagon train and get to his niece.

Sebastian also focuses on the job at hand. He heads towards the livery, trying to work out where his brothers could be with the wagon and at what point to travel to in the hope of intercepting them as soon as possible.

* * *

Some distance away in the French countryside, Henrey and his crew are preparing the horses for the day's journey. They all are tacked up, hooves picked out, and are now being assembled at the front of each wagon. James approaches Henrey and helps to strap in the horses. 'I did not know Emma was in the wagon.'

'I know.'

'I also did not know her history or motive for her coming along, as I would never have agreed to it. I give you my word on that.'

'I know.'

James pauses and scratches his head. 'I cannot send her back as she will not go, but I also do not wish to endanger her life as I care for her dearly. But if we reach Paris and she asks questions in the wrong places, it will surely put her life at risk.'

Henrey looks at James, steely-eyed. 'Again, I know that too.'

'Well then, do you have a plan, Henrey? As at this moment I do not know how to resolve the situation.'

Henrey puts his hand out towards James and tilts it left and right four or five times. 'I am, as you would say, working on it.'

'Is there anything I can do to help?'

'Just keep Emma with you and protect her at all times, while I work on how we fix the problem.' Henrey finishes the last strap connecting the two horses then begins working on his own animals, leaving James to mount the wagon and collect the reins.

Emma climbs up to sit beside him, leans over and kisses him on the cheek before speaking. 'You have been very quiet all morning. I hope you are not still angry with me.'

James nods his head. 'A little, Emma. I had no idea what you've been through in your life, or even who you really are. If I had, I think I would still have done everything exactly the same as we have up until now. For I cannot help how I feel about you as it seems you have lit something in me that has been long since hidden away. But the risk you have put yourself and others in by being here is a lot to take in. Are you really ready to do this?'

Emma is quiet for a while; she stares blankly at the back of the wagon ahead of them. 'Since my uncles and Henrey rescued me as a baby, I have been loved and pampered as my mother's daughter by all of them. I've been ze memory of my mother to them all, protected and sheltered from life and all the dangers it has to offer. Outside of my family, you are the first man I have met who stood up for me, defended me when I was afraid and needed comfort. The first man I have met who really interests me and is not around just because I am my mother's little girl. I do not want to miss the chance of 'appiness because I was afraid to act on instinct and take a leap of faith.' She puts her arm through his. 'When you spoke about what happened with your family and wanting to find out about your sisters and see if they were still alive… I can relate to that. I want to 'elp you find out what happened to them too, and me speaking French will 'elp in Paris. It is a risk, I know. But I want to be with you when you search for the truth, even if what you do in Paris endangers us both. I like you, James, and you need to understand that I am not afraid of death anymore. It has been with me too long, hiding in the shadows and keeping watch over me. Holding me in fear and dread of what might happen my whole life. I see now that I was more afraid to live, and to reach out for what I wanted, than I was to accept obscurity and loneliness. But now things are different. I want to share what time I have with you, a man I feel passionate about.'

She pauses before opening up to James about things she has never spoken about with people outside of her family, such is the trust she has in this man. 'I also need to find out about things in my life, like who my father is! Confront Madam Kelly and make her suffer as badly as my mother did all those years ago.'

She reaches down and holds his hand. 'If you were to turn back now and give up looking for your sisters, I will give up looking for my father and vengeance on Madam Kelly. We could go and live our lives far away from the evils of Paris, carefree and without knowing what happened in our past. But I 'ave a feeling this is not who you are. Like me, you must finish off what others 'ave started. Close what has been dealt us before we can move on and live our own lives.'

James has been listening to Emma intently while, in a similar way to her, blankly staring forward at the horses as they wait to move off along the road. But now, as she finishes speaking, he turns and looks into her tear-filled eyes. He knows that she has put it all on the line for him to hear and left no stone unturned. All that she has said has come from her heart. There are no tricks or sleight of hand to get him to do her bidding, just what she is feeling and thinking.

He slackens the reins and turns to kiss her softly and tenderly on the lips. She responds, kissing him back and putting her arms around his neck and broad shoulders, holding him tightly against her. They keep this passionate embrace for a few minutes or more before James leans back and she releases him from her grasp.

'Emma, I cannot put into words how I feel about you. I just don't have the tongue for it, but I think you have said it well enough for the both of us. I will not stop you going to Paris with me as it will hopefully resolve both our needs in this one venture. With luck, we will find what we are both looking for and finish all the nasty things that have been started by others and left for us to endure. Once we are done here and all issues concluded, the time left will be ours to enjoy and use as we see fit. I cannot promise how this adventure will end but be certain of this. I will not leave Paris alive without you. We will leave together or not at all.'

Just as James finishes speaking, the wagon in front starts to move off. He releases the wheel brake, collects the reins and flicks them on the backs of the two horses. They instinctively set a pace behind the wagon in front, allowing James to put his free arm around Emma and tuck her into his side. He kisses her cheek as she snuggles up to him and swings a small blanket over her shoulders to keep warm.

CHAPTER 3

The Underworld of Paris

The convoy of wagons has been travelling for four days. James has realised that the pace being set and distance travelled each day is not by any means as fast or far as it could have been. They are moving considerably slower than they did on the first day, before they had found Emma hidden on one of the wagons. Also, by his calculations, the hours on the road each day have also reduced by at least two. He has not spoken about this with anyone but has an idea that Henrey is waiting for someone to catch up with the group. His thoughts are that it will more than likely be Emma's uncle Bernard, or his brothers.

To James it is not too much of a concern. He was bound to meet up with them at some stage as he and their niece have become close and from what he has heard, they are very protective of her. That being said, in his mind it is James who needs protecting from Emma as she is a strong-willed woman with a fiery temper and passion to match her spirit. That in itself might cause a small issue, but how her uncles react to them being nearly on the borders of Paris is a different matter, especially now he knows about her past.

The danger Emma is taking just by being at the capital plays heavy on his mind, for should she be recognised or found out, he would have another problem to deal with. He still does not have a complete plan on how to search for his sisters, or where to even begin looking for them. How does he ask the questions, not knowing the local language? Even if he did, it is not as if he can walk up to people and ask, 'I am looking for three kidnapped girls from around seven years ago. Do you know where they might be?'

Using Emma would indeed help with the language barriers, but it would need to be done sparingly. And they'd have to carefully plan their questions, to prevent too much interest in her and in why she is looking for these children, as the people they would encounter would be from the nastier, more seedy side of Paris.

So many thoughts weigh heavy on his mind as he drives the cart along the road. Did they really send his sisters to Paris? Are they still alive? Would they recognise him, the way he looks now? Even more so, will he be able to recognise them if he finds his siblings, now that they are several years older?

The closer they get to Paris, the more villages they pass through, each one a little larger than the last. At mid-afternoon, they pass a marker stone on the side of the road that states: *Paris 12*. At a shallow bend in the road, Henrey pulls off the main route onto a less used grassy side track. He travels down this narrow path for about two hundred metres before pulling up in a floodwater meadow on the side of a large, wide river. The far side is a steep hillside lined with mature trees that overhang the river and dip their fully leaved branches in the water below. The near side, where the first wagon has pulled up, is a gentle slope leading into the water's edge. The fauna on this bank is different – thick layers of reeds and marsh grass, a few spindly shrubs, with any trees present being small and deformed or withered by flood damage.

With the far side bank being steep, the rising river would burst its banks on only this side, creating a vast expanse of shallow marshland. Typical of a flood meadow in winter when the area would be immersed with the extra water that the river carries from upstream during the heavy rains. Along this nearside waterline, the reeds grow thick and have been cut down in various areas, then stacked in large bundles and leaned against each other in groups of three to make a tripod.

James has seen this before and knows that the long straight reeds are used for thatching houses and barn roofs. With no way of building houses on this land due to the flooding, growing reeds is a good use of the meadow. The track they have just travelled down would have been made to transport the bundles off the riverbank when they had finished the season's harvest and the reeds dried out enough to store ready for use.

After securing his wagon, Henrey climbs down and heads to the others, speaking to each driver in turn. Emma has been asleep by James's side for the last couple of hours, curled up in a blanket with her head on his lap. As James stops his wagon with a bit of a jolt, she stirs and sits up. Stretching out her arms as she looks around, then up at where the sun is in the sky.

Henrey has just reached them. 'We will stop here for tonight and head off to the warehouse first thing in the morning.'

Emma is quick to comment. 'But the sun is still high in the sky. Surely we can travel for a few more hours yet.'

Henrey looks at Emma and scowls. 'The water is good here; the grass is green and good for the horses to eat. They need their rest from hauling the heavy loads all day, even if you don't. What's more, I say we stop here for today, and as I am wagon master, you will do as I say.'

Emma stands up, dropping her blanket, and salutes him. 'Yesserrr, we will stay here today.' She holds the salute as Henrey shakes his head and walks away.

She turns and smiles at James, then sits down and kisses him on the lips, holding him in her grasp. 'It would seem we will have one more night under the stars, my dear. I hope you are up for the challenge.'

'My dear, I have held up my end so far. I have no doubt I can make a good account of myself again. I have a feeling I might not win, but it will be a close enough second in my reckoning.'

She gently slides her finger along the tattoo that runs down the side of his face and onto his neck. 'Were you ever afraid when you were whaling? Or are you one of those men who's afraid of nothing?'

James thinks for a moment, experiencing a flashback to his time at sea chasing down a large bull sperm whale in a rowboat, watching as it turns in the distance and charges back at him. With nothing more than the harpoon in his hand between life and death, he holds his nerve, waiting for the perfect moment.

He now looks down at his hands, rubbing the backs of them as if to wipe off some invisible dirt that only he can see. Emma watches as he scrubs harder and harder, then he looks back at her with an icy cold stare as if death was in his eyes. 'Those that showed no fear were usually the first ones to die,' he says while still rubbing his hands. 'As they were too confident, and those big whales are not as stupid as you think. Especially if they have been chased and stuck before or have watched you pick off others from their pod. From the moment you spot a whale, launch the long boats and start rowing after them, you are terrified. As you plunge that spear into the head or back of the huge beast and they accelerate off at speed, you pray that all ends well. Once they realise that they cannot outrun you, the whale takes its first deep dive. Now you are terrified as you wonder how deep it will go. Thoughts like, *Do I have enough rope to slow it down?* Or *Will it pull to the end of the line and drag the boat down as well?* come to play on one's mind. I have seen so many people get their foot caught in the hundreds of loops of rope in the boat and as the whale dives they are pulled overboard, never to be seen again. When the whale eventually does come back up, you always wonder how each one will react, as they are all different in their actions.'

He pauses and thinks on his past experiences. 'Some come up under the boat, smashing it high into the air with the impact they deliver, killing or injuring most inside. While others start to run the surface again and wear themselves out, towing the boat around in circles behind them. The scarier encounters are with the big bulls or a mother protecting her calf who has fallen behind the pod. For they will turn and ram you or leap out of the water and land on top of the boat, smashing it to pieces along with its crew. If you're lucky and survive the fight, the tow of the boat that follows and if needed, another killer blow with a harpoon or have a second boat attach to the beast to help slow it down. The whale eventually slows to a stop, blows red out of its air hole due to the blood spilling out of the lungs, covering all around in a mist of red water as if from the very gates of hell itself. At that point you are relieved and thank God that he has seen fit to keep you alive for another day.'

James lowers his head as if ashamed. 'The worst for me was when the whale rolls over on its side. You look into its eye as it stares back at you with that last cold empty gaze of pity before it slowly closes and the animal dies by your hand. For these beasts are God's creatures just as much as us, and I am sure they have a part to play in his grand plans.' Taking a deep breath, he turns to look at Emma. 'From this point in the hunt, my work is done. While for others, their work is just beginning. Some men would instantly jump upon the whale's back and start to cut up the layers of blubber into strips to melt into oil, sometimes even before the animal had drawn its last breath just to beat the sharks to the prize. You see, once a whale is taken, it always becomes a race to get as much of the blubber aboard the ship to melt before the sharks below have eaten their way up through the carcass. And there were always a lot of big sharks around every kill, brought in by the smell of fresh blood leaking into the water.

'Unlike most on the ship, I did not choose to be a whaler. It was forced upon me, so I killed to survive and keep my place amongst the crew. I became a harpooner as the smell of boiling oil from melting the blubber was so rancid that I could not stand to be on the main ship anymore. So, I took to the boats and chose the better of two evils. I would sooner have tried to give them a swift death than spend days melting their bodies down and storing them in barrels below deck. To my shame, right from the beginning I was good at what I did, taking out my anger at being at sea on any of those poor beasts that happened across my path. I killed so many of them gentle giants. For most, the first time they ever saw a man on a boat was their last. But it came at a cost, for each one I killed seemed to take a little piece of my soul with them. I felt so dirty and ashamed for having taken the life of an animal just to light a lamp or fill a woman's dress with parts of its body on some distant shore.'

Emma listens intently. She is saddened by the shame he now feels. 'Were there many men killed amongst the crew of the ships you were on?'

'The ship that brought me back to Holland from the islands needed me due to all the harpooners in the crew being killed by whales. To fill the hull and make it a profitable return home, I killed thirteen whales at the cost of eleven crew members who will never see their families again. Seven were lost to the whales and four more fell foul to sharks grabbing their feet and pulling them down through the middle of the whale's carcass as they were slicing blubber into strips for rendering. They are the ones you remember most as you hear the screams and watch the fight as they try to pull back up and get away, holding on to the whale's bones as the sharks tug at their legs before finally pulling them down into the depths below.

'You see, the cost of oil and whale parts can be high on the numbers of crew lost at sea. But if you make it back, your share of the prize is a small fortune and can last a person a long time. That is if you are able to leave the port with what you have earned. As there are many more sharks that wait on land to take what you have worked and bled so hard for. Each trip out on a whaling ship will see your pay get better as you have more experience. However, I for one will never go back out and hunt those beasts again. I have done my time and paid with enough of my soul. I want to keep what's left for myself.'

He wriggles free of Emma and dismounts the wagon. Taking two wooden stakes, a large hammer and a length of rope from the back of the vehicle, he pegs out the line a few metres away from the convoy. He then unhitches the horses, removes the harnesses from each one and tethers them to the rope about ten feet apart. He does the same with all five carts while Henrey fills and places a bucket of water by each horse.

Thomas is checking the hooves on every horse and picking out any stones and clumps of earth that might have lodged in place. Pierre and Jack look round for any firewood and start to build a small campfire while Phillip pulls out and assembles the table then starts to prepare vegetables and meat for the pot. Emma dismounts and joins Phillip in preparing the food. All is going well until Henrey walks over with a whole piece of his famous cured sausage and speaks up.

'Perhaps you would like this to help spice up the stew, yes?' Emma and Phillip look at each other then back at Henrey in disgust. She curses in French before speaking in a more civil manner.

'Take that evil thing away from here. It has no place near good food.'

The rest of the group have heard the conversation and are chuckling or laughing at Emma's answer. Henrey goes quiet. He sheepishly steps closer to the table and places his offering on the corner. 'I will leave it here in case you change your mind.'

Again, Emma and Phillip look at each other before Emma grabs the offending offering, storms over to the riverbank and hurls it into the river. For a small flock of mallards that just so happens to be swimming by at the time, this unfortunate event will have consequences. The heavy foot-and-a-half-long projectile goes crashing into the group with the impact of a brick. The birds split up, running to take flight, squawking and quacking. Two of them dive under the water before one re-emerges, taking straight to the air and flying off. The other is slow to respond; it has taken the full impact of the missile and has been left in a semi-unconscious state. As it resurfaces, it flounders on the surface.

While the rest of the party are now roaring with laughter, Thomas runs into the water. With it being a flood meadow, it is a shallow gradient into the water, and he swiftly makes ground on the flapping duck, grabbing it by the neck and raising it into the air with a roar of achievement.

James and the others cheer and laugh at what they have just seen and Thomas heads back to the bank and presents the duck to Emma.

'Your prize, my dear, for the finest throw ever made,' he says in French. 'However, I must point out that the weapon of choice was a bit extreme, and I do fear for any creature that may come across said weapon on the bottom of the river.'

Everybody but one laughs. Even James, who does not fully understand the words but gets the gist of it, is chuckling and shaking his head. The only person not to laugh is Henrey. He walks over to the river, arms held out in front of him and a sad expression on his face. He looks mournfully into the water to try and spot his cured delicacy. But it is now murky and visibility is poor due to Thomas walking around and kicking up the soft sediment on the bottom.

Pierre walks up to Henrey and puts his arm on his shoulder. 'Do you have any more of that cured sausage?'

Henrey's face lights up and he excitedly replies, 'Well, yes, I have another stick in my wagon! Would you like some?'

Pierre nods. 'Yes, please, I would like a piece about this big.' He holds his hands out, showing a distance of around ten inches.

Henrey looks at the gap and says, 'That is a lot of sausage, my friend! Are you that hungry?'

Pierre looks at him in shock. 'Eat it? Don't be so stupid! It is disgusting. But it seems to make a great weapon and I want to have a go like Emma.'

Henrey roars with anger, curses in French, then swings a fist wildly in Pierre's direction. Pierre swiftly runs away as Henrey storms after him, flailing his arms in an attempt to land one on him. Phillip, Thomas and Emma are in fits of laughter, having watched everything unfold. As Emma regains some composure, she explains what has happened to James, making him laugh and clap his hands.

As things start to quiet down, Thomas dispatches the duck and plucks it. He draws out the guts and throws them into the water before taking the dressed bird to Emma. It takes her just moments to cut it up and add it to the stew pot, while the remaining carcass is tossed into the fire to burn away. The makeshift camp settles down for one last night. The horses are content, grazing the grass they can reach from their tethered positions on the rope, while Emma and the men have grouped up around the campfire and stew pot. They use the time to teach James some more French words to help him understand their language better.

It's a slow and painful process, as James is not the fastest learner, but he makes progress while the others kill time talking to him and each other. When the stew is finally ready, Emma dishes it up into bowls, breaking off a chunk of French stick to go with each meal. It is a few days old now and getting a little stale, but as they dunk it in the stew, it soon softens enough to eat.

The evening wears on, and there are many references to the new duck-hunting method, using a type of barely edible hand bomb that can be used as a last resort if you ever run out of shot. Henrey takes it all in his stride. It is all part of the banter he has had with his friends over the many years they have known each other.

The shadows move in as dusk settles and the light fades from the sky, and James and Emma leave the comfort of the fire to bed down for the night. He had previously flattened the ground under the wagon, placed down piles of abundant reeds on the floor and spread a blanket out over the top. With some of the cloth from the wagon now wrapped round the wheels on one side for a bit of privacy, it is not too bad for an overnight stay. There is a comfortable silence between the two of them as they lie quietly together with different thoughts rushing through their heads. James still does not have a clear plan set out for how he is going to begin his search for his lost siblings, while Emma wonders who her father really is, and what she will do once she finds out his name.

For once, the couple are in a more sombre mood and passion is not on the agenda as they settle down for the night with just a few kisses. Tomorrow is going to be a big day for the pair of them, and they know they will need all their wits about them when they enter Paris and begin the search. They finally fall asleep with Emma tucked into James's chest and his arms holding her tightly.

* * *

James is awake early; the sky is only just starting to lighten as dawn breaks and the first of the birds begin to voice their opinions. He carefully removes himself from his embrace with Emma, puts on his large jumper and boots, then walks along the river for around fifty yards before taking a seat on an old tree stump. Rolling his neck and stretching out his arms, he views the water's edge and far bank. The odd bat darts through the air, twisting, turning and swooping to get the last of the small insects that are present in the still air. He does not hear Henrey approach until he is within a few feet of him and by then he knows exactly who it is by the strong smell of garlic and pipe tobacco. As he sits down quietly beside James and looks out across the river, he speaks.

'You must have a lot on your mind today, James.'

'Hmmm, more than I would like. For many months I have been focused on one goal. I had no idea a week or so back that I would happen across a woman who would turn my life upside down again.'

'They can do that to a man, which is why I need to ask of you some more questions while Emma is not present.'

James nods. 'Ask what you need to, and I will answer as best I can.'

'You say you spent several years living on the islands once you were abandoned, and I see by the tribal marks on your face, neck and arms, you must have adopted their culture heavily. Could I view the rest of them under your clothing before I ask my question?'

James stands up, takes off his jumper and lays it to one side of the stump. Henrey walks around him, looking at all the pictures tattooed on his body. With some he can follow the pattern of symbols in a kind of trail around his torso and arms, while others seem more random. Henrey observes every one of them for several minutes, then nods and sits back down while James puts his jumper back on. 'Well, now you have looked at them, what do you wish to ask me about?'

'I can see by the marks that you killed many men in defence of your village. Not just from other tribes but some were pirates from large ships, men from your own part of the world.'

'Yes, tribal disputes all over the islands were not uncommon to start with, but with the vision of one tribal chief in particular, they soon united as one people to deal with the bigger threat, as these tribesmen needed to protect the lands that feed them from foreign invaders. Twice I fought with Spanish pirates and once with a Portuguese navy frigate trying to steal people for pleasure and labour from our village.'

'The marks say that you were gifted a great reward by a chief. That would mean that you either saved his life or that of someone close to him.'

James nods. 'It was both – him, his family and his grandchildren. From men who wanted to use them as leverage to get the black pearls the villagers were famous for collecting and using for trade with Europeans.'

Henrey gets to the meat of the question. 'Did you take a woman from the village?'

James looks at Henrey. 'I was offered many, but finally I took one of the chief's granddaughters, Dela, to be my woman. Looking back, I think it was for company more than love. I had been alone a long time.'

Henrey nods at his honesty. 'No doubt a child was soon to follow.'

James smiles. 'Yes. We had a son called Pele, named after the woman's brother. He was lost in a battle with the Spanish raiders long before I met her.'

Henrey nods again as he rubs his chin. 'That would put the chief in high status with the other villages and secure his granddaughter and your son's position in the village for the rest of their lives, now that you have left.' He thinks for a moment before continuing. 'Tell me, did they advise you to go and find your sisters?'

James looks at Henrey with a surprised expression. 'I was having bad nightmares, more so when the stormy season arrived. The tribal chief and spirit shaman concluded that it was the spirits of my lost siblings calling for assistance. They advised me to come home, face my dreams and find out what had happened to them if I wanted to put to rest the nightmares.'

Henrey does his usual nod. 'They paid you with something special and found you passage on a ship. Then, before you left, they gave you that final tattoo of three wavy lines and, above it, that cloud-like creature, yes?'

James is now very curious. 'Yes, that tattoo was done a week before I left by the tribal shaman. And the tribal elder gave me a bag containing a dozen large, highly prized black pearls. All the people from the tribe were helping to look for a way to get me home. Finally, a nearby village approached a Dutch whaler in need of hardwood for repairs after a heavy storm. They had lost all their experienced harpooners after some bad luck whaling. But how did you know all this?'

'Ah, that all makes sense to me now. You see, your story is marked all over your body, but to read it you must think like a child as these people are not as advanced in society. Their way of keeping records and expressing themselves is by very simple markings. Because you already had many tattoos of whales and dragons and mythical beasts all over your body, their story of you has been put between these existing marks and needs to be followed by one that knows what they mean.

'For example, the wavy lines with a canoe and a stick man on the side means a large ship, so big that people live in it rather than a man on a canoe – that would represent a dugout canoe. You see, to the people of what became your village, you were found at a time of great need and healing, hence the first tattoo is your arrival to them. So that monster facing downwards covered in marks and trailing smoke represents you with your tattooed and scarred body arriving as a warrior ready for battle. All the other tattoos are your story – events and battles that you have had to unite the villages and defend the people and their lands. You would have wanted for nothing, and your gift of a son, well, that is a true honour from you to them as he will defend the village in the future from any enemy.

'Your nightmares would have been read by a shaman as the ancestors asking for the return of their champion. Your tasks having been fulfilled, the village is now safe, and your son has been left to continue in your footsteps and defend his people. Your time of being needed by that village was over, but not the tasks the spirits have set for you. For now, other people need your help, and it would be down to the village to help you on your way as a thank you to their ancestors.

'The final mark on your body of a cloud-shaped animal above upward-facing wavy lines is the final part of your story. It depicts you ascending back to the ancestors, your task fulfilled and the people safe.' Henrey pauses and looks at James sternly before continuing. 'Despite what you think, you are not expected to return. And if you did, I doubt it would go down well with the village as their need of you has been completed. However, there is something odd with your last mark. The small dots below the wavy lines represent the gift of pearls as a thank you from the village. But they also put what looks like an eye with a dagger in a round house. That symbol would be the village, so if I am reading this right, it would mean that the whole village has given you a curse to put on someone or something! That is very powerful and dark indeed. Do you know what they are talking about?'

'I have an idea. But that would be between my brother and me should the day arrive that we meet. But I must ask you a question now. How is it that you know all this? It would not be common for a man from these parts to understand the island natives and their ways.'

Henrey gives a small grimace. He slowly lifts up his tunic to show a tattoo similar to James's. 'Thomas and I both have these marks on our bodies. We were the only two survivors of a battle between our navy ship, D'hautpoult, and a renegade buccaneer named Red Rogers, who was fighting for the English. We chased each other for over a week until the wind dropped. Then we fought each other on the drift of the ocean currents. Finally, our ships were tied together with grappling hooks, each of us trying to board the other across broken rigging. Both captains had the same idea of a full broadside, close in, but as they fired someone hit one of the powder magazines below deck and both ships went up in a huge explosion.

'Thomas and I were fighting on a part of the rigging being trailed behind the ships at the time and got blown into the water. In total, seven men survived that blast. We were in a good enough condition to be able to work together to survive. We lashed bits of both ships together in an effort to try and make something that would float long enough to reach land. We piled on all the injured and wounded who were still alive from both sides until we could take no more. But it soon became clear that finding land was not our biggest problem. The explosion from the ships and the bodies and blood in the water soon attracted the sharks. A few at first, then they got bigger, much bigger. Twelve, fifteen then twenty foot in length. And as time went on, they got bolder. First it was those hanging on the sides of the raft that got their attention, then they started to push and bump to dislodge more of us. By the end, they were launching themselves onto the makeshift raft, pulling it apart as they worked their way through us. The following day, there was just Thomas and I left alive, hidden inside a cabinet strapped to a piece of the deck.

'We were picked up by native fishermen a few days later and spent four years in a community much like yours. We fought like you and survived against many enemies and raiders. I took a woman. Thomas took two. We started families and made the best of what we had. We did not know if the likes of us would ever be found, such was our remote isolation away from the main sailing routes. It was by chance that an East India trade ship, looking for water and fresh fruit to fight a serious bout of scurvy, came across our island. With so many of the crew dead and dying, they were only too glad to have two new and healthy members of crew to help sail the ship back home.

'In the four months it took us to return, we talked a lot and decided that it was best to keep our women and children to ourselves and not go back for them. We had left their community in a better state than when they had found us, and there was no way they would understand how to live here in France. It was better for all involved to close that book and never talk about it with those who would never understand unless they had been through it themselves.

'That is also my advice to you, dear boy. Close the book. That part of your journey has ended. Feel proud that they will live in a better place because of your help and never speak about it to Emma. It would do more harm than good. Move forward now that you have returned to your own part of the world and don't look back as it can serve no purpose for either side. You did what was needed to survive at a time when you knew not what the future held. Now you are back, and you have yet another battle to overcome.'

James thinks on the story told by Henrey, who he now realises is far wiser and knowledgeable than he first thought. He may not like all what he has been told, but his words do make good sense to him. Not only that, but he has also been through a similar event to James and came out with a good perspective as well as learning how to accept his past while still moving on with his life. 'I will think on your advice, Henrey, and take it under advisement for later. But I also know you have been slowing down this convoy to allow Emma's uncles to catch up. Is there anything I should know before they arrive?'

'You noticed then.' Henrey nods before continuing. 'I have been slowing us down in the hope Emma's uncles would arrive before we hit Paris. It is the only thing I could think of to get more help here to protect her. They are all four good, honourable men. Bernard is the oldest. He holds them all together and will be the one to call the shots. He is not stupid and thinks before he acts. I am sure that, before he arrives, he will have worked out some of the situation you are in with Emma.

'Sebastian, on the other hand, will react with fire and passion and think later. He is the youngest of the four, quick with the words and faster with his fists. Unfortunately, he will come at you first, then ask questions later. Gaston and François are the middle brothers, big and powerful; they are the engine of the group. When they are set a task, it gets done. The four of them have one thing in common. Having loved their sister deeply, all feel they failed her in her time of need. As for their niece, Emma… well, make no mistake. They would poke the devil in the eye and walk to hell and back for her. So, you have your work cut out to get through this, but they are also good men and respect honest and true people.'

'So, Henrey, where do we go from here? Is there a store or building in Paris that we are heading to?'

Henrey stretches out and yawns. 'We have a large warehouse on the outskirts of the city where we sort and sell our goods to the local traders. If we leave in around an hour, we will arrive before lunch. From there, what you do is not in my hands, but it is the best place for Emma to be kept safe until her uncles arrive.'

James nods in agreement and stands. 'We had better wake the

men and get the horses and wagons ready to go then.'

Henrey grabs his arm and pulls him back down. 'Before we get going, I must ask you something.'

'Ask what you will.'

Henrey takes a deep breath and clears his throat, then looks round to ensure that no one is present. 'It is about my cured sausage. Is it really that bad?'

James stares hard at Henrey. 'Oh yes, my friend, it's that bad. But as I have seen with my own eyes, it is able to get good food, as a weapon.'

He stands up and walks off, leaving Henrey to shake his head and mutter to himself. Moments later he wakes Emma with a kiss. 'It's time to get up,' he whispers before leaving to prepare the horses for the day's travelling. It has been the same routine for the last few days: feed, water, hooves checked and picked out, and a quick once-over on the horses' bodies as he brushes them down to ensure no injuries or wounds are present. Any sores or chafing that have been caused by the tack rubbing against the horses' skin are rubbed with soothing lavender and rosemary oil to prevent infection while reducing the attention of flies to the area.

While James is tending to the horses, Emma is rekindling the fire and, after collecting a large pot of water from the river to make a morning pot of coffee, she also prepares the last of the cheese and cured meats. Cutting both into slithers, then slicing the remaining tomatoes and sieving off the final jar of pickled onions. It will clear out all their food stocks, but by lunchtime she knows they should be on the edges of Paris at the family warehouse.

The men are just finishing assembling the horses on the front of the wagons when Emma yells out, 'Coffee's ready! Come and get it while it's hot.'

For some reason, there is a more sombre mood in the air, perhaps because they all think that today is going to be an eventful one. Whatever the reason, barely a word is spoken as they eat and drink what Emma has prepared. After around ten minutes of near silence, Emma starts to clear away. The last thing she does is take the plates and cups to the river to clean. As she reaches the water's edge, she lets out a scream and stares down at the reed-lined edge.

James is the first to arrive, followed by the rest of the men, who are all stopped in their tracks by what they see. Thomas and Phillip take off their caps in respect. 'Poor thing never had a chance,' says James.

Emma translates his words into French for the others to understand.

Phillip shakes his head and speaks while Emma translates for James.

'My God! Death by poison! What a terrible way to go. Cut off before it even had the chance to grow. Taken before it even had time to live and experience life.' She turns to Henrey. 'This is what you have done, you murderer! Taken an innocent's life with that poison. This could have been good food if it had not been contaminated by that evil you make.'

Lying in the margins is a four-foot baby wels catfish, belly up but still twitching, with two inches of Henrey's sausage still hanging out of its mouth. Henrey looks round at the others. 'What are you talking about? It will still make good eating.' He goes to reach for the fish, but Thomas pulls him back.

'No, it is too late,' he says. 'Look at its mouth. The poison is in its system. It will kill all who try and eat it. This one we will just have to leave for nature to take its course.'

Henrey looks at them all with a blank expression. He does not understand what they are talking about. Finally, he fumbles in his pocket for his spectacles and puts them on. Then he looks back down at the catfish in the margins. This time he can see what the others have seen all along, his homemade sausage hanging out of the fish's mouth. No doubt the catfish had tried to swallow the sausage whole and had choked to death.

He looks back at the group of friends around him. All of them are desperate not to be the first person to laugh. Emma is barely holding on, while Phillip and James are shaking and covering their mouths with their hands. Thomas looks away in the hope he will not be seen as he starts to let out little giggles.

'Bastards, the lot of you,' Henrey bellows before storming off past them all and climbing up onto the front of his wagon. The rest of the group burst into laughter; they can contain themselves no more as they point and laugh at the unfortunate catfish. Henrey sits up straight, head held high, choosing to ignore them all.

While everyone is laughing, Emma moves upstream above the dead catfish to the next gap in the reeds and washes the plates and cups before returning to the wagons and placing them inside a wooden box with the other crockery. She then moves around to the front and steps up to join James on the wagon.

With a flick of the reins, Henrey leads them back up the track towards the road and on to Paris.

The group continues for around an hour, winding this way and that through small woods and open farmland before heading up a long incline to the top of a small hill lined with trees. As they reach the top, the trees thin out and there, spread out before them in the distance, is the city of Paris. A mixture of new and old buildings and monuments. Church spires like the one from Notre Dame Cathedral break up the skyline, along with other high-profile buildings such as the Sorbonne and the Pantheon. A huge heaving mass of people that live below a dirty grey smog of soot and dust being produced by bellowing fires of the factories and household chimneys.

All the wagons stop as the drivers view the city intently. None of them have even noticed the lonesome figure of a man standing by his horse under a large hazelnut tree. As his horse stamps at the ground impatiently, Emma looks round. She grips James's hand tightly as her heart skips a beat. James too looks across and sees the man staring directly at him. 'Wait here, James,' Emma says before dismounting.

She walks over and kisses the man on both cheeks, while being watched by the rest of the men in the convoy.

'Hello, Uncle,' she says before hugging him. He does not move a muscle, just looks at her with steely eyes. He passes Emma the reins to his horse before walking towards the group. He looks at all the men one at a time, with each man nodding back at him, before fixing his gaze on James.

James has been expecting this meeting for a while, so the stare does not intimidate him one bit. What he does wonder about is whether his first communication with Emma's uncle will be with his words or his fists.

Bernard does not say a word to anyone. He moves on and climbs up on the seat next to Henrey, takes the reins from his hands and flicks them at the horses. As the wagon moves off, the rest follow. Emma ties the horse to the back of the wagon and goes to mount up next to James.

Bernard yells, 'I gave you that horse to ride, so ride it!'

Emma goes to step down, and as she does, James's hand reaches down to her.

'Come, Emma,' he says. 'Sit next to me. We are in this together now.' His eyes do not break contact with Bernard, who just stares back at him. James does not know what Bernard said, but he will not allow Emma to be spoken down to.

Emma pauses for a second before taking his hand and stepping back up to sit beside him. Bernard says nothing, just turns around and looks forward as he flicks the reins again.

For the next hour, they follow Bernard's lead. James can hear a continuous and heated conversation between Bernard and Henrey which goes on for the best part of thirty minutes, with plenty of arm throwing and fist clenching. It peaks with a finale of words and the wagon abruptly stopping, bringing the rest of the convoy to a stop as well. With a few more words, waving of arms and this time finger pointing at each other, then at James, it goes quiet, and the wagon train moves off again.

Emma chuckles to herself. 'What is so funny?' James asks.

'My uncle said that if he finds out you are lying about your sisters, or I am harmed in any way, he will beat you to death. Henrey replied and told him that you are of good character and if he tried it on with you, he would be the one to be flat on his back. To be fair, I think this is the first time I have ever heard Henrey stand up for someone other than my uncles or me. Perhaps there is hope for us yet!'

James says nothing. He knows this is only the start of things and there will be a lot more problems to overcome in the coming hours and days.

Bernard takes the convoy deeper and deeper into the streets of Paris. As they venture to the more established areas of the city, the roads and buildings become better made and to a finer standard with all types of stone and marble being used to outshine one establishment from the next. The people of the area are also dressed to a more fashionable standard – each person trying to be trendier, better dressed and more opulent than the next.

The route is lined with cafés and bistros and the smell of coffee and cake fills the air. Each shop has their own signs, tables and chairs out the front to attract more people to stop for beverages and food. Women are wearing more elaborate and larger dresses with even bigger matching hats while still keeping their waists as narrow as possible to make themselves more desirable. Paris has become centre stage in Europe for displaying fashion, wealth and social standing. The women walk around in female groups or are shown off on the arms of men as a statement of how rich they are to be able to dress their women in such fineries. These trophy women can easily be spotted, as they are the ones who will only sit at tables furthest from the establishment's doors, even if the closer tables are empty, for they must be seen by as many people as possible in order to attract the attention of a wealthy gentleman.

Bernard turns his team of horses down one of the side roads. At the end of the short lane is a large blue arched doorway on the front of a warehouse. As the wagon approaches, the doors start to open, revealing a huge interior space, large enough for all the wagons to drive straight in and have space to spare.

James follows the others inside and looks around. He can see it has been split up into several areas. As he moves through, it opens into a courtyard with many stables in a line, a storage area for wagons, and a building for tack with a small blacksmithing area adjacent.

Along the far walls of the warehouse and down the sides are hundreds of large wooden barrels stacked several high. Most are filled with wine and brandy, with some containing salt and salted or cured produce stacked in a column down the middle. There are dozens of shelving units full of different materials, clothing, metalwork, furniture and produce from all over the world, even separate areas for tea, spices and coffee. In front of this mixed collection of storage goods is a line of tables.

On one of them, three men are haggling over a large roll of highly decorated cloth. They argue for several minutes, each sticking different numbers of fingers in the air before finally reaching a value that they can all agree on. With the nodding of heads and shaking of hands, the deal has been struck. The man then hands over some kind of payment before picking up his roll of cloth and leaving the warehouse.

Within minutes of their arrival, people start to appear from different areas of the building and descend onto the wagons. A man with a red bandana wrapped round his head takes the bridle on one of James's horses and leads the wagon team to the tables at the far end of the line. As they stop, another person opens up the back of the vehicle and within seconds the contents starts to be unloaded. James is amazed at just how much can be stacked in the back of one wagon, as the tables fill with all he has been transporting.

Crates of wine and brandy are stacked along the floor, and all kinds of trade goods he did not even know were aboard are placed on the tables ready for sorting and pricing. The bandana man marks everything down on a ledger and places a tag on each item before yet more people move them from the tables and into the warehouse stock. Emma explains the system to James.

'The goods belong to many of the people in the village. Being a coastal port, we have the opportunity to buy all types of unusual items, particularly after a storm like the one we just had. As a community, we pool all the goods and send them down here every month in a convoy. Whatever the items are sold at, my uncles get ten per cent, while the wagon drivers are paid a fixed price for transporting the stock. The rest of the money goes back to the person who commissioned the items to be sent and sold, hence the name tags on the goods.

'Some items sell straight away. Others take a little longer, but all make a lot more money selling in Paris than they would do anywhere else. Doing our trade this way, we can also employ people all year round – some months in the fields harvesting, other months in the warehouse sorting or selling the goods to the local establishments. It has made everybody who works here a good living, and we have a well-respected reputation of supplying quality merchandise.

'Come tomorrow when the word goes out about new stock, we will have buyers in and out all day haggling for the supplies. Every quarter we auction off any stock that has been around for too long. Sometimes that gets a better price as more people want the same items, other times it is just good profit. When the wagons return to the port, we transport the money back in hidden compartments inside the wagons' frames known only to us. My uncles do this when all the other staff have left for the day. The money is then distributed back to the people who sent their goods via the café or warehouses on the port.'

'It seems a good way to benefit all.'

Henrey calls out to James and Emma to join him. James dismounts first and assists Emma down from the wagon. He leads them into a large wooden structure just off the side of the stable block.

Emma is apprehensive and grabs for James's hand as she tenses up a little. She knows they are going to meet her uncle, and this will not be a pleasant encounter. Henrey enters the room first followed by Emma, then James, who looks around the inside of this large room. There is a huge open fireplace in the middle with a brass fireguard made in four sections surrounding it in a circle. Several armchairs are scattered around this focal point. Across from them is a large rectangular dining table that has around twenty chairs lined up against it. Leading off this main room is another containing a kitchen and pantry. On the other side of the room is a long bar with several racks of wine and spirits. Bar stools with burgundy cushions are propped up against the marble-top bar, and there is a long coat rack with multiple coats hanging from it.

Bernard is sitting in one of the armchairs. Beside him on a giant blue pillow is a grey Irish wolfhound. As it captures Emma's attention, it stands up, the excitement in its face plain to be seen. As soon as Emma smiles, the dog bounds over to her.

It is still quite young and not full-sized yet and its long gangly legs are going everywhere as it bounces around with excitement. Emma pats him as he rubs against her.

'Napoleon,' yells out Bernard. The dog stops and crouches slightly, looking at Bernard sheepishly before staring back at Emma. Bernard points at the dog's bed, but he just sits down by Emma, leaning his head against her for protection.

Bernard looks up at the ceiling and shakes his head. 'Even my own dog loves that woman more than me. Emma, you are a bad influence, now send him back here to his bed.'

Emma pats the dog one more time, then flicks her head in the direction of Bernard. The dog bounds over and dives onto its pillow, rotating several times while looking at Bernard with its dark brown eyes and its cute scruffy teddy-bear face. He fixes his gaze on Emma as he lies down, waiting for the opportunity to run back over to her.

With a hand gesture, Bernard offers James the chair next to him. He moves forward and takes the seat while Emma pushes another armchair close to James and sits. Henrey sits on the other side of Bernard, twisting another chair slightly before resting his bones.

'So, you are the man who has won the heart of my niece, Emma. I can understand that as she is a fine, beautiful woman.' Emma automatically translates what Bernard is saying.

'I also understand that you protected her when some sailors were getting out of hand at the café, and again I thank you for defending her honour.'

James just gives a slow nod.

'I do not even blame you for Emma smuggling herself aboard the wagons. The story of your sisters and their fate is quite compelling, and she can be a determined spirit at times when she wants to help people. But what I do not understand is, when you found out about Emma's past, why the hell you did not send her back? More so if you care for her the way Henrey says you do.'

Emma attempts to speak to Bernard, but he cuts her short, slamming the arm on his chair with his fist and giving her a stern look. 'Just translate what I say or go, and I will have Henrey do it.'

After hearing the translation, James responds for the first time with Emma translating his words into French. 'Emma was determined. If we were to send her back, she threatened to go it alone to get to Paris and find out about her father and seek vengeance on Madam Kelly for her mother. Now it seemed to me that she was better off with me beside her than no one being there as you were not around. In the case of my brothers and sisters, I have been acting on information since I first found out foul play was at hand, and I will not stop until I know the truth. Many men along the way are already living with the consequences of their actions and I will continue until satisfied.'

James sits up in his chair. He looks at Bernard and continues in a firmer voice. 'What I do not understand is why it took you a whole damned year to act upon information when you knew where your sister was and who was holding her prisoner. I myself would have never waited so long to get my sister back and I would not have rested until those responsible were either dead or punished or I had been killed trying. By the time you did grow the balls to do something, it was just too late. Emma's mother was lost to you forever.

'Now, many years down the line, she wants answers to questions that should have been known about years ago. Because of your failure to act, here I sit with you thinking you can blame me for Emma looking for these answers.'

He waits for Emma to catch up with the translating before he continues. He can see he now has Bernard's full attention. 'Let me tell you something I have learned over the years. When you choose to hide in the shadows away from people who have been searching for this young lady for years, rather than confront them and fix the problem, this is what happens. You knew this day was going to come, whether it was me or someone else by Emma's side. It was always inevitable.'

James pauses again for Emma to catch up her words. 'Now you can choose to act on it, try to take me out or get the hell out of my way. Because I will find out about my sisters, then I will do what is needed to help Emma with what she wants to do. It's your choice.'

Emma is translating but pauses as James's words make her think about what she is doing in Paris. 'Tell him!' James barks at her while staring back at Bernard.

Bernard sits up in his chair. He grips his fists and stares at James with dagger-like eyes. James has really hit a nerve with the words he has spoken, but that was his intent. He has not come here to be used as an excuse for someone else's mistakes.

Bernard thinks on the comments James has said and it takes his mind back to past events. At the time, he put far too much faith in the law, public outcry and diplomatic solution to his sister's situation. All of them had played him and his sister in a human form of chess. They had all been pawns, pushed around the table by the rich and powerful that control the big pieces. He sits back in his chair and thinks on it for a while. For as terrible as it sounds coming from a stranger, James is hitting all the points that he knows are true.

As tension mounts in the room, the main warehouse gates can be heard swinging open, then the clipping of horseshoes on the stone floor followed by people shouting and dismounting from another wagon and horses. Seconds later the door to their room bursts open and Sebastian steps in. He looks around and spots James, spurting profanities in French as he moves towards him.

Emma and James stand up and turn to face the oncoming Sebastian. He approaches, pointing his finger at his niece, still spilling out words. Emma looks down at the floor as the barrage of words continues. James reaches out to comfort Emma just as Sebastian lets fly with a fist that – because of James's movement towards Emma – glances down the side of his face, turning his head and cutting his lip on his teeth.

James looks back at Sebastian as he takes another swing. This time, he catches his fist in his left hand and grips it tightly, while spitting some blood in his mouth onto the floor. He then looks at

Sebastian before head-butting the bridge of his nose with a bone-shuddering crack, splitting his nose wide open as blood starts to flow. James grabs Sebastian's crotch in his other hand, and lifts and throws him over the armchair, leaving him in a heap on the floor.

Sebastian tries to sit up, but he is totally disorientated. He touches his nose and yells out as the pain bites hard. He gets to rocking on his hands and knees in an attempt to stand up but falls back down onto the floor.

By now, his two brothers have entered the room. They see Sebastian on the floor with blood dripping profusely from his face. Standing across from him is James. Instantly, they set towards James, who himself is preparing to take them both on by raising his fists. Emma moves in front of him, trying to shield him from the advance of her uncles.

'Enough,' yells Bernard. 'Sebastian got what he deserved. He attacked this man, not the other way round. Henrey, take Sebastian out back and clean him up, will you? He is bleeding all over the floor and making a mess.'

Bernard turns to look at Emma, who is still covering James. 'That man does not need you to protect him – I can see that for myself. Just translate for me and tell him to relax and sit down. He will not come to any more harm. Then go out back and get some food prepared. This is going to be a long night and I haven't eaten in days while trying to catch up with you. Gaston, François, take seats round the fire and for God's sake relax while I think for a bit and work this out.'

James sits back down while Gaston and François take seats in the armchairs to his left. The atmosphere is somewhat frosty to say the least, but a brawl has been avoided and there is an uneasy truce. Henrey helps the staggering Sebastian to his feet and out into the other room to get cleaned up, while Emma kisses James on the side of the head before leaving to prepare some food.

Bernard walks over to the bar. He takes out seven glasses from under the counter and places them on top, takes a bottle off the rack and looks at the label. With a small knife he has pulled from his pocket, he cracks the wax seal from around the top and twists out the stopper. He pours a generous amount in all the glasses, then places the bottle down and carries four glasses to the waiting men. Handing each one of them a glass as he passes before sitting back down in his chair, he looks at his brothers and then at James. His eyes are welling up as he relives the pain of holding his sister in his arms as she died. Pausing to think on the right words to say, he raises his glass. 'To our sister Juliet du Grande, the Lost Angel of Paris. May God continue to allow her to sing to all in his kingdom. For her daughter, Emma, and with what we are about to do, keep her safe and protect us all from harm.'

Gaston and François look at each other before raising their glasses. James has got an idea of what has been said as he recognises Emma's mother's name and raises his glass as well. They all drink deeply of the apple calvados, a powerful but tasty drink that warms every part that it touches before the strength of the alcohol kicks in.

Emma is in the kitchen, rushing round to get food together as fast as she can as she does not want to leave James on his own for too long with her uncles in case another fight ensues. She layers assorted meats, cheese, tomatoes and chunks of bread on platters, along with pickled vegetables and fish, then starts to bring them out and place them on the large table. In and out of the room she rushes, watching the men every time she leaves the kitchen. Finally, she brings out some plates and cutlery, places them on the end of the table and calls out, 'Food is on the table. Come and get it when you are ready.'

She watches as her three uncles get up and make their way to the table, grabbing a plate each and piling on the food. Noticing that James has not moved from his chair, she picks up a plate and fills it with food and passes it to him with a smile. She then moves over to the bar to collect one of the glasses on the counter and sniffs the contents. Realising instantly that it is calvados, a drink she likes greatly, Emma takes a sip then sits back down beside James. 'I'm sorry to have put you through this, James. I did not want it to go this way.'

James pats the back of her hand. 'Fear not, Emma. I have a

feeling these uncles of yours have been itching to do something for years. You growing up and doing what you did just ignited the flame and gave them a reason to get on with it. What's more, I think Bernard already has a plan in his head, as he is just too composed after I rattled his cage like I did.' He leans over and whispers into her ear. 'I have a feeling that he is going to let us know his plan tonight once Henrey returns with the other one who swung at me.'

James puts the plate between them on the arm of the chair so they can share the food together while they wait.

The three brothers are still in deep conversation around the dining table. Bernard is doing most of the talking while the other two listen to what he has to say. Every now and then one or more of the brothers looks at James and Emma, then they continue with their debate. Henrey appears from the other room, closely followed by Sebastian, who makes straight for James. The other brothers watch him intently but do not interfere as he approaches him.

'I, er, um, have been speaking with Henrey, yes, perhaps I was wrong in what I thought of you. But you must understand I love her as if she was my own daughter. I thought that you had took her. For that I am sorry.' Sebastian puts out his hand in friendship. James stands up and shakes it while nodding in acknowledgement, then he sits back down.

'Good, now I get some food, for I am starving,' Sebastian comments as he turns and leaves James.

The conversation around the dining table by the now four brothers continues for some time, with each of them adding their opinions. Bernard walks to the bar and picks up the bottle of calvados and goes around topping up all their glasses. As he fills Emma's glass, he speaks. 'You have made things very difficult for me, Emma. Do not get me wrong; I knew this day would come. But not with you in Paris and an Englishman we do not know by your side. Are you sure we can trust him?'

Emma nods. 'I am sure. But above all, I need him around. He is the first man outside of my family that I trust, and he has as much to lose as I do in being here.'

Bernard rubs his chin. 'If that is the case, then I need you to ensure that this man and my brothers do not come to blows while I go and visit some old friends. I will be gone for an hour if not longer. Hold down the fort until I get back.'

He knocks back the rest of his drink and places the empty glass on the bar as he leaves the room. His brothers watch as he departs before all moving to the armchairs around the fireplace, each carrying their own plate of food and drink with them. Gaston prods at the fire with a poker, then adds a couple of logs to bring up the heat.

It is an uneasy silence with Emma and James sharing a plate of food together and the three brothers and Henrey talking amongst themselves on the other side of the fireplace. Emma only has eyes for James and lets her uncles banter on in the background. She asks him about the different tattoos on his chest and arms and their meaning before suddenly chuckling and shaking her head.

'Did I say something funny?'

'No, James. I just heard Sebastian talking with his brothers about you. I think he is a little bit afraid of what you might be. He was asking his brothers and Henrey if the tribes you lived with were cannibals who ate their enemies.'

James chuckles and thinks for a moment. 'Shall we have some fun with them?' Emma nods with excitement. 'Then just play along with what I do.' He coughs loudly to ensure he has Sebastian's attention, then he starts to slowly roll up Emma's sleeve. With one eye watching Sebastian, he licks all the way up the inside of her forearm. Sebastian watches intently as James starts to sprinkle salt and pepper on the wet part of her arm. With his head lowered and his face obscured from Sebastian's view, he squeezes the cut in his mouth so that it bleeds again. Smearing the blood around his mouth and lips, he then attaches his mouth to Emma's arm and gives her waist a pinch.

She jolts up and squeals as James growls and shakes her arm in his mouth, then looks up and takes a satisfying 'Aahh' as he pulls away from the limb.

Sebastian can see the blood around James's mouth and Emma's

arm. He slowly starts to stand, his plate falling from his lap, as he points at James. 'Ooooohhhhuuuuuu,' he murmurs as he gets to his feet, still pointing.

Emma collapses back into her chair as if she has passed out, turning her head away and biting her lip hard in a desperate bid not to move or laugh.

James looks up. 'Do you want some while it's still warm, boy?' he asks, licking his lips in satisfaction.

Sebastian is terrified. Still pointing, he speaks. 'Looooook! Heeeee's eating our Emma! Stop him, somebody! Stop him!'

James throws Sebastian a wicked grin, tilts his head and gives him a wink, then licks his lips. 'Fresh blood be right tasty. Sure you don't want some?'

Beside him, Henrey can hold it no more. He has been watching events unfold and is now near wetting himself trying not to burst into laughter. Gaston has looked the other way in an attempt to laugh without his brother noticing and François has closed his eyes so he can concentrate on staying serious. With all around him hanging on for dear life and desperately trying not to laugh, Sebastian is in absolute fear of the man sitting opposite him across the fire. As for James, he just stares back at him with no expression on his face at all.

James stands up and turns to Emma. He flicks her head one way then the next. Her head rolls around lifelessly and her arms flop down the sides of the chair as she starts to slip onto the floor.

Sebastian screams. 'Mother of God! Somebody do something! He has killed her!' he yells, still pointing at James.

Henrey is the first to crack. He bursts into laughter, quickly followed by Gaston and François. Soon all three are roaring with laughter. Emma is next to break, her whole body shaking as James helps her back to her feet and gives her a hug and a kiss. He is the last to start laughing as Sebastian looks round at them all. It takes a few seconds to sink in that he has been had. 'You, you bastards, you all knew all along and let me go on believing he was eating her!' He tries to be angry, but it does not last long. Soon he also starts to chuckle as he realises how stupid he has been. The chuckle turns into laughter as his brother Gaston stands up and gives him a hug. 'Never mind, little brother, it happens to us all.'

Emma walks over and kisses her uncle on the cheek. 'Oh Sebastian, what a wonderful fool you have been! Did you honestly think James was a cannibal and that he would eat me in front of you all?'

Sebastian grabs James by the shoulders and shakes him while beaming a huge smile. 'I continue to get you wrong, yes? I must learn to be a better judge of people going forward.'

The rest of the evening is less eventful as they wait for Bernard to return. The joke has eased tensions in the room as they now all have questions about James's adventures on the whaling ships and the islands. Emma translates for all of them as best she can as they settle down for the evening and wait.

It is around nine o'clock when Bernard finally arrives back at the warehouse. The fire has burned down to a mellow glow, and he walks over to warm himself as it has become quite chilly outside. Looking around, he notices that everyone has waited up for his return.

The room is lit by oil-filled lamps hanging around the walls that keep the area in a semi-light condition. As they all get up to greet him, Bernard waves them back down with an arm motion. Gaston has moved to the bar and pours a drink from one of the open bottles and passes it to his brother Bernard. He takes it and salutes him with the glass before taking a sip. Collecting one of the lamps from a wall hanger, he takes his seat at the head of the dining table. Pulling a silver case from his chest pocket, he takes out a small thin cigar and lights it over the flame of the lamp. He draws a couple of breaths and blows a smoke ring into the air, before composing himself and speaking. 'Come, everybody, please take a seat around the table. Emma, would you translate for James, so he understands all I have to say?

'I have been with friends, asking about Madam Kelly and what has been happening in the past few months since we were last here. It would seem that she has been very busy obtaining favours for an expansion of her enterprises. Intending to invest in a pleasure house in London, England, as well as a retreat in the country with private services for the rich and influential. She has also raised the bounty to find our Emma to fifteen thousand gold coins and five thousand on the heads of each culprit who attacked her that night. It would seem that Emma's father is still important to her plans and his leverage is needed for something she wants. As for the rest of us, it would be revenge for what we did to that spiteful woman all those years ago.

'However, it does seem like she learned from past experiences, as there is a special ledger where she keeps a record of all favours and deals done for her clients. If you like, a marker book that could be called upon if ever it was needed. From what my friends were saying, Madam Kelly herself had to give some quite explicit performances of her own to save her neck from the scandal of our Juliet. For years she has been working to rid the stain of these men and women from her past. Destroying them in society, enslaving their families into her service or just killing them. Even grooming some of their young children into canaries for her use in the future. She is a dangerous woman, vengeful and far more powerful and influential than before. Even some of the clergy from the Vatican are now on her books.

'I, more than anyone, wish revenge for what they did to our sister and you, Emma. But by starting this all off again, you must understand that if we go down this route, there is no turning back. We would have to finish her for good this time as we could never be able to hide away again and get away with it. That woman has become far too powerful and well connected to be fooled by the likes of us a second time.'

Emma looks round the table at all present. 'I am not sure about all of you, but I have hidden away too long, constantly looking over my shoulder at shadows. I need to know who my father is. I also want Madam Kelly to pay for what she did to my mother. She did not deserve to have her life ended the way it did. If I get caught, I know the fate that awaits me. It has been spoken about many times and it is not a pretty one.' She turns to James and grips his hand. 'I will hold you to your word, James. You will not leave me if you still draw breath. For outside these men here, you are all I want in life. Should the worst befall you and death come your way while I should live, take pride in knowing, arms or not, I will bite the cock of any man fool enough to get too close to my mouth.'

All the men round the table react in different ways – from sucking air through their teeth to chuckling at her tenacity. Only James does not flinch. He looks her straight in the eyes. No words are needed between them, for she can see that he will stand by her no matter what happens.

Bernard turns to James. 'This may be of interest to you, James. Lord Fitzgerald Senior and the new one are well known to Madam Kelly and her establishment. I believe it is your brother who she has been in contact with to help expand her business in England. If indeed your siblings were sent to Paris, that book may have information on their whereabouts or fate as they were from high society and may have been worthy of favour or blackmail in the eyes of Madam Kelly. Perhaps some or all are still alive. To that end we can only hope.

'There is a great hatred between the French and English monarchies at present. No doubt war will soon be upon us, and it will be us fighting for the rich on both sides again. I think that her establishments in England will be a way of getting information to and from powerful people on both sides of the Channel. That is, for the right price, of course. It would take a lot of influence and negotiations for her to expand into England. She may well be using what she did for him in the past as encouragement to get him to pull strings in political circles for her.'

Bernard takes a few puffs on his cigar and puts it out in a brass dragon-decorated ashtray. 'I have had many plans for this day over the years. Some good, some not so good. Now we are all here thanks to our niece forcing our hand, perhaps this is the time we act and take vengeance on those responsible. Finish what was started all those years ago and bring closure to our sister's tragic demise. I for one do not want to delay any longer, preferring to take my chance now while I am still strong and able, rather than wait another year or so. All of you make your own choice. Those who wish to stay remain at the table. Those who want out of this should leave now and go as far away from here as you can. Failure will have them hunting down all my relations and friends with a passion.'

There are a few looks around the table, but no one moves from their positions. Several nods later and the decision is made by all to stay. Bernard explains his plan and all of them listen intently. It soon becomes very clear this is a plan that has been thought about for a very long time – not just the last few days, but maybe even years. The only update seems to be the addition of James, who will now be taking a pivotal role as he is a total unknown to Paris and will not need to be in disguise.

Three hours later, Bernard has finished the outline of the plan and sums it up. 'This will be very fluid in its timing, but if we are going to do this, we only have five days to get prepared as it is said that Madam Kelly is due to leave for England in a week's time. So, get some rest and we will start preparations in the morning.'

CHAPTER 4

Entering the House of Pleasure

It's mid-morning and the streets of Paris are bustling with people from all walks of life looking to make a living. Merchants are travelling from shop to shop in an attempt to move on bulk deliveries of goods. Others are displaying their wares in small shop windows or from the sides of mobile carts, trying to attract passing people to buy their produce or gifts. Almost anything can be bought on the streets of this fine city – you just need to know who to talk to or where to look. Some people are just browsing the windows or looking for a few special items to take home, while others with deeper pockets have sent out their servants or housekeepers to collect the many items they desire.

For safety reasons it has become more fashionable in these modern times to meet people or make business transactions over coffee or a meal in one of the many cafés or restaurants that litter the streets – rather than invite them home – unless you know the person well. As crime and theft go hand-in-hand with wealth and prosperity, and people always want to protect their families and possessions from the more undesirable members of society. Not allowing strangers and business associates to know where you live helps protect what you hold most dear.

France is a melting pot of cultural heritage and a Mecca for people wanting to enjoy the very best that life has to offer. Paris is still the most desired destination, with visitors from all over Europe filling many of the hotels and pleasure houses of the capital all summer long, bringing much-needed money and opportunities to the city. Those who can afford it would often own a townhouse to use when visiting the great city, allowing other family members to use it when not in residence. The sheer scale of so many wealthy people keen to spend their money on the finer things in life brings with it the darker side of society. Thieves, pickpockets, house-breakers and gangs of organised criminal syndicates thrive in this environment. And all are prepared to supply any service required, from the murder of a competitor to the abduction of somebody for ransom, if the price is right.

On the outside, the elected government of Paris takes this threat very seriously, wanting to encourage and promote spending while deterring villainous gangs. To this end, they have a large organisation of thief-takers and police commonly known as 'Sûreté' or its more modern title, 'Police Nationale', who are under the control of the ministry. It is their duty to serve and protect the people of Paris, be a visual deterrent and patrol the streets of the city to reduce and deter crime. But, as with anything, corruption and bribery can be found at all levels and having senior members of the ministry in your debt helps to smooth over, adjust or just delay the outcome of some very sensitive issues. Such as in the case of the Lost Angel of Paris, where delays, evasion and political interference were used to impede investigations and drag out the case for as long as possible – thus allowing time for cover-ups and bribery to hide those responsible for this atrocious act. It just goes to show what can be achieved through wealth and influence, even successfully hiding such a crime from their own monarchy.

No business does as well as the entertainment houses in this great capital, for pleasure has no bounds when you have unlimited funds to spend. Some of the guests and long-term residents of these places will spend many months living lavish lifestyles, being pampered by a vast army of people dedicated to fulfilling their every need and desire. Each suite in these establishments is a palace of its own, filled with exquisite decorations, the finest furniture, pictures and statues, all commissioned and created by only the best master craftsmen from all corners of the globe. The restaurants serve only the finest foods, while the entertainment shows and cabarets put on in their great halls are amongst the most popular in France, with many selling out in the first days of bookings being taken.

In the case of the most famous establishment of them all, La Fleur Blanche, such is the quality of the service and entertainment that over half the suites are leased all year round by guests who include royalty, diplomats, foreign dignitaries. There are even rooms reserved for members of the Vatican. Not that it is widely known, as discretion is also key to the success of such places. These retreats command a price tag few individuals can afford out of their own pockets, which is why many of them are leased by royalty. The people of those countries pay with their taxes for their monarchy and representing diplomats to reside there. On more than one occasion, a country has been brought to its knees and near bankruptcy by the actions of its leaders wishing to maintain their stay within the walls of this renowned building.

This establishment is run by the infamous Madam Kelly. She, and her entourage of providers, are the best of them all. For over twenty years she has delighted her guests with a service better than any other in the known world, with the muscle and influence to ensure that what happens in the hotel stays in the hotel. This kind of service means that business is constant and reliable as people feel safe to unwind and live out their wildest fantasies in private. No criminal gang or police force would dare take on this kind of organisation. For if they were caught interfering, they would never be seen alive again, such is the power at her command.

Up until the events of the Lost Angel of Paris. Madam Kelly's grip on society had been vice-like, but during that turbulent time period, she had seen her position heavily weakened for several years and her reputation tarnished deeply. It had taken nearly a decade to fully repair the damage caused by her actions that day. The King of France and many other envoys from around the world (including the head of the Catholic Church, the pope, who himself had watched Juliet du Grande perform several times) publicly frowned upon the actions taken by Madam Kelly. Just their words alone decimated the popularity of La Fleur Blanche and her position of power, as nobody in high society wanted to be seen to offend the king, the Catholic Church, the pope or God himself.

But now, years later, she is back on top, all people appeased, smoothed over, or in many cases deceased and removed from society. Through her manipulation and scheming, she has now returned, more powerful than ever and ready to expand into London and enlarge her growing empire.

As with the way she always works, Madam Kelly has plied the officials and high society of London for the past couple of years with women, favours and generous bribes. With the more resolute and resistant objectors, blackmail in the form of compromising information has been collected and used to break their resolve – threatening their families or exposing their innermost secrets if they do not support her new ventures. The only thing that would seal the deal even better would be to find the daughter of the man who would help open the country of England to her in an instant to prevent public scandal in the royal household. Many years have passed, and the power of a grown woman would not have the same impact as a child. But all monarchies have enemies who would pounce on the chance to disgrace a member of the royal family. Using her as leverage would aid their plans in undermining the authority that governs.

* * *

Outside La Fleur Blanche, a large red-and-gold-trimmed coach pulls up. As the horses stop and the driver locks the wheel brake, one of the footmen on the back jumps down and opens the carriage door. He pulls out and unfolds the double step then stands to the side.

After a few minutes, a man's head appears and looks around before stepping down from the coach. It's James, and he is decked out in the latest fashion – burgundy knee-length shorts, burgundy tights, a white no-frills shirt and a tight-fitting burgundy waistcoat with similar colour shoes and triangular hat. The whole set-up is finished off with a long, tight-fitting jacket and a cane sword with a silver-tipped scabbard and an eagle's claw grip.

The modern fashion of the day is to ditch the old horsehair wigs, frills and bows and show off the man's physique, and with the size and shape of James, this outfit does just that. He is a mountain of a person and the clothing, if anything, makes him look even bigger. He turns around and presents a hand into the carriage. Seconds later, he helps a woman down from the coach. It's Emma, and she is wearing a full-length pale peach muslin dress built up in layers and held in tight below the breasts to show off a robust hourglass figure. Her outfit is finished off with a pair of thick-heeled peach shoes, a white lace parasol with a peach trim and a petite hat held to one side. Since the start of the revolution, ladies' fashion has changed in style, becoming far more influenced by comfort and flowing lines that enhance a woman's figure. Out with the tight-fitting corsets, frills, thick bulky dresses and hair wigs and in with light, elegantly fitted dresses with more comfort and style in mind.

James and Emma are dressed to show the height of Parisian fashion and they look the part perfectly. James offers his arm to Emma and escorts her to the entrance to the hotel. As they reach the door, they are greeted by the doorman, who smiles and tips his cap at them while more people open the doors behind him. He is trained to observe the people arriving at the hotel and what they arrive in and estimate their importance and social standing. Based on his observations and signals, the people inside put on a show to match the clientele arriving. He now gestures to the people inside, using his hands and a twist of the head. As James and Emma enter the building, they are immediately offered canapés and glasses of champagne and are personally escorted to the reception area.

With drinks in hand, they are greeted by a woman speaking French. 'Good morning, sir. And what can I do to assist you this morning?'

'I'm sorry, I only speak English,' James replies.

Instantly she responds in perfect English. 'That's no problem, sir. We speak all languages here. Now, how may I help you?'

James looks round the front reception. It is a fabulous sight, beautifully decorated with rich red curtains tied back at all the windows with gold sashes. Huge chandeliers hang from the high beams. Paintings and statues are displayed everywhere, and in the distance a large lounge area is filled with assorted suites and chairs. On one side of the room is a full-length bar made from dark mahogany. The wall behind it is lined with mirrors, enhancing the appearance of all the bottles on display. Everything in the building seems to be finished with gold trim, from the covings on the top edges of the walls, to picture frames, light mounts and even the banister rails going up the ornate marble stairs. Everywhere he looks, well-dressed people are being served or just relaxing and making conversation.

'Well, my dear, I have just spent the last few years in the Pacific Islands amassing my fortune in trade. Now I have returned, I wish to be entertained and pampered with my fine lady here. So, I am looking to reside in one of your suites for a month, possibly two depending on how good the service is.'

The receptionist smiles. 'Well, the service here is the best in the world and the entertainment the finest that can be found. But do you have a reservation?'

James smiles. 'Alas, no. We only arrived in Paris this morning, and this was our first stop, but I do have plenty of gold to spend.'

The woman smiles at him. 'Everybody who comes here has plenty of gold to spend. But at the moment we are near to capacity. I am afraid the only suites we have left are reserved for special clients that may arrive.'

James swiftly thinks on his feet. 'Oh, that is a shame. I was hoping to meet Madam Kelly as I have a special gift for her to open up commerce and negotiations.' He leans forward and places a small black velvet bag on the counter for the receptionist to look at.

Curiosity makes her pick up the bag, place it on a small silver tray and pour out the contents for display. Out rolls a dozen of the largest black pearls she has ever seen, perfect in form and identical in size and shape. As the light reflects off their surfaces, a warm glow of rainbow colours shimmers through the room. They are exceptionally fine quality, and the receptionist is aware that they may be something rather special that Madam Kelly may find desirable. 'If you would like to take a seat in the lounge, sir, I will make some inquiries for you,' she says while placing the pearls gently back into the bag.

James holds his arm out to Emma, who smiles and hooks onto him as they head over to the lounge where a porter is removing a red rope from a reserved area especially for them. As they take their seats, the porter asks in French, 'Would you like something more to drink, sir and madam?'

Emma is quick to respond. 'It is the beginning of the holiday season for us, so two glasses of calvados would be a good start.' The porter nods and goes to the bar to request the order.

James speaks to Emma. 'It's likely they are watching every move we make from a distance, so hold your posture and act like you own the place.'

She nods ever so slightly in response. 'I have never been so terrified as I am right now, sitting here in the place where my mother suffered so badly at the hands of Madam Kelly and her enforcers.'

The pair sit and watch the establishment service all its patrons. For most of the people present, it oozes style and elegance, but it does not take long to see the cracks in this utopia. A group of elderly men all dressed up in black suits are becoming rowdy on the far side of the bar, no doubt as the alcohol takes its grip on them. The young server is topping up their glasses with wine when one of them grabs her by the waist and pulls her down onto his lap, tearing at her dress as he fondles her breasts. The others join in as if it is some kind of game as she screams and fights to break away from his grasp. Dodging past the others, she runs out of the lounge holding her torn dress together over her semi-naked body.

The old men are laughing with each other as a more senior member of staff tries to calm them down. It soon becomes clear that they want to continue their fun with the young server even though she is not a working girl, and they demand that she be returned to them, stating they are prepared to pay well for the privilege.

The member of staff disappears for several minutes before returning to speak to the group of men. Emma is listening intently as the men start to cheer and roar with delight. Within minutes, they are finishing their drinks and then the group of seven men head off towards the stairs.

Emma looks down and shakes her head in dismay.

'What is it, my dear?' James asks quietly.

'That poor girl. They are putting her in their suite so they can 'ave their way with her, all seven of them!'

'Surely not! She is only a young girl – maybe fifteen or sixteen if she is lucky.'

Emma is saddened and near to tears. 'Young or not, she will not be the same when they 'ave finished with her, that's for sure.'

Before James has a chance to speak, a group of people led by the smiling receptionist approaches the table. Both of them stand up, to be greeted by her and the two well-dressed men who accompany her. James can tell instantly they are enforcers by their build, their eyes that are constantly on the hunt, and the pistols that are neatly tucked inside their waistcoats but still bulge out to give their presence away.

'I have the honour and privilege of presenting you to Madam Kelly,' the receptionist says as she steps to one side and sways her arm to the left. A woman in her late forties, immaculately dressed, steps forward. Her pale make-up and red lipstick along with her perfectly positioned hair are stunning and have James immediately looking her up and down. She has a small black heart-shaped patch below her left cheekbone and her figure is set off by the full-length, bright red crushed-velvet dress that enhances her large, half-exposed cleavage. Either side of her are two handmaidens, one holding her glass of champagne and the other the tray containing the bag of black pearls.

She reaches out towards James as she speaks. 'It is not often that somebody piques my interest these days, but you did get my attention with such fine pearls.' James holds her hand and kisses the back of it before coming closer and kissing her on both cheeks. Her security swiftly steps forward but are quickly waved away as she takes a minute to look James up and down, instantly attracted to his size, build and tattoos. 'It's a little more than I usually allow when greeting a stranger for the first time, but you are a very handsome, rugged man and your pearls are amongst the best I have ever seen. Where did you find such exquisite examples and how many do you have?'

'Oh, those trinkets. They come from an island in the Pacific where I do some trading with the local chief. Seems that they have a small area of deep coral reef that holds a specific type of clam that produces huge black pearls. Every time I visit him, I trade for all his village has collected. If I remember rightly, I exchanged the latest batch for a boat and some brass cannons, shot and powder. When I return home every three or four years, I bring some of them back for trade. This time I brought around two hundred and fifty with me as it is wise not to flood the market with too many and lower the value of such a rare commodity – especially as so few are known to exist and even fewer of this size and quality.'

Madam Kelly nods in agreement. 'Well, it seems that you have perfect timing, as I am going through a dark period in my fashion. I wish to purchase all the black pearls that you have to offer and reserve all that you will have available in the future.'

James thinks about it. He looks round at Emma, who glances at him then casts her gaze down at the ground. She is trying to control her emotions and not look HER in the eye in case she reacts. It is the first time she has seen Madam Kelly in the flesh, and the hatred welling up inside is getting difficult to control.

'Well, we came here for a fun time, but you seem to be full, so—'

Before he can finish, Madam Kelly speaks up. 'We are only full to the common public. I always have rooms for special guests and potential new clientele. If you would like to trade all the pearls you have in exchange for a stay at my establishment, I could offer you a choice of the President's Suite or the Rose Garden experience. I would have also been able to offer the Canary Suite, but I have some people coming tomorrow for a special treat.' She leans forward and whispers in James's ear. 'Last minute and from the Vatican, they are a bit particular and unusual in their taste to say the least. So, I am afraid I only have those two suites available at present.'

As she talks about the Canary Suite, Emma tenses up as she recalls her uncles talking about how her mother was found slowly deteriorating in that awful yellow suite. James knows it will be difficult for Emma not to get too emotional and swiftly makes the trade. 'The President's Suite sounds divine. I am sure it will be fine for our entertainment needs. And please keep the pearls on the tray as a thank you gift from me, as I am certain you do not visit all your guests as you have so graciously done for us.'

Madam Kelly smiles and nods. 'You are too kind, now please, Margarette, show the young lady to the suite while I finalise the details of our transaction with…?'

'James, just James to my friends,' he replies as Emma is escorted to the suite by Margarette, one of the girls who arrived with Madam Kelly. As the two women turn a corner and disappear from view, Madam Kelly speaks up. 'James, your lady does not do you justice. She seems, well, to put it bluntly, a little out of her depth in a place like this. Whereas on the other hand, you have me curious, sounding and speaking like a gentleman, but looking like you do.' She steps forward and rubs her hand up his firm chest. 'I think a man who has been on as many adventures as you needs a little more stimulation than she could possibly offer.' She turns her hand and moves it back down his body, rubbing his crotch area to feel the size of his manhood. Her eyes light up and a smile appears on her face as she is pleased with what she feels in her hand. 'Why don't you call on me when she retires for the night? And I will show you how to make the best of my establishment, for I am sure we have a lot to offer each other.' She lifts his chin up with the tips of her fingers and gently kisses him on the lips, then moves around to his ear and kisses that as she whispers, 'Perhaps I will be able to teach you a thing or two, and I now know you are equipped with what I need. It just boils down to whether or not you best know how to use what you have been given. I am around all night, so don't be shy.'

She turns away and glides into the bar area to greet the rest of her guests, leaving James and the receptionist behind. James cannot help but watch as she moves across the floor, as she knows how to walk and shows off her assets to their maximum effect. He snaps out of his trance and turns to the receptionist. 'Would you have somebody go out to my carriage and have my servant and luggage sent to our suite? Also, someone show me the way to my room, for I am yet to know where I am going.'

'But of course, if you would but follow me to the main desk, you can sign in while I organise the people needed to assist.'

James follows her to the desk and fills in the ledger while a porter waits to escort him to the President's Suite. The man leads him up the marble staircase and along a long corridor, then knocks and opens the door. As he turns to leave, James tries to tip the man, but he refuses to take payment. 'I'm sorry, sir. We do not accept gratuities here; it is all included in the price of the room. But thank you for the consideration.'

James waits for the door to close before walking up to Emma. She grabs him round the neck and holds on to him tightly while he cups his hands round her waist. He can feel her trembling as she presses against his body. 'I was so nervous I would give us away. When she started talking about the Canary Suite, it was all I could do to restrain myself from ripping out her eyes. That evil, nasty woman.'

'My dear, you're the lucky one. That old woman had more than just her eyes on me. If she finds out that those pearls I gave her are all I have, it may well be my balls that get served up on the next tray.'

Emma thinks curiously for a second or so. 'How do you know she wanted you? I 'ave only been apart from you for a few minutes and I did not notice anything.'

'Ha,' James snaps, 'in those few minutes that woman made sure she found out all she needed to know. But worry not, my dear. You are the only one for me. I would fear your wrath more than hers when it comes to my manhood up for grabs. Now our cases should be here soon with Sebastian, so let's get ready for his arrival.'

It's only now that James begins to look around the room. It is exactly as you would imagine a presidential suite to look. A large wooden desk with a leather-bound top, brass inkwell of a hunting scene and an upright stuffed armadillo. Boldly coloured walls decorated with flags and paintings of prominent men, several brass ornaments and two large busts of Napoleon Bonaparte. There are three double bedrooms branching off from the main lounge, all with plush, wooden four-poster beds with silk sheets and plenty of matching pillows.

The suite would be exactly where a young diplomat or politician would want to be pampered and entertained if he had ambitions in life. James turns to Emma with a grin. 'I wonder how many people have been had over that big desk.'

Emma gives him a stern look. 'I do not know how many, but I do know one that won't be joining zat number. Eerrru! It makes my skin crawl just to think of it.'

There is a knock at the door, then it opens. It's the porters bringing up their luggage and behind them is Sebastian, dressed as a butler, carrying two small bags. The porters drop off the cases and chest in the main bedroom and leave, closing the door behind them as they exit the room.

As Sebastian hears the footsteps fade away, he starts to speak. 'Bernard and the others are in the coaching house across the road, getting changed out of their footman clothes ready for the next part of our plan.'

Emma translates the conversation both ways with James and her uncle as usual.

James thinks for a minute. 'Good. We can get them in tonight when the place starts to fill up with clients and customers, for now we just need to wait for time to pass.'

Sebastian takes a seat and sits back. 'Do we even know if she is here?'

Emma grimaces. 'Oh yes, she is here alright. James has just been talking to her. In fact, I think she has taken quite a fancy to him.'

This time it is James giving the death stare back at Emma. 'It was not my doing. Anyway, I am more concerned for that girl serving those old men in the reception area. I hope she will be alright.'

'Girl?' asks Sebastian. Emma explains what they had seen happen in the bar earlier. This seems to sadden Sebastian as he has not been brought up to treat women that way and he does not like to see or hear of people who do.

The three of them cannot afford to compromise who they are, so for the next couple of hours, they stay in the room, drinking a few glasses of wine from the selection of bottles on the rack of the small bar while beginning to work out how to get the ledger from Madam Kelly's grasp. Later that afternoon, Sebastian gets up from his chair. 'I think I will go downstairs and order some food for you and my brothers, for I am sure they will be hungry when they arrive here. Is there anything in particular you would like me to request for you?'

Emma smiles at her uncle. 'Well, manservant, I would like a selection of cakes and sweet pastries covered in sugar frosting, along with the usual assortment of cheeses and cured meats.'

Sebastian looks at the cheeky grin on her face. 'You get away with this just this once, but next time I will tan your behind, young lady.'

She laughs at him. 'I do not think so, Uncle, not with my James watching on. He might get a little jealous or protective of me.'

'No,' says James with a grin. 'I feel you are tough enough to fend for yourself, Emma. But if you would ask your uncle to see if they have the arm or leg of a human, I am feeling a little peckish.' Emma smiles as she translates the request to Sebastian.

He looks back at James, chuckles and shakes his head while commenting a few profanities in French before he exits the room, leaving James waiting for the translation from Emma that never comes.

Emma walks over to the sofa where James is lying down, hitches up her dress and straddles him across his groin, leaning forward to kiss her man. Between kisses she says, 'I reckon we have five minutes before he comes back. Time enough to show you why I am ze best thing that will ever 'appen to you.'

James grins as his hands slide up to cup her firm breasts. 'I do not need convincing of that, but five minutes is not enough time to satisfy a rabbit like you and I do not want to be caught by your uncles.'

'So, we had better make the most of five minutes to make sure I am content to wait for your full attention another time then, yes!'

Sebastian has made it down to the reception area. 'My master would like a selection of cakes and sweet pastries with sugar frosting sent to the President's Suite. They are feeling somewhat hungry after their efforts.' The receptionist writes down the request as he turns to walk away. Suddenly, he stops and looks back. 'Oh, I nearly forgot, my niece Emma also asked for a selection of cheeses and a large platter of cured meats as well.'

The receptionist adds this to the list and passes it to a porter to take to the kitchen, then watches Sebastian leave the reception area. She thinks for a bit then walks out to the back office.

Sebastian is heading back along the corridor to the suite when he hears a noise. He stops and looks around but sees nothing, so continues on his way. Again, he hears a faint noise. This time he pauses and listens more intently and makes out a quiet sobbing. Following the sound, he moves to a gap between a potted palm tree and a statue. As he approaches, he sees a small girl curled up tight in a corner. What's left of her clothes are torn apart. She has blood all down her legs, on her hands and smeared all over her face. He goes to approach her, but she screams and swings out wildly with a long thin ice pick. As he looks at her, he can see her face is bruised, battered and swollen.

Sebastian is right by the door to the President's Suite and calls out loudly to James and Emma. Moments later, the door opens, and they both come rushing out to see why he is calling. Sebastian points to what he has found wedged in the corner by the statue. James and Emma look at her then at each other. They know exactly who the girl is and what she has just been put through. Emma rushes over to help her, but again she lashes out frantically, stabbing at the air and screaming. Slowly, Emma manages to calm her down and several minutes later she talks her into lowering the ice pick. As she drops it to the floor, the girl breaks down, tears flowing down her face as she sobs her heart out.

'James, pick her up and bring her into our suite. Quickly, before anyone sees us,' Emma snaps as she moves out of his way. He steps forward and slowly shuffles the girl into his huge hands, gently lifts her up out of the corner, then starts to move towards their suite. The girl is in a great deal of pain and any movement hurts as they bustle her into the room.

Sebastian picks up the ice pick and looks about before swiftly entering the room and closing the door behind them. 'Is this the girl you spoke of earlier?' he asks curiously.

Emma just nods as she tries to check the girl over.

'But she is barely a child,' says Sebastian in shock.

Emma rushes to the bathroom and starts to fill the large bathtub with warm water. 'James, hold her until I am ready.' She opens a cupboard, takes out some spare sheets and walks back into the main room. Taking the ice pick from Sebastian's hand, she places it on the large desk, then passes him the sheets.

'Sebastian, tear them up into strips and get some of my night clothes from the wardrobe by my bed. Place them by the bathtub with as many towels as you can lay your hands on.'

Emma takes off her shoes, dress and other items of clothing, moves back into the bathroom and climbs into the bathtub. 'Lower the girl into my arms and leave us until I call for you.' She holds out her arms to take the girl as he lowers her slowly into the bath. There are several moments that the girl whimpers with pain, but eventually they get her into the water. It takes a little longer for her to let go of James's neck, but soon she releases her grasp of him.

Sebastian arrives with the strips of sheets and Emma's clothes and drops them by the side of the tub. 'Go and get your brothers and be discreet. While you are out, find some laudanum from somewhere, for I fear without it this girl may do something stupid.'

Emma turns to James. 'Close the door when you both leave and do not let anyone in here with me. I need to get her clothes off and find out what they have done to her down below and I have a feeling it may take some time.'

The two men leave Emma to work on the young girl. Sebastian looks at James and shakes his head, clearly deeply upset with what he has just seen. 'I go now, yes!' He exits the room, leaving James standing by the large desk. James is beyond angry. All he can think of is what he would do to the men who did this to that little girl, should he come across them. He can hear moaning and crying from the room next door but stays away as he knows she is in far better hands with Emma than anyone else.

Just as he takes a seat, there is a knock at the door. 'Come in,' he yells, thinking it is Sebastian returning for some reason. But as the door opens, he realises it is a waiter with a large trolley. Before he has a chance to get up, the man is pushing it into the room. It makes a lot of noise as it rattles and shakes with all the plates and trays on it. What is strange, though, is that an enforcer follows him into the room. This piques James's interest, and he stands up to receive both men. As the waiter looks at him, James points to the large desk.

With a slight nod of acknowledgement, the waiter puts down a tablecloth and starts to unload the trays of cakes, pastries and cheese and a large platter of assorted cured meats along with cutlery and plates. The enforcer is doing his best to discreetly look around the rooms to see who is about, but it is not good enough to fool James. He steps towards the only closed door, which just so happens to be the bathroom. As he does so, there is a lot of splashing and Emma yells out, 'Hurry up, darling! The water's getting cold, and I need your attention if you know what's good for you.'

The enforcer is in two minds to investigate further or leave, but before he makes up his mind, James starts to take off his waistcoat and shirt and yells back. 'Coming, my dear.' He looks back at the man who is still too curious for James's liking. 'You finished, man? My naked wife is calling for me and I'm feeling lucky tonight.' The enforcer thinks better of taking on James, tilts his head at him and leaves the room, closely followed by the waiter.

James thanks them both as he follows them out of the room and watches them walk down the corridor. He notices another enforcer standing at the end of the hall before he steps back into the room and closes the double doors. As he turns and approaches the desk full of food, he cannot help but think something is not right, but he has made no mistakes, so how can that be? For now, he puts it down to the security being raised for the night's entertainment to ensure nothing gets too out of hand. But it is on his mind as he eats a slice of cured ham. With nothing more he can do at the moment, he sits back down and waits.

Nearly an hour passes before there is a tap at the door. As James gets up, the door quietly opens and Sebastian enters, closely followed by his brothers. They smile as they see James and the selection of food on the desk. James eyes up their clothing and shakes his head as he starts to chuckle, for Bernard looks quite the fashion statement, with pale blue as the main colour of his clothing. But Gaston and François are in bright red and orange, both with frilly shirts and looking more like a couple of peacocks. James cannot control himself and continues to laugh. Bernard knows what James is chuckling about and says, 'I tried to tell them it was too much, yes! But this is what they liked.'

While James shakes his head, there are a few comments in French as the two brothers pull at their clothes and admire their choices, much to the disappointment of Bernard and Sebastian, who is still in his personal servant's uniform.

The clothes are soon forgotten about as the two peacocks start tucking into the food, while Sebastian moves towards the bathroom. James taps him on the arm as he passes and shakes his head. Sebastian gets the hint and stops; he sadly looks down at the ground in disappointment that he cannot check on them himself.

It is another hour before the bathroom door opens and Emma peers out. She looks at the men and quietly speaks. 'Bernard, open the sheets on one of the beds. Sebastian, I hope you got what I asked for?'

Sebastian nods and lifts a small bottle into the air.

'Very good,' Emma says. 'Now come and carry her to the bed. She is in a lot of pain but has asked to speak to you. When you have finished speaking, make sure she takes a small sip from the bottle and stay with her in the room. She does not want to be left alone at the moment.'

The men quietly do as Emma asks. Bernard opens the sheets, and Sebastian carries her gently to the bed and lays her down. Bernard closes the door, leaving the two of them alone together.

He is reminded of the time he carried his sister out of this very building. It is a painful memory that can be seen by the others on his face.

Emma comes out of the bathroom carrying an armful of torn clothes, blood-stained towels, sheets and makeshift bandages. She has tears running down her face as she throws them into a large waste bin, then walks to the bar, pours a glass from the nearest bottle and downs it in one. As she goes to pour another glassful, James puts his hand over the glass. 'That will not help, my dear.' As she looks up at him, he opens his arms to her. Emma starts to cry again as she steps forward to be comforted.

Turning to face her uncles, Emma speaks. 'Those men were French diplomats. Most of them old enough to be her grandfather. They took their turns with her, beating her with riding crops if she resisted. Not being a working girl, she fought back as best she could. It was only when she stopped fighting that they lost interest in her.' Emma looks at her brothers. 'They have torn her insides apart. It is a real mess down there. The poor child never stood a chance.'

She wipes the tears from her face and tries to control her emotions before speaking again.

'Do you know what they did next? They sealed her up with red candle wax to ensure the best chance that one of them had impregnated her. The girl did not even know what that meant, let alone what they were doing.'

Emotions are running high as she continues to speak. 'Six weeks ago, she was a farm girl on the outskirts of Paris. Madam Kelly's scouts spotted her and snatched the girl away from her parents because they thought she was pretty, killing them both when they fought back to save their child from abduction. When Sebastian found her, the girl was digging out the candle wax with the only thing she could find.' She walks over to the desk and picks up the weapon. 'This bloody ice pick.' Emma points the item into the air before stabbing it up to the hilt into the stuffed armadillo on the desk. 'She has done even more damage to herself punching holes than what they did to her. I only hope that infection does not set in and finish her off.' She bursts into tears as her emotions get the better of her.

James steps forward and holds Emma in his arms as he looks in the direction of Bernard. He does not understand all what she has just said but gets the rough picture of what has happened. 'This all ends today, no matter what,' he says.

Bernard also does not need a translation for what James has just said. He can see by the expression on his face and feels the same way himself. They all take seats around the room, and with Emma translating, the next stage of the plan is discussed. Once they have outlined who is to do what and when, James adds that he had an enforcer enter the room and that he saw another one at the end of the hallway earlier. With a good chance they saw the brothers enter the room, they decide to change the plan slightly, something Emma is not too happy about as it involves James taking a further risk. For now, they will have him distract the enforcer in the hallway while the others go their separate ways. He will then go and find Madam Kelly, joining her so that they can keep an eye on the woman's whereabouts, leaving a reluctant Emma and Sebastian to stay in the suite and monitor the girl.

Bernard takes a couple of bottles of brandy from the shelf behind the bar and passes one to François. He then turns to James and gives him a nod that they are ready. James puts on his jacket, collects his cane, opens the door and steps out into the corridor. Tapping the floor in front of him as he goes, to ensure he gets the attention of anyone watching him, he walks straight up the hallway past the enforcer, who has now moved out from behind a statue to observe his movements. James swiftly turns around. The man is surprised, and he turns and pretends to be looking at the statue.

'Can you tell me where Madam Kelly is?' James asks, but the enforcer ignores him, so James taps him on the shoulder with his cane. The man's response is to grab the cane with one hand and reach into his waistcoat pocket with the other. Unfortunately for him, James is far faster. He pushes the man's hand against his chest and the small pistol held within, grabs his throat with the other hand and lifts him a foot up the wall. While this is going on, Bernard and his two brothers slip out of the room and move off up the corridor in the other direction.

'As I politely asked before, where may I find Madam Kelly? She has requested I meet up with her tonight. Now if you persist in going for your peashooter, I will rip out your throat. Do you understand?'

The enforcer is still trying to draw his pistol, so James applies pressure to his neck with his thumb and fingers and holds the struggling man, watching as his face starts to turn from red to purple. As he begins to lose consciousness, James drops him to the floor, picks up his cane and gives him a whack with the handle to knock him out. 'We don't want you to shoot me in the back, now, do we?' he says as he steps over the body and moves off towards the stairs.

Downstairs, James is approached by a young, long-haired blonde lady in a dark green evening dress.

'Can I help you, sir?' she asks in French.

James has no idea what she has just said, but replies, 'I am looking for Madam Kelly. She invited me to join her tonight.' Before the woman has a chance to respond, he feels someone rub their hand down his back and squeeze his bottom.

'I see you have taken me up on my offer, James.' He turns round and before him is Madam Kelly, beautifully decked out in a gold, figure-hugging dress. Her make-up is still pale apart from the red lipstick, and a real gold and diamond tiara in her hair finishes the look sublimely. Above her left breast, she has a brooch containing three black pearls within a gold frame.

'You like it? I had the piece already made, but I have been waiting on the right pearls for a very long time, that is until you gave me your gift. I had my people work on it all afternoon in the hope I would see you, now let me thank you.'

She steps up to him, slides one hand down his chest and up his side, while the other moves up the back of his neck as she kisses him on the lips. She strokes his neck, then starts to add her tongue into the action. James responds and they get into a passionate grasp as his arms wrap around her. They hold their embrace for a few minutes before she steps back with a smirk.

'Baby, we are going to have so much fun. I'm going to show you a whole new level of desire and satisfaction, for I am feeling somewhat generous tonight. Now come and join me. I wish to show you off to some of my special friends.'

James pauses. 'You better know I had one of your enforcers try to pull a pistol on me when I asked where you were. I was forced to take action and put him down just a short time ago.'

She grits her teeth and lets out a sharp huff as her expression instantly turns to anger. With a flick of her wrist and a look at the reception area, she instantly has three enforcers by her side. Looking back at James, she calmly speaks. 'Did he hurt you, my dear?'

'No. I asked where you were so I could join you and he ignored me. From there it just went downhill.'

She swears a lot in French before calming down and composing herself again, then points at one of the men. 'Go check it out, and you two finish the job I asked to be done earlier. If it proves to be the case, let me know and open the G room, now go!'

Madam Kelly looks back at James, who has no idea what she has said. 'I am so sorry for the interruptions. It seems I have so little time to myself, but now I have sent away my security on errands, would you please walk with me?'

She leads James into the best entertaining lounge and continues over to the far side to a private section marked off with red velvet cords. On the way, she greets lots of people and introduces them to James, while many more approach her for conversation and to wish her well. It takes a good fifteen minutes to reach the plush corner suite, but its position and vantage point allows her to view the whole lounge, being up four steps and with a wooden balcony round the front. It is a very cosy spot to watch all the action and cabaret performances from, while the lights around them are set low, making them nearly invisible to the rest of the well-illuminated room.

Champagne arrives in an ice bucket and is positioned beside the table by a waiter who promptly leaves as they take their seats. They are served only by one of Madam Kelly's canaries, a beautiful young girl in a skimpy yellow silk and feather outfit. The scantily dressed woman smiles at James as she places two glasses down in front of them, then pours the champagne.

'Beautiful, isn't she, James? I train them all myself for many years to create perfection. Only a handful make the final grade and they are always very special, coming only from the finest stock around, and are absolutely loyal as well as pure.'

The girl smiles at them both as she finishes pouring the drinks and then takes her seat in front and to the left of Madam Kelly. 'Now, James, don't get any ideas with her. It's been many years since a man has stirred my blood and had my favours. I can be a very jealous woman if you should stray.'

She moves closer beside him and sips on her champagne topped with a pair of raspberries. They watch as the room fills with people all out for a fun time. The twelve-piece orchestra play wonderful music while entertainers move about the room presenting their skills to the people who are coming and going in couples and groups on a continuous basis. One of the entertainers attempts to approach Madam Kelly first but is discreetly waved away by her little canary.

Madam Kelly places her glass down and turns to James. She kisses him tenderly on the lips, encouraging him to touch her breasts. Her hand slides down the inside of his trousers and starts to caress his penis.

Whatever else she may be, Madam Kelly knows how to work on a man. It does not take long for her to get a firm reaction. Slowly, she slides down his body, taking his trousers down at the same time. Within moments she is below the balcony eyeline. As she looks up at him, she comments, 'If you were to stick with me, this would be only a taster of what would come your way.' She kisses the end of his penis before sliding her rich red lips down the full length of his manhood. James struggles for breath as the woman works on him, sliding her lips up and down while massaging his balls in her left hand.

* * *

While James is keeping an eye on Madam Kelly, Bernard and his two brothers reach the hallway outside Madam Kelly's private quarters. Bernard knows from his associates that two enforcers will be guarding the door to her room. He puts his plan into action. Opening and splashing some brandy on his clothes, he takes a couple of swigs from the bottle before grabbing the arms of his brothers and staggering round the corner of the corridor. They are swinging their bottles and singing. Instantly, the two men standing outside the room turn and watch. As the brothers get closer, they move forward to intercept the drunken trio.

François falls to the floor laughing. As he does, Gaston leans forward to try and pick him up while Bernard takes a drink from the bottle and falls back against the wall.

'We… we have come to find Madam Elly… no, Madam Kelly… and thank her for a great night.'

These are not the first drunks to have tried to visit Madam Kelly in her private quarters, hence the need for two men on the door. Shaking his head, one of them reaches down to pick up François, but is swiftly met with a punch to the jaw from Gaston, who twists round on his heels to deliver another powerful blow followed by a kick to the head. As the second man reaches into his jacket for a pistol, Bernard brings the bottle of brandy down on his head. It is not like in the movies where the bottle shatters into a multitude of parts, but more like a dull thud as the hard bottle cracks down on his skull, splitting his head on impact.

Both men are on the floor in seconds and remain motionless. Even then, Gaston gives his victim another kick just to be certain he is out cold. Bernard walks over to the door and starts to pick at the lock with a hooked wire pin while also sliding a thin, curved piece of metal down between the lock and the seal of the door. It takes less than thirty seconds for him to force the lock and spring the door open.

He looks inside for any more people before signalling his brothers to enter. They waste no time in dragging the two enforcers inside the room before closing the door. Ripping the sash cords off the curtains that hang at the windows, they tie the two men up and bundle them into a walk-in shoe closet before shutting the door and leaving them to their fate.

Bernard had been given a hint by his friends to look around the huge desk, as it was rumoured that the ledgers would be hidden there or somewhere close by. As he lowers to his knees and looks around under the table, he gets the fright of his life as he comes face to face with a double-barrelled blunderbuss pointing straight at him. It would seem anyone sitting opposite her could be in for a nasty surprise if she chose to pull the trigger.

The other two brothers are looking round the rest of the room. They find two safes, one large and one small. The smaller one is not locked and inside is some poor-quality jewellery, a small stack of cash and several documents. Bernard expresses his opinion.

'It's a fake one to catch the eye of any stupid thief. Most of it will be worthless trinkets.'

The other safe is a lot larger and hidden behind a false wooden bureau front. It could be what the men are looking for, but Bernard is still searching round the desk. He is about to give up when he notices some scuff lines on the inner edge of a side support bar. He feels about but no button or lever can be found. In frustration, he punches the under panel and to his surprise it clicks and lowers the whole shelf in a hinge-like motion.

Running along the lip of the lowered shelf is a large ledger and a smaller black leather-bound book with red velvet clasps hooked over the corners to keep it closed. 'Yes,' he comments as he places the books on the desk before closing the hatch back up.

Taking out his reading glasses, he opens up the smaller black book and begins to read the entries. It takes him a while to understand the format, but it soon becomes clear that it is a record of payments to prominent and influential people, as well as favours she has done and debts owed. The more he scours the pages, the more he is shocked by what he is reading as it lists many people well known to society, including nobility.

He then moves on to the larger of the two books. On opening

it, he finds the dates go back many years. It is the true inventory of La Fleur Blanche. From the arrival of staff and people to the establishment, to all the antiques, cost of renovations, payments of people hiring the rooms, the list is endless. But his first search is for the date of his sister's abduction. A silence befalls the brothers as he finds entries around and before that date, and payments after, including the person who is responsible for the abduction of their sister.

'Bastard! I will fucking destroy you for what you have done, I swear it on my sister's soul.' Both brothers come over and look at the book and then at each other. The man's name shocks them all. Bernard then looks forward in the book for James's sisters. He finds a whole section on the Fitzgeralds and the entries for the three girls. There are several updates as to their history as it unfolded, and their fates are documented. Reading the last entry on the girls, he closes the book and turns to his brothers.

'It's time to go. Gaston, just leave the safe. We do not have the code and it is too big to move. These books are all we really wanted and the two together have all the information we need. François, find a bag or cloth to wrap these in, then take them to Henrey. Ask him to prepare the carriage as we will be leaving within the hour. Gaston, come with me! We need to see if we can help our friend out.'

As Bernard places the books on the sheet his brother has provided, he opens the hard front cover on the ledger to see who first made entries in the book and he makes a discovery. On the front sheet are the letters and numbers R10, L5, R21, L67, R44. He thinks for while on what they could mean. *Surely it cannot be that simple*, he thinks. *But then again, just maybe!*

'Gaston, go over to the safe and put these numbers in as I call them. From zero, right ten.' Gaston moves to the big safe and starts to dial the numbers as Bernard calls them out.

'Then left five, right twenty-one, left sixty-seven, right forty-four.'

To their surprise, the safe clicks with the final number. Gaston pulls open the heavy door and all three peer inside. It is full of files and documents, and there is a small black velvet pouch that

Bernard recognises instantly. A huge quantity of money and eight thirty-two-ounce gold bars are spread out on the bottom shelf.

The brothers look at each other and start to laugh as their eyes light up. 'Slight change of plan. We will take the gold, coin and James's pearl pouch. Pile the rest of the contents and documents into the fireplace, pour brandy on everything including the carpets and furniture and burn the fucking lot of it.'

François and Gaston look at each other dumbfounded before turning to face Bernard. They do not even get a word in as he continues to speak. 'Look, we all know it will be full of secrets, blackmailing documents and political leverage. We are not the type to bribe and extort people. Knowing what's in those documents will only make us all targets for everyone wanting their secrets kept safe. I myself do not want to be looking over my shoulder for another ten years or more. So just burn it all and go – the gold and money are already an unexpected bonus. Let's just give the people of France the chance to try again from a clean slate, because after today, I never want to come back to this place or any other like it.

'Besides, Madam Kelly will be too busy fearing for her life when she sees that all her leverage is burned and ledgers missing. What better revenge could you ever want than her being hunted by those she has crossed?'

Gaston and François look at each other, exchanging a few words before they turn to Bernard and nod in agreement. Collecting up all the files, they throw them in and around the fireplace. Gaston then splashes the brandy all over the parchments followed by a match thrown on the pile. Instantly, the fire bursts into life, roaring and spitting as it takes hold and spreads over all the documents and surrounding floor. The paperwork is burning well as they open the door to leave. With one last careful look around, they move off cautiously. François has the books in a bundle and the rest of the items in a small leather travelling case he found in the room. He heads off down the corridor and makes his way towards the reception area and out of the building. Bernard takes his brother down the stairs to the basement to investigate a new lead that has only just come to light.

* * *

While Bernard and his brothers are holding up their part of the plan, James is doing his best to hold up his end, more so with the help of Madam Kelly, who is still entertaining him.

An enforcer approaches Madam Kelly's booth and the canary stands up and steps down the stairs to intercept him before he can disturb them or see what Madam Kelly is doing. He passes on a message and the girl nods. There are a few words exchanged, then she sends the man off to wait a few yards away. Returning to her master, she slides a hand along her back to let her know she is there as she kneels down beside her, whispering a few words into her ear.

Madam Kelly pauses for a second before continuing. After a few more strokes, she releases her grip on James and looks up at him. 'As bad as the timing is, my dear, I have just had some good news and must attend to some unfinished business.' She continues to stroke the end of his cock as she thinks for a second. 'I will leave you in good hands until I can return.'

Turning to her little canary, she whispers her instructions. 'Finish him off, he is nearly there, then do all that is needed to keep him entertained until I return. Anything he wants, you give him, understood?'

The girl is a bit shocked by the request, as it is not what she is used to, but she nods in agreement and as Madam Kelly gets up, the girl slots into position between James's legs.

'I will be back as soon as I can, darling.' She blows him a kiss as she turns and walks across the lounge. Within seconds, she is joined by two enforcers, who latch on to either side of her. The young girl attempts to continue what Madam Kelly had started, but she has absolutely no experience and he soon starts to go soft. This isn't helped by the fact that James's mind is now thinking about where she is going and if Bernard and his brothers have completed their objectives.

Realising things aren't going right, the young girl frantically tries to rub his cock without success. It becomes uncomfortable for James, who grabs her hands to stop her. He raises the canary's arms to lift her up to her feet and sits her down beside him. The girl becomes upset and panicky as she has failed to carry out Madam Kelly's instructions and does not know what to do. James looks at her as he does his trousers and clothes back up. 'I'm sorry, lass, the woman is good at what she does, and my body reacted as any man would, but I personally felt as uncomfortable as you do now, so stop worrying.'

'But I failed her. When she finds out, I will be—'

James interrupts her. 'Nothing is going to happen. To my mind, you were amazing. And she will know no different. But for now, you need to wait here while I check something out.'

The girl looks at him, reaches out with a hand and puts it on his shoulder. 'But I must keep you here until Madam Kelly returns. That was her instruction to me.'

James smiles at her. 'What is your name?'

The young girl thinks for a moment. 'I'm not sure, I am just number fourteen to all who speak to me. That is until I am named by the man who I will serve when Madam Kelly instructs me to do so. However, I remember as a child being called Lillibut, but that was a very long time ago.'

He thinks for a moment. 'Lillibut is usually a nickname for somebody called Elizabeth. I would think that you were once called Elizabeth. Now listen to me, Elizabeth. Is this what you want to be for the rest of your life? To be that woman's property? To go down on anyone and do everything that Madam Kelly tells you to do?'

The girl is already nervously shaking her head before he has finished speaking.

'No, I did not think so. Now I need to know, what message did you pass on to Madam Kelly, as it is very important that I know all that has just gone on.'

The girl pauses as she plucks up the courage to go against her mistress's wishes. 'He said that they had found what she was looking for and that the G Suite was being opened, ready for her to attend.'

'I've heard that before – G Suite. What does it mean?'

The girl looks at him strangely. 'Why it is Madam Kelly's personal Guillotine Suite, a torture room filled with all the old relics from the past, like the rack, iron maiden, all the way up to the guillotine of modern times.'

James's expression turns more serious as he thinks on her words and puts two and two together. 'I must go. You stay here and do not move, yes?'

The girl looks at him.

'But Madam Kelly sai—'

James interrupts her again. 'Please, do as I say and wait here as it will be safer for you, for I must go immediately.'

The girl looks at him and slowly nods. 'Yes, sir.'

James is up and across the lounge in minutes. Not too fast, as he doesn't want to be noticed in the crowd, but at a good lick of speed. He takes the stairs and heads back to the President's Suite, hoping he is not too late.

As he arrives, the doors to the suite are partly open. He steps in and calls out, 'Emma, are you here?' With no answer, he calls out again, but there is still no reply. Swiftly, he checks in all the rooms for any signs of Emma or Sebastian, without success. The room that the injured girl was in has some chairs knocked over, and on the far side, ornaments that once stood on the bedside table are now scattered across the floor, broken. He goes to check on the young girl lying motionless on the bed, fearing the worst. As he moves the sheets, a voice calls out from behind him. 'She be alive at the moment, but not for much longer.'

James turns around and is confronted by two men with pistols drawn and pointing in his direction. One of them is the man he had taken out in the corridor earlier. The other is new to him but is of a similar size and stature to the first.

'Small world, isn't it?' he says in English. 'Now if you would be so kind as to sit down at the desk, I would feel more comfortable.' The man flicks the end of his pistol at the desk, encouraging him by cocking back the hammer on his weapon. Slowly, James walks over to the desk with both men watching his every move.

'Now take a seat like a good little boy while we wait a while.'

James obliges, not taking his eyes off them. The man James had the altercation with collects an ornate wooden chair from a back wall, places it opposite him on the other side of the desk and offers it to his associate. He then takes a seat between James and the girl in the bedroom.

'It would seem that we are to watch you for a while until she returns, but the girl in the bed, well, she scratched one of the clients and he desires satisfaction. The house thinks that the girl will be a liability from now on, so wants her removed, if you get what I mean. Still, she has already made us a small fortune entertaining them old diplomats. It will be far better to get rid of her now while she is asleep than wake her up just to kill her, don't you think?'

He looks up at the man ahead of James then continues. 'Frank, we may as well do her where she be and wrap her in the sheets she is on. It will save a lot of messing about later,' he comments to him in French.

James watches the man behind him via the mirror on the wall. 'What about the girl, Emma, who was in this room?'

The man smiles at James. 'Girl? What girl? There was no girl here when we arrived, was there, Frank?'

James discreetly looks round on the desk for something that could be used as a weapon, but nothing catches his eye until… *Yes! That will do*, he thinks to himself.

The man in front of him slowly places his pistol on the table in an attempt to get James to grab for it. But James does not take the bait. He waits, biding his time until his opponent makes a mistake. As they sit staring at each other, the man starts to get a bit impatient and irritated. 'Kill her now, Luke, and get it over with. That way we can work on this one next.' James watches in the mirror as Luke turns his back and moves towards the girl. As he reaches the doorway to the bedroom, James swiftly makes his move.

He pulls the ice pick out of the stuffed armadillo and thrusts it into the eye and through the brain of the man in front of him. The man barely moves or makes a sound, just twitches as James rotates the ice pick in his brain, scrambling all that it contacts inside his head. Frank just judders as he slumps down on the desk, dead.

Pulling the ice pick back out, James stands and swiftly turns to the man in the doorway, throwing the pick in his direction with the power and strength that only a harpooner would have.

The weighty metal spike hits the man just below his right shoulder blade and drives in a full six inches to the hilt.

'Aaaaahhhh,' he yells as he drops the pistol on the floor and tries reaching up his back to grab at what has impaled him. He has barely moved an inch before James grabs him and pulls him back into the main room, throwing him to the ground with force. He closes the bedroom door out of respect for the girl inside, then turns his attention back to the man he has downed. Rolling him onto his stomach and grabbing the ice pick, he starts to rotate it in his shoulder. The man screams out in pain.

'Let's start again, shall we? Where is the girl who was in this room?'

Somehow, the man resists telling James anything, so he pulls out the ice pick and rams it into the back of his leg and twists it.

'Aaaaahhhh.' The man screams again, yet still he holds out without saying a word. James pulls out the pick and slowly pushes it into the left shoulder and socket joint, and this time the man yells out to him.

'Enough, for the love of God, enough. I will tell you what you want to know.'

James grabs his hair and lifts his head. 'Where is the girl who was in this room?'

'Oh, that girl. She has gone to the Guillotine Room to have her arms removed,' he says with a smile.

James takes exception to his attitude and pushes the spike across his shoulder to rip the socket joint apart, causing the man to scream louder than ever.

'Did that hurt? Now where is this Guillotine Room and how do I get there?' He applies more pressure until the man speaks up.

'Next floor up and along the corridor to the end. It's on the right with an axe and block painted on the door. But I would hurry if I was you as she may not live long enough for you to see her again.' The man lets out an evil cackle of laughter at James. 'Sounds like she meant something to you. Shame she will soon be clipped of her wings, as they say. Never to hold a man again in her arms.' He chuckles as James releases his head and pulls out the ice pick.

The man lets out a grimace of relief as the pain reduces, but it is short lived as James moves it to the back of his neck. Holding down his head, he slowly pushes the point into Luke's neck and drives the needle-like blade hard into a gap at the top of his spine, rotating the pick forwards and sidewards and severing the spinal cord inside. The body twitches for a minute or so before finally the man lies motionless.

James retracts the blade and rolls him over to face him. 'You see me.' He taps the man's face and watches his eyes move slightly and blink. 'I don't know how long you will live like this, but I do know you will never move or walk again. In fact, unless someone looks carefully, I doubt these people will even know you're still alive! However, what I do know is that either way, nobody will bother or want to look after a man like you. So, I wonder if they will just bury you alive or do what I hear is the usual thing around here – weigh you down and slip you quietly into the canal in the dead of night to sink to the bottom and drown, while they watch from above. I have seen many a man dragged to their deaths before, being pulled down by whales while caught up in the ropes. The look on their faces say they know it's a one-way ticket, but yet they still take a deep breath in the hope they will come back up and breathe again.'

He pats the man on the shoulder. 'How will you do it when the time comes, I wonder? Take a breath and try to hold on as long as possible or breathe out and end it sooner. Not that I really care. It's the price you pay for touching my woman and threatening to kill that girl in the next room. Now I will leave you to think of the many ways you could meet your fate. I personally hope it lasts at least a few days, if not longer. I want you to get a real taste of what it is like to be helpless and vulnerable. Between now and then, you can think what it is like, being on the receiving end of a fate most foul, for once I leave this room, I will think on you no more.'

James gets up and walks over to the armadillo. He thrusts the ice pick back into its body, then moves to the bed he was going to share with Emma that night and kneels down beside it. Reaching underneath, he pulls out a long travel case and places it on the mattress above. Undoing the catches, he flicks open the lid to expose its contents.

On top of his clothes is a large thick belt with all his attachments, including his modified sword, two pistols and several knives. Taking the belt out, he clips it to his waist, rotates it into a position where he is comfortable, then heads out of the President's Suite. On his way past the other man he killed – Frank – he picks up the small pistol that had been dropped on the desk. Placing it in one of his large pockets on the side of his trousers as he leaves the suite.

CHAPTER 5

The Hand

At the same time James is heading to the President's Suite, the door opens on the Guillotine Room and an enforcer steps in. He looks around then turns and watches as Madam Kelly enters with the grace and finesse of a jaguar, gliding across the floor in her elegant attire, locking her eyes on her prey.

She looks straight at Emma, who is sitting in a chair with her hands tied together in front of her. Across the room, behind a large upright guillotine, sits the beaten body of Sebastian. His hands are tied to the chair's arms, and he has a blood-stained gag in his mouth and heavy bruising across his face and neck. His waist is held tight with a leather strap securing him to the backrest and his feet are locked in place with large metal clamps that reduce any movement to a minimum.

Madam Kelly focuses her gaze on Emma and walks over to look at her closely. 'Is it really you? My long-lost child.' She slides her fingertips down the side of Emma's face and looks deep into her eyes. 'You're about the right age and very beautiful in your own way – without make-up and the benefits of a fine wardrobe. Yes, I can see you in there. You have your mother's eyes and nose and your father's ears.'

Emma just stares at her intently. Madam Kelly walks round behind her and places her hands on her shoulders, gently massaging them with her fingertips as she speaks. 'Oh, how I have wanted to find you for so long, my dear. One of the only things in my life to get away from me, never to be found. Yet here you are, located in my establishment, staying in one of my very own special suites. Who could have possibly imagined that?

'All these years spent searching for you, at great expense I might add, only to have you return to me on your own terms. Even then, if it were not for that stupid clot over there, we would never have known it was you in the President's Suite. You see, my staff brought it to my attention that a manservant had asked for food for his niece called Emma!'

She walks around Emma to face her again. 'Well, ask yourself, what manservant could afford to have their niece here in this establishment, in one of my special suites? Unless they were working for me?'

Emma stares at her with a hatred that would burn through walls. 'Murderer. You killed my mother.'

Madam Kelly's head snaps back to stare at her. Her expression changes to rage as she stretches out her hand and is about to slap her before pausing as her self-control returns. 'My dear, all your mother had to do was pleasure a man for a few hours. Just a few hours and she would have been rich beyond her wildest dreams. But no. Instead, she refused, fought him at every turn and nearly destroyed me in doing so. For what? Something that every woman loses at one time or another. Why not get well paid for what you would give freely to some unworthy man at some stage in your life?'

The hatred between the two of them wells up as Madam Kelly starts to rant about how defiant her worthless mother was. 'Just because she could sing and act so innocent, she was no better than me. Your mother only entertained the masses. I now rule them all. The rich, the powerful, even the religious have found their way under my sheets. Hell, most of the nobility of Europe are controlled by me and what I require of them. If only she had just given in and played along with me and accepted her fate, your mother would still be here today. Still, that matters not anymore. I've made dozens of women in her image over the years, all of them far better than she ever was.'

'My mother was a decent woman, honourable and loved by all. Not because they were threatened by her, but because she brought kindness and joy to all she met. For that, you snatched her away just to show the world what you could do for money if it was requested of you. Despite all that you did to her, the abuse, suffering, isolation and threats to her life, you could not break her. She never sang for you. Never once smiled or did as you demanded. All this power you think you have, yet she passed away defiant of you, beating you with nothing more than her sheer will.'

'Silence, you little bitch. You have no idea what your mother put me through when she died. Nearly six years I suffered, crawling over and under people of all ages, male and female. Groups and individuals prodding and poking me from all angles, in every hole possible just to save my skin and keep this place going. I called in every favour I could lay my hands on, handed out more money and bribes than this entire city earns in a year. Bedded more men than I can count. But worse was to come. My entire collection of precious jewellery and stones, dished out like they were confetti in the wind. To people who did not even appreciate what the pieces were, the history and people who had once worn them going back to Egyptian and Byzantine kings and queens of old.

'But now, after all these years, I am back on top. My debts all but settled. Those that opposed me appeased or dead. Almost every politician, diplomat and head of state in Europe now frequents my rooms, even the King of France has time for me at court when I request it of him. Hell, I even have a special suite reserved for the Vatican all year round for when their cardinals come to visit Paris. And believe me, their tastes are somewhat unusual to say the least.

'You see, I have collected something on almost all of them now. That's power, my girl. All I have left to do is take my vengeance out on your father for abandoning me, and on the men who attacked me that night. Then I will be complete. Which is why you are so important to me, for now I will be able to lean on your father and use him to do my bidding, before exposing him for what he is and ruining his reputation. Now you can see why having you back under my control is so important to me. He will suffer like I did, only much, much worse.'

Madam Kelly looks at Sebastian, then back at Emma. 'I wonder, is he one of her brothers? Could he be one of those who ripped me up that night? Was it them that broke into my beautiful establishment and took away my little canary and her daughter all those years ago?'

She looks down at the floor and ponders for a while then looks back at Emma. As she does, her hands start to undo the side of her dress. 'Could he be the one responsible for this?' Madam Kelly opens her dress to show Emma the twelve-inch jagged scar across her stomach, and a second one from her naval down several inches towards her crotch. 'Being pushed through that glass window left me with this! What woman wants to see this every time they look in the mirror? What man wants to see this on the woman he is in bed with, scarred and disfigured for life?'

Emma does not even look at the scars. She has heard about them her whole life and does not need to see them now, or ever. She prefers instead to just stare at Madam Kelly's face, itching for the opportunity to get at her and take revenge.

Madam Kelly does her dress back up and reshapes her clothes into the perfect position. 'Now that I have you again, I can complete my revenge on your father.'

'You took his payment, didn't you? Stole my mother's life and dreams from her in the deal. If it was so bad for you, why not let her go and let him take the blame for what had been done?'

Madam Kelly grabs hold of Emma's chin and slams her head back against the chair. 'Listen here, you little bitch. If it was not for me, you would have never been born. So have a little more appreciation for the person who set up your conception.'

She pushes Emma's face away and steps back. 'I was younger and very naive then, thought that those powerful and influential people would stand by their words and agreements. But I was wrong, so very wrong. They do what they want, when they want, to get what they desire, then walk away and deny all involvement. Having you, a baby, by my side gave me some protection from those who wanted me gone. But when you were stolen, it left me without any defences. Within days the wolves came knocking and by God did they feed on me.'

She pauses for a moment, reminiscing. 'You leave me in

somewhat of a dilemma, my dear. Being older now, you do not have the same impact on your father as you had as a child. I could still use you as leverage, but most of what I wanted I now have. Perhaps I could better use you now as an example to put the fear into those who would think of opposing me in the future.' She taps her lips with her finger before running it along her dress where it covers the scar as she considers her options.

'I wonder. Maybe I should do what I always threatened to do should the opportunity ever arise. How would he feel if I was to cut off his precious child's arms and make her earn her keep in the suites of this establishment? Having men crawling all over his daughter, fucking you from dawn till dusk, giving birth to bastard child after bastard child. Each one with a birth right to the throne of his country.'

She looks at Emma. 'How would it feel, never being able to hold one of your children in your arms? Then again, would you want to hold them, not knowing who their father really was and the way they came to be?

'What would it be like for you, being fed and cleaned at my discretion or left stinking of dirty drunk men? Do you think he would come to your aid, being his only child? Well, the only one that we know of, anyway. Or would he deny you and leave you to your fate, like he did your mother and me all those years ago?'

Emma has not stopped making eye contact with Madam Kelly since she entered the room. 'There is something wrong with you. You suffer with the delusion of grandeur from your own self-importance. You believe that you are some kind of supreme being, dictating your will on others when in fact you are a bitter, twisted, lonely old woman. With nothing better to do in her life than make other people suffer at your hands to make your own existence tolerable.'

Madam Kelly strikes Emma across the face. 'Insolent fucking child. I do this for power. Power that will ensure no one will ever take away my position in society again. As for lonely, well, maybe that will change as well, as I have taken a fancy to your tattooed man, James. It would seem that I have a lot more to offer him than you do, my precious.'

Emma laughs at her. 'You have got nothing he wants; you are just an empty shell. I doubt that it is even blood that runs through your veins, just a grinding bit of old granite for a heart and poison for blood.'

'Well, if that is the case, my dear, why is he downstairs waiting for me to return at this very moment? He seemed more than satisfied with the service I was providing just a short while ago.' She smiles and gives a seductive wink towards her captive.

Emma laughs again, even louder than before. 'He is only down there because we wanted him th—' Emma stops speaking. She has so nearly slipped up and hopes it has not doomed them all.

'He is downstairs because I asked him to join me. This is what your man gave me as a gift.' She points to the black pearl brooch pinned to her chest. 'You know, I think you have just helped me finally make up my mind on what to do with you. Just like your mother, you do not know how to handle a man, but I will change that. By the time I have finished your education, you will have serviced thousands of them.'

She pauses as she looks over to the guillotine. 'Have you ever seen one of these at work, my little soon-to-be wingless canary?'

Emma just stares at her, hatred still filling her eyes.

'No! Allow me to show you what it can do.' Madam Kelly walks over to the guillotine, taking her two enforcers with her. She slaps Sebastian across the face to bring him round. 'Time you did something useful for me,' she comments as she moves to the large hearth and stokes the orange coals with a brass shovel. Pulling out one of three irons that have been heating to an amber glow, she inspects the flattened end herself before placing it back in the hot coals. Then she turns to the table beside the guillotine where she inspects the quality of the work on the leather cups and straps spread out before her.

Looking back at Emma with a smirk, she speaks. 'Seems like everything is in order and ready to go.'

She clicks her fingers at the enforcers, along with a sharp nod of the head. They immediately move to Sebastian and rotate his chair in front of the guillotine, clicking the two front legs into purpose-built metal grooves in the floor to hold him firmly in place.

Sebastian took a vicious beating and is still only semi-conscious and not fully aware of what is unfolding around him, but he tries to resist at every opportunity he gets. One of the enforcers moves to the side of the guillotine and pulls down on a thick white cord. The huge blade starts to ascend into the air. The cutting edge is at a twenty-degree angle, making it deeper at one end than the other, supported with a thick wooden block on the top keeping the blade square in the runners and adding weight to the cutting edge. As it reaches the top, the man pushes a metal pin with a T-bar-shaped end into the frame and loops the cord over it, holding the blade in position. He then stands back from the machine and nods at her.

Madam Kelly turns to look at Emma. 'What would give you the best demonstration of our machine, I wonder?'

'There is something very wrong with you. What kind of person would have a contraption like that in their possession? You are a very sick woman.'

Madam Kelly ignores her. She is in her own world now and is tapping her lips with a finger as she decides what to do next. 'I think we will go for the left hand for this demonstration.' She looks to her second enforcer.

'Claude, if you would do the honours? Put a rope on it and thread it through.' The man obeys and puts a loop over Sebastian's left hand and pulls it through one of the three holes in the stock at the bottom of the guillotine. Sebastian tries to fight, but he is so weak it is to no avail. The enforcers close and lock the stock in position, trapping the hand at the wrist. Sebastian looks up at Madam Kelly and quietly murmurs something. She does not hear what he says, but it has sparked her interest, so she moves closer. 'What was that you said?'

Emma yells out, 'Leave him alone! That man has done nothing but be in a room with me and for that you have beaten him senseless!' Madam Kelly ignores Emma and moves closer, leaning down to hear the words Sebastian is trying to speak.

Sebastian coughs up mucus and blood and spits it out before speaking again a little louder. 'We should have killed you when we had the chance. I pray we do not make that mistake again this time.' He then spits a load more blood on Madam Kelly's dress and laughs as she tries to wipe it off and just smears it over a wider area.

Enraged at his actions, she yells, 'So you think that is funny, do you? Well then, get a load of this and see if you are still laughing.' She stands upright and moves to the side of the guillotine, grabs the pin and pulls it out. With a grating sound, the blade comes crashing down with a thud as it hits the stops, severing Sebastian's hand at the wrist. He screams out in agony as his hand falls into a waiting wicker basket below.

Emma looks down at the floor, helpless, tears flowing from her eyes. There are no words or sounds coming from her; she just has utter hatred for this evil woman. The two enforcers swiftly jump into action. The first man binds the wrist of the severed limb with a strip of leather, then holds the arm down while the second man grabs a hot metal iron from the fire and seals the wound by burning the end of his limb. Sebastian again lets out a blood-curdling scream before passing out with pain as the room fills with the smell of burning flesh. The two enforcers continue their work. First, they bandage the wound and then push it into a leather cup, finally strapping the arm across his chest. From the very start of this procedure to its dire conclusion, you can see that these men have done this many times and have their technique down to a fine art.

Emma looks up at Madam Kelly, tears flowing down her face as she cries for Sebastian. 'No matter what happens to me, I will see you pay for this injustice,' she comments with a scowl.

'Do you see how efficient this is? Almost all our subjects now survive the procedure.' Madam Kelly walks over to the basket, picks up the hand and looks at it. Moving over to a side table, she drops it into a clear glass jar of alcohol, submerging it fully in the liquid before placing a wooden stopper in the top to seal the jar tightly. She turns to one of the enforcers and summons him with a flick of her wrist. The man obediently picks up the jar and follows Madam Kelly to a long curtain running the length of the far wall.

He pulls down on a cord at the end of the rail and the entire curtain rises up, exposing three rows of shelves filled with jars full of severed limbs. Madam Kelly points to an empty spot and the man places the jar in position before stepping away.

Emma shakes her head as she looks at the assortment of jars containing hands, arms, feet and even a severed head and what looks like a man's penis.

Madam Kelly smiles at Emma. 'Do you not like my collection? All of these at one stage belonged to someone who insulted or rebuffed me. But the middle spot has always been reserved for you, my dear. And now I think it is time for you to fill the space.' She turns to her two enforcers. 'Clear him away and put her in the chair.'

The two men oblige, undoing Sebastian's straps and dragging him off to an adjacent room. They return swiftly to collect Emma and escort the resisting woman to the vacated seat. Emma fights back, kicking and screaming, twisting her body all the way to the guillotine, giving her all to break free of the enforcers. But she is no match for these men and is easily overpowered and locked into the seat in front of the machine. With her waist, legs and feet clamped down, the blade is raised and locked in position with the pin. The men then put loops of rope around both her wrists and pull them forward through the two smaller holes in the stocks, this time up past the elbows, then lower the stock into place and lock the wood into position. As they prepare for Emma's fate, they hear thumping sounds from outside the suite. Both men look up at the same time and stare at the door. One of them starts to walk over to investigate, while the other holds position beside Emma.

* * *

Outside the room, other events have been unfolding. James has just reached the last turn in the corridor before reaching the Guillotine Room. Walking at an extended pace, he has his sword in his right hand and a knife in his left. As he turns the final bend, he spots the two men standing at the sides of an ornate door adorned with a picture of an axe and a block painted on the centre panel. He accelerates until he is nearly sprinting, raising his sword as the men react to his approach. They reach for their pistols as he strikes the first enforcer with his blade, hitting the man on his left shoulder. The jagged teeth cut him right down to his navel, separating one side of his body from the other. The second man has pulled out his pistol, but before he can aim it, James's knife is plunged into his neck and twisted forward to cut clean through his throat and jugular with the same stroke. Both men are dead within seconds and lie heaped on the floor, bleeding profusely.

He pauses in an attempt to calm his racing heart, cleans his sword and knife on the jacket of one of the downed men then clips the weapons back on his belt. He can hear Emma screaming on the other side of the door as he pulls a pistol out of his pocket, and one from his belt, and cocks them both.

Facing the door, he takes one more deep breath before kicking it open and stepping in with the follow-through. Both pistols are raised and looking for their targets. He spots Emma strapped to the guillotine. An enforcer is standing beside her, and another is in front of him. Madam Kelly stands with her mouth wide open. Aiming the pistol at the man next to Emma, he fires, hitting him in the centre of his chest. The impact knocks him backwards and down to the floor. The other man attempts to run at James, but with a gap of around twelve feet, James has time to focus his aim and fire, hitting the man between the eyes and killing him instantly. Dropping the pistols, he unclips the sword from his belt and raises it above his head, ready to strike, as he does not know if anyone else is in the room and can take no chances. He moves cautiously, looking in all the doorways leading from the main room.

He stares at Madam Kelly. 'Do not move if you value your pathetic life,' he says as he moves past her to check the last two adjacent rooms. Madam Kelly is not stupid. She knows the game is up for now and needs to come up with something to save her skin, but her options are very limited. She can either get to the guillotine and use Emma as a bargaining chip to get away, or she can pull the pin and at least get her revenge on the girl before trying to convince James that she is the one for him.

It takes her seconds to decide. After all, it's her place and her rules. She will beg to no man ever again. As James reaches the last doorway, she makes a run for the guillotine. He spots her movement out of the corner of his eye and swings his sword back over his head. She is reaching for the pin on the guillotine as James lets loose the sword with all his might. It rotates through the air towards the guillotine as Madam Kelly grabs the pin. She slips on the blood oozing from the man on the ground, pulling the pin out of the column and activating the blade. There's a deadly grating sound as a shocked Madam Kelly falls to the ground. Emma screams as she hears the pin release and the blade drop down, then closes her eyes as she waits for the inevitable.

An eerie silence falls across the room, like time standing still, or being in the centre of a storm when all has just gone calm, but you can see chaos strewn all around. Emma can hear her own heart pounding as if to jump out of her chest, but she can feel no pain. After several seconds have passed, she tilts her head to the side, opens up one eye and looks up at the guillotine. It rests about two feet above her head, held up by James's sword, which is firmly imbedded in the woodwork. The sheer thickness of the sword's edge is like that of a line of small axes and has the strength to hold the blade fast to the side of the guillotine.

'No!' screams Madam Kelly. 'I will not be denied my vengeance,' she yells, grabbing the blade and pushing it down with all her might. But the sword is imbedded too deep into the post. Within seconds, James pulls her off and strikes her across the face, knocking her to the ground. He turns his attention to Emma, releases the stocks and helps her sit upright. He undoes the restraints to get her out of the chair. As Emma hugs and kisses James, she hears Madam Kelly moan as she attempts to get to her knees. Madam Kelly slowly looks up and is about to speak when Emma steps back, lunges forward and kicks her in the head, knocking her back down to the floor.

There is still a faint moaning in the air and Emma takes another look at Madam Kelly. She is definitely out cold, so where is the noise coming from? Suddenly it dawns on her. 'Sebastian,' Emma yells as she rushes into a side room. There lying prostrate across the bed, Sebastian is barely conscious and in a lot of pain. But he's alive.

As Emma attends to him, she tells James what happened, and as much as she can recall about all that Madam Kelly said. James shakes his head in disgust. 'That woman is no good and you will never be safe with her still around.'

They hear a noise coming from the corridor outside. James heads over to the guillotine, grabs the sword and tries to free his weapon, twisting and pulling with all his might. But all he succeeds in doing is pulling the ten-inch stem from the main body of the sword. Tapping it in his hand, he decides it still has enough weight to do damage and moves quietly over to the broken door, with half a sword in one hand and a loaded pistol in the other. He leans up against the wall as the door is pushed open and somebody slowly enters the room. He raises his sword ready to strike, but at the last second stops himself delivering the blow as he recognises a crouched Bernard entering the room with a pistol in his hand.

Bernard, on the other hand, is slow to respond. He cautiously pans round the room before looking up to his right and seeing James's towering form. 'Hello,' he says, before standing up. He points at the two dead men in the hallway, and then at the two in the room.

'All you, yes?'

James nods. 'Uh huh.' Bernard looks at him, suitably impressed with what James has done to all the enforcers strewn across the floor. Recognising his voice, Emma calls Bernard and he swiftly heads off to join her. James continues his own work, putting his sword hilt into the hot coals of the fire. He then picks up Madam Kelly and takes her to the guillotine. Bending her over the back of the chair, he straps her hands into the ankle cuffs. Pulling her dress up to her chest, he winds the waist strap round the back of the chair and around the backs of her legs, tightens it and lets the bottom half of her dress drop back down.

He hears Bernard yell out, 'No, Sebastian, what has that bitch done to you?' In French. He does not understand all the words but can take an educated guess as to what he is saying.

Seeing what has happened to his brother's hand and the beating to his face, there are many words between Emma and Bernard in French before they both come out from the room. Bernard has tears running down his face. He notices that James has slumped Madam Kelly over the chair connected to the guillotine. He goes to speak to James but stops when he sees all the severed limbs in the jars on the shelves. He has to do a double take as he does not believe what he is looking at, then shakes his head in disbelief. 'No, this cannot be. Who would do such a thing to another person?' This only adds fuel to the fire as he clenches his fists and turns towards Madam Kelly, swearing in French.

Madam Kelly is starting to come around, trying to move her hands and legs. She slowly becomes aware that she is clamped over the chair of the guillotine. Staring at the advancing Bernard, she screams for help, pulling at the clamps wildly as she does so.

In French, Bernard speaks to her.

'It will do you no good. You have told your enforcers in other areas of this building to ignore any screaming and shouting from this room. You see, we heard them talking in the reception area when the two pistol shots went off. No one will come, no matter what you do. You are all alone. Just like my poor sister was all those years ago.'

Madam Kelly turns her head to see who is speaking to her. She pauses for a moment to think. 'I seem to recognise you, but I do not remember where from.'

Bernard leans down to her and grabs her hair in his fist and turns her head. 'It was a long time ago, when I was here to get my sister and her daughter, you wretched animal. I was the one who threw you through the glass door. And looking around now at what you have done, it's a shame I did not kill you then.'

Madam Kelly growls and curses at him, pulling at her restraints. 'When I get out of here, I'm going to cut off your head and your balls and add it to my collection on the wall over there.' Realising she is in a vulnerable position, she changes tack and goes to the only person who might ally themselves with her. 'James, my dear, are you going to let them harm me, when you know I can give you so much? Anything you desire, just ask and it will be yours. I can even elevate you in society if that is what you want.'

James looks at her. 'Woman, all I want from you is to know about my sisters and what happened to them.'

'Darling, just get me out—' Bernard hears the word 'sister' and interrupts.

'Emma, translate what I say for James to understand.' He looks straight at James. 'We found the ledgers in Madam Kelly's private suite; I took the liberty of looking through the book for references of your sisters. It would seem that this thing in front of us and your brother Lord Fitzgerald's relationship goes back several years. He frequented here many times in the past, along with your father before him. Having a debt to pay here for services rendered and your father unwilling to pay his son's expenses anymore, the younger Lord Fitzgerald struck a bargain – full payment of the debt if she would wait a few months for the collection, allowing him time to take over his father's empire and affairs, plus three thousand gold pieces and three young high-class girls in exchange for her support of his plans to expand.'

James stares angrily at Madam Kelly as Bernard continues. 'Brace yourself, my friend, for it gets worse. The book has details of all their important girls and in some cases their preferred clients from the start to the finish of their involvements. It would seem that the oldest sister, Harriet, fought back in a tussle with some Spanish dignitaries who paid heavily for the privilege of breaking her in. It got violent and she hit one of them with a vase and cut him across the forehead. After the brutal raping that followed, she managed to slip their grasp and chose to take her life by jumping from a window rather than give them any more satisfaction. It would seem that Madam Kelly here laid her to rest in the bottom of the canal to avoid the scandal, in return for certain favours from these Spanish diplomats. Their names are in the ledger if you need it for later.

'As for your second sister, Elizabeth, they used her as a cleaner for a year or so until she was older, then they moved her on to one of the suites. But she was a wild one, and they could not break her will as she was too strong. It would seem from the book that after several escapes, and a stabbing of a client with a letter opener, they decided that they could not control her. So, they used Elizabeth on that machine as a punishment and to try and stem her ferocity. They did to Elizabeth what they were going to do to our Emma here.'

Bernard walks over to the rack of severed limbs, closely watched by James. He reads the names marked on the bottom of each glass container until he comes across one containing two complete arms. At the bottom of the specimen jar is a name – Elizabeth Fitzgerald – and a date that matches the notes in the ledger. Bernard lowers his head with sadness, then turns and puts his hand on James's shoulder. 'I'm sorry, James,' he says quietly. 'Those are your sister's arms. Her name is listed at the bottom of the jar. She was one of the first to be guillotined but died from the shock of it.' Emma struggles to translate her uncle's words as she chokes up, weeping heavily as she continues as best she can.

Tears also begin to roll down James's face as he stands motionless. Slowly, his body seems to expand as he tenses up. He goes to move against Madam Kelly, but Bernard's hand on his shoulder holds him fast as he speaks again.

'Wait, my friend. That is not all. I also read about your third sister, Anna Marie. We went to the basement of this building where they groom the special girls to be canaries, and we found her. She does not know of your existence yet, nor why we took her, but one of my brothers and Henrey are with her in our carriage outside. She will be waiting for you when we finish here.'

As Emma finishes the translation, James's face begins to light up just a little and he looks to the heavens as if to thank somebody for the good news.

Bernard grabs James's shoulders and shakes him. 'We found her, yes!'

James is numb as Emma comes over to hug him. 'You still have a sister, James. She is alive and waiting for us,' she says as James puts his arms around her.

'Oh God, Anna Marie still lives,' he comments.

As the three of them stand in a small circle, a sound comes from one of the rooms. Sebastian is standing in the doorway, trying to support himself, the arm of his severed hand still strapped to his chest. Emma rushes over to hold him up as he tries to speak. 'The girl in the room, is she still alive?' he asks.

Bernard smiles. 'Yes, Sebastian. When I left, Gaston was carrying her down to our coach. She is still very weak, and it will be a close thing, but we know good physicians and she has a fighting chance.'

With Emma's help, Sebastian staggers towards James and Bernard. 'We were talking before they broke in and took me. You know they killed her parents when they fought back to keep her safe. She was so sad, wanted me to end her life as she has nothing to live for. The child is only fifteen and thinks her life is over!'

Sebastian shakes his head before he turns to Madam Kelly. 'I wish you to suffer like nothing on this earth, you destroyer of lives. I do not think that God himself would ever forgive such a vile creature. Even hell would be too good for the likes of you.'

He turns back to his brother. 'I promised that I would look after the girl as if she were my own daughter, brother. I will not let her down. Not another one. Not after Juliet. I could not take losing one more to this place.'

He staggers, but Emma holds on to him.

'Do not worry, Sebastian,' says Bernard. 'We will look after her. Now go with Emma and get to the carriage. I will join you shortly after we have finished here.'

Bernard has his stern, cold expression on his face as he looks at Emma and signals her to the doorway. 'Take Sebastian to the carriage, Emma. This will not be something you want to see.'

She looks at James and he gives her a small kiss on the cheek before whispering in her ear. 'Before you go, tell Bernard to go with you or to not interfere with what I do next. For I do not wish to fall out with him when you are gone, and I cannot communicate with him like you. I will deal with this woman in my own way.'

Emma passes on the message. Bernard looks at James before speaking back to Emma and she then turns to James. 'My uncle will not leave you here alone, but he will also not interfere with what you do. However, you must ensure this evil is gone forever, or he will finish her himself.'

James turns to Bernard and gives him a deep, slow nod. The two men then watch as Emma helps Sebastian through the shattered door, looking back only the once before they disappear.

When they are gone from sight, James turns to Madam Kelly. 'What makes you think you can treat people this way? Does it not bother you that people suffer and die at your hands?'

She looks up from her position. 'My darling, some people are born to lead and influence the masses, others are sheep to be used as we see fit. I merely ensure the people with influence get what they want, that's all. Think of me as a negotiator for them that deserve more from this life.'

'Two of my sisters are dead. Bernard's sister is dead. The men round your feet are dead. By the door, two more lie with their guts hanging out. Does it mean so little to you, the life of another, or are you beyond all help?'

She stares at James. 'What about my needs? I am a woman who desires things as well. Nobody thinks of my requirements and what I would like from life. I do what I need to survive, that's all. If it is not them, it would be me, so I choose me.'

James is shaking with rage. This woman shows no remorse for the things she has done, no matter what he says. She will never understand the levels of suffering she has caused. Like his brother, she is just too full of her own self-importance to even acknowledge the rights of others.

'Now, James, darling, release me from this ridiculous position and I will forgive you. But not him. He will pay for what he has done to me.'

He looks at her in disbelief as he walks around behind her. 'I'm going to give you something you have never had before.' He grabs her dress and rips it open across her back. Then, taking the knife from his belt, he cuts round the dress and drops it to the floor, exposing her bent-over naked body from the waist down to her shoes.

Madam Kelly looks back at James in shock. 'Darling, there is nothing there that I have not done before, I can promise you. But do you really think this is the right time for that now?'

Undoing the strap, James kicks her legs apart and ties her ankles to items of furniture with the cord that was used to pull the limbs of the victims through the stocks.

All of a sudden, Madam Kelly feels very vulnerable, held in a compromising position where she has no control of the situation. Her tone changes as she continues to speak in a more reserved manner. 'But then again, if this is what floats your boat, I'm willing to give it a go with you.'

Bernard is watching everything unfold from the other side of the room. He is curious as to what is happening but is willing to see where it leads as he can see the rage in James's face, even if Madam Kelly does not. He watches as James picks up one of the leather straps and wraps it round his right hand.

'I've seen this done once before when I was on the islands. A man had sneaked off a ship anchored off the beach near a village where I was staying at the time. He came ashore against the wishes of the captain and the islanders. They were in negotiations for hardwood from the forest to repair their storm-damaged ship and supplies to replace their dwindling stocks before resuming their hunt for whales. This man decided he wanted a woman, and nothing was going to stop him. He thought that taking a native girl would be fun and surely nobody would worry about a savage being taken. So, late that night, he swam ashore and stalked round the village until he found one he could discreetly snatch. In this case, a diving girl carrying a jug of fresh water to her father's house. As she came out of the treeline, he grabbed her and dragged the woman, kicking and fighting, back into some bushes.

'He had his way with her for an hour or so before he was finished. At that point, with his lust satisfied, he let her go. Then he watched as the young woman stood up, redressed as best as she could and walked slowly back to the village, head held high but with tears running down her face. The man thought he could sneak down to the beach and return to the ship without anyone being aware. But he did not bank on running into some late-arriving fishermen who noticed him in the water. Knowing that he should not be around the island, they dragged him back to the village to stand before the chief.

'The villagers were in uproar, for the girl's father was a tribal elder and she was promised to the son of a neighbouring chief. It was intended to be a bonding of the two tribes and was most anticipated by both sides to ensure a lasting peace between them. With the daughter now violated, the marriage could not go ahead, and the girl was in disgrace. That night, the man was tied to a tree and left to his own devices until the morning.

'He awoke at sunrise to see the whole village standing on the beach looking out to sea. The girl he had violated was in the centre of the group. None of the villagers would even look at her. He watched as she tied a length of rope to her wrist, then got into a wooden dugout canoe. Two men in the boat paddled her out to the edge of the reef, where there was a drop off to much deeper water. They stopped and the girl stood up, turned to the villagers, lowered her head, then dived off the boat into the water. As she left the boat, the men paddled back to the beach, and the women and children moved off and got on with their daily tasks.

'The girl had let the village down and was in disgrace as the tribes would now go back to hunting each other and the killing would start over again. She would have been an outcast to the village from that moment on, so she did the only honourable thing left to her: diving down as deep as she could go. The young woman then wrapped the line around the coral and took her own life, offering her body to the spirits and gods of the sea.'

James grasps the handle of his broken sword and pulls it out from the coals. The glowing orange and yellow metal is bright on the eyes and sparks fly as he taps it on the side of the grate to remove any loose debris then walks towards Madam Kelly.

'As for the man who had caused this tragedy, it was going to be a different story, for he was about to be given a week to think about what he had done. Or, as the tribal elders called it, the dreams of the damned. For me, it would seem more like a week of intense pain and suffering that can only end one way. As once it is done, there is no going back; you just slowly fade into a trance-like state as infection sets in. But with nothing you can do, you think back on your life, what you have done with your time on this earth and how you got to be in this situation. Moving around is limited due to the pain, and eating and drinking is almost impossible as it will kill you sooner if you indulge too much. So, setting your affairs in order is as good as it gets for you.'

Madam Kelly stares at James as he approaches. 'What the hell do you think you are going to do with that?' she screams, finally realising that this is not going to end well. She tries to free herself of her bonds by pulling and tugging with all her might.

'Now you, Madam Kelly, have caused more pain and suffering to people than any person I have ever known. Kidnap, murder, torture, blackmail and so much pain and misery. Yet you feel no remorse for what you have done.' By now, James is standing behind Madam Kelly and positioning himself at the right angle before placing his spare hand on her lower back.

As he touches her, Madam Kelly yells out, 'What the hell are you doing? Get that dammed thing away from me. I will have your heart cut out while you still breathe and served to me on a plate for this, do you hear me?'

James continues to talk in a calm voice. 'That's the spirit. Now where was I? Oh yes, I need to get this just right. Too deep and you will not have enough time to contemplate the error of your ways.' James slowly pushes the rod into her rectum.

'Aaaaaaahhh,' she screams with a blood-curdling yell as the skin and flesh burns, spits and bubbles. As he inserts the sword hilt deeper, her body vibrates on the red-hot metal and the air fills with the smell of burning flesh, while Madam Kelly continues to scream. He is careful to only insert this object around eight inches deep and retracts it after only ten seconds or so. As the hilt is removed, she finally stops screaming.

Her face is bright red and covered in sweat, and her eyes are glazed over as she stares forward. She is panting fast like a dog that has been left in the sun too long. The pain has made her whole body go into shock as it twitches and shakes uncontrollably. 'Now I bet you've never had that done to you before,' James says as he watches her pant and shudder. Slowly, she manages to turn her head and look at him.

'I think seven days will be about right. Let's see how you plan what's left of the rest of your life, see what thoughts come to your mind during your time of repentance.'

Bernard has been watching in total silence. Now, he grabs James by the shoulder. 'Perhaps, if I was as brave as you, my sister would still be alive, yes?'

James pauses for a second, then speaks, knowing Bernard won't understand much of what he says. 'I could not have done this myself, years ago. It has taken another lifetime and a world of changes to turn me into this. Pray you never become what I am now, for I look back with regret that I left my family at the mercy of my brother. Besides, without you being who you are, I would not have found my last sister.'

He turns to look at the jars on the wall, spots the one with two severed arms and allows the tears to swell and slowly flow down his face again. He stares for a while, allowing the many terrible thoughts of what she must have gone through and why he was not around to protect her. He swings his arm back and launches the sword handle at them. The hilt hits one of the jars and shatters it, and as the liquid contents touches the hot metal, it bursts into flames, covering the floor and some more of the jars with fire. James swiftly moves back over to Madam Kelly and removes her restraints, slinging her over his shoulder as he heads to the door that Bernard is now holding open for him. They exit the room as the first of many jars explodes into small fireballs, catching the rest of the room on fire.

At the top of the stairs, James lowers Madam Kelly's part-naked body to the floor, leaving her leaning against a marble statue of Aphrodite. She is still in shock and cannot speak or move, just trembles and pants as she stares blankly at the wall.

As they reach the bottom of the stairs, a door bursts open, and a young girl runs out screaming. She is holding her arm across her breasts and what's left of her dress is clutched in her other hand. Moments later an elderly man with an erection runs out after her. He turns in the doorway to his friends inside, raises his hand and says, 'I will be back, gentlemen, for I feel I must fuck her at least one more time to be sure.'

The men in the room cheer him on as he staggers after the girl in hot pursuit. By now, the girl has passed James and is hiding behind Bernard's legs in the hope he does not see her. The man catches James's eye. He instantly recognises him as the gentleman he saw abuse the girl in the reception room. James cannot help but grab him by the throat and push him up against the wall. 'This is for the girl you savaged earlier, you animal,' he says as he unclips his knife from his belt and – with a sharp downward strike – slices off the end of his penis, then turns the knife sidewards and cuts into the man's scrotum, pulling back and severing his balls.

The man drops to his knees holding what's left of his manhood in his blood-stained hands, moaning in pain and numb with shock. Before he even has time to yell out, James and Bernard are off and away.

As they pass the reception area, James speaks to the two women present. 'There is smoke coming from the Guillotine Room. I think there might be a fire.'

One of them instantly shouts for assistance, directing the porters to investigate, while the other calls to the enforcers in the lounge area. In the confusion, James and Bernard slip out the main entrance into the street and cross the road to the waiting carriage.

Henrey has hold of the reins, while Gaston and François are sitting beside him. James opens the carriage door and the two of them step inside. Emma bangs the roof to let Henrey know they are in and to quickly drive off. As the carriage moves, James looks around at the people inside. Sebastian looks in great pain but is hiding it well as he has the young girl curled up tightly in his good arm. Bernard is sitting back in the seat, staring at his brother, and Emma is holding someone who is tightly wrapped in a blanket and hidden from view.

James leans forward and gently pulls back the fabric. He sees the top of a trembling head, but as the moments pass the person slowly looks up directly into James's face. She is taken aback as she sees a scary tattooed face looking at her. But the more she stares, the more she starts to see something in him. Her trembling slows and when James smiles at her, she finally recognises him.

'James, is that you? Why are you painted? You look all funny,' she says in a quiet voice. A hand slowly reaches up from the blanket and touches the side of his face. He nods gently as he smiles, and the tears start to flow from her eyes.

'Is it really you?' she asks so softly, as if afraid of what the answer may be.

'Yes, it's me, Anna Marie. It's your brother James.'

Her face changes from that of a terrified girl into someone who has just been given a little hope. She reaches out with her other arm and holds both sides of his face in her hands. 'We thought you were gone forever, eaten by hungry sharks,' she says with the beginnings of a smile.

'We?'

'Yes, silly, me and your sisters, you know Harriet and Elizabeth.' James looks at Emma, who shakes her head at him. 'I have not seen them for a while, but I am sure they will be happy to see you and know that you are really here.' She retreats into her blanket, as James starts to tread carefully with his words.

'Anna, when was the last time you saw your sisters?'

She thinks for a bit. 'Umm, on my birthday. Yes, it was my tenth birthday and we had cake.'

James leans forward and whispers in Emma's ear. 'By my calculation, she is a month away from being fifteen years old.' He looks at his sister with the saddest of expressions, desperate to ask what she has done for the last few years but far too afraid of what the answers might be. He stares into her eyes. It is quite clear that she is heavily sedated, more than likely with some form of opium. Whatever they have used on her, it will take time to get out of her system. Sitting back in his seat, he looks directly at Emma. She responds with a wry smile for a while as they bounce around on the uneven cobblestone road, before finally asking him, 'Is she dead?'

'In a way, yes. She has not gone yet, but she will soon enough.'

She looks at James with disappointment in her eyes and is about to say something when Bernard beckons her close with his finger. As she leans forward and comes within range, he starts to whisper into her ear. The more he speaks, the more shocked the expressions on Emma's face become. She looks up at James regularly with an expression of disbelief. This slowly changes to a smirk, then to a smile of satisfaction. 'Will she suffer badly?' she asks.

'Knowing what that woman is like, she will have an army of physicians around her by tomorrow. All will offer different solutions and will cut, prod and poke her for the next week or so, making her suffer more and more. She may get an extra day or two, but her fate is definitely sealed. The building will also be a mess – assuming they manage to get that fire out. If not, it will take many years to rebuild – for it will never go. The demand for places like that is fuelled by people with deep pockets and a lust for the good things in life, regardless of cost.'

Emma is content and sits back with a satisfied look on her face for the rest of the journey back to the warehouse. It's a journey in which no one else speaks, as they reflect on what has just happened. All are deep in their own thoughts over the night's events. With it being the early hours of the morning, there is little in the way of traffic on the roads. And most of the people who are walking about stagger with the amount of alcohol they have consumed, oblivious to all around them. The lighting is not good but is sufficient to navigate the large coach and four horses, especially with Henrey as he is an exceptional driver.

As they approach their destination, the large arched gates swiftly swing open, allowing the coach to drive straight in. Inside the warehouse, several close friends have been waiting patiently for their return and they spring into action as the gates slam shut.

Bernard has planned for every possible outcome. There are people to deal with the coach and horses, and the large room is warmed by a roaring open fire. Food, coffee and various spirits are waiting on the table, and most importantly, he has his old friend – a physician named Albert – waiting to assist.

The brothers are first to step down from the front of the carriage and help to unload the people inside. Albert checks out each one quickly before deciding who needs his attention first. In this case it is Sebastian. Despite his insistence to check out the young girl, it is him that Albert attends first. Helped to one of the large chairs, they move more lamps around him to improve the lighting before taking off all the strapping and slowly beginning to unwrap the bandages. It soon becomes clear that they are stuck to the end of his arm with all the dried blood and pressure of the leather cup. The pain is intense, and he needs to be anaesthetised if the physician is to work on the severed limb. Albert makes up a tonic and Gaston ensures his brother drinks the entire foul-tasting brew.

'Gaston, stay with your brother and let me know when he falls asleep,' Albert says. 'I will check on the others while we are waiting.'

The two girls are in separate bedrooms. James is with his sister, who is still curled up in the blanket he carried her out of the carriage in. Although she is now on the bed, Anna Marie is refusing to release the blanket or let go of her brother's arm in case she loses him again. Every now and then she has called out for her sisters to join them and does not understand why they do not answer.

As the physician arrives in the room, Anna Marie spots the older man and smiles. 'Are you here to play with me?' She flings back the blanket to expose a very skimpy yellow canary outfit and begins to wiggle and squirm, rubbing her hands over her small body. 'What part of me do you want to touch first?' she asks, beckoning him forward.

James and Albert are taken aback by the girl's change in mannerisms. While it saddens him to see his little sister like this, it is something James had anticipated and tries to play it down.

'Please continue and check her out. Let's see the full extent of what we are dealing with,' Emma says to Albert.

The man moves in and checks her eyes, and he does his best to check the rest of her over in a professional manner, asking her a few questions as he goes. After five or six minutes, he covers her back up and turns to James and Emma.

'It's not as bad as you think. I will check out the other girl then get back to Sebastian. When I have finished with everyone, I will give you my opinion on them all.'

Albert leaves James with his sister and moves to the next room to see to the girl's wounds but receives a very different reception from her. The girl is terrified as he moves towards her, and she pushes back into the bed. He pauses and waits for Emma to sit by her side before he tries again. This time he gets beside her, but he can see the fear in her eyes as she tenses up. Emma explains what happened to the girl, the assistance she gave, what injuries she saw in the bath and the measures taken to improve her situation. Albert is horrified, but he sits down beside her and calmly talks. 'And what is your name, my dear?'

The girl cautiously responds, 'Josephine.'

'Well, Josephine, do you trust Emma?' The girl looks at Emma and nods.

'Do you believe that she and all the others here want to help you get better?'

She pauses before answering. 'Yes, I do,' she replies while also giving a slow nod.

'I was the man who delivered all of Emma's four uncles when they were born. I have also looked after Emma since she was a little girl. Now I need to add you to that group of special people and check on your wounds to ensure you are well. It will be a little embarrassing, I know, but Emma will be here with you, and I will be as quick as I can.'

The girl tenses as fear wells up inside her. She is not stupid and knows she needs help, but is so afraid to trust a stranger, especially after what she has been through. Albert continues to reassure her, and after a small period of time, she allows him to inspect and treat her wounds. It is a very uncomfortable ten minutes or so and the girl sheds a few tears as he checks all the damage to her body. Albert finishes his work, then covers her back up. He gives her some comforting news. 'I think you will be alright, young lady. Quite sore and uncomfortable for a week or so. But the damage is not too bad, as I could see no puncture marks leading into the bladder. Now I will be back tomorrow to check on you. Until then, I think you will be in good hands with Emma by your side.'

As Albert gets up to leave, he turns back to Josephine. 'Oh, I almost forgot… Bernard was talking in the other room. Do you know what Emma's man James did to the person that led the attack on you?' Josephine looks at him blankly.

'Well, according to Bernard, the man who caused this terrible experience ran past him and James in the corridors when they were leaving. He was chasing another woman, bare as a newborn baby, with his manhood sticking out. Unfortunately for him, James recognised who he was. It would seem that with a swift flick of the wrist and a sharp knife, he sliced off the man's you-know-what, and the bits below for good measure. He will never be able to touch a woman again. That is if he ever recovers from his wounds.'

The girls look at each other before Emma bursts into laughter. Even Josephine starts to smile at the thought of the man losing his bits.

'On that note, Emma, a little bit of laudanum will help her for a few days, but no more than a spoonful at a time and in moderation. Now I need to go back and see Sebastian and tend to his arm, so I will bid you goodnight, ladies, and I will see you tomorrow, Josephine.'

He picks up his bag and returns to his first patient in the main room. He greets Sebastian but receives no response and looks into his eyes to see if they are totally glazed over.

'That is what I have been waiting for,' Albert says, summoning François and Bernard to help with the dressings. Between the three of them, they get all the old bandages off and the physician makes his inspection. After a full check of the exposed wound, he comes to only one conclusion.

'The skin has to be stretched over the wrist and sewn up. To do that, we must cut the bones back a little more as there is not enough skin to stretch at present. It's going to be tight on the arm for a while, but it will help seal the end and prevent infection and rubbing from the edges of the exposed bone below. Even then, there will be a lot of pus and weeping for a while, but if the bones heal up with a callus at the end, he will be good. He will have ongoing pain for a few months, but I have seen many army and navy veterans with similar wounds go on to have a good normal life. It just becomes a case of adapting to being one-handed, more than surviving the loss of the hand. But we do need to work on the skin now, while it is still wet and alive, to have the best chance of it sealing well.'

'What do we need to do this procedure here, Albert?' asks Bernard. 'As we can go nowhere else for a while.'

Albert replies instantly. 'I have the tools in my bag. Move him to the big table with bright lamps and place a blanket under his head. We need plenty of boiling water, white cotton sheets pulled into strips. Use alcohol to clean out that leather cup as it seems to fit his wrist well enough. I have the needle and thread on me, but we need to start now while he is unconscious.'

Bernard calls out to his brother Gaston to get the necessary items ready, while James comes through and helps him lift Sebastian onto the table. Albert sits down and gets to sterilising his tools in a flame and then pours brandy on the equipment before starting work on the severed limb. While the others stand ready to assist, they watch him at work and are amazed at the skill and finesse he shows as he removes unwanted bone pieces and rebuilds a new surface over the end of the limb with the stretched skin. Barely an hour has passed, and Albert has finished his work. The stitched area is completely bandaged up, put back into the leather cup and strapped to Sebastian's chest to prevent him bumping the end.

'Keeping his arm raised will also help reduce the swelling,' says Albert as he packs his tools away.

Gaston and François carry their brother to one of the many bedrooms while Albert speaks to Emma and James about Anna Marie. 'She has been drugged for many years. I would think she has also suffered some malnutrition to keep her petite. The child has very little understanding of morals and has been exposed to all manner of things we would consider unacceptable. With time, all this can be overcome, but her dependence on opium is going to be difficult for her to cope with. We are going to have a challenging few months, ridding her body of its addiction safely. So, we will need to keep her using it and slowly reduce the dosage over time. We must also ensure that she is always occupied and away from people who would take advantage.

'Josephine is another matter. If she has punctured her bladder, the infection will probably kill her. But I did not see any signs of leaking, so I am hopeful the damage is superficial. Her internal wounds will fix themselves in time, but the scars will always be present. Again, it is her state of mind that may take longer to heal. Now it is late. Time for me to be going home. I will call in tomorrow around lunchtime to see how my patients are doing.'

Albert is a true family friend and his word on medical issues is highly regarded by all in the profession of healing. Bernard sees him out of the warehouse, handing him payment for his trouble. Albert tries to refuse the offer, but Bernard is insistent due to the risks he has taken by helping them.

For the next ten days, the group lie low at the warehouse, keeping up-to-date on the situation with Madam Kelly and her establishment through a network of well-positioned friends. Madam Kelly's hunt for Bernard, James and the others has been intense. A huge reward of five thousand gold coins has had every villain, gang and bounty hunter scouring Paris along with her own enforcers and assassins. Looking for clues as to where they can be found.

But at the same time, many high-ranking officials and prominent people are relieved to hear about her fate and soon to be demise – especially after Bernard's associates have spread the rumours that Madam Kelly's stockpiled material for bribery and debts owed are now destroyed. The ledgers that once held sway are no longer in her possession and will be disposed of once the search is over. This has ensured that the government and the ministry's force of Police Nationale have no interest in pursuing her attackers, restricting her ability to force a legal search for the assailants.

Albert visits every other day and is pleased with all his patients, as their recoveries continue to go well. Anna Marie and Josephine have become inseparable. Wherever one is, the other is usually within a few feet – and most of that time, it is beside Sebastian. Tending to his every need has also helped to occupy their time as they regain their independence. With his help, they are beginning to cope with what happened to them at the hands of Madam Kelly.

However, Emma is becoming restless. She has been away from her beloved café for some time now and worries for the elderly she has left behind. She also wants some private time with James as she has something to discuss with him.

Sebastian's arm had kept him in bed for the best part of a week, while the two girls were always by his side, fussing over his every need. It was like he had his very own pair of nurses, but now he is mobile, he spends most of his time watching over them and their menacing and cheeky behaviour – ensuring they are safe, guiding them whenever they need help or have a question that needs answering. As a surrogate father figure to Josephine, there is no one better than Sebastian. He observes her and Anna Marie from a distance, allowing them to gain their confidence while they have a guardian angel to watch over them. He has also changed during this time. No more the quick, rush-in and react foolishly type, but a man who thinks before reacting, very much like his older brother Bernard.

On the eleventh day, Bernard organises people to start loading the wagons for a journey the following morning. With so many bored people looking for things to do, the warehouse is now more organised and up-to-date than it has ever been. And their loyal employees are more than able to run the business without him and his brothers being around for a while.

He says nothing of their destinations, just what and who is to be put on each wagon. Throughout the course of the day, he spends time with each family member and friend, speaking to them one-on-one. Later, he starts to place packages on the large dining table and labels each one with a name. He then informs everyone to be at the table for seven o'clock in the evening for an update. But still he explains nothing of his actions.

As the time nears, there is great excitement in the group as each person knows a little something that the others do not know. By ten to seven all the seats are filled with people eager to know what is going on. The excitement must be infectious as at five to seven, Bernard also arrives early and places both the ledger books down in the middle of the table. He serves everybody a glass of wine, although when it comes to the two girls, he mixes their wine with water. The girls are still excited as it is something they have never been offered before. He moves around the table and takes his seat, places some notes down in front of him, puts on a small pair of spectacles and raises his glass to all around the table.

'Well, ladies, gentlemen, and of course Sebastian, we have been hiding in here for nearly two weeks now.' Everyone chuckles at Sebastian's expense, while Emma translates her uncle's words for James to understand, though his French has been improving all the time. 'I dread to think how many people have been looking for us again, yet here we still are. Bounty on our heads or not, they still do not know who they are looking for, let alone where to look, so we are still safe and will be from now on.

'For many of us, this news has been a long time coming and I am delighted to announce that this afternoon at around three o'clock, Madam Kelly passed away from her injuries.'

There is a huge cheer, and much banging on the table from all present. Bernard puts his arms up to quiet the group before continuing. 'I have it on good authority from Albert that not only did she suffer from James's method of revenge, but even more so from the many physicians that cut, slashed and poked her around, just as he said they would. So, my first toast is to James.' He raises his glass, closely followed by all round the table. 'Thank you, James, for a job I should have done many years ago. To James, we salute you.'

The whole group responds, 'To James,' and they all take a sip of their drinks.

'As for the hotel itself, the damage has been severe and most of it is closed for repairs that will take a year or two to complete. Without the ledgers and documents for blackmail and Madam Kelly to organise her empire, many of her enforcers are being hunted down by vengeful people. Some have already met their fate and have joined her in the fiery pit below. When the place does finally reopen, it will be a proper entertainment venue. Not a life-destroyer like it has been up until now.'

Bernard looks at his notes, then continues. 'The second toast has been requested by young Josephine, who wishes to offer a special thanks to James for a little flick of a knife that severed a nasty man from his weapon, and to Sebastian for finding her and not walking away like so many others that day. So, to James and Sebastian, we thank you.'

Again, everyone calls out, 'To James and Sebastian,' then takes another sip from their drink.

'Now there is a man among us who has endured the wrath of almost all of us in the past month. Including myself, yet without his cunning and courage to stand up for what he believed, we would not have been here today. So, without further ado, all raise your glass to a true friend of us all, Henrey.'

The group responds again. With glasses now empty or near empty, Gaston and Emma go round topping them up while everyone talks amongst themselves for a moment. Once the glasses are filled, they sit back down, eager for the speeches to continue.

Bernard taps his glass, bringing the group to order. 'Now I know you are all aware we found the ledgers. In the near future, at a time and place that my brothers and I have chosen, they will be destroyed.' His voice lowers as he speaks. 'But for that, we need to be with another who is no longer with us, so we will have that moment later amongst ourselves and close the books for good.' His voice rises again. 'While we were searching for the hidden ledgers, we came across a code, and this code took us to a rather tasty find. Now, as we were all in this plan together, Gaston, François and I decided it should be shared between us all. So, if you would please open the package in front of you, you will find a gift that we hope will make up for some of the pain you have all suffered. Now you will find it is different for each and every one of you and I will explain why once you have opened your particular package. So please, open them up.'

There is huge excitement as the packages are torn open and the boxes looked into, followed by a deathly silence as a yellow glow appears on many of the faces round the table. They all look back at Bernard, shocked but smiling.

'To Anna Marie and Josephine, there is half a bar of gold each, and a pouch of coin as a gift for your futures. But for now, we also have an offer for the both of you. James and I feel that it would be to your advantage to spend time at our family château in the country, as a place to reside and recover, make a home for yourselves should you choose. I still cannot believe this, but my wayward brother Sebastian has offered to be your guardian for as long as you need him, and I would be delighted to have the pair of you stay with me and my brothers.'

The girls look at each other with huge smiles on their faces, then turn to Bernard, nodding with excitement. Josephine gets up and runs round to Sebastian, hugs him round his shoulders and gives him a kiss on the cheek.

'Henrey, what more can I say about you? A true friend and protector of us all, a bar of gold and coin, but it does come with one request from Emma and James. In fact, it is from all of us who have suffered… that is… never to attempt to make that stinky, awful sausage again. It is an insult to all good French salami makers.'

Everybody roars with laughter, including Henrey, who shakes his head at the same time. 'Yes, I do feel it is time to retire that recipe. This money should keep me in good sausage until I am long gone.'

As the people laugh, Emma speaks. 'Yes, but not for a very long time yet, Henrey. We still need you around.'

'To my brothers Gaston, Sebastian, François and myself, a bar of gold and a share of the pot to do with as we see fit. So, I will collect it all up from you and spend it on myself later.' The group once again roars with laughter as François and Gaston, who are sitting either side of Bernard, move their gifts further away from his reach.

'Finally, to the two people who have been the cause of so much controversy and trouble recently. Emma, words do not do justice as to how the others and I feel about you. As for James, though you may be English and to some an enemy of this country – not that I have ever met an Englishman that looks or acts the way you do – it is a privilege and an honour for us to call you our friend. We have given you both a share of the prize and each of you a deed. To you, Emma, our house in the port to live in, with the livery yard as a personal income. You cannot continue to live in the storeroom anymore. Not with a man in your life.

'For you, James, we have given you the deeds to the café, as it is Emma's love. With luck, it will keep her by your side for at least as long as it takes her to get it away from you.'

Again, the group bursts into laughter as they celebrate the gifts. Emma turns to James and kisses him passionately as her hand slips across the table and collects the deeds for the café from James's pile and moves it onto her own. Bernard and his brothers see the sly move and grin, while James, who has also seen the move, winks at the brothers and smiles before putting it back, much to Emma's disappointment.

As the laughter calms, Emma stands and addresses the table. 'A lot has happened in the last few months – finding love, revenge, sadness and happiness. I now know who my father is, but I do not care anymore. I do not wish to share you all with him, nor do I want him to know me or us. That side of my life has finished – well, to be fair, it never really started, and that is the way I feel it should remain. I do, however, expect to have my uncles stay with us as often as before, and now bringing Anna Marie and Josephine along with them. My home and MY café will always be open to you all. As for you, James, you are beyond special to me. Little did I know one could be so happy in love. And I also have a gift for you.' She takes his huge hand and places it on her stomach. 'I was going to keep this quiet until I had spoken to you first, but it feels right to say it to you all as some will be travelling in different directions for a while. It's very early days, but I think that we are going to have a new member of the family.'

A deathly silence fills the air as James looks into Emma's eyes. Gaston and Sebastian are taking a drink as James speaks in French.

'Well, to be honest, I was hoping for a bit more practice first.'

The room echoes with the loudest laughter of the evening. The brothers both spit out their drinks as they choke and laugh so hard. Emma slaps her man round his face and gives him an angry expression, before they both smile and hug each other.

'Really?' he asks with an excited smile.

'Well, it would seem so. Clockwork is clockwork, and the clock has stalled, but it will be certain in another seven or so months, my dear.' There is excitement all around the table at the thought of Emma and James becoming parents together for the first time.

Bernard taps his glass again and the group quiets down. 'With that news, the final announcement is even more important than before. You see, we still have two bars of gold and a little part of the pot left. My brothers and I have decided to build a small chapel on the plot overlooking the valley where our sister – your mother, Emma – Juliet lies. It would now be so fitting if the first ceremony performed in it was to be your wedding, Emma.'

Emma is brought to tears. As she turns to James, her sad eyes and trembling bottom lip melt James instantly and he gives a shallow nod to the idea. As she looks back at Bernard and the others, she speaks quietly as a smirk appears. 'The dowry for my hand will be the café. I will take nothing less.'

The roar of laughter erupts again.

As the night draws on, Bernard makes his final speech to all present. 'Tomorrow is an early start for Henrey on one empty wagon and James and Emma on the other, so say your goodbyes tonight as I doubt you will see them in the morning. We will also be leaving for the château at about seven, and it will be a while before we see each other again with the harvest due soon.'

Over the next half hour, they talk and say their goodbyes as they go. Anna Marie walks up to James and hugs him. They have spoken a lot in the last few days, and as the drugs slowly filter out of her system, she is becoming more aware of her surroundings and better able to hold a conversation. James has already explained that their sisters have passed on, and that they have gone to join Emma's mother in a better place. Though how they went has yet to be explained. Having Josephine around as well has been a godsend as the two of them are in a similar state of mind and will be excellent at helping each other through these difficult times.

'I expect you to write to me while I get better,' Anna Marie says as she starts to get upset.

James holds her in his arms. 'Dear sister, I will visit you often and you will visit me, but for now you and Josephine need to look after Sebastian and make sure he gets well.' James knows that, for her own safety and wellbeing, a château in the country is the best place for her to mature. This family that he has become a part of would move mountains to help her get well. As fast as she arrived, Anna Marie is off to sit the other side of Sebastian.

'It has been a long time since Sebastian has put other people before himself, my friend,' says Bernard as he joins James. 'I think this will be good for them all.' He puts his hand on James's shoulder. 'I have not yet thanked you for what you have done for us. I did not treat you well when we first met, but we are an old people and tend to mistrust outsiders – even more so the English. Although, with the tattoos and changes you have been through, maybe you are now a man of many countries, yes?'

James smiles. He has to think on Bernard's words for a while but now understands most of what he says in French. 'Maybe I have changed. For I fear I was once spoilt and selfish like my brother, Lord Fitzgerald. But now with so much that has happened in my life, perhaps you are right.'

Bernard digs round in his pocket and pulls out a small bag. 'I also found these when we were looking around Madam Kelly's rooms. I believe they are yours, along with a few other bits from her safe.'

James opens the bag and pours the contents into his hand just as Emma arrives by his side. Nine large black pearls roll out, along with a dozen precious stones, including a large pink diamond, some smaller samples, a pair of deep blue sapphires, three rubies and a selection of polished black opals showing traces of many colours.

'They are indeed nice, but black is not my thing. I have all I want in Emma. I do not want these st—'

James is interrupted by the dribbling excitement of a wild-eyed

Emma, who is staring at all the precious stones and bouncing up and down on her toes with anticipation.

James thinks for a bit before speaking. 'Well, if we are to be married, we would need a ring and I suppose we could use one of these.'

Emma's sad-puppy-dog face looks at him.

'Two of these?'

An even sadder face looks at him.

James sighs. 'If we were to use three of these stones to make a ring, the rest could go towards the chapel your brothers are going to build.'

'Gimme, gimme, gimme,' Emma says, already reaching for her favourites: the pink diamond and the two deep blue sapphires. As she lifts them from his hand, James quickly slides the rest back into the pouch and passes it to Bernard.

'Please use them as you see fit. Maybe, when it is built, you could leave a space for me to put something in memory of my brothers and sisters.'

Bernard is not an emotional man, but in James he has met his equal. A decent man who has not yet taken anything for himself and has put his life on the line for Emma and his brothers many times already, without reservation. He looks James in the eye with a tear in the corner of his own. 'I am proud of the fact I can call you my friend, and I will be honoured when you become part of my family. Of course a place will be reserved as a memorial to your lost ones. It is only right. More so, my friend, if ever you have need of me or my brothers, we will be there for you.' In typical French style, he steps forward and kisses James on both cheeks. 'I will take these and hide them before Emma starts working on me for more.'

James laughs loudly. 'Good luck with that one.'

As Bernard walks away, James looks at his lovely Emma. She is holding the jewels over her finger and lifting them up in the air, observing them in different positions. He thinks of how much his life has changed in the past couple of months. How this little ball of fire has altered his perspective on what he now wants going forward. He is so lucky to have met a young lady who is hard-working, caring and passionate, but also brave beyond words and forgiving should that be the better option. She has been through so much yet was prepared to risk all to help James when he was going to Paris. Now, when she finally knows who her father is, she is prepared to walk away, content with what she has at this moment in time. Could he be as strong as her and let go of the past with his brother? James decides that he must try and put aside his thoughts of revenge, for he can do no less than what Emma has done for him.

As he watches her move around the room, he realises that with just one smile or a cheeky look, this woman has his heart pounding. It could not get better than this for him. For surely there would not be many out there who could live with a man who looks like he does. Let alone knowing what he has done in his past and yet still love him all the more. Has finally found the peace and happiness that all men crave but few find. The test will be to see if it lasts or the nightmares of what his brother has done return to haunt him again, just like the shaman prophesied.

* * *

Some two weeks later on a hillside in the Rhone valley, four men are sitting on chairs overlooking fields of vines heavy with fruit. Below them, two girls are running along the lines of bushes, playing hide and seek, peering at each other between the rows then running off. One wears a light blue dress, the other is in pink, laughing and giggling as they enjoy their freedom.

In the middle of the four men, a fire burns in a fluted iron barrel, glowing orange through the exposed grooves. Every few minutes, a flame comes out of the top of the barrel as one of the men throws in another sheet of paper and it bursts into flames instantly with the intense heat.

To the left of the quartet of men on the only visible flat spot in view, several labourers are digging out the foundations to a building yet to be started. Others around them are bringing in and dropping down timbers and stone slabs ready for construction.

Bernard is taking a sip of wine from a glass as he looks over to see his brother Sebastian taking a gulp straight from another bottle. He shakes his head in disgust at the heathen way his brother drinks a fine bottle of wine.

'What?' says Sebastian. 'You have your way of drinking wine and I have mine. It still tastes the same and I appreciate it just as much as you, if not more.'

Gaston and François are chuckling at the antics of their two brothers. Each one of them has a book on their lap and is pulling out a page at a time. They scan each sheet and if it is of interest, they read it out. If not, it goes in the fire. Even the ones of interest eventually go in the fire to be destroyed.

Gaston sits up in his chair. 'Listen to this,' he says. 'The mayor of our region visited Madam Kelly's last summer. He spent ten thousand florins on two women for a week in the President's Suite. Seems he lost a lot of money on the cards as well.'

Bernard smiles and looks to his brothers. 'Perhaps we will use this information if he does not declare our wine a vintage year at the festival!'

François looks at Bernard as his brother Gaston burns the evidence in the fire. 'How will you do that if we are burning every page as we go? Besides, we agreed not to use anything we find as leverage or blackmail.'

Bernard shrugs. 'Well then, perhaps I will whisper it into his wife Isabel's ear the next time we are in bed together.'

The hillside echoes with the laughter of the four brothers as another page gets chucked into the fire to burn away in seconds. Bernard takes another sip from his wine glass. 'You do know that when the harvest is in and our niece's wedding is over, I will be paying him a visit. King or not, it cannot go unpunished. Honour is at stake here.'

Sebastian sits up. 'It's a big palace with lots of guards and there are not that many of us, brother.'

Gaston rolls his eyes and knocks back the last of his drink. 'Next, you will be flirting with the queen and taking her to bed for good measure.'

Bernard sits up, wild thoughts rushing through his head. 'Now that's not a bad idea.'

François looks around at his brother. 'You have got to be kidding me!'

'No! Hear me out! They have been married, what, five years now? With no living children to show for it. He is old and must be riddled with the pox from the places he has visited. Probably unable to produce a child of his own to take the throne. While she is still young and fertile – as she has lost at least one child that I recall. All it will take is for me to get in there and we could have a relation on the throne. What I need to do now is find a way of getting her alone so I can use my charms on her.'

'Bernard! Coveting the mayor's wife is one thing, but the queen is quite another. We would be executed at the block. No! Let it go,' Gaston cries while his brothers are laughing at the thought of it.

'Just let me think on it for a while. There must be a way. Perhaps in their private chapel at prayer time during Sunday mass.'

'What! Under God's own roof? No! One more word on this mad idea and I will tell Emma and get her and James down here to sort you out,' replies Sebastian as he downs the last of his bottle while listening to the chuckles of his brothers.

CHAPTER 6

The Finding of Edward

Back in England, it's the start of another Friday at the village school. Jennie sits at her desk perplexed as she looks around the classroom and waits for the teacher to arrive. Two weeks have passed since Edward was apprehended for crimes she does not yet fully understand. It feels a cold and empty place for her now that several of the people she once knew are no longer present. Yet she's amazed at how little the events have changed the other children in the class. Joking around in the lessons, wet paper balls being flicked across the room, and messages being passed between the classmates make it all seem normal on the surface. But there is a feeling of uneasiness that she cannot quite put her finger on, a quietness and look in their eyes as if they are avoiding her, or as if there is something she does not know about. It is like the children are actively removing Edward and the others from their memories, rather than thinking of them as missing or gone. *How can this be?* she wonders. *Does nobody remember Edward? He sat just here at this now empty desk, beside Susan, who is also now gone.* She leans across and rubs her finger over the scrape marks on the corner of his desk left by the lock on the blue diary he always carried.

She often wondered what secrets it contained as he guarded it so carefully and never let it out of his sight. The thought of him and the others being forgotten and gone forever saddens her deeply. Especially as it was only a few weeks ago he was the brightest boy in the classroom with people hanging on his every word. Now you would have difficulty realising he and the others had ever existed at all.

During playground break, Bowen and Georgia approach Jennie as she passes the corner of a building. With a quiet whisper, Bowen speaks. 'Meet us at the old oak tree by the footbridge after supper.' They do not stop, but walk straight past as if they are strangers, vanishing into a crowd of children playing tag at the bottom of the yard. Jennie knows the place well as she crosses the bridge twice every day, going to and from school. But why so secretive?

The rest of the day seems so uneventful as she wonders what the two of them want to speak to her about. She goes through the motions in different lessons, without really paying attention to any of them. Finally, the handbell rings in the hallway, signalling the end of school for the day. All eyes are on Miss Gibbons, awaiting the nod that will allow books and bags to be grabbed, followed by the mad rush to the classroom door and the freedom of the weekend.

Eventually, after a few minutes of waiting, the dismissal comes in the form of a slow downward motion of her head, followed by, 'Do not forget your homework is due in on Monday. I want to see it on my desk first thing.' The children are off, bolting out the door like stabbed rats. Only Jennie is in no rush as she passes Edward's old oak desk with its chipped glass inkwell. She is immersed in the memory of how she chipped it while flicking marbles at Edward on the first day she arrived at the school. With a wry smile, she heads to the front of the classroom and turns to the open door leading to the corridor.

'Jennie? Could I have a word with you?' calls out Miss Gibbons, in that piercing voice that only the strictest of teachers can produce.

She turns and approaches with her head held low. 'Yes, Miss Gibbons.'

'You do understand what your father and mother have sacrificed for you to be here in this fine school? It has cost them a great deal of money and hard work to move to the country just to give you a better life and a proper education. Unfortunately, there are those who do not deserve or appreciate the importance of what we do in this school. Teaching young children like yourself the knowledge needed to have a good future, helping you to expand your mind and prepare you for adulthood.

'I am sad to say that your friend Edward turned out to be one of them. A deceitful, devious and disruptive child. I know his kind well. From the moment I set eyes on him, I knew he would be a troublemaker. Even after all that his family had done for him and his younger brother. They both bring such shame on their parents and this school, just like the others who did not deserve the opportunity to be educated here and have now departed.'

Jennie is desperate to say something back, but she has learned to keep quiet until the right time is found to express her opinions, so for now she just listens.

'I am so glad you saw through his disguise and called him out that day. It must be a big relief to you that he was captured and removed from decent society.' She sighs heavily. 'All that time I wasted on trying to educate them. Shame on them. Shame on them both.'

'I never knew Edward had a brother,' Jennie says, as a reaction more than a question.

'Oh yes, his name is Oliver. He would be ten, no, eleven years old now. I can never quite rightly remember, as it was over a year ago he was removed from here to be home schooled due to his disruptive nature. Now we know why, as he also ran in that group with his older brother. In fact, it was only when Oliver and, later, his brother Edward were captured that all the troubles in the village started to subside. Before then, things were regularly going missing or being stolen around here. But it was not just the villagers having problems. New machines were sabotaged in the factory, then there was the death of our local news printer and his wife. I mean, this is Pippinsford, a respectable village. We should not have a criminal element here. Why would anyone do such things, except to cause no good, mischief and ill feelings? For two years them two and their friends ran amok in this village. I tell you now, we are better off without their kind causing all those problems around here.

'As for you, Jennie, I just wanted you to know that the school is very proud that you stood up to these bullies. But be vigilant, as I am sure there are a few of his group still at large. Now it is time you went home, or you will be late for your own supper.'

'Yes, Miss Gibbons,' Jennie says before she moves out of the classroom and down the white-walled corridor to the coat rack, collecting her blue bonnet, scarf and coat before leaving the building.

A brother, Jennie thinks. Her mind is a whirl of unanswered questions as she heads out through the school gate. Edward had never told her about his brother or that he had been accused of being a thief. Why had he never said anything to her about him? And what did he have to do with Edward's actions that night? She recalls the fear in his eyes when they grabbed him and dragged him out of the building. His continuous yelling and screaming of something about Oliver, who she now knows is his little brother. The crack that she saw open up in the fireplace wall just before he was captured. And what was in the sack he was carrying and threw across the room in such a hurry? So many questions are going through her head that she does not realise how far she has walked or where she is.

'Watch out!' comes a shout from behind her as she feels a tug on her arm pulling her back just as an open-backed cart being pulled by two bay mares whizzes past at breakneck speed. The metal-rimmed wheels rumble and slide on the cobbled roads like thunder as it races past.

'That was close,' says the voice.

As Jennie turns around, still shaken from the event, it is a relief to see her sister, Isabelle, still holding on to her arm. 'Father told me to keep an eye out for you and by the look of it, it's a good thing that I did. You could have been killed by that wagon. Now be on your way home and mind you look where you go, as next time I might not be there to save you.'

Isabelle releases Jennie's arm and strides off. She has far more important things to do than look after her baby sister, having been tasked with purchasing good brandy and cigars for Father's study. Important people are expected tonight and a good impression, along with a fine table, are the order of the day.

Jennie continues her walk home, but this time paying more

attention to her surroundings. As she looks up, a smirk appears on her face as she notices the largest man she has ever seen walking directly towards her in a waddling manner. His right hand is clasped over the top of a dark wooden cane with a brass handle. With every second step he takes, the man swings the stick up into the air and down onto the ground, making the shiny metal tip tap on every contact with the stone path. He wears a bright green waistcoat with a big chain connecting his pocket watch to a clasp in his buttonhole.

'Mind the way,' he yells as he approaches, acting as if he owns the very path he walks on. Jennie steps into a doorway to allow room and watches as he shuffles past, his wife directly behind him, and following her are five children dropping in descending heights as they pass. The two boys in the group are wearing the same colour waistcoats as their father, while the three girls wear the same colour and style of dress as their mother, along with matching hair and bonnets.

She chuckles as she wonders how a man so big could have sired so many children without crushing his wife. Having never seen them before, she presumes they must be some of the new people, recently arrived in the village with lots of money. For there is no way he could be that large and be a working farmer – as he would never catch his animals or even ride a horse. After one last look back at them walking in a line, she giggles before stepping back onto the path and continuing on her way home.

Turning the corner and walking down Albert's Lane, she can see a house at the end of Brook Street is being cleared of its furniture. The cart pulled by the two bay mares that had so nearly run her down is out front, being loaded with all the goods. Brannigan and Sykes – men you could never forget as they wore big hobnail boots, long dark trench coats and tall top hats with a red band round them – are deep in conversation while filling small clay pipes with tobacco. Both men are shouting orders at the labourers who are frantically filling the cart high with the furniture and belongings from inside the house. She slows to a stop behind a stone garden wall to watch.

'Hurry up, damn your eyes,' Sykes yells. 'We haven't got all day; I want this house completely stripped by Sunday or so help me you'll be the next people for a visit from the reaper.'

Whatever he means by that, she has no idea, but it has the desired effect as the four labourers begin running in and out of the house carrying all they can get their hands on. In less than ten minutes, the cart is filled to capacity and a large sheet is slung over the top, followed by several bands of rope to hold it all in place.

With the nod from Sykes, the driver cracks his whip, and the horses step forward to take up the slack. It's a heavy load to get moving, so it is slow at first, but as the momentum builds up, the horses begin to roll the sunken wheels out of the soft ground and onto the stone road. They pick up the pace as the wheels roll easier and are soon moving at a brisk walk in the direction of the factory.

Brannigan turns to the labourers who are now standing around catching their breath. 'What are you waiting for?' he shouts. 'Start on stripping the tiles from the roof as he'll be back from the factory in an hour.' The exhausted men slowly get going again, moving two large ladders into position to get up on the roof.

Brannigan reaches down to his belt for his club. 'Move, you scum.' They do not need a second telling as the pace quickens and the men climb the ladders and begin lifting the tiles and stacking them into ten-high piles. Sykes spots Jennie watching them from over the wall. He nudges Brannigan and points in her direction. She swiftly looks away and ducks down.

She does not like these two enforcers and decides on a course of action to avoid going directly past them by crossing the road and walking along the front of the general feedstore. Without looking across, she can feel them watching her every move as the hairs on the back of her neck stand on end, sending a cold shudder down her spine. Walking soon moves to a jog and on hearing deep bellowing laughter, she runs. Heart pounding and pulse racing as she makes for the safety of her home, she only stops as she reaches the steps to the front door. With a quick look back to see if they followed her, she grabs the handle and swiftly opens the door just enough to slip inside and close it behind her. Pressing her back up against the wall, she lets out a huge sigh of relief. She pauses for a moment to collect her breath before moving down the reception hall, up the large mahogany stairs and into her room to get changed, washed and ready for supper.

Barely twenty minutes pass before Jennie is bounding back down the stairs and into the dining room. The first action of this well-rehearsed routine is to greet Father, ask how his day has gone, followed by greeting Mother and asking how her day has been. Then she explains what she has learned at school during the day. Only after this does she take her seat at the table with her three brothers and one sister, ready for supper to be served.

Her father has done well financially since moving here. Although he is not one of the wealthiest new members of the village, he can now afford a cook and a housekeeper to help run the house, as well as the housemaid, Molly, who he brought with them from the capital – she did anything that was asked of her by the family. Being on duty six days a week, all three staff reside in the house, in rooms located in the attic as part of their wages. Each one in turn takes a day off in the week and time off on Sunday should they choose to go to church.

Jennie and the housemaid are more than friends. Having been with the family most of Jennie's life, Molly has become her best friend and her confidante when needed. But to the rest of the family, she is just someone to do their bidding when asked and, for the most, treated quite poorly – something Jennie is never comfortable with.

Supper always starts with soup, usually a seasonal vegetable but on occasion seafood or oxtail, followed by a main meal, and for dessert, fresh fruit, cakes or other sweet pastries. But her parents prefer fruit as they are now in the country, and it is easily available. In the city, fruit used to be an expensive luxury and rarely affordable to them. But now, their choices are endless, with a wide selection available, depending on the time of year. After dinner, the children will leave the table, allowing Father and Mother to talk and plan the following day's schedules.

Conversation at the table today is all about tonight's important meeting and ensuring all is in place to make a great impression. Father has planned all the entertainment, while Mother is still stressing over what to wear and how to present her home and family in the best manner for the occasion.

Jennie knows that Father's appointment will make it easy for her to stay out late and attend to her own objectives, and she is determined to meet up with Bowen and Georgia as they had asked. With luck, a few of her other friends will be around later that night to join them.

'I'm just going outside to play, Mama,' she says, heading for the coat rack. Mother is far too tied up in what she is doing to hear Jennie's words, but her father does reply.

'Be back by dark and take Oscar with you. It will give your mother a break for a while and the fresh air will do him good.' This is not what she wanted to hear, but then again, at least she was getting out of the house, even if she had to take her younger brother with her.

'Yes, Father,' she replies, putting on her shawl and pale blue bonnet and actively looking around for her younger brother. *Where can he be?* she wonders as she walks to the front door. Then, as she is just about to open the door, she can see a shadow through the frosted glass down the side of the doorframe. *Hmm*, she thinks. *It seems about the right height.* As she opens the door, Oscar jumps forward, roaring like a dinosaur with his hands grabbing at the space in front of him while wearing a big beaming smile on his face. Jennie pretends to be shocked, holding her hand over where her heart is, as he laughs and puts his arms out to give her a big hug.

Oscar is already wearing his coat, has his chequered scarf wrapped round his neck, a flat brown cap on his head and clasped in his left hand is a half-eaten apple he has just pulled out of his pocket.

'Where are we going and what are we doing?' he asks, still beaming. As she looks at his excited expression, Jennie realises that he would never leave her side without causing a huge commotion, so, like it or not, Oscar is coming along.

'We are going for a walk down to the brook,' she replies while squaring his cap on his head and grasping his spare hand in hers.

'Yippee!' shrieks Oscar as he wriggles his hand free from Jennie's grip and starts to run towards the brook.

'Slow down, Oscar! It's not a race,' she calls out in the forlorn hope that he will listen. With a big sigh, she realises there is only one option, and begins running after the escaping child. She soon catches him up, runs past him and continues on, laughing as she goes.

'That's not fair! You're bigger than me! I only have little legs,' moans Oscar as he loses his early advantage. The two of them continue playing around across the meadow and along the slate wall that follows the side of the field almost all the way to the little wooden footbridge over the river. They continue past the end of the high hedgerow made up of a mixture of bramble, hawthorn and sloe bushes, to a more open area of grassland beyond. In the distance, Jennie can see a group of four children moving around by the oak tree. Three seem to be talking together, while the other one is standing on the footbridge, looking into the water below.

Along the side of the footbridge is the well-worn and rutted lane that travels from the village to the factory about a mile away. All carts and carriages heading for the new factory from this direction must go through the ford by the side of the footbridge as it is the shortest route and shallowest area to cross the small river.

This is not to say it is the safest place to cross anymore as heavy usage in the last few months by the factory wagons and cartloads of building materials for the new houses have damaged the ground below the waterline. The large slabs and thick-cut flagstones that make up the base of the riverbed road have started to move apart and become unstable – mainly due to the weight of the loads travelling to and from their destinations. Deep gaps and widening cracks have opened up and wagon wheels often get wedged in them, causing problems for inexperienced drivers making the crossing.

Now they are closer, Jennie can see Bowen, Harvey and Georgia talking by the oak tree, with Ellie standing on the footbridge looking down.

Oscar sees Ellie and calls to her as he runs over and greets her with a hug. They are classmates and sit next to each other in many of their lessons. Jennie has almost reached the three friends by the tree when she hears a distant rumbling followed by the crack of a whip. She needs no second telling of what the sound is. 'Oscar, Ellie, come here now!'

They both look up. 'Quickly, I say. Now hurry up!' The children scurry over the bridge and run round to meet up with the others. At the same time, the wagon being pulled by two bay mares comes cantering over the brow of the hill, down the dip and whooshes into the brook. The over-stacked cart shudders into the water, veering violently left and right on the mismatched riverbed. Bumping up onto the next level of stones and bouncing a large chest off the back of the wagon, it pulls up onto the track on the other side of the water.

The chest lands half on the footbridge and half in the river with a thud, flipping the lid open and spilling much of its contents into the water. All the children look at the chest and what has been thrown out of it. Floating along on the water's surface with the current are a few small dresses and other items of clothing, while submerged in the water by the chest are silver candlesticks, cutlery and part of a silver tea service.

The driver by now has stopped the cart and the labourer beside him jumps down. He runs back to the chest, pulling it onto the footbridge, and begins filling it with the spilt items. He attempts to collect what he can of the drifting clothing, but with the current pushing some of the items into the footbridge stakes and bramble bushes, pulling them out just tears them up, leaving parts of them behind. 'Forget them. They are only clothes. There's no value in what's caught up,' the driver cries to his companion. The labourer drags the chest to the back of the wagon and, with a mighty heave, lifts and pushes it over the tailgate of the cart and slides it back into position before getting back up on the wagon himself.

'Hey yah,' shouts the driver as he flicks the reins and starts the horses on their way again. Jennie and the others have watched the event unfold. It happened so fast and was over so quickly that it is only now that they begin to move and talk about what they have seen.

Georgia looks down at the water's edge. Something has caught her attention and she is now curious. Kneeling down, she leans over to fish out the item that is pressing against the step of the footbridge. Standing back up, she squeezes the water from the small cloth doll.

'I know this doll,' she says. 'I saw it only yesterday. It belongs to little Margaret. You know, the girl who lives in the end house on Brook Street with her grandmother.'

'That's right, she's in my class at school,' says Ellie. 'I sit behind her some days. Mind you, she was not there today. Perhaps she was poorly or her grandmother had fallen again. She is very old and often falls over and hurts herself.'

'Are you sure she was not in school?' Georgia asks.

'Yes, I'm sure. The teacher put our homework books on her desk, and we collected them on our way out of class. This doll, it went everywhere with her. Why would it be in a chest on its way to the factory?' Ellie asks.

'Perhaps she packed it, ready for the move,' replies Jennie.

'What move?' asks Ellie.

'Well, after school, when I was walking home, I saw Brannigan and Sykes with some other men clearing out her grandmother's house. They were intending to have the building demolished by Sunday.'

She looks at her. 'No, that cannot be right. Margaret is my friend. She would have told me if she was going away.' Ellie's eyes are starting to well up at the thought of not seeing her friend again.

'Don't worry, Ellie. Once I've spoken to Bowen and Georgia, we will go down and see if she is still at the house. I'm sure she had no intention of going anywhere without saying goodbye,' Jennie says in the vain chance it will cheer her up. Then she has an idea that could solve a couple of problems!

'In fact, why don't you, Oscar and Harvey start walking up to the house, and we will catch you up. It is only over the top of the hill and a hop, skip and a jump away. We will only be a couple of minutes behind you.'

'Yes, let's go,' says Harvey. Ellie looks at Oscar, who is torn between staying with his sister and going with the others.

'Come on, Oscar. I won't go without you. The others will be along shortly. They have grown-up things to talk about – I can see it in their faces.'

Oscar steps forward and hugs Jennie then turns and runs up the hill with Ellie to catch up with Harvey, who is already making his way up towards the house.

'Now that was quick thinking,' Bowen says to Jennie.

'Yes, but we had better be quick, cos I know Oscar and it will not be long before he starts missing me. What is it you two want to speak to me about, and why all the secrecy?'

'Have you not noticed all the teachers watching you? We've not been able to approach you all week without someone watching our every move. Even my mother and father have told me to stay away and not to talk to you,' Georgia says nervously.

'Since the day they caught… or should I say the day you worked out that Edward was the leader of the gang that all the village has been looking for, we have been treading on eggshells. I feel that everything I do is being studied, and what's worse is that all our friends are avoiding us too. Don't get me wrong, when we do talk, they are not nasty or rude, just very careful about what they say or do around us. But that's not the worst of it. No one comes to visit me at home anymore. It's like I have a disease or something,' Bowen explains.

'Well, I have noticed the change at school. Nobody ever talks about Edward anymore. Even the registration book has had his name removed along with several others I knew, like Susan and Maddi. But I did not know it was affecting both of you as well,' Jennie replies. She pauses for a moment to think, then continues, 'I still don't understand why Edward did all these things, or should I say, has been accused of such terrible crimes. I mean, why was he dressed in dirty rags? And what was in the brown sack? As for running into that derelict old forge, he must have known as soon as he set foot inside the building he would be trapped as there is no other way out. Especially with half the village chasing him. It just seemed a stupid thing to do.' Jennie sighs and shakes her head.

'Nothing makes sense to me anymore. He used to sit at the desk in front of me in class, yet nobody had a clue it was him everyone was after. There has to be more to it, something that we do not yet understand. Even his best friend Susan along with Topper, Harriet and Dicky have gone in the last month or so.' Jennie thinks more and more about Edward and what has been going on lately. 'You both have known him a lot longer than me. Had he always been so quiet and reserved? Hell, I did not even know that he had a brother until Miss Gibbons spoke of him today.'

'That would have been Oliver. He liked to wear his pirate bandana and speak like he was a real pirate. Edward was never the same after his friend Susan and her family left the village. Then, when they took his brother Oliver out of the school, he virtually cut himself off, stopped speaking to everyone. He changed and became very secretive, always on his own, walking around the playground like a caged lion with his blue diary in his hand,' Georgia says.

'I have so many unanswered questions in my head and by the look of it, only the few of us to solve them,' Jennie says, beginning to walk after their friends.

'Us?' Bowen replies in a shocked voice.

'Yes, us, Bowen. We both saw Edward kick that grate, opening the crack in the corner of the fireplace, even if the adults did not. Also, that sack he threw across the room; I wonder if it is still there. If it is, we can find out what was so important that he would risk so much to have whatever was inside.'

'Oh no, don't involve me. My father would give me six of the best for even thinking about going to that old forge, let alone going inside it,' Georgia hollers, backing off and shaking her hands.

'We must, for the sake of Edward. Surely you want to know what happened to him. Or at least what he was doing there?'

'It's too much to risk. If we are spotted or caught and my father finds out, he will have the skin off my back. I doubt that I would be able to sit down for a blooming month with the thrashing he would give me,' says Bowen with a shake of his head.

Jennie can see that both Bowen and Georgia are afraid of being caught. Somehow, she must come up with a good plan before it's too late and they lose all courage. 'I know, why don't we catch up with the others at Margaret's house? From there, we have a good view of the old forge and can see who's about. If nobody's around, I will take a quick look inside while you two keep an eye out for anyone approaching. If you spot anybody, you can call out an alarm and I will come running out and leave in the other direction, away from you. How's that for a plan?'

Before either of them can utter a single word, Jennie adds, 'Good, then it is settled. Let's go while it is still daylight.' She instantly accelerates up the hill with a cheeky little smirk on her face, as she knows she has just duped them into doing what she wants.

Bowen and Georgia stop and look at each other in confusion. After pausing for a few seconds, they turn and chase after Jennie. 'What will the alarm be?' asks Bowen.

'I don't know, make it one of those bird calls you do all the time at school. They are very good, and I would be sure to hear it.'

'Yes, that's what I'll do. My best one is a turtle dove. No, that is too common. I will do a barn owl.' Bowen practises all the way up the hill, much to the annoyance of the other two.

By the time they reach the others, Georgia has had enough. 'Bowen, for the love of God, please give it a rest, just for a little while.'

'I've got to practise,' he snaps. 'This could be the difference between life and death, Georgia.'

Georgia laughs loudly as Jennie responds. 'I don't think it's going to come down to that quite yet, Bowen. But it's nice to think that you have my best interests at heart.' They all chuckle and share a moment before stopping to look at the approaching Harvey. Tears are streaming down his face as he looks at them utterly devastated.

'The house. It's nearly all gone.'

They turn and look in the direction of where the house once stood. Sure enough, all that remains is the timber frame, the stone fireplace and chimney stack at the far end. They can see the basis of the wooden stairs, spiralling up through the middle of the building to the two rooms above. Strewn around the shell of the framework is a pile of tiles, timber strips and broken bits of furniture and rubble. All the windows, doors and doorframes are stacked neatly in a line, ready for collection or reuse.

'I cannot believe they have done all this so quickly! They were only taking out the belongings and furniture when I left school this afternoon.' Jennie turns to Ellie. 'I'm sorry, Ellie, I think we must have missed Margaret. When we go back to school on Monday, we will ask the teachers for a forwarding address and write her a letter. I know it's not the same as saying goodbye in person, but at least this way you can let her know you're thinking of her.'

'I suppose so. I just thought she would have told me herself that she was moving away. I thought we were close friends,' she says, attempting to come to terms with the situation.

'I'm sure you are friends, and if she'd had the time, you would have been the first person she would have spoken to. But from the look of it, they must have left in a terrible hurry. Can you imagine how much packing they would have had to do in just a few days?' The more Jennie thinks about what she is saying, the more it does not make sense. Margaret's grandmother is elderly and frail. Where would they go, once they left here? The clothing falling out at the brook, along with the silverware left behind in the chest destined for the factory. The driver and his mate speaking about what was of value. No 'fare thee wells' with friends, or anyone for that matter. This is a very strange affair indeed. Jennie looks around the outside of the building frame. In the doorway leading into the house, broken crockery and glass are strewn everywhere, along with items of clothing and a child's shoe. Stooping forward, she picks up a cracked hand mirror with a mother-of-pearl handle. 'It's beautiful,' she says quietly. 'There's something wrong here. Margaret's grandmother would not have left this beautiful mirror behind. It is far too precious. I wonder where they went in such a hurry and why.'

'Yes, Jennie. I am now thinking the same thing. But like you, I cannot work it out. Why would anyone leave such pretty belongings behind and go without some sort of planning or talking about it with their friends before they left?' Replies Ellie

Jennie is starting to think that everything that has been going on lately is connected in some way, but a few key pieces of the puzzle are still missing, including what part Edward and his brother played.

'Edward!' Jennie shouts loudly as she has an epiphany. 'That night when I confronted Edward and asked him what he was doing, he said, "If you follow the signs, they will lead you down a path you can never return from, then you will know this place's deepest secret." At the time, I thought he was talking in riddles to throw us all. But now I think it was a clue. The only signs we had were him, the sack, and the fireplace. We must take a look inside the old forge. The answers we need are in there, I'm sure of it.'

'Are you mad? My father said that place is dangerous. It could fall down at any minute!' Ellie says with a frown.

'Remember my plan. I said that if you kept a lookout, I would go and check it out myself. All you have to do is warn me if someone comes along, that's all.'

'No, that's not what we said,' remarks Bowen. 'The first thing we were going to do was to take a look from here and see if anyone was around, then if the coast was clear, you would take a look inside while we kept watch.'

Oscar grabs his trouser belt, pulls it up, sticks out his chest and bellows, 'I'm not afraid, even if you are. You're not going in there without me, Jennie.'

A small debate between the children takes place for the next few minutes before Jennie takes control of the situation. 'Stop it, all of you. This is not helping us one bit. Besides, we've not even been looking in the direction of the old forge yet.' With that statement, the bickering ceases as all eyes look firstly at Jennie and then in the direction of the old forge far in the distance.

Looking at the building from their position, it is a curious mismatch of workmanship. A two-up, two-down thatched cottage that on one side is butted up against a much larger rock protruding out of the ground. The chimney on this end of the building seems to run up the side of the rock face, curving as it goes. On the other side it has the extension that attaches the house to the forge. The forge itself has an open-fronted wooden frame that has long since seen better days and is partly collapsed. Inside is a large, raised horseshoe-shaped red-brick coke pit. There are also the remains of a barrel-shaped air-bellow system. Above, the remnants of the old flume and chimney are hanging down from the decaying roof. Outside the structure are pieces of the old well – most of the frame and winch mechanism are gone, but the ring of rocks that raised the sides are still present along with the horse watering trough. A large wooden cover has been put over the top of the well to prevent people falling in, but even that is now showing its age. Around the back of the building (although not in view) is a small wooden outhouse that leans so far to one side it seems to defy gravity, but still, somehow it holds off falling to the ground.

Due to the location of the old forge cottage – hidden from most of the village behind the large protruding rock and set back from the main track by around one hundred metres – it is easy to enter the building without being seen, as long as no one is travelling along the road from the village to the factory.

With nobody in view, Jennie moves off towards the cottage, closely followed by Oscar. The others reluctantly follow her lead until they all end up about thirty yards away, hidden behind a large thicket of scrub willow.

Now, being closer, they can see the 'Danger' and 'Keep out' signs on the floor in front of the building. They can also see some wooden boards that were once attached to the windows and doorways, which were ripped off by Brannigan and Sykes when they forced their way into the building to drag out Edward.

'Remember, make that call like a barn owl if anyone comes along,' whispers Jennie as she moves towards the house.

'Wait, I'm coming too. I need to see this for myself,' says Bowen. With that, all the children start vying for Jennie's attention, all trying to put their case forward as to why they should be allowed to go with her.

'Quiet,' Ellie says in a low voice. 'I can see someone coming down the road from the factory end.' All the children crouch down low and watch the people approaching. Within a few minutes the small figures seen in the distance have become a lot larger and are nearing their position.

'It's Brannigan and Sykes,' Jennie says quietly. She recognises them from the clothes they were wearing earlier in the day. The closer the men get, the more the children can hear their hobnail boots clicking on the stones in the track. As they pass by, their discussion can be heard.

'Yeh, we've got plenty of time. Let's get into the tavern and knock down a few ales first, then check on that little puke. For I have a special job for him tonight. One that will finally see an end to it for good,' says Brannigan.

'It's about time. It should have been done when we got him the first time. Christ, when was that now? I don't seem to remember now I think about it.'

'Near two years ago, around the time that bastard Springer killed Fletcher. Man alive, what I would not give to get my hands round his neck and rip out his throat. I still think that he and the woman Victoria planned it together, for we have not seen hide nor hair of them since that day.'

'Aye, that just about be the truth of it,' comments Sykes as they pass the children and head towards the village.

Georgia follows the men with her eyes. 'That was close,' she whispers. 'I wonder who they were talking about to do a special job. Whoever it was, it does not seem like they are in for a very nice time.'

Jennie looks at her friends. 'We cannot all go into the building at the same time. For one, it is dangerous, and for two, someone needs to keep an eye out for people walking by. As the oldest, I have decided that Bowen, Georgia and I will go inside. The rest of you will keep watch. Before any of you start moaning, understand we will do this my way or not at all!

'Oscar, you stay here and watch the factory end of the road with Ellie. Harvey, you watch the road coming from the village. And remember, with Bowen now with us, one of you will have to make the barn owl bird call to alert us if somebody steps off the road and heads towards the building. If not, say nothing as they are just moving past.'

After a brief glance around, the three of them head towards the cottage. Jennie reaches the doorway first. The door is already ajar, and she pushes it open a little more and peers into the gloom. Her memories of the day she chased Edward into this very room come flooding back. How much her life had changed from that moment on. She can still see the terror in Edward's face as Brannigan and Sykes, along with a few others, dragged him off to the magistrates. She shakes her head as if trying to remove the horrid memories before stepping inside and checks out the first small room. It contains a large stone sink, a few broken cupboards and a pile of rubble. She moves through another doorway into a larger space and looks around.

To her left is the large open fireplace with a rusty grate. The room itself is in a poor state of repair and bits of broken wood from the walls are scattered over the floor. Cobwebs hang from all corners of the room and a couple of broken stools are pushed up against the far wall, along with a well-warped wooden table turned over on its side.

To her right is a narrow set of wooden stairs that leads up to the next floor. It's fairly dark in the room as wooden boards cover the back windows, blocking out most of the light, and the damp musty smell of rotting wood hangs in the air.

Past the table on the floor, Jennie spots the brown sack that Edward threw down while trying to escape. 'Edward's sack! It's still there!' she says as she moves over to investigate.

Bowen and Georgia are right behind her as she shakes out the sack's contents onto the floor and pushes it around with her foot to take inventory. A small child's jacket, five mouldy loaves of bread, a dozen or so apples, four used candles, a box of matches, a used pair of child's shoes, Jennie's red scarf that went missing the day of the chase, three blankets, a shirt, and a small bag of boiled sweets. 'This is hardly what you would call a master criminal at work!' says Bowen.

'What would he want these things for?' asks Jennie. 'He wore better clothes than these and ate better food. There has to be more to it than what we see here.'

She looks round the room for other clues. At first, nothing stands out. But after a while, with her eyes adapting to the low light, she notices that the banister rail on the stairs is shiny, reflecting light from the doorway. She slides her hand along the rail and turns it over.

All three inspect her hand. 'It's clean. Someone has been using these stairs recently.' They look at each other and then up the steps to the top.

'I'll go first,' says Bowen. Putting his left foot on the first step, he slowly moves up the stairs, closely followed by Jennie with Georgia bringing up the rear. As they reach the top and turn the corner, a closed door confronts them, making Bowen hesitate. Jennie steps past him, reaches for the door handle, turns it until they hear a click and slowly pushes it open. The three of them peer inside and view the open space.

The first thing they notice is a white sheet on the floor, pegged out in the four corners. Jennie walks onto it and stands in the middle, turning clockwise and viewing the whole room.

On the wall to her right, six sets of clothes are hanging on pegs. Three contain different-sized trousers, shirts, jackets and caps, and below each set is a sturdy pair of boots. Then there are three beautiful dresses, with fine shoes or short boots below each one.

Georgia picks up a pair of red shoes with big silver buckles. 'These are beautiful. Why would someone leave such great things here in this filthy old building?' she asks as she puts the shoes back.

Jennie thinks for a while. 'I've seen that distinctive dress and those red shoes before. It was some time ago. Yes, now I remember. It was the first time I saw Edward in the park. I was with my parents, and we had just finished our Sunday picnic. We were leaving when I dropped my shawl. Edward was walking past with some of his friends. He picked up my shawl and passed it to me. I thanked him very much and turned away. With him was a girl wearing this exact same dress and those red shoes with the big

silver buckles. They were laughing and joking. Her name was…'
Jennie ponders for a second or two. 'Of course, Susan!' she cries.
'It was Susan, and in her hand, she had a red parasol to go with
the outfit.'

Georgia walks over to the dress and pushes it to one side. Sure
enough, behind the dress is the red parasol. 'What is going on?
Why are these clothes left here? What has happened to these
children? They can't have just disappeared.'

On the opposite wall, Jennie sees eight more pegs knocked into
the wall. Two of them have worn-out, tatty clothes hanging down
from them, and below are two pairs of well-weathered shoes that
have seen better days. She touches one of the pegs, then looks at
her hand and the dirt and soot that covers half of it.

Wandering back to the centre of the sheet, she looks at the
clothes on the wall, the shoes on the floor and then the pegs on the
far wall. Then she looks at the floor while mumbling to herself, as
she tries to work out their significance. 'I've got it, I think,' she says
quietly. 'I think I know what was going on here.'

The other two look up. 'What is it?' Bowen asks. 'Do tell.'

'This is where Edward and his friends got changed – they
would come here in their nice clothes no different from the rest
of us and they would get changed into these rags and dark cloaks.
That's why no one knew who they were. They were in disguise.'

She thinks for a minute. 'Bowen, check out the boys' clothes for
names. If I am right, one will be Edward, and another will be his
brother Oliver.'

Bowen starts to look for names in the clothing. On the neck
of a jacket, he finds a faded name. 'This one says, "Oliver the
pirate". I would presume that is Edward's brother.' He looks at
the next set of clothes. On the back of a grey flat cap, he reads
'Topper Harley'. Moving on to the third set of boy's clothes, he
looks everywhere but does not find a name. As he goes through
the large jacket pockets, he pauses and looks at Jennie as he slowly
pulls out a blue book with a lock on it.

Jennie recognises it instantly. 'That's Edward's diary!' She takes
it from Bowen and looks at the front of it. 'I have seen him with

this many times.' She clutches it tight to her chest before placing it in her pocket and continuing with her theory.

'Once changed, they would go off and do all the things they did in disguise so nobody would know who they were. But it still does not answer the question, why?'

Bowen looks at her. 'Well, if that's the case, how come their clo—' He stops in mid-sentence, thinks for a second, then speaks again. 'They never came back for their clothes, did they? That's why the other pegs are empty. They were still wearing the rags when they were caught,' Bowen says quietly as his head lowers and he looks at the floor. 'They were only children like us. Where did they go? Surely their parents would be looking for them. It still does not make any sense to me.'

A chilling silence comes over the three of them. 'I know, Bowen,' Georgia replies. 'It does seem strange that we never hear about our friends again, once they have gone. Perhaps they have been grounded by their parents, or in shame they have been moved away to stay with relatives until things settle down.'

Jennie frowns at them. 'It still does not answer the question, what were they doing, and why?'

'There is only one place left we have not looked.'

Bowen and Georgia look at each other and at the same time they utter, 'Fireplace.' Without any more words, all three of them head off down the stairs and make their way over to the hearth.

For such a small house, it is very large. They dip under the flume and look up at the back wall. In front of them, at head height, scratched into the stone are the words *pieces of eight.* Below the words are eight scratched-out circles about two inches in diameter, all in a line from left to right. Seven of them have an X cut through them, and the eighth circle is empty.

'I wonder what this means?'

'Is it not obvious to you yet, Georgia? The last disc without the X through it is Edward. All the others had already been taken; in the end he was on his own. That's why he had become so quiet and secretive at school. He had nobody left. All his friends had gone, leaving him all alone,' Jennie says.

'But why all the secrecy? Where did they all go? What happened to them all?' Georgia asks.

They look to the right along the edge of the wall and see the open slit in the corner. Georgia leans forward and starts pushing. With a grating sound of stone on stone, the crack opens wider. Bowen starts to push as well, forcing the gap until it's wide enough to squeeze through.

Jennie peers through the gap. 'It's very dark inside.' On the far wall, she can see small cuts in the stone with half-used candles stuck in them.

'Georgia, go and collect the matches that we found in the sack.'

A moment later, Georgia passes them over to Jennie, who promptly strikes one of them, settles the flame, then leans forward and lights the first candle inside the gap. She then steps inside and looks around the lit area. 'It is a tunnel.' She moves inside and lights a second candle. Moving down deeper into the depths, she lights a third before… 'Ouch,' she squawks as the match burns to the end and the flame singes her fingertips.

'There's a path in here that seems to head downwards in a large spiral through the rock. Shall we follow it?' There is a quiet pause before the sound of shuffling as Bowen and Georgia enter the tunnel behind her and move down to catch her up. Behind them, the wall of the fireplace slowly moves back under its own weight, not fully, but enough that the children turn round in a moment of panic. As they realise it seems to be designed to close back to that position, they regain their confidence and slowly walk down the stone-cut steps. Jennie has lit three more candles on the descent before they come to a narrow slit between two large boulders. The path does carry on down, but something has caught her eye and she needs to check it out.

Scratched into the surface of the rock is a round disc about two inches in diameter. 'This is exactly the same as the eight discs on the fireplace,' she says to the others. 'So, I guess this means that we go through here.'

Instead of climbing over the rock to go through the larger part of the entrance, Jennie bends down onto all fours and starts to squeeze through the lower part of the gap. But she is becoming a woman which means that her body shape was changing, a fact that doesn't go unnoticed by Bowen as her rear is wedged in the narrow slit between the walls.

'I knew I should have turned sideways. Bowen, give me a push, will you?' Bowen looks carefully at his target, trying to work out what part to grab without causing offence. After deciding there is no dignified method, he puts his hands to her cheeks, grips her tight and rams her through the gap with force. Jennie shoots through, rolls over and sits up all in one motion, with an unladylike comment and a fierce stare back at Bowen as she stands up and readjusts her dress. She composes herself as the others wriggle through the small opening. There is some dim light – enough to see that they are now in a large domed tunnel made of red bricks with a narrow trench cut in the floor about two feet wide and half full of water. 'What a smell,' Georgia says as she stands up.

'I think we are in the new sewer system they are building for the expansion of the village,' replies Jennie.

'And how would you know that?' Bowen asks.

'My father came here to help complete the design of it. He has Lord Fitzgerald and the build supervisors at our home tonight for a review of the modified plans and where it is going to next. They now want to build additional areas to store water in two underground reservoirs for the factory and more drinking water for the village expansions.'

As she looks around, she can see another disc cut into the wall. 'The marks say we go this way,' she says with confidence. As they walk along the tunnel, the yellow glow of a low flame comes through missing bricks in the wall, about two feet up from the ground and spaced evenly along the entire length. They take turns looking into the small hole left by one of these missing bricks and see a piece of two-inch metal pipe running through the gap. In the top, two small squares have been cut out and a piece of wick placed inside each of them, soaking up an oily liquid. Dancing on the top of both wicks is a small flame. 'How clever,' Bowen says as they straighten up and continue walking along the lit area of the tunnel.

About one hundred yards further on, the tunnel splits into two. The left side takes the trench and water onwards as far as the eye can see in the low light, and to the right the floor becomes level with no gully of water, and it slowly starts to widen out.

'Which way now?' Georgia asks.

'Look for another disc,' says Jennie.

The three of them all look in different areas and after a couple of minutes, Bowen yells out, 'Found it.' The others soon join him, and they continue down the right-hand tunnel for another five minutes. As they progress, the tunnel changes its structure. The bottom two and a half feet is still brickwork, but above becomes parallel metal bars in strips about ten yards long, then a block of square brickwork holding the bars in place and so on as it continues. Behind the bars, small open areas can be seen. The more they move along the tunnel, the larger the spaces behind the bars become. The lighting in the brickwork has now gone, so their side of the tunnel remains in semi-darkness. All the light is now coming from the ceiling on the other side of the metal bars, natural light shining through large squares exposed in the roof above at even distances apart. On the far side of each of these long rectangular rooms is an open door that leads to a well-lit path which they can see leading off into the distance before curving out of sight.

They continue for about another twenty yards before the tunnel just finishes. The brickwork around the edges stops and they are confronted with a rock face and loads of masonry tools, pickaxes and shovels.

'What now?' Georgia asks the other two.

'I don't know,' replies Jennie. 'There must be more than just this. We have not seen any other doors, paths or tunnels leading off, so there must be something here.'

After looking around for a while, Bowen shouts out in frustration. 'There's nothing here. We've come all this way for nothing.'

He looks at the floor and sees a large stone sitting right in the middle of the path. He runs up and kicks it as hard as he can. The stone shoots sideways, ricocheting off the brick wall and heading straight into the rock face ahead of them. It hits with a soft, cushioned blow.

They all look up at the same time. 'That didn't sound right,' says Bowen as he leans forward and touches the rock face in the corner where the stone had impacted. It's soft and spongy. He grabs a handful and pulls it towards him and upwards. A large sheet of cloth the same colour as the rock face moves. As Bowen lifts the sheet, a tunnel approximately three feet in diameter comes into view.

'I don't believe it,' he says, looking down the tunnel. It's too dark to see very much, but they can just about make out the end of a thick piece of rope. Jennie grabs it in her right hand and pulls it towards them.

'There's something attached to the end,' she says quietly.

As Jennie pulls on the long length of rope, a large trolley just narrower than the diameter of the tunnel appears. It's about seven feet long and has a rope connected to the front of it, where two glass lanterns are attached. Sitting on two small metal rails, it rolls along the tunnel floor smoothly.

Fishing around in her pocket, Jennie pulls out the matches and lights the lamps, then puts the glass fittings back over the top. 'I think you lie on this thing and pull on the rope to move yourself along.'

She looks back at Bowen and Georgia. 'I'll go first. When I get to the end, pull it back for yourselves.' She climbs on and slowly pulls herself along. Within minutes, she gets the hang of it and moves herself through the tunnel in a smooth rhythmic motion. After about fifty yards, brickwork appears on the left side again. Within a few more metres, the metal bars and brick pillars appear just like before as the tunnel curves off to the left. She pushes the trolley forward another few feet and it grinds to a halt. Putting her hand out, she feels a solid wall in front of her. 'This is as far as it goes,' she mutters and climbs off. 'Pull it back,' she calls down the tunnel. 'I will wait for you here.'

As the trolley moves off, she looks around. This area looks incomplete, with piles of unused bricks, rock rubble and building material. Jennie waits for the other two to arrive before moving on. First, Georgia appears, then a few minutes later, Bowen.

They move along the new tunnel on the left side for about twenty yards until it stops at a line of parallel iron bars. 'Well, that's the end of this tunnel,' Jennie comments as she looks through into the huge open space beyond the bars.

Although more lit than before, it is still quite dim. There is patchy straw on the floor, with a few rags scattered amongst it. Evenly spaced around the open room are large brick pillars which open up into great arches above, forming the ceiling. Square beams of sunlight illuminate the ground every thirty feet or so.

Jennie notices a shadow against one of the pillars. As she studies the object, a form starts to come through. It's a child, sitting on the floor, leaning against the pillar. Their knees are lifted up and she can see what looks like a pile of rags on their lap. The child is wearing a tattered shirt, torn trousers and has no shoes on their feet. Jennie deduces that the person must be a boy. 'Hello,' she says. 'Can you hear me over there?'

The child lifts his head up and stares back at her. Now she can see him a lot more clearly. His face is covered in soot, with two clean shiny lines running down his cheeks. He raises his hand over the top of his eyes to shield them from the dim light above, as he waits for his eyes and mind to take in what he is looking at. Then he lowers his hand, clasps the rags on his lap, leans forward and whispers, 'I told you she would come. All we had to do was hang on until they got here.'

The three of them watch intently as the pile of rags starts to move. It twists around slowly, and a small face appears through the sheets. It stares in the direction of Jennie, holds this gaze for a while, then covers back up and turns away. The boy leans forward again as from within the pile of rags, a faint whisper is heard.

'I can't see her very well. Is it really Mother?'

'Yes,' the boy answers. 'It's Mother. You didn't really think she would forget her little pirate son, did you? She is here to take you home.'

'Home? I've nearly forgotten what home looks like. Will Father and sister Victoria be… be… there.' The voice is getting fainter.

The boy tightens his grip on the rags and lifts him closer to his chest. He looks down into his arms and then at the three of them. They can now see the tears running down his cheeks as he begins to quietly weep.

The emotion Jennie sees in his face is ripping her heart apart, but what can she do from the other side of the bars? The boy looks up as if into the heavens, as an arm falls down from the child in the rags. As it hits the ground, his hand opens and something rolls towards Jennie, stopping against the wall.

Reaching through the gap under the bars, she grasps at the ground until she finally puts her hand over the object. Clasping it tight, she pulls it back through the gap. She strikes a match to view the item with the flame. Before her eyes is a large glass marble with two red streaks through it. As she rolls it around in her hand, she sees a letter scratched into the surface. 'E'. A sudden feeling of dread courses through her veins as the marble drops from her hand.

'Oh my God. What have I done?' She turns to look at the boy. 'Edward,' she shrieks loudly. 'Is that you?'

He slowly looks up, still clasping his little brother, Oliver, in his arms. 'Can't you see you are too late? You cannot help us now. Just go before you are seen and they get you too.'

Bowen, Georgia and Jennie have too many emotions going through them to just walk away. A friend they haven't seen in nearly two weeks is stuck behind some metal bars in a dark dingy sewer and they cannot get to him. Georgia by now has tears of her own running down her face while Bowen is shaking the bars frantically in a hopeless attempt to break them free.

'I will get to you, Edward, I promise you,' yells Jennie, tugging at the bars to try and break through. 'Oh God, I will help you,' she says.

What the three of them don't realise is that in a strange way they have already helped Edward. The fact that they have seen him in this situation and managed to piece the clues together means they are halfway to understanding what is going on. The burden Edward had carried all these weeks and months on his own is starting to lift from his shoulders as it has now been shared with others. He knows with his body all bruised and broken that there is not long left before he will join his brother in another place. But seeing these three friends will make the passing easier and hopefully they can help more than he could do on his own. All he needs is a little more time to explain what has been going on. The part Lord Fitzgerald has played and what he is planning to do next.

Edward tries to sit himself up a bit. As he opens his mouth to speak, he hears something and looks over his shoulder. He can hear a faint rhythmic shuffle coming up the tunnel, and he turns back to Jennie.

'Quiet,' he whispers, as he listens to the all too familiar sound. 'They're coming. Blow out the lamps and keep quiet if you value your lives.' The three of them fall silent as Jennie and Bowen snuff out the flames on the lamps.

'Listen to me carefully if you want to help. Please stop shaking the bars and just hear what I have to say. Don't make a sound and they will not see you. Wait until they have gone and go back to the fireplace. Up the stairs, in my jacket, you will find my diary. If you can get it to my sister Victoria and Springer, you may yet save the village and yourselves. I now know from some of the others here that my sister is near the village of Stockton. Find a farmer named George Todd. I repeat, George Todd. He can take you to them. But tell no others of what I say as it is hard to know who to trust these days.'

'We have already found your diary. It is in my pocket,' Jenny comments.

'What about you and your brother? We cannot just leave you here,' Georgia whispers as she still tries to pull on the bars.

'Oliver's strength fails as we speak. It's already too late for him. As for me, I am so weak and just about out of time. Now be silent and don't trust any of the new adults from the village, including your own families. Find Victoria and Springer, give her that marble and she will know I sent you. Please do this for me.

There are others you could save. It's not too late for them.'

The shuffling sound slowly draws closer. Within a couple of minutes, ghostly shadows start to appear, at first just a few, but the numbers keep swelling. With barely a sound, people move into the open space and sit or lie down. In the background, they can hear another sound, a clicking that gets louder and louder. 'Come on, you scum. Hurry up and get settled down or feel my boot on your head.' It's Brannigan and Sykes. They walk straight through the crowd directly towards Edward.

'I told you they would not move,' Brannigan says.

'Is the brat dead yet?' Sykes asks Edward, stooping down and grabbing Oliver by the neck. He picks up his near-lifeless body and looks into his eyes.

'Yeh, he be near enough for me.' He opens an old coal sack and bundles Oliver's body inside. 'We'll chuck him on the wagon on the way out.'

They turn their attention to Edward. 'Well, are you ready to earn your keep? You've got a lot of making up to do for all the damage you've caused us, you little shit.'

Jennie wonders why Edward has barely moved. Even as they snatched his brother away from him, he did not put up a fight.

'We've got you a lovely little number down the hole holding the pressure hose, boy,' Brannigan yells in his face. 'The longest anyone has survived down there is four days, and that was a fit boy, not a sickly puke like you.' He grabs Edward by the shoulders and lifts him up. Edward lets out a small yelp and tries to twist away. But Sykes has him in a tight grip and shows him the back of his hand, knocking him back against the wall. 'Shut up, you mangy bleeder.'

It is only now that Jennie sees the extent of Edward's wounds. His left arm is in a thin sling made from a piece of sheet and strapped to his body above the elbow. Around his right thigh is a strip of cloth stained dark with what looks like dried blood. His foot on that side is held off the ground as if unable to support his weight and there is a nasty wound on the side of his head that has yet to be cleaned up.

She tries to sit up and grab at the bars, emotions tearing at her very soul as she struggles with what she is seeing. But as she moves forward, Bowen grabs her and pulls her back down. Tears flow down her face as she realises that all his suffering is down to her. She desperately tries in vain to get up and reach him, forcing Georgia to join in and wrap her arms around her legs to help pull her back down. Bowen covers her mouth with his hand and the three of them remain in this tight clench, while still observing what is going on.

'Let's go,' Sykes utters, pushing Edward sideways around the pillar.

Edward shuffles along, part hopping.

After a few seconds, Sykes speaks out. 'This will take all bleeding night at this rate.' He grabs Edward by the arm and pulls him along.

Edward yells out with pain as Brannigan grabs him by the waist on his other side and together they pull him along even faster. In Brannigan's other hand, he drags the coal sack containing Oliver's broken body along behind them.

The children watch helplessly as Edward and his brother are hauled down the tunnel for the final time. They can barely see Edward's features as he looks back at the three of them for one last time, before he disappears into the shadows. It's a haunting sight that will be etched into their memories for the rest of their lives.

Jennie is breaking apart, tears flowing ever faster as she realises that all his suffering is because she thought he was a thief and a murderer running from the law. As the sound of the hobnail boots begins to fade into silence, she now understands that he was only trying to get food and clothes for his brother and the others trapped in this hell.

The three children relax their grip on each other as they sit there trying to take in all that they have just witnessed. There is not a dry eye amongst them, but at the same time there is no sound of crying either. They are just numb; it is as though the whole world has gone empty and dark and makes no sense.

Little do they know that this is the last time anyone will ever see Edward alive, for tonight in the cold of the deep pit, holding a pressure hose, the life will finally drain from his broken body. That fire in his eyes that had burned so brightly, that will that could not be easily broken, his passion and drive that could not be stopped, his smile that lit up the room and all that was in it – extinguished and crushed by the greed and brutality that only man can inflict on another.

Georgia turns around as a small hand reaches through the bars. Seeing it out of the corner of her eye, she panics and leans back to the far side of the tunnel. The hand now slowly closes together and points to the pocket on the front of her dress. She looks at the chest pocket and sees the little cloth doll. 'Please, miss, can I look at that doll?' comes a quiet voice from just the other side of the bars.

Reaching to her pocket, Georgia draws out the doll, looks at it then passes it to the waiting hand. 'There you are, Katie,' the child says. 'I didn't think I would see you again.'

Georgia moves forward and looks through the gap between the bars. 'Margaret? Is that you?'

The little girl looks back at her. 'Georgia!' she squeals. 'Can it really be? I thought I would never see anybody again.'

'How did you end up here? We thought you had gone away with your grandma.'

'I, I don't… I don't know.'

Jennie and Georgia both reach forward through the bars to hold her. They can see in her eyes that she is totally confused. 'I was in bed asleep when I heard a loud crash. Grandma was screaming, and someone grabbed me and carried me down the stairs and… and… I don't remember any more. But I'm so cold, scared and hungry, and they are nasty to me.'

Before the girls can say more, they hear more footsteps and voices coming up the far side tunnel. 'Quick, Margaret, sit down and be quiet. People are coming.'

Margaret lets go of Jennie but refuses to release Georgia.

'Margaret, you have got to be brave and let go of me,' she says in a quiet reassuring voice.

'But I'm scared and afraid.'

Georgia realises that she must act fast. 'Alright, sit down and hold my hand, and we'll cover our hands with that cloth beside you.' They cover their grip just in time, as out from the far tunnel, several people come into view.

Lord Fitzgerald in his entire splendour swaggers in and stands in one of the natural spotlights. The three of them recognise him instantly. For he can never be mistaken as the clothes he wears are so vivid and, on his head, he always wears the largest of hats.

Burgundy trousers, burgundy waistcoat, dark red jacket with gold thread, knee-high boots with gold buckles up the sides, a large wooden cane with an ivory and gold handle. This is topped with a black velvet triangular hat with burgundy trimming to complete his attire. Whenever stationary, his left hand swings a large gold full-hunter pocket watch, and when he moves, it is always popped back into his waistcoat pocket.

To get where he is in society, Lord Fitzgerald has made himself more than a few enemies, so is always accompanied by two or more burly armed men and today is no exception. They stand back about five paces behind him, watching their surroundings intently. In this case it is just the poor wretches strewn about the open space, not that they have any fight left in them. For they are beyond half-starved and drained of life, just ghosts of people waiting for the end to come and free them from their suffering.

Three other men are with Lord Fitzgerald, but at present only one can be seen. A thin weedy character, dressed in dark clothing, with small round spectacles hanging off his nose. The other two, at present, are obscured by one of the support pillars and cannot be identified.

'This, when fully completed, will be part of the main storage area for the raw materials needed for my other project. At present, we are using it to house these poor unfortunates. But this is only a temporary measure until they have served their purpose.'

'Are you not concerned that other people will find out what is going on and inform the magistrate?' the weedy little man asks.

'My dear fellow, I own the magistrate. He is my second cousin on my mother's side, so don't worry,' he explains with a coldness that would chill a normal person to the bone. 'What you fail to understand,' he continues, 'is that this whole process runs itself. Let me explain. The village has a large fruit-growing industry, supported by a few others but mainly myself as I own most of the land. This gives much-needed work to the locals and a healthy profit to us. We use this profit to improve the village, with better roads, lighting in the streets, new drainage system, schools, and clean water pumped in from the reservoirs on my land to the village and factory to keep them running.

'Even the factory is about to be refitted with the latest steam-driven machines, to be more efficient and profitable. On the surface, this makes this village a very appealing place for wealthier people to settle and invest their money.

'Now, here's the good part. At present, the new drainage system is a mask for the mining we are also doing way under the village along the rock line. You see, it's an ancient underground river course. While we pump some of the water to the park to fill up the lake and run the fountains, the rest we use to pressure mine the bed of the underground river for silver ore and small amounts of gold.

'We process all this material on the far side of the cotton and wool factories, in the new extension, crushing the rocks to get at the precious metals, ore and other useful components before sending it on to the factory smelters. It is not ideal to have it so far away from the source, but it needs to be kept out of sight of our expanding properties. We use some of these tunnels and these unfortunates as labour to move the material about. The tunnels will later be used for sewers as the village grows and the mining moves along.

'The profit from this purchases the materials to build new modern shops and houses in the village. When we need more land and space, we offer the existing village residents good prices for their homes and once they have accepted the offer, we help them move out. With the main way out of this valley being past the new factories a few miles away, they are seen to leave the village by their families and friends, only to be collected by us later. Then we take the money back, burn their belongings in the furnaces and add all those that are able to work to the labour force. Until finally, they end up down here.

'Those that show resistance or don't want to sell, we intimidate, provoke, encourage them to leave or create a response that allows us to legally involve the magistrate. Our magistrate. It always ends up the same way, with us getting what we want. For those that oppose us, there's a late-night visit from my associates and a permanent move to the factory quarters for them and their families. The houses are stripped of all worth in a matter of days, demolished and rebuilt in a matter of months, ready to sell to those with ambition and drive, who will join our cause and have a much-improved lifestyle.

'The workforce we collect is used at the secure far side of the factory until they are controlled and broken. Then they move to mining and finally when they are too weak or too young to do anything else, they end their days doing the sewer and tunnel expansions. At present, we are also working on a large underground water reservoir to store more water. The rock around the village is a bit porous, so it needs to be lined with a thick layer of clay, hence the ghostly grey colour to their skin.

'Unfortunately for us, people do not last long in this environment. But there is always new stock to harvest if you know where to look. The old and weak just get removed and, well, shall we say that our furnaces are some of the most efficient burners in the land.

'We only sell the new houses along with attractive positions within the company to hard-working and visionary people like yourselves with large families and skills that can benefit us. Thus, we all continue to grow and prosper. I am telling you this now so you fully understand there is no turning back if you want to advance yourselves here. To be wealthy and prominent in this community, you will have to abide by our rules.

'Work hard. Protect the enterprise. Enjoy what WE have to offer. Never – I repeat never – interfere with my business. Oh, and don't get too friendly with the locals, as some may not be around long. You're far better off sticking with our own kind.

'If, like in the past, one of your children involves themselves in company business, control them. If not, well… you can always produce plenty more, can't you! I am afraid it can be the price paid to become extremely wealthy and live this lavish lifestyle.'

Lord Fitzgerald slowly leads the group along the tunnel, past the three children. The men behind the pillar move forward into better light.

'Now down to business. I need to continue the expansion of this area and down to the right of where we are now. But the floor on the tunnel leading to the factory is not holding up to the weight of the ore wagons. This is a priority as it is starting to damage the structure of the floor and the wheels on the carts.'

'I have a theory on that,' says a short, stocky man wearing a top hat. 'We could lay metal tracks down on wooden plinths and roll the ore down them in interlocking carriages on grooved metal wheels. That would protect the floor and be easier to pull along.'

'That sounds like a splendid idea,' Lord Fitzgerald replies. 'I will have people look into this and see if we can modify the carts to fit such a design of track.'

Jennie recognises the voice she has just heard and continues watching him as they pass one of the light spots on the ground. 'Father,' she utters in a shocked but quiet voice, disbelieving that he could be part of such a terrible scheme. The party continues walking down the tunnel, with the conversation fading the further they move away. Jennie sinks to the ground, shock taking its toll. 'I cannot believe my father would be party to this. There must be some mistake.' She looks at the others. There is no room for any more tears, just utter disappointment as she comes to terms with the fact that he is not the person she thought he was.

'We need to go,' Bowen says as he turns and slowly heads off down the tunnel. Georgia leans over and looks at Margaret.

'I need to find a way to get to you, Margaret. You must let go of my hand to—'

'Nooooo,' she yells.

'Margaret, you must be brave. We will be back as soon as we can. I will also bring you some food and find a way to get you out of here. I promise, now hold on to Katie while we work out what to do.' She starts to cry as she reluctantly lets go of Georgia's hand.

'Don't be long,' Margaret says as she releases her grip through the bars and drops down on the other side.

Georgia turns and joins the others moving back through the tunnel. Not a word is spoken as they return to the cottage above. The experience has left them numb. The three of them are drained physically and emotionally, for what these young children have just witnessed leaves nothing to the imagination.

Walking up the spiral stone steps, Jennie pinches out the candles as she passes each one. They pull open the back wall of the fireplace and step through the gap. Standing up in the open hearth, they all look up the chimney and see a gap in the stonework. Jennie picks a brown rag off the floor and wraps Edward's diary in it, then wedges it tightly into the crevice.

'We'll leave it there until we have a plan, but at least we know why Edward had those items in his sack. He was trying to keep his brother and the others alive.' She looks around the fireplace, picks up a rusty bent nail and scratches a cross through the last disc on the wall.

'You will not be forgotten, Edward. I'm coming back,' she says in a quiet voice. Jennie is watched by the others as she moves towards the sack in the corner of the room, stoops down and picks up the red scarf. She looks at it for a while, then wraps it round her neck and walks over to the door, followed by Georgia.

Bowen turns back to look at the fireplace. He closes the back wall and watches as the brass fitting clicks back into position. He pauses for a moment to look up at the eight discs, then joins the others at the doorway. 'I'll go first,' he says, lifting the catch.

Outside, night has started to creep in. There is a cold chill in the air that makes him shudder and gives him goosebumps on his exposed skin. It takes a few minutes for his eyes to adjust to the light, after which he carefully views his surroundings. Reassured that nothing outside has changed, he slowly steps outside.

Suddenly, a movement catches his eye. Instantly, his heart begins to pound as he turns towards the broken-up area of the forge. He sighs with relief as he sees the rest of his friends beckoning him with hand gestures and flicks of their heads. He is greeted by the arms of many, all wanting to show their affection. The still of the air is broken by the whispered barrage of questions that are fired at him from all angles.

The girls follow him and after a lengthy debate the group head off back in the direction of the brook, moving along the grassy pathway with barely a sound between them.

* * *

Two weeks later, the still of the night is broken by the cracking of a twig and shadows begin to form in the distance. They can be seen crisscrossing this way and that under the pale moonlight, always moving closer and closer. In and out of the darkest patches of cover below trees and hedgerows, the shadows move at pace and with purpose.

At the last moment, all the figures converge into one loose group and the collective mass runs into the old forge cottage. A foot kicks the brass fitting, and the wall is pushed back. Children in rags, carrying full brown sacks, scurry down the tunnel.

The last one pauses and looks up into the ducting above the fireplace. Below the eight discs is another line. This consists of seven perfectly carved crescents about two inches high. One of them already has a large cross scratched through it. Below these marks, two words are neatly written into the surface. *Night Owls.*

A candle, held in a small broken clay cup, moves across to the left and Jennie can be seen. She quietly sighs as she stares at the two rows of symbols. Her hand reaches up out of the darkness and follows the outline of the end disc, then moves down to the first crescent with the cross through it. 'You are not forgotten, my friends,' she whispers. 'None of you.'

The light from the candle dances away as she moves towards the tunnel. The tip of the flame flickers and arcs towards the dark passage within, and without a sound she disappears. There is the grating sound of the wall rotating back as the gap closes, followed by a clunk as the mechanism locks into position. Then there is silence.

CHAPTER 7

Looking for the Lost

The village streets are busy with people, even more than usual for the start of market day. Victoria is pushing her pram around the stalls, accompanied by Cook, who is collecting produce for the kitchen. Inside the pram, baby Molly is rolling the toys connected to the bar across the front of her transport. She dribbles and makes all kinds of bubbly sounds as she grabs, pushes and rolls the attachments in front of her.

It's her first outing away from the estate and it is also a big day in Victoria's eyes, as she has not had time to leave their farm or George's estate for many months. So, to have the opportunity to come to the village on market day and have a look around and shop is a real treat. 'Looks like it will be one of the last nice days of the season. There was a frost this morning and the trees are beginning to drop their leaves,' she says to Cook, who is holding the hand of a young child barely two years old.

'Yes, you're right. But it's been a good year. Look at all that has been achieved in such a short space of time.' The young child at Cook's side pulls at her hand. Which means only one thing – he wants to be carried by Aunty Cook. She obliges instantly, swinging him up and onto her side so she's still able to view all that is on offer while also holding her godchild who she adores so much.

'Well, Edward, what apples should we go for today then? Red ones or green?' Edward looks at the apples on show and points to the large pile of bright red apples, followed by the word 'Cooky'. The young child's vocabulary is still very limited, but to Springer's frustration and Cook's delight, his favourite words are 'Mummy',

'Cooky', 'DanDan' and 'George'. No matter how much he tries to get him to say 'Daddy', it comes out as 'Gargar'.

It would be fair to say that these people who have known each other for just a few years have become a very close-knit group of friends. They have flourished in each other's company and with the addition of the hard-working families that moved up to join them on the estate, they have become a great community. The estate is prospering beyond all expectations, allowing George to help his tenant farmers as well as promote projects in the village.

George himself, with his new boost of confidence and zeal for life, has recently become close with a widowed lady called Bernadette, or Bebe as she prefers to be known. She is a good lady who has a fine sense of humour and a passion for life that is a match with George's. She has lent a hand on the farm as a seasonal worker for several years and stayed on to look after the animals the last two. In particular, she tends to the ever-growing herds of sheep and cattle that George loves so much.

Bernadette has no family of her own, since a terrible accident robbed her of her husband and two sons many years ago. They once had their own farm in Wales, but tragedy struck after a very wet spring and a severe flash flood. Bebe was in the hills, staying in one of the wooden sheds and checking on the newborn lambs, helping deliver any problem births within the flock. Her husband and two sons were patching a leaky roof on the farmhouse when there was an almighty rumble that shook the ground as if there was an earthquake.

When Bebe went to investigate, she found that there had been a huge landslide. The whole side of the valley had slid down and swallowed the entire farm. Such was the size and volume of the earth moved, the landscape changed forever. They had never even tried to find the bodies, as it would be an impossible task. So, she placed three graves on top of the new hillside, put a small picket fence around them as a memorial to her family and left Wales forever, vowing never to return to such a tragic place.

She treats everybody on the estate as if they are family, pitching in with everything that needs doing. In the last several months, her and George have spent more time together and they seem stronger for it. The pair of them treat Victoria and Springer as if they were their own and their children as grandchildren.

That is when Cook allows it, as it seems Victoria and Springer's children – who have George, Cook and Dan as godparents – actually have a number of people who watch over them all the time, just as Victoria and Springer watch over George and Cook. Despite not being related by blood, they are truly a family unit.

'So, Cook, are you and Dan looking to start a family of your own any time soon?' Victoria asks as she purchases a bag of apples.

Cook looks back with wide eyes. 'Steady on. I'm just getting used to waking up and seeing Dan still beside me in the morning.' She laughs. 'It's funny. Dan has changed so much! He takes a bath regularly, does not smell half as bad as what he used to, even shaves and cuts his hair now and then. But he still loves to be out in the woods and along the river doing whatever is needed to better the estate. Do you know that he now does not like to kill or take any more game than he needs to feed all of us?'

Victoria looks at her, wide-eyed and mouth open.

'It's true, he has started drawing and painting what he sees when he is out patrolling instead.'

Victoria is shocked by Cook's statement as her lips turn up into a slight smile. 'Well, I am not sure what surprises me more – an ex-poacher that does not like to hunt or the fact that Dan is becoming a bit of an artist!'

'It's true, he has become a bit of a softy as he gets older. Not that I am complaining, as he has become far more affectionate with me as well. Who knows, if it is not too late, we may well be blessed with a little one like this little nipper Edward,' she says, bouncing him on her side.

Suddenly, a commotion breaks out on the other side of the street. Victoria and Cook look up as a stall owner yells, 'Stop, thief! They are stealing my wares!'

Cook and Victoria look over to see a person running along the stalls, trying to collect food as they go. They grab at many things, but most seem to just fall out of their hands. Eventually, with a few things tucked under an arm, the thief makes a break for it, running along the street, away from the growing crowd of people chasing after them. As the thief passes the blacksmith forge, their luck runs out as a large muscular arm swings out from behind a stationary cart, hitting the person across the chest and knocking them backwards to the ground.

They remain motionless as several people crowd round. It is not long before two constables arrive on the scene and on hearing what the person has done, they grab the thief and start to drag them away.

During all this commotion, a wagon has pulled up beside Cook, Victoria and the children. It's George and Bebe. They have bought the animal feed they need and are ready to collect the others before heading back to the farm. 'What's been going on here then?' George asks.

'They just caught a thief stealing food from the stalls over there,' Victoria replies.

George thinks for a bit. 'That is a bit odd. Why would anyone need to steal food? It's the end of autumn. There's plenty of food everywhere, not to mention every farmer around here needs seasonal pickers at the moment. You can get fed and paid at any number of farms for a day's work.'

The constables have dragged the thief across the road and are approaching George's wagon. As they pass, the thief grabs the wheel, tucking their whole arms through the spokes and clutching it to their body. While doing so, they grab something from their chest and wedge it under the cart into a small gap in the wooden boards. The constables pull and tug to release the felon from the wheel as George looks down to see what's going on. The thief's clothes are shredded, and they have no shoes on their feet. Filthy strips of cloth are wrapped round their wrists and arms. As the men pull, the arm finally comes back through the spokes, dragging down one of the strips of cloth and exposing their hand.

George stares for a second then shouts at the top of his voice, 'In the name of God!' Everybody stops moving as George climbs down from his wagon. 'Can you not see this person is injured?

Look at the state of that hand.'

The arm is purple around the wrist and the hand and looks deformed. The constables release them, and they just curl up in a ball on the floor, trembling.

'Who are you? What happened to your hand?' asks George.

The person murmurs some words, but it is so quiet he cannot hear what is spoken above the noise of the growing crowd.

'Say that again? We could not hear you.'

The thief looks up at all the people surrounding them and, slowly lifting themselves up a bit from the floor, they speak a little louder. 'I am looking for a man named George, George Todd. I was told he could be located in this village.'

Everyone goes silent. Victoria and Cook look at George and he looks at them before turning back to view the person on the floor.

'Who are you?' George asks again.

'I must find George To—' The thief drops back to the floor, unconscious.

George looks at the constables. 'What has this man done? What are the charges against him, can I ask?'

'They tried to steal some vegetables as they ran past the stalls,' one of the officers replies.

George looks round at the crowd of people. Most of them he knows well or trades with on a regular basis. Some even rent small farm holdings from him. 'How much do you want for the damages? I will pay any storekeeper for the loss of stock this poor person has caused.' Nobody answers him, so he raises his voice. 'How much do you want for the damages this injured person caused? I will pay anyone who is out of pocket.'

After seeing the unfortunate's injuries, most people now feel ashamed for the commotion they made and shake their heads or just walk away.

An ex-employee of George's, Big John – who was once removed from his land by Springer for inciting rebellion as well as theft and corruption and who now tends one of the stalls – takes advantage of the situation. 'Five shillings for the loss of goods and my time away from my stall,' he yells.

There is shock on the faces of all the people around him, for only a few carrots and some apples were found with the thief, but George does not hesitate. He puts his hand in his pocket and tosses the coins on the floor in front of Big John. 'There's seven. Keep the change,' he says in disgust to the man who once ruined all George held dear.

John smiles as he kneels down to pick up the money, but as he does, he hears a voice behind him. 'If thee touch a penny of that coin, I'll throw you such a beating that God himself would not be able to see who thee be.'

Springer is standing right beside him. He had been in the crowd watching and now steps forward to say his piece to this horrible man. John's expression instantly turns to fear. He goes to move to his left and bumps into another person. As he looks up, he recognises Dan, the man who set him up for stealing livestock and supplies. Though the charges against him were valid, they could never be proved in court as he was not there when the trap was sprung. Nor would his associates confess to him being involved, as so-called honour amongst thieves prevented them from naming him.

Lowering his head, he shuffles backwards on his hands and knees in an attempt to squirm his way out of the situation he has put himself in. Then he turns, stands up and runs, much to the laughter of the crowd. For all of them know the man and what he is. They also know George was very lenient after what John did to him and his wife. George looks at the constables. 'Would it be alright for me to tend to this person? I know not who they be, but they are injured, and I will take responsibility for them until they are well enough to answer for what they have done.'

One of the constables laughs. 'For a couple of vegetables and a few apples, I think this one can be forgotten for a round of drinks for everyone present?'

George smiles and nods, and Dan passes the constable the coins that he has just picked up from the floor. 'I think this will cover a few rounds,' he says, and the crowd cheers before they all head off to the tavern, still laughing over John running away from

Springer and Dan.

George turns his attention to the would-be thief on the floor. He gently lifts them up with Springer's help and lays them in the back of the wagon, covering them with a sheet before the group all climb aboard and head back to the estate.

'I wonder why they were looking for you, George,' Bebe says.

'Be damned if I know. I'm sure that I do not know them or recognise whoever they are. It is a real mystery to me at this moment in time.'

Victoria speaks up. 'Whoever they are, they seem to know your name, George. Even if they do not know who you are, as they did not recognise you.'

It takes them around thirty minutes to get back home, and while Cook, Bebe and Victoria take the children and purchases into the farmhouse kitchen, George and Springer collect the unconscious person from the wagon. They carry them into one of the guest rooms, place a sheet over the bed and lay them on top. The person is absolutely filthy and stinks of excrement, but the first thing they do is unbandage their hands and remove the strips of rags covering them. 'Oh my godfathers, what has happened to you?' says George.

Both wrists are the same – deep purple and yellow in colour, heavily bruised and scuffed. The hands seem distorted, and the thumbs are out of position, along with two of their fingers.

Dan looks at the hands. 'I have seen this before. She has been hung up in cuffs until her hands have pulled through.'

'She?' asks George.

'Yes, she,' answers Dan as he removes her cap and uncovers her long matted hair. 'Her hands are smaller and softer than a man's and she is either a young lady or an older child.' Dan gently lifts one of the arms carefully.

'She has been hung up by her cuffs and her thumbs have dislocated with the weight of her body. Then, she would have fallen through and no doubt escaped her captors. That is why her hands are out of shape. As for the two fingers, that could have happened at any time. Her bare feet wrapped in rags will also need looking at. Her captors would have taken her shoes to stop her escaping. Perhaps because she had already run away once before, hence being hung up by her cuffs. This person must have been in agony for some time and would have struggled to pick up food or even wipe her behind. That is why she smells so bad.'

George is clearly distressed that something awful has happened to this young lady, especially as she was looking for him. 'Can we help her in any way? Fix her hands or something?'

Dan looks at the hands again. 'They have been dislocated for some time now; it will be very difficult to put them back in place without damaging them further. But if it can be done, and we get it right, we would see the colour and warmth coming back. If not, she will lose her hands for certain, and that's if she has not already, as the blood circulation is poor.'

'How do we do it?' George asks.

Dan looks at him. 'We don't. But I do know someone who has done this twice, and we need to do this while she is unconscious, as the pain will be almost unbearable.'

'Who is it that can do this for her?'

'She will say no, as she does not like to hurt people, even if it is to help them get better, but she can do it if you can convince her,' says Dan.

'What, Cook?'

Dan nods.

'Really? Well I be blowed, that there woman of yours be full of surprises,' replies Springer.

'She has done my hand and a friend's before, but she hates doing it as the pain makes people scream and she feels bad. Also, I cannot watch as it makes me feel sick.'

Springer thinks for a minute. 'If we be wanting Cook to do this deed, we be needing to get Victoria, for she be able to work her womanly ways on Cook and get her to do what needs to be done.' After a few more minutes thinking, he continues, 'Dan, go and ask Victoria to join us and stay thee with Cook, Bebe and the youngerns, for I be workin' a plan in my mind.'

Dan is off like a flash and a short time later Victoria arrives in the room. The first thing she sees is that it is a girl lying on the bed, then she sees her exposed hands. 'It's a girl! But what has happened to her hands? They look awful.' She goes to feel her fingers and they are cold to the touch. 'What is wrong with her hands? Why are they cold?' she asks.

'They be disjointed, my dear. The blood does not flow right good. We be needin' to push them back in right quick for fear she be without them if not done quick like. Poor lass could lose them there hands anyway, but back in place, she has a fighting chance that they could be of use again.'

'Well, why have you not done it then?'

Springer looks at her. 'A sawbones be a day's ride from here. Only Cook be knowing what needs doing and Dan be reckonin' she be reserved in her trying as she does not like to inflict the pain needed to fix them there bones back in place.'

'Cook,' Victoria yells. 'Cook, I need you at once.'

They hear Cook rushing down the corridor and then into the room. She looks at Victoria and then to the person on the bed. 'Well I be, it's a girl,' she says before moving in for a closer inspection. She looks at her face and the matted hair and filthy clothes and catches the unpleasant smell. Her gaze moves down the girl's body to her wrists and hands. Gently, she lifts one hand and feels along the joints. The girl's body twitches even though she is unconscious, making Cook jump a little. She lowers the hand and strokes the side of the girl's face. 'We need a doctor now, or she could lose them hands for good.'

Victoria looks at her. 'We need to do it now, Cook. Dan says you can do this procedure. That you've done it before on other occasions.'

'Uh uh. Hell no! We can get a doctor in from the local town. They would be here for tomorrow if we sent somebody to get them now,' Cook swiftly replies.

Victoria gives Cook the look, staring hard at her. 'No. I won't do it.' She continues her relentless stare at Cook. 'No, no, no. I don't like hurting people and that will really hurt her.'

'I risked the safety of my unborn child and Springer's very

existence to give you and Dan a better life. And George was shot at trying to rescue you from peril.'

Cook raises her eyebrows. 'Are you going to pull that old chestnut on me every time you want me to do something that I do not want to do?'

'Absolutely. You know you need to do it now. I saw it in your eyes when you felt her hands.'

George and Springer are keeping quiet and are trying hard not to chuckle at how Victoria works on Cook. Dan is just around the corner, listening but staying out of sight. He dares not get between Cook and Victoria in these sorts of confrontations, for fear of Cook venting her wrath on him.

Cook takes a deep breath as she thinks. 'She is filthy and cold to the touch. We need to warm her up, especially her hands and legs, as well as clean the filth off her body. Dan! I know you are hiding round the corner. Get all the water you can on the stove and over the fire. We need to give this young lady a soak in a hot bath. It might even take two to get her warm and clean.'

Dan instantly pops his head round the door, tilts his cap and heads off to the kitchen.

'George, find some loose-fitting clothes we can put her in once we have cleaned her up, then start a fire outside to burn these clothes, rags and bandages once we have removed them all. Springer, cut a white sheet into strips for bandages and find some strong alcohol – brandy or something stronger. Get the iodine from the medicine cabinet, for we may need it later.'

Cook shakes her head and sighs. 'Victoria, we need to start stripping her down. Then once the bathtub is ready, Springer can carry her through, wrapped in the sheet she is on now.' She looks around the room. 'Well, move, all you men, and give us some privacy!' she bellows, ushering them out of the room. George and Springer leave to do their allotted tasks while Cook and Victoria start to undress the young lady, slowly taking off each item of clothing and placing them in a pile. As they do, they go through her pockets in the hope of finding something that might identify her.

Her clothing is beyond any kind of repair, and the only item they find is a small rag doll in her petticoat pocket. Victoria places it on the side as they continue to remove all her clothes and wrap her in the sheet until the bath is ready.

Cook turns to Victoria. 'She is very thin, and some of the cuts in her feet are infected and need lancing, and the thorns need drawing out. Once we have bathed her, we will look at them and see what can be done to help.'

Around thirty minutes later, there is a tap at the door and George speaks. 'The bath is ready. Not too hot to start with, but we have more water on the go. I would also like to ask if I could carry her to the washroom rather than Springer.' It is plain to see that George has been deeply affected by the state of this young girl.

'Of course,' comments Victoria. He bends down and picks her up in the sheet, then follows Cook and Victoria to the bathtub. Cook checks the temperature of the water and adds some more cold. 'She is so cold we had better not put her in too warm a water to start. It might be too much for her to handle. Now lower her in with the sheet wrapped round her, George, and we will call you when you are needed again.'

Half an hour later, Victoria opens the door and asks the men in. 'George, if you could lift her out and you others drain the water, we will give her another warmer soak.'

The first thing the three men notice is how filthy the water is, near brown in colour, as George picks up the girl still wrapped in the sheet. The others get to work, emptying the water down a shoot to an outside gutter system. When the tub is full of warmer water, George lowers her back in.

Cook speaks. 'If you could get the fire going in the bedroom and lay out the bandages on the side along with the clothes we asked for. We will warm her up for a while then carry her through to the bedroom and work on her hands. Being warm and supple will help with what I need to do, I think.'

'You think?' George asks in concern.

Cook puts her hands on her hips and stares at him. 'You pay me to cook. I am not a physician. I do what I can. If you want to get someone else—'

George interrupts. 'No, no. I'm sorry, Cook, that just came out wrong. I am just worried for the girl, that is all. I apologise for how it sounded.'

The men leave the room again. Dan deals with setting and lighting the fire while Springer lays out the clothes and bandages. George waits by the door, ready to carry the girl once Cook and Victoria summon him. Sure enough, with half an hour gone, Cook beckons to him for assistance.

Once she is out of the bath and dry, they cover her with a clean cotton sheet and George carries her through to the bedroom and places her on the bed. Victoria and Cook slide one of Victoria's old nightgowns over her head and down her body, gently pulling her arms through the large sleeves.

Cook sits on the side of the bed and picks up her right arm. She feels round the hand and then the thumb joint, twisting and manipulating as she goes. She rotates the thumb until she is happy with the position, and then applies pressure and pushes the thumb hard to the hand. There is a loud crack as the parts of the joint are reunited, and as Cook massages and rubs the hand, the dark purple colouring starts to pinken out and the hand takes on some of its normal colour. Cook takes one of the girl's fingers and does the same again with a crack as it goes back into position.

Cook is nearly in tears as the hand begins to return to a more normal shape. 'This poor girl must have been in so much pain. I wonder how long she has been like this,' she says while working on the second finger. It takes a little longer, but eventually she gets the finger to position itself correctly.

Victoria just nods as she starts to wrap the hand in bandages while Cook moves round to the other side. She does the same procedure with this hand, but this time there is no crack. 'It's not right,' says Cook as the hand begins to swell and go dark purple. She pulls apart the thumb and hand and they separate easily. 'I trapped some tissue or veins in the joint. I don't think this one will go back.'

Victoria can see Cook is about to panic. She looks at George for support. 'I know you are her best chance, Cook. I've seen you handle all kinds of problems and come out on top. Now this girl needs your help and the best chance of saving her hand is you, so please don't give up now. I know it is within you.'

Cook nods at George and takes a moment to calm down, then starts to massage the hand again. With the gentle rubbing, the swelling subsides, and she lines up the joint, pulls the digits apart, and twists and pushes them together with force. The joint resists for a moment before finally cracking into place. The girl twitches and tenses up before relaxing again, making Cook jump a little as well as bringing more tears to her eyes. She continues massaging the hand, but this time the improvement is far slower. But with persistence and continuous rubbing, eventually some of the purple swelling starts to turn pink. Cook takes some deep breaths and calms herself, wiping the tears that run down her face.

'What a relief. This poor child has gone through so much. Who would do such a thing to you, my dear?'

George walks over to Cook and hugs her tightly. 'You never cease to amaze me. How you always seem to know what to do and how to get it done.' Cook goes a little red in the face as she nods at George.

After Victoria and Cook finish wrapping the second hand, they move down to inspect the wounds on her feet, digging out some large splinters and thorns and squeezing out the pus, wiping them down with brandy then wrapping the feet in more bandages.

George leaves the room, only to return minutes later with Springer carrying his favourite armchair, closely followed by Bebe. They put the chair down beside the bed as George speaks. 'Bebe and I will take turns to watch over her. Victoria and Cook, you have the little ones and food to attend to. As for you, Springer, both you and Dan need to run the farm's affairs for a few days. For I will not be leaving this girl until she is awake, improving and can tell us why she is looking for me.'

All in the room can see how greatly this girl has affected George, for it is written all over his face. He takes his place in his favourite chair and settles back as the others slowly leave the room. Bebe sits on the edge of the bed and holds the young girl's hand as Victoria passes the bundle of rags and used strips of sheet to Springer.

'Burn these in the fire outside, my dear,' she says. 'They cannot be saved.' As they leave, they take one last look at the girl and George. He does not even look up as Cook, who is the last to leave, closes the door quietly behind her.

Over the next couple of days, George barely leaves the room except for the call of nature. All his food is eaten in there, everything he does is done in that room or not at all. By his leg, as always, is Fern, for she will not leave her master unless it is Dan taking her for a quick walk. Bebe and the others visit him often. They offer to watch over the girl so he can take a break, but he never accepts, just remains vigilant by her side.

On the third day, the girl begins to open her eyes. Firstly, she looks up and stares at the ceiling, then around the room with a small movement of her head. Finally, she locks eyes on George, scared and having no idea where she is or who the man is watching her. She remains as still as possible while considering her options. Her hands are very sore, but she can now at least move them without the agony they once caused. She moves her fingers and thumbs around under the bandages, watching the dressings move while assessing how much movement and grip they provide before the pain is too much. She lifts the sheets and looks down just enough to see that she is wearing a nightdress before lowering them back down and looking around the room again. Spotting the two windows slightly ajar on the far wall of the room, she considers making a run for it, but as she looks back at George, he is smiling at her. 'You need not be worried here, my young lady. For I will not harm you. In fact, it was my friends and I who fixed your hands and helped to clean you up. I have to say, you were in a bit of a mess.'

'Where am I?' she asks.

'You, my dear, are in a guest room on my farm.'

The girl spots the water jug on the bedside table with a glass by it. She reaches for it but touches it with the tip of her thumb and grimaces with pain.

George quickly stands up as the girl dives under the sheets to hide from him. 'I did not mean to scare you; I was just getting you a glass of water,' he comments, pouring the water and holding it out to her.

Slowly, the sheets move, and the girl peeks out from under them to look at him. After a while, a bandaged hand reaches out for the glass, takes hold of it and disappears back under the sheets. It is only a few seconds before the empty glass reappears for a top-up. George fills the glass back up, and again it disappears below the sheets before returning empty. This time, the young lady places it back on the bedside table before retracting the arm and falling asleep. Around an hour later, the girl stirs again from her slumber. As she looks about, George is still in his chair watching her. She begins to sit up, wriggling and using her hands as best she can to better position herself.

'How long have I been here?'

'Best part of three days now.'

She thinks a bit and then asks, 'What day is it, sir?'

'Why it be the afternoon of the twenty-fifth of September.'

The girl is a little shocked as she calculates things in her head. 'That would mean I have been travelling for a little over five weeks so far.'

'Five weeks travelling with hands like that?'

The girl tries to work out the timescale in her head. 'No! I was captured by them some three weeks ago. They caught up with me on the road and were taking me back. That night they were drinking heavily. He said I needed to be punished for the inconvenience I caused and that he was going to administer his own retribution. He grabbed me like a wild animal, tearing at my clothes and forcing himself on me. But I fought him off. Biting, kicking and scratching at him until he fell down drunk and eventually left me alone. The next day I got away from them and made it to a village inn, but they were waiting for me. They put me in cuffs and dragged me behind a horse until dusk. That night they hung me up in a tree by the chains. It was then that he came at me again. I was so tired when he dragged me into the woods, and I could not fight him off like before. I tried but just did not have the strength, and he… he… oh God.' The girl starts to cry as she thinks back on what happened. 'When he had finished, he hung me back up and left, saying I deserved it and would get the same treatment every day he was away from home. I just collapsed and hung from those chains until I suppose my hands broke and gave way, pulling them through the cuffs. I woke sometime later, got up and fled into the woods. This time I did not stop moving, stayed off the roads and hid from anyone I saw. They didn't catch up with me again, but I was lost, and it took a while to reach the village. That was the day I got in trouble. I was so hungry I could not help myself; I went into the village to see if there was anything I could get to eat.'

She pauses to think about what she did next before continuing, clearly upset and ashamed of what she had done. 'I am not a bad person, honest. But I was so weak and hungry. I desperately needed food, but my hands would not work, and I kept dropping the things that I took from the stalls. I did not want to steal, honest! I am not that kind of person, but what else could I do? And who could I trust to ask for help? So scared was I, when more and more people started chasing, then something hit me. It all became a bit grey and confusing for a while until I saw a wagon wheel and I held on to it. Now I wake up here, I know not how or why.'

George smiles at her. 'That is another story, but for now you must be very hungry, as it has been several days since you last ate anything.'

The girl pauses before speaking. 'A little, but I have no money to pay you. They took all I possessed when they captured me.'

He looks at her in shock. 'You do not need to pay me for some food. We have plenty to spare. Now you wait just there, and I will sort you something to eat.'

As George opens the door, his young collie Fern squeezes through the gap and runs into the room. She jumps onto George's armchair, spins around and lies down, watching the girl with total focus.

'Pay no mind to my young Fern. She's been dying to see you for days.' Having noticed the way his guest looked at the window,

George thinks better of leaving the room. 'Cook,' he calls. 'Any chance of some food for the lass? For she be brave enough to sample your cooking.'

He closes the door and returns to his armchair. He can see that the girl wants to stroke Fern but does not know if she should. 'If you want her to come to you, just call her by her name. She would be very obliging, given the chance.'

The girl looks at the dog. 'Fer—'

Before her name is even finished, the dog leaps to the bottom of the bed, crawls up the sheets and rests her head on the girl's lap, ready to be stroked. The young lady readily obliges as best she can with her hands in such a condition.

'It seems to me that the proper thing to do now would be to have an introduction. So do you think it is about time you told me your name?'

The girl looks at him, still stroking the dog. 'My name is Jennie. Jennie Meadows.'

'Well, hello, Jennie. It is nice to make your acquaintance. My name is G—'

The door opens and Cook walks in with a tray in her arms. Instantly, the dog jumps up and faces her, hackles up and showing her teeth in an attempt to protect her new friend.

Cook takes no prisoners. She flicks the dog out the way, forcing her to jump back on the chair, as she places the tray across Jennie's lap. 'It's nice to finally see you are up, my dear. I am Cook and I have some nice chicken stew and fresh bread for you here. So, tuck in and I will be back later to check your hands.'

Cook nods at George as she leaves the room. Now that she has seen the girl awake, there is something about her that she recognises. It's gone for now, but she will remember by the time she returns, she is sure of it.

Jennie struggles to hold the spoon with the bandages wrapped round her hands.

'Shall I take them off for now?' George asks in a gentle quiet voice.

She nods her head, and he slowly undoes the strips of cloth. Jennie looks at her hands and moves her fingers and thumbs.

'Who fixed whatever was wrong with them?'

'Your thumbs and a couple of fingers were dislocated, and it was Cook, the woman who was just here, who put them back in place. She is an amazing woman with unlimited talents, and we are so glad she is with us.'

Jennie picks up the spoon and starts to eat the stew. She is very careful with the way she eats, so as not to put pressure on her hands, but being so hungry there is a compromise between eating and the pain. George watches as she polishes off the stew and bread in just a few minutes.

'Do you want some more?' he asks as he removes the tray from her lap.

'No, thank you, not just now. But perhaps you could help me. I am looking for someone, and as you live in the area, maybe you would know him.'

George looks at her. 'I have lived here many years, so I do know a great many of the people nearby and further afield.'

'I am looking for a man named George Todd. Have you heard of him? Or better still, know where he might be found?'

George looks at her and plays the situation carefully. 'The name does ring a bell, but why would a young girl like you be looking for a man like him?'

'I am hoping he can help me find some people. I was informed some time ago that he might know the whereabouts of two people – Victoria and Springer from Pippinsford village. I have something for them, something from a friend who could not bring it themselves as they are no longer with us.'

Her eyes start to fill up again as she remembers it was her mistake that cost Edward his freedom and left him in captivity. The recollection of Edward's younger brother's last moments, watching the life slip from his body as they bundled him into a sack, then seeing Edward disappear down the tunnels, is too much for Jennie. Tears flow down her face and her emotions get the better of her.

Ever since that fateful day, she has slowly lost all her friends to the factory and underground caves. Before she left on this last desperate attempt to find help from Victoria and Springer, she watched as her father give up her best friend Georgia and her family after she confided in him. He sent her younger brother, Oscar, abroad to who-knows-where just for standing up for her and refusing to obey his instructions. Never has she been so alone in her whole young life: abandoned and betrayed by her family, abused and violated by those that hunted her down. If anybody knows how Edward felt in those last months of his life, it is Jennie. For she is now living the very same nightmare he went through.

After months of fighting those people, living on the edge of fear and with the loss of her friends, she now finally breaks down. Sobbing her heart out on a bed in a stranger's house, utterly broken in body and will. George moves forward and comforts her, holding the girl in his arms. He is also affected by her breakdown, for he is beginning to think she is a victim of the same fate as his brother and the rest of his family.

As she slowly begins to regain some composure, he speaks. 'Jennie, listen to me, I was trying to tell you earlier, my name IS George Todd. You have found me.'

She continues to cry as she grips him a little tighter. Then, after taking several deep breaths to calm herself, she relaxes and allows him to sit back up. 'Are you really George Todd?' she asks, wiping her eyes with a strip of bandage.

'Well, I have been known by that name for sixty-odd years, so I think I am sure by now.'

Jennie steadies herself for the big question then calmly asks, 'Do you know the whereabouts of Victoria and Springer? For it is vital that I find them.'

George smiles at her. 'Of course I do. They are without doubt the best friends that I have ever had. I think many around here count it a privilege to know them and have them as friends.'

'Is it possible you could get a message to them from me?'

'Yes, I can do that, but I think it is important that my friends check out your hands first. At the same time, I will also get you another bowl of Cook's stew, for you look like you could do with it.' As he stands up from the side of her bed, Fern takes advantage and leaps from the chair to the bed and lies down with her head on Jennie's lap again. George looks at his dog then back at Jennie. 'That dog does not give her affections lightly and never to anyone when I am around. I'm not sure what has come over her with you. Perhaps she knows something I do not.'

He picks up the empty bowl and walks to the door, then turns around and says, 'I will be back shortly. Please watch over Fern for me.'

Jennie smiles at him and nods as she strokes the dog, scratching the sides of her ears as she turns her head in appreciation. There is a cold, empty feeling inside Jennie, for she may well be near the end of her journey. If so, what does she do next? There is nobody left to care for her. All her friends are dead or missing. And she knows full well that 'missing' means they are also dead or near dead by now. So, what will she do?

The door reopens and George enters. 'Here we go, young lady, another bowl of Cook's chicken stew.' He places the tray on her lap, allowing room for Fern's nose as she refuses to move from the girl's side. As she starts to eat from the bowl, two people enter the room.

'Jennie, do you recognise these two people?' George asks.

She looks up at the man and woman in front of her and shakes her head, then continues to eat her food. Victoria approaches the girl and takes off her locket, opens it and shows the pictures to Jennie. 'Do you know any of these people?' she asks quietly.

Jennie takes the locket carefully and views the pictures closely. Her face instantly saddens as she realises that she is staring at a picture of Edward and Oliver. Looking back at Victoria, she nods her head.

'Could you lift up the tray, please?' she asks quietly.

Springer obliges and puts the tray on a side table. Jennie sits up and puts her legs out of the bed, then stands and staggers over to the sideboard, picks up the small rag doll and passes it to Victoria.

'Inside its stuffing,' she says as she sits back down on the bed and wriggles back under the sheets.

Victoria puts her fingers in the small nick and pulls out a marble. Rolling it in her hand, she notices the marks making the letter E scratched into it. Jennie watches Victoria as she takes a breath. 'You are their missing sister Victoria,' she says, then turns her head towards Springer. 'Which means you are Springer.'

Springer nods as he holds Victoria in his arms. 'That be me, and this here woman be my beloved Victoria, sister to them there youngerns.'

Jennie continues. 'Under the wagon that I held on to, I wedged something into the floorboards. It was Edward's. He asked me to get it to you as it might help save people.' Her face saddens as she looks down at the bed. 'But that was some time ago and I don't think there is anyone left to save now. They are all gone. Edward, Oliver, their friends, all my friends. There's nobody left but me.'

Victoria is taken aback. 'What do you mean, all gone? All gone where? What happened to Edward and Oliver?'

Jennie takes a minute or so to compose herself, then starts to explain. 'I do not know how it began as my involvement started much later. But Edward and Oliver worked out that their friends who supposedly left the village so suddenly with their families had in fact disappeared. I do not know how, but they found out where they were being kept and by whom.'

Jennie looks up at Victoria. 'They were the ones going out at night with their school friends, stealing food and clothes in the village to give to those trapped in the sewers and tunnels below the streets. Not thieves or murderers, but children trying to get food and provisions for their friends as they had no way of getting them out of their imprisonment. They had nobody to go to for help as everybody of influence was involved, including their own parents. I know as my own father betrayed my best friend and her family when I confided in him for help. All any of us could do was try and keep them alive as best we could.' She bursts into tears and cries profusely as Victoria rushes over to hold her tightly in her arms. 'I led them to Edward; it was me who got him caught. I am so sorry, but I did not know what was going on at the time.'

Cook and Dan have been outside the doorway while Jennie has been talking. They now both move into the room as they heed what has been spoken and stand behind Springer.

After a few minutes of comfort from Victoria, Jennie continues to explain how there were eight of them to start with in Edward's group, but she only knew Edward and a girl named Susan personally. His other friends she had only seen by sight or from others talking about them. Oliver was not known to her until his final moments as she was new to the area, and he had already been removed from the school. She continues to explain how she herself had started with seven of her friends, but one by one they were caught or sent away by their parents, while trying to do the same thing as Edward and his friends.

'Do you know what happened to my brothers?' asks Victoria.

Jennie nods, as more tears run down her face as she explains, 'I was with them at the end. I watched behind metal bars when they came and grabbed them in the darkness. Edward begged me to be quiet or they would see us. He wanted me to see who was involved and for you to have his diary. So, I had to watch everything until they took them away. Edward said the diary would help to save the village and the people in it.'

Between floods of tears and more than a few pauses as she breaks down, Jennie goes on to explain about Oliver being on Edward's lap, calling for his mother, the condition of Edward with all his injuries, the little girl and her grandmother who were kidnapped and the role that Brannigan and Sykes played as they took Oliver in a sack and dragged Edward away. Jennie holds nothing back, explaining everything to them. Even the part she unwittingly played in the capture of Edward as he tried to help his brother and got cornered in the building they got changed in.

'Oh God,' Victoria yells. 'My baby brothers! Why did they not tell me? I would have gone back for them had I known the truth.'

Springer looks to Cook, who rushes in to take Victoria from his arms. Springer then turns, walks past George and out of the room. He leans against the doorframe for a moment to think. Tears flow from the rock of a man as he moves off towards the kitchen. Instinctively, George leaves and follows him down the hall. 'Don't be stopping me, my old friend. I be needin' some air afore I leave.'

He grabs Springer by the arm. 'I will not stop you, because I'm going with you, but we need a plan.'

For the first time in his life, Springer walks into the kitchen, places his hands down on the kitchen table and breaks down. 'Did you hear what them there bastards done to them youngerns? I said I would be there for them there boys should I be needed and now they be gone.' Even for such a hardened man, the thought of Edward and Oliver suffering cuts deep into Springer's soul. He goes to open the kitchen door but does not lower the handle enough. In sheer frustration, he leans on it with his forearms, brings up his knee and rips it off its hinges, throwing it to the ground outside with a crash before stepping out into the yard. George is right behind him, following his friend until he stops.

Springer turns, holds George's shoulders and tries to keep his emotions together, but it is to no avail. He drops to his knees. 'I swear to thee I will tear life from limb from all that be doing wrong in that place. But Brannigan and Sykes, they will feel a pain that when I be finished even hell will refuse me a place for such will be my reckoning.'

George, who is also distraught, thinks with a slightly clearer mind. 'Let's go get that diary, my friend. Perhaps that will help us with what we do next.' He helps Springer upright and walks him to the barn. It only takes a few moments to reach the wagon and Springer is under it like a shot. He finds the gap in the boards where the diary wrapped in a piece of cloth has been wedged.

He removes the sheet to reveal a blue diary. He is tempted to open it, but also realises it should be left to Victoria to read first as it belonged to her brother. 'Would you give this to Victoria? For I be needin' to be left alone.' He stares blankly into the distance. 'I think it be time I finished repairing that there stone wall in my meadow. The stones be a right size and I could do with letting off some steam.'

George pats him on the shoulder. 'You go and start that, my boy, and I will deliver the diary. But I think I might also join you and start from the other end.'

* * *

It's been several hours since Jennie revealed the terrible events, and it is well after dark when Victoria walks across the meadow to see Springer. In the pale light of the moon, she can see several men working on the wall at all distances along its length. Springer is lifting and laying the larger boulders in the middle of the wall. His shirt is off, and he is dripping with sweat that reflects in the light from the lanterns on sticks around him. He is pushing himself beyond what any normal man should be able to do with the heavy rocks.

News of Jennie and what had been going on in Pippinsford has spread fast amongst all the farmhands who now reside on George's estate. Most of them, originally being from the village themselves, feel the shame like Springer for the loss of friends, family and the children. All the men of the farm are working along the wall, filling in the gaps and levelling up while George is ensuring everything is as good as he did it nearly thirty years ago. Victoria is fully aware the men will not drop tools until their friend Springer stops, as they will not leave his side while he is so angry and full of remorse.

To an extent, they all feel his anger as well, as most of them come from Pippinsford and all of them and their families have been mistreated – with most losing their family homes through eviction, or who have friends that left without goodbyes, never to be seen again.

She stands in front of her man as he turns to pick up another large boulder. He is breathing heavily, and his eyes are blank as he stares motionless at the next rock. 'It's time to stop, my dear,' she says. 'The men are tired, and they will not relent without you being the first.'

Springer says nothing. He just stands there blank to the world. A minute or so passes and still he stands. Tears roll down his face again, but still he does not move. Finally, he speaks. 'I failed them there youngerns, my dear. Let them down when they be needin' me all the more.'

Victoria puts her hands on his shoulders. 'No. My brothers

loved you and they did what they thought was the right thing. They called it their "quest" and did what they could to help others for months. I have read all the entries in Edward's diary, along with the additions Jennie put in. All the parents allowed their children to be removed from society, so they could have a better life for themselves – including my own mother and father. Those children showed more decency and maturity than their own families. Put their lives on the line many times for what they believed in.'

Victoria is upset as she thinks about her brothers and all the others who she knew and are now gone. 'You have no right to blame yourself for what others have done.' She looks round at the men who are now crowding round her. 'My baby brothers cared for the people of Pippinsford and fought the corruption Lord Fitzgerald brought with him. It cost them their lives, as it has cost all of you something as well. Now this is our home and we have made a new start, a good start. All of us have fine lives through our own hard work. Can we not just leave the past behind and live going forward? We cannot bring these people back, no matter what any of us would like to do. They are gone from us.'

Springer looks at her, then all the men around them, still breathing heavily. 'I be done here. Thank thee kindly for your help,' he says as he picks up his shirt.

There are several sighs of relief as the hard work is finally over. All the men stood by their friend when he needed them around him but are exhausted and relieved that it is over. They collect their belongings and quietly head off to their homes on the different parts of the estate.

George walks with Springer and Victoria to their cottage. 'I've been thinking about this while on the wall. Jennie has nothing to go back home to or anywhere else to go. I was going to offer her a place here on the farm if she would like it. Bebe and I think that between us we could give her a good place to stay. What do you think?'

Victoria smiles at him. 'It's a wonderful thought and an offer that I doubt she would refuse. But it will not be easy to bring up a resourceful teenage girl. You would have your work cut out. Not to mention that you will have to set rules and stand by them, even when she does not agree with what you say. It would be a challenge for you, that's for sure. But if anyone could do it, without doubt it would be you, George, and we would support you all the way.'

George nods. 'I think I will speak with her and offer the proposition when I return from my trip.'

Victoria stops and looks at him. 'Trip? What do you mean, trip?' she asks in a stern voice.

George looks at her with a smile. 'Ease up there, Victoria. It's late September. You know, the time I go up north to buy more livestock for the estate. I go every year, but this time it will be a few more animals, as some of the working tenants want me to purchase some animals for them as well as for myself and Springer. You remember, I went last year and brought back those big red Highland cattle, Gloucester Old Spot pigs and some black turkeys.'

She thinks for a moment, remembering a little about the trip they made as she has two of the Highland cattle in her own meadow grazing, but the time of year eludes her. With what has gone on in the last few days, she is suspicious of what the men in her life might do next and is cautious of the idea. 'When do you intend to leave? And how many of you are going?' she asks.

'Well, let me think… Springer, Dan and myself, four others with a wagon for the pigs, turkeys and supplies. Then four more on horseback to drive the cattle, sheep and whatever else we need all the way back from the stock farms up north. As for leaving, I reckon the sooner the better, as it will keep Springer's mind occupied and hopefully calm him down after all that we have just been told. I think we should aim to prepare everything tomorrow and leave early the following day, with an intention to be back here six days later with our new stock.'

Victoria cannot find fault in the plan, but it seems far too convenient that the trip is organised just after what they have been told by Jennie. As for Springer, he just walks along with them, not saying a word. She hatches a plan of her own to speak to Cook tomorrow and ask her to question Dan and find out if it is all above board. In her mind, there is no way Dan can hold a secret from Cook – she is far too wily and will get the truth out of him.

She turns back to look at George. 'Well, tomorrow I had better see about getting some food together for the journey. I cannot see that you and Springer can survive six days without food in your bellies.'

George nods before leaving the two of them to head back to his farmhouse. He has a lot on his mind and even forgets to say goodbye as he turns away. Even so, Victoria and Springer stop at the gate to their land and watch him walk away until he is out of sight before they enter their own cottage and close the door.

CHAPTER 8

The Secret's Out

It's the morning of the cattle drive and the men are finishing offloading the wagon with supplies for the journey. Four horses are saddled, and wives, girlfriends and family are saying goodbye to their loved ones as their men ready themselves to purchase animals from the stock farms up north.

Victoria, Jennie and Bebe are with George and Springer, talking about the journey and what they have packed in the way of food for them. Victoria passes Springer a hand-drawn miniature sketch of Victoria with the two children. 'Take this with you, my dear. One of the farmhands drew it for me. It is a very good likeness of the children and me.'

Springer looks at it, turns it over and reads the inscription she has put on the back. 'Forever yours, Victoria.' He smiles and then kisses her goodbye before placing the picture in his pocket.

Further up the track, Cook and Dan are alone, deep in a conversation about the trip. Cook has her serious face on and is pointing at Dan, shaking her finger at him as she talks in a stern voice. 'Don't you be getting in any bother, you hear? It's taken nearly ten years for us to have a place to call home and now we are here, I sure's hell do not want to lose you.'

Dan looks towards the others to see if they are ready to leave, angering Cook, who clips him round the top of his head for looking away from her. 'Are you listening to me? Just get it done and come home, you hear? Finish it for good this time and let this be the end to it.' She grabs her man and hugs and kisses him before she turns and walks with him towards the horses.

George, Springer and Jethrow are already mounted up as Dan gets to his horse, steps up over the saddle and corrects his riding position. They wave as they turn their horses and move off, closely followed by the wagon with the four men on board. They are watched by their families and friends as they move off up the track and onto the road that sweeps around to the left and disappears behind high hedgerows.

The group follow the road for around half an hour before George leads them down a small tree-lined path into an opening beside a wooded area. There, hidden in the bushes waiting for them are three of George's neighbours on horseback. 'Hello there, my old friends,' George calls out as they approach.

'Just like you to be exactly on time, George,' one of them says as he raises his hand. George introduces his party to the Underwoods. Brothers Robert and Bill and their father, Ernie, are George's oldest farming tenants, leasing near three hundred acres on the far side of the village for the past twenty or so years. George charges them less than half what he could for the land, but he is not greedy, and they use the land well, which is all he ever wants from his tenants. 'It's good to see you, Ernie, and the boys look well. Seem to grow bigger every time I see them.'

Ernie smiles. 'Aye, that they do. Near eat me and the wife out of house and home these days,' he says with a huge amount of pride.

'I appreciate your help on these matters. Here is the wagon and supplies, along with four good men to help bring the stock back. Young Ivan is the driver, and a good shot should you come across some game on the way.' Ernie flicks his hand in the air at George. 'I be owing you more than I can ever repay, George. I am only glad to be of assistance. Anyway, it gives us a chance to get a couple of animals for ourselves. A few pigs and a few dozen new hens would not go amiss, even a new bull if we can find one as good as your old Winston, for that bull is a legend in these parts after what he did.'

'Well, we are on a tight schedule and must go, as we have a long way to travel. God willing, I will meet you back here six days from now, old friend,' George says, passing Ernie a thick money belt. 'Use what you need to get the animals I have asked for and don't be afraid to top up your own poke should you find a good bull and the price a little high. Add one for me if they look top quality and have a size to them.' He shakes Ernie's hand and turns his horse to leave.

'I know better than to ask, George, but I wish you well with all that you be up to and come back safe,' Ernie says as he watches the four men ride away.

Springer has already taken a large bag full of supplies from one of the men in the wagon as he passed by. He now lays it over the front of his saddle as they make their way back onto the main road.

The four men take to a mixture of walking, trotting and the odd canter to get the best time and distance out of their mounts without wearing them out. They are careful not to push too hard and incur injury or throw a shoe as that would delay them and there is no time to spare. Conversation is sparse as each man contemplates what will happen in the coming days. For this is going to be a particularly bloody and violent affair and they will need to always have their wits about them if they want to survive.

Finally, after several hours, George turns to Springer. 'I have waited for this to happen for a long time, my friend. It hasn't come about in the best of ways, but it was always going to happen at some stage.'

Springer has barely spoken to anyone in days. He looks at George with eyes that would put the fear of God into the devil himself. 'I have an anger in me that be fit to burst. I think on them there youngerns, Oliver and Edward, constantly. The suffering they be forced to endure by them that are wicked and evil beyond reproach. What they did to that there lass, Jennie, it shames me as a man to have stood by and not took to arms sooner.' He thinks for a moment as he calms himself down and settles his rage inside. 'Promise me, George, that what I do in the here and now will never be mentioned to my Victoria. For what Brannigan and Sykes along with them there others of low standing are about to receive will give her many a bad night's sleep.'

George reaches over and puts his hand on Springer's shoulder.

'I think that goes without saying, my boy. But how is this all going to play out? Do you have any sort of plan from here on out? Or are we just going to trust in fate when we get there?'

'There be a plan alright, but it be in my head for now. Saying that, tonight will be a cold night by the fire with nowt but the stars for a roof. Come the morrow we call on old friends of mine and Dan's for hopefully a warm barn and some hot food. That is, if the good lady of the house so wishes it. Then it be time for that there Dan to weave his magic and dangle a bait to trap a fool.'

George nods as they up the pace and ride on at a canter, continuing until an hour before dusk. Then, at a small wooded area fifty or so yards from the road, they make camp. With two long logs to sit on, good grass on the ground for the horses and a fast-flowing brook within a few yards. It is an ideal location that has been used for this purpose many times before, judging from the ring of stones that mark an old campfire.

Springer strips down the horses and picks out their hooves, giving them a once-over to ensure no problems are evident, while George rubs them down with a brush and tethers them to a rope between two trees, giving them enough line to feed on what lies around them.

Dan sets a fire and starts to boil water, the pot being the one he has always carried with him when poaching. He believes it to be lucky and brings good fortune when used. Getting some food out from the sack, he finds nine tightly wrapped muslin bags about two inches round with a length of string attached to the top of each one. He turns to George. 'What the hell are these things?' he asks, throwing one in his direction.

George catches it and gives it a sniff then laughs. 'Dan, it could only be your wife and my cook who would do this for me! It's tea. If you want to make that boiling water into tea, just drop a couple of these in the water for five minutes or so. No doubt there will be sugar and a vessel of milk in that bag as well.'

Dan rummages around in the bag and sure enough he finds both items. 'Well I'll be! Looks like we will be drinking like proper gentlemen tonight rather than nettles and pine needles in water.'

He tosses two of the balls into the heating water and looks for something to drink from in the food sack.

Jethrow cuts some willow branches from the nearby trees to act as insulation from the ground and spreads them around between the two logs and the fireplace. With all the duties done, they settle down around the fire for some food and scoops of tea they pull out of the pot as required.

'I wonder what the place looks like now,' Jethrow says. 'Do you think there be anyone left who we know from the old days? For it's been nearly a year and a half for some of us, and even longer for others.'

Dan speaks up. 'Words from some of my contacts say Lord Fitzgerald has continued in his conquering ways. Buying up people's homes, knocking them down and rebuilding larger houses in their places then selling them on to city folk. Even started to stretch out into the little village of Baddow View to take over the wool dyeing and cleaning sheds, much to the detriment of the people who once lived there. Take poor old Ma Jessup. She was found murdered in her kitchen and her husband was convicted and hung for the deed. The land and all the sheds somehow ended up in Lord Fitzgerald's hands, while their three sons were never seen again.'

'Would have taken more than a few to put her down. She could probably take even you in an arm wrestle, Springer,' says Jethrow. 'I've watched her carrying two rams at a time to them sheds, and I mean carry, not drag. We always thought she slung her husband on her shoulder and carried him down the aisle and across the threshold. Strong as a bull was that lass.' The men around the fire chuckle as they remember her and her family.

Springer is staring hard at the fire, poking it with a stick. 'I be saying it now so it comes as no shock to thee all later. This be no pleasure trip for me. I be in a fearful rage for what be done to all of them there youngerns and mercy has long since left my ways. My intentions be to end the days of Brannigan, Sykes and them that be alike to those men in one night and be done with that place by the morning. So be fair warned, if thee decide to stay the course, you will be party to the ending of more than one life. For I cannot forgive what they did to young Oliver, Edward and them there others. And it will not go unpunished. They be right deserving of a reckonin', and I intend to be the one to serve it, even if the price be my own as well.'

The group goes silent for a moment as they think on his words before George speaks up. 'Seems that from the day we first met, this has been building to fruition. All here know what is at stake and are prepared to throw in our lot with you. But if you do die on us, and by some miracle we are able to carry such a big, heavy man as yourself all the way home, we will just take you back to Cook, for I'm sure she will have a way of bringing you back to us. So fear not, my boy.'

'I've not seen my Cook perform that miracle yet, but I would not put it past her abilities,' Dan replies with a smile on his face.

The group settle down for the night with a growing anticipation for what the morning holds. All know the danger they will be in when they enter the village tomorrow night, but for now, they pick their spots around the fire and try to get what sleep they can.

* * *

It's dawn the following morning when George begins to stir. He gets up and heads off into the woods to relieve himself before returning to the group. Springer is sitting up and stretching out, while Jethrow is upright and looking around for Dan after noticing his belongings are gone. 'Where's Dan?' he asks.

Springer looks at him with a yawn. 'He be gone near an hour afore ye be awakin'. For he must get the going early and find out about that there man he intends to bait, then make what's needed happen afore we be able to do our part.'

Jethrow has not long woken up, and it takes him a minute or so to work out what Springer has said. 'Oh, so he has gone ahead then?

The men waste no time getting ready to travel. Within thirty minutes the horses are tacked up and ready to go. After one last kick of the embers to ensure the fire is fully out, they mount up and get on their way.

They make good time during the day, keeping to their strategy of walking, trotting and the odd canter. By late afternoon, they are at the track leading down to Bull Farm. 'We be here,' comments Springer.

'Bob and Emily run this here farm with their son, Robert. They be a good sort with no love for Lord Fitzgerald, that's for sure.'

As they approach, a young man is sitting on the cross poles of the fence at the entrance to the farmyard. Moving closer, Springer makes out that it is Robert. 'Afternoon, young Robert,' he says. 'By God, ye be grown near a foot into a full-size man since I last set eyes on you! How be thee on this fine day?'

Robert laughs. 'Better than you three will be. Dan said you would be only an hour behind him. It's been nearly three and Ma's been keeping some food hot on the stove for an age now.' He hops off the fence as the three men dismount. 'I will take your horses and tend to them while you head to the house and see her.' He collects their reins and walks the mounts to the large barn while the three men move off towards the farmhouse. As they approach, the door opens, and three collies run out. They check out each of the men in turn with excitement and vigour but instantly make a beeline for the crouching George. He does not disappoint them, stroking and making a fuss of each one. 'These be a fine set of working dogs,' he says as he strokes them all with an even distribution of attention.

'Here,' calls Emily and the three dogs turn and bolt for the door and rotate inside the entrance to face their guests, lined up abreast. Emily walks up to Springer and puts her arms out to give him a hug. 'It's been too long, my dear. How are you? And more importantly, how is that young lady of yours?'

As she holds him in her arms, he speaks. 'She be fine and busy looking after our youngerns.'

Emily's jaw nearly hits the ground. 'You have children?'

'Aye, that we do. A boy named Edward and a little girl named Molly.'

A huge smile appears on her face. 'Well, I be blowed, and when, may I ask, will I get a chance to see these fine offspring of yours then?'

Before Springer has a chance to answer, Emily turns her attention to the others. 'You must be George and you are Jethrow, from the descriptions Dan gave me.' She looks hard at Jethrow. 'I've seen you before. I know you from somewhere, but I cannot quite put my finger on it.'

'You have a good memory and a better eye, for you and Bob purchased fruit trees from the estate I once worked on. But that would have been many a year ago.'

She thinks for a minute. 'That would be Steven Todd's old place. I remember it well! You and Steven came all the way over here to help plant our trees and advise us on how and when to prune them. Well, it is a small world, I must say! And it is good to see you again, and still alive. For there be many that say all who lived in that old barn in the woods have long since gone from this world.'

Springer adds to the conversation. 'The world is even smaller than thee think, Emily, for this here be Steven's brother, George Todd. A good man by all accounts. Jethrow, and those that thee be thinking gone, live and work on his estate. Make a fine team and good life for them and their kin now they have been given a fair chance.'

George smiles and tips his cap. 'It is a pleasure to meet you. And what a fine set of working collies you have there.'

She looks back at her pack of black-and-white canines. 'Oh yes, they are as good as you can get and work as hard as you push them. Could not want for a better team for rounding up stock in the fields. As for the lead dog, Flash, he heard you approaching and gave warning near five minutes ago.'

George smiles. He loves dogs and has a soft spot for working Border collies. 'What word do you use to set them off?'

Emily laughs. 'If I say that word, you would be no longer a friend to them.'

'True, true,' says George as he nods his head. 'For mine it be the word R-A-B-B-I-T-S, and with that they take up a guard position and await instruction. Though in recent years I have been trying to add D-A-N, so I can try and keep an eye on that illusive man.'

Emily bursts into laughter then steps forward and leans towards George's ear. 'I use the word F-O-X-E-S,' she says before stepping back. 'And the last time I used it in anger, it was against a certain acquaintance of ours and he near shit himself. Well, to be more precise he decided not to step off his horse and take me on. For our boy Flash and his companions did not take kindly to him, and nor should they.'

Hearing his name, Flash shoots out of the doorway and sits beside Emily, closely followed by the other two, who sit down behind him.

'Please come inside the house. I've had some food on the stove ever since Dan dropped his horse off and gave us a warning you were on your way. Funny though, he would not say why you would risk coming back to this neck of the woods, Springer. Just that you would be arriving and need food on your way through to somewhere else.' She leans down and strokes Flash on his head and shoulders before continuing. 'I had heard bad things about what went down on your brother's farm, George. Also, for those that were loyal and worked there on the estate like you, Jethrow. Being evicted and forced to live in that old barn in the woods was not right. For that I am truly sorry as I know only too well the levels that man will stoop to in his drive to get what he wants. The extremes to which he is willing to go to satisfy his greed and ambitions are well known to me and Bob.' She lowers her head as sadness starts to take hold.

George steps forward and gently lifts her chin back up. 'My dear, thank you for your kind words on my brother. I am under no illusions over what happened to him and his family. I also know who is responsible for their fate and am aware I will not be seeing Steven or his family again in this lifetime, the same as you will not see your father.'

Emily looks at him sharply before turning to Springer.

'Yes, my dear, Springer did tell me of your family's fate when

I wanted to rush in for revenge without thinking. At the time I was not ready or prepared for the occasion, just angry and full of rage. He explained to me that others had been waiting a lot longer than I for the right to claim satisfaction and that we needed to wait until the time was right. As always with Springer, he was right at the time, but fate has now shown its hand and it seems that the time has come for action to be taken. More so after the arrival of a young girl called Jennie at my estate. She had suffered horrendous injuries and abuse and travelled for weeks in that awful condition to find Victoria and Springer. In her possession was a diary belonging to Victoria's little brother, Edward. His last wish was that it be delivered to his sister and Springer as it contained information that could help save some of the people living in Pippinsford.'

Emily raises a wry smile and a nod. 'Let's get you warmed up and some hot food in you, then we can talk some more afterwards.' She takes the lead, moving the party into the house with Flash ever by her side. Through into the kitchen they go, and she offers her guests seats round the large table. She wastes no time dishing out large bowls of hot stew to the three men, then places down a whole loaf of warm homemade bread and a stick of her finest butter. 'Now eat up. I have plenty more on the stove should you be needing it.'

The men heartily tuck into the meaty offering, breaking bread and dipping it into the juice as Springer speaks up. 'And where be your old man? Surely, he be not delivering this late in the day?'

'He would have been here to greet you himself, but I sent him on his way to finish the groundwork for our piggery as I want it up and running for next year to bring in more income. It would seem the need for bacon, chops and legs of pork are in high demand around here and I want us to be taking advantage of every opportunity that comes along. So, we have started building an eight-pen piggery for sows with an enclosed hut for each animal and a back door to deal with farrowing and delivering their piglets.'

Before any of them have a chance to speak, the front door clicks open, and they can hear the sound of boots being pulled off on a boot hook. Within a few minutes, Bob and his son appear in the kitchen. He has a huge smile on his face as he sees Springer for the first time in more than a couple of years and wastes no time in shaking his hand before hugging him. 'They never found you then, my friend. I cannot say in words how good it is to see you again.'

'It be damned good to be seeing you again too. Come the morrow, things may change enough and ye be free to pay us the honour of visiting our farm, for she sure is a sight to be seen, cut back in a valley an' all.'

Springer introduces George and Jethrow to Bob and his son Robert as they also sit down for some stew. Finally, with all the people served, Emily takes her place at the table and starts to eat with them.

While they are eating and talking, George cannot help but hear the quiet whimpering and scratching at one of the doors leading off from the kitchen. Finally, he asks, 'Do you have a giant mouse or something in that room?'

Bob laughs as he gets up, ushers his three dogs into the hallway and closes the door. 'No. Something far worse than that. It's an Oscar.'

George looks at him with a puzzled expression. 'An Oscar? What is one of those? If you do not mind me asking.'

'It's not a what. It's a who.' As he opens the door, a four-month-old puppy comes bounding out of the room. Wild-eyed and so excited to see everyone, it dribbles a little wee on the floor as it runs around from person to person, thrashing its tail and spinning in circles between the chairs. Soon it is with George and desperate for every bit of attention it can get from him, something he is only too willing to share with the puppy.

'It be from Flash and Hazel's first mating together; we had a litter of six and I decided to keep the best-looking one as I was planning for a future working dog. But Flash and the others are but four and five years old themselves. They don't take too kindly to this one jumping around everywhere and pouncing on them all the time. Flash has started to take offence to him and has pinned him down twice already, while the chickens have all but stopped laying eggs due to him constantly rounding them up and moving them round the yard all day.

'So reluctantly I must keep them apart. In the long term, I now realise it was too soon for another, but he has such potential that I am struggling with the fact that he will need to go, and I must wait a few years before considering keeping another one for the pack.'

George thinks for a minute before replying. 'I seem to have the opposite problem. I kept two from my last litter. One bitch is with Springer and Victoria on their farm, and the other is my Fern. The parents of these two puppies are getting on a bit now and in the last year or so of their working use before I retire them. Winter hits them hard now and they are a little stiff in the limbs during the cold months when I use them most. If you were in a mind to let Oscar go to a working estate, I would be willing to pay for him or return a pair of puppies in a few years from now after a mating between him and my Fern. It would be a good way of introducing a new blood line into both sets of dogs, for they are also working Border collies.'

Bob thinks on the offer for a while. 'What do you think, Emily?'

She looks at the rascal as it continues to leap and bound about the place, still full of excitement and wonder. 'Well, if he stays here, I fear our boy Flash will put him in his place and that might be fatal for him. But also, I will not take money from a friend of Springer's. Oscar would be going to a working farm, and I think the offer of a pair of puppies in a few years' time would be a worthy investment for our farm's future. I would say yes. It is a good offer and a worthwhile trade for both sides. But we would have to come visit and collect them, as I could do with looking forward to visiting Victoria and their children in the future.'

'Children? What children?'

'Be true, Bob. Victoria and I have two youngerns now, a lad and a lass, and they be a fine pair.'

Bob has a huge smile on his face as he gets up and shakes Springer's hand. 'Well, don't that top all! Springer and Victoria with children, who would have thought it?' He turns to George. 'The wife said it how it is. It be a deal on the puppies as trade for Oscar.'

George willingly accepts, but as he is shaking his hand, he does comment in a sceptical tone, 'Mind you, it does depend on the outcome of the next couple of days, for the events about to unfold could change all our fortunes.'

Bob looks at him. 'Well, that does drive me to ask the next question, why are you all here? And what is all this about the next couple of days? Dan was right prickly when I asked him of your return to the area, young Springer.'

George looks in the direction of Emily and Robert. 'Do you think it is right to talk about this in front of Bob's wife and son, Springer?'

Emily gives George a serious frown and Robert stops eating to look up as Springer speaks. 'I be thinking that for a while, but with all having suffered in loss and hiding like us for years in the shadows of evil, it would be poor and wrong not to explain, especially with us being guests an' all. We be putting them in harm's way, just by being here. So, aye, they be deserving of the knowin'.' He pauses to think his words through before continuing. 'That there man Fitzgerald and his men have killed, imprisoned and murdered many a good family. Caused enough suffering and wrongdoing to more than I can count these past few years. More than a dozen youngerns, including my Victoria's little brothers, Edward and Oliver, have been put to passing. For doing what us adults should have done years past. Them there youngerns gave their very lives to try and save their friends from that evil man. I be ashamed when young Jennie turned up all broken and near death, looking for us with stories that tore the good and decentness from my bones and pulled at my very soul.'

Springer goes on to explain about the contents of the blue diary, Edward and Oliver's fate, how the families of the rich put their better standard of living above their children, and what the children had been doing to get food and clothing to the people of the village imprisoned as slave labour to the factory and its mine. He explains what really happened to all the people who sold up and left the village and surrounding area.

Emily has tears running down her face. Bob's eyes are watering and near fit to bursting, while Robert, who knew some of the children, leaves the room as he has heard enough. By the time Springer finishes explaining all that they know, there is not a dry eye in the room.

After a period of quietness from the group, Emily is first to speak up. 'The bastards, I never knew it had got so bad for the people of Pippinsford.' She pauses to wipe the tears from her eyes and blows her nose. 'So, what exactly are you four going to do?' she asks as the tears still flow.

Springer looks at her with such rage on his face. 'Why, I be here to end Brannigan, Sykes and all others that had a hand in them there youngerns' suffering. Not least Lord Fitzgerald, if God be willing. I will rip the very life from their evil bodies, so help me. They will do no more harm to folk I know and love, an' if hell be where I go for doin' what be needin' to be done, I will pay the price to the reaper willingly. For no more will I run or take to hiding from such men, not when youngerns are prepared to do more than grown men should.'

'Do you have a plan, Springer?' Emily asks in a serious voice.

'I know how I be getting the first of them there wrongerns with the help of Dan. I also be knowin' where all the people are below ground who be needin' help to get free. Even knows a secret way to get to them without being seen.'

'How many of them do you think there are to be rescued? And what about disposing of the bodies of the men you remove while covering your tracks so that none find you when you have gone?'

Springer looks at her blankly. 'Well, I will just leave them be where they fall. They be not deserving of anything better in my mind.'

Emily shakes her head. 'No, no, no, Springer. There are many wealthy people in the village now. People with power and influence with the law and able to pull strings in high places. If you do this, you need a better plan and the bodies can never be found, not ever! Theirs and yours, they must be hidden well, as identifying just one of you would risk capture to the rest of us.' She sighs heavily. 'Now you lot eat your food while I go for a walk and think on the matter for a while.' With that she gets up and leaves the room, puts on her coat and departs the house with Flash and the other two dogs tight to her side. She can be seen through the window walking across the yard and into one of the orchards before disappearing amongst the trees.

'I've not seen her this way since we first came out here,' Bob says as he watches her go. 'Then again, I have a fear for all involved when a woman thinks that hard, for they are a vicious breed when they be rattled. And what you see there is the worst of them in the meanest of moods with a mind set on vengeance.'

It's nearly half an hour before Emily returns to the house. Robert has already taken his place back at the table as she walks straight into the kitchen with the dogs in tow. 'Bob, dear,' she says.

'Oh hell,' Bob replies. 'That means she has a plan. That will be more work for me, I'm sure of it.' He receives a glare from his beloved wife as she takes a seat at the table.

'The piggery foundations, where are we with them? Are the footings dug down the two foot and are the broken tiles and bricks for hardcore put in the bottom?'

'Yes. The footings are in, fifteen feet wide by nearly eighty feet long. No, the hardcore is not down – it is in four large piles around the outside of the footings. I will be starting to fill it in tomorrow.'

'Well, that's not going to happen now.'

Bob looks perplexed. 'It's not?'

'No, it's not. I want another trench along the middle, three feet deeper. Three foot wide and forty foot long in the centre of the area.'

Bob looks up at his wife with an open jaw. 'You got to be kidding me.'

Emily looks at him with steely eyes. 'I kid you not. And I want it done by end of play tomorrow night. Get them two worthless labourer friends of yours to help. They have eaten well for the last few months while here picking crops. Now they can do some real work if they want me to feed them again. Tell them it's for drainage and that once they are finished, we will pay them off for this season in full. Explain that we now have family here to conclude the harvest, for we dare not have them around for the next few days with all that be going on.'

Jethrow starts to chuckle, a sight not unnoticed by Emily. 'And what are you laughing at? You're too old to do what needs doing in the village. So you will help my husband dig that trench and help burn those many boxes of oyster shells for making the lime for the mortar.' The chuckle soon turns to a shocked look as the wrath of Emily strikes another blow.

'Robert, you will take the heavy wagon and head towards the village mid-afternoon tomorrow. That means you will arrive a few hours after midnight. Load up any bodies that Springer and George have come across and bring them back here to go in the pit before filling it in and packing the earth down tight with your father.'

She sniggers a bit before speaking again. 'Ironic, isn't it? Going forward, every time our pigs piss and shit, it will be soaking down onto the biggest pigs we have ever known. Weather permitting, by the time George and Springer get back here, we will have the bodies, soil and hardcore down. So, all can help with the mixing and laying of the base. God willing, within a week nobody will ever know where those evil men lie or what happened to them.'

Emily turns her attentions to Springer. 'Well, that's my plan for what we do with the bodies, even though you did not ask for my help. The rest is up to you, young man. Just don't disappoint me as we are digging a big gully and expect to fill it.'

Springer puts his hands out in front of him. 'Easy, lass. I be just the man who be putting right the wrongs done to others. We will leave late tonight; horses best be staying here as they be not the easiest to hide and keep quiet. By morning we be meeting with Dan and can put to use what that there man be working on at present. Now is there a place George and I could put our heads down for a while? For it be a long walk ahead.'

'Emily has already set you up in the back room by the fire,' replies Bob. At the same time Emily gets up and leads them down the hallway, opening a side door into a room with makeshift beds made up ready. She turns to the two men and speaks.

'Listen to me, for I will speak quietly so my husband does not hear my words. It is nearing Lord Fitzgerald's birthday and there is to be a huge gathering tomorrow at his estate. There are many people from far and wide arriving to celebrate with him over the coming weekend. As you would expect, many powerful, influential people will attend. I was sent a letter from a dear friend I knew well from years ago in the days of my father. He may arrive at the village around the same time as you, or already be there. He is big, very big, an ex-whaling man with tribal tattoos on his face and body and as powerful as you, my dear Springer. You may not recognise him as an Englishman, but he was and still is. James is his name, and he is the only surviving male sibling of Lord Fitzgerald after his treacherous plan to have all his brothers killed at sea on whaling ships.

'If the man arrives for his brother's birthday, it will be to give him a fate far worse than any death you could imagine, for it would involve lifelong pain and suffering that will never stop causing problems until his demise. So, if you see him, do not set to him as if he were one of Lord Fitzgerald's protectors, as he will be working his way close, very close to him, so that he can execute an attack.

'Should you meet such a man, mention my name and Bob's and explain your plans to him. If not, just clear the way of all the other enforcers to let him get on with his intentions.'

She looks back down the corridor to ensure nobody is around before continuing. 'I do not want my Bob to know James is coming here, or he will insist on going to help him, for he knew him well. You see, although my husband can stand up to many a man, he is not as strong or as vicious as those you know are waiting for you. I do not think he could live with taking another man's life. It is just not his way.'

Emily steps forward and kisses both men on their cheeks. 'I wish you both well and thank you for finally doing something to rid the world of such evil men. May God understand and grant you both safety and strength to stay the course and protect you in your endeavours,' she says, then leaves Springer and George to their thoughts.

As the two men take off their jackets, George speaks. 'Do you think this man James will show up?'

Springer shakes his head. 'I be doubting it. Besides, I've never heard of a good Fitzgerald. Anyway, let's be getting some rest for there be work enough for the both of us tomorrow.'

The two men settle down. They will need all their wits about them if they are to make good their intentions and leave with their lives intact.

CHAPTER 9

Returning Home

George and Springer emerge from their room a little after ten in the evening. The house is dark and quiet as they put on their boots and jackets. Oscar, the puppy, has been moved to the hallway with his blanket and water bowl to make room for all the additional people in the house. He is excited to see George, but like most collies he does not yap or bark. Instead, he makes lots of facial expressions and jumps around wagging his tail, demanding attention.

George has no problem with supplying the puppy with some affection for a short while before they leave through the kitchen doors and head out of the house as quietly as possible. As they make their way up the track to meet the adjoining road, they can see the outline of a small carriage and a pair of horses. Moving closer, they can see young Robert sitting on the front of the transport lit by two coach lights either side of him. 'What be thee doing here then, young Robert?' whispers Springer.

'Pa thought you might like a lift part of the way. We borrowed this buggy from a friend. It's light and quick, but as Pa cannot see too well at night, he asked me to take you as far as four hours will allow. Then I must turn back and get on with the work around the farm. I've been waiting here to get used to the dark, so get on and let's go,' he says eagerly.

George hops up first, closely followed by Springer. 'Good on your pa, young man,' says George. 'For I was dreading the long walk even though I would have done it.'

Springer gives George a wry smile. 'Them there old bones finally feeling their age, eh, George?'

As Robert flicks the reins to get the horses moving at a good trot, George turns to Springer. 'Certainly not! I just like to store my energy for the challenges ahead. For I am sure there will be a lot to overcome when we get there, and I would sooner not waste it on walking. Besides, it seems to me that the only time I am in danger or mortal peril is when I am doing something with you or Victoria.'

Springer and Robert both chuckle. 'Don't worry, Mr Todd, I will make good my four hours and get you as near as I dare, you being so elderly an' all.'

George leans forward and gives Robert a light clip round the top of his head. 'That be enough of that, my young whippersnapper. It's bad enough the trouble young Springer gets me into, without you adding your bit on me being a more mature gentleman.'

Springer and Robert laugh as they continue down the road, illuminated with only two candles and the pale glow of a half-moon when the clouds part and a gap in the overhanging trees allows. It is a challenge for Robert to keep on the road and make good time, but apart from a few wayward excursions, he makes good his word and such excellent time that within the four hours he is just two miles from the village.

'I think this be close enough, young Robert. Thank thee kindly for saving old George's "mature" bones. Pull up and we be on our way from here.'

Robert grins and slows the horses to a stop, allowing the two men to carefully look around for any people before they disembark. There is a sharp chill in the air and George lifts up his collars and does up the button to keep warm before stepping down.

'Now take it easy going back, young man. You pushed them there horses 'ard to make good time. There be no needin' to push going back. Let them rest a little aways up the track from here. Now fare thee well, and with luck we be seein' you in a day or so,' says Springer as the two men move into the woodland.

Robert watches as they melt into the gloom of the darkness. Just a few moving branches give their position away before they slip into the trees and disappear for good. Now gone from view,

Robert carefully turns the buggy with expert precision and returns home. His first part in this adventure is now complete. For now, the rest is up to Springer and George and the trap being set up by Dan.

The two men walk through the wood for around an hour with Springer leading the way. The trees have begun shutting down for the winter, losing their green canopies in exchange for reds, bronzes and browns. The ground is covered in a carpet of dead leaves, making it hard to spot any obstructions like stumps and roots in the darkness.

George trips over for around the fifth time and yells, 'Are you sure you know where you are going, my boy?' as he gets back to his feet and brushes himself down.

Springer ignores him and continues for another hundred or so yards before he comes to a small clearing that allows the moonlight to peek through. Sniffing the air, he can smell a wood fire, but cannot see any smoke. In the better light, he makes out the shape of a small log cabin tucked tightly into a thicket of scrub. He looks around before heading in its direction, closely followed by George. He pauses at the doorway leading into the cabin, putting his arm out to stop his friend behind. On the ground before the slatted entrance is an empty plant pot. As Springer moves it out of the way, a connected thread rattles another metal box containing stones, highlighting their presence to those inside. Springer is not bothered by the noise and just opens the door and slowly enters the cabin.

It's darker inside and he takes his time looking around. There is a small coke fire in the fireplace, which is why he could smell the fire but not see the smoke – as coke burns with very little smoke, if any.

By the window, a man is moving backwards and forwards on a rocking chair, holding a pipe to his mouth. 'You do know you have walked past this place once already tonight without finding it, don't you?'

Springer chuckles. 'I thought I could smell the Old Hobb burning in your pipe, but I was not sure, Dan.'

On hearing Springer speak, the cautious, crouched George

slowly enters the dwelling. 'Hurry up and close the door, George. You're letting out all the heat.'

George stands upright, closes the door behind him, walks straight over to the fire and starts to warm his hands over the comforting heat. 'If you knew we were out there, you could have at least called to us, you canny old fox,' George says, rubbing his hands together.

Dan looks at him. 'Now that would spoil my fun. Anyway, it gave me time to get your tea on the go.' He points with his pipe towards a pot on the side of the fire.

'There be a jug of milk and sugar on the table behind you and some of them flashy cups or a mug. Take your pick.'

George takes two of the mugs and dips them in the pot to fill them up. As he does so, he notices a bit of string attached to the handle. He lifts it up, pulling a tight muslin ball of tea leaves up with it. 'No need for me to ask where the tea came from, then!' he says with a chuckle.

'I be nowt but a humble gamekeeper and ex-poacher, m'lord. I cannot afford such fineries as tea with what I earn.'

'Dan, there is nothing humble about you, good man, and I know how much you earn as I pay you each month – and that is just what I know of. I shudder to think what you really cost me.' Springer laughs out loud as he knows George still does not know how to handle Dan.

'But, guvnor, don't I make sure your estate runs well and free from them that would take advantage?'

George gives a big sigh. 'Oh yes, better than at any time I can remember. I eat well – fantastic food no matter how many guests or hunting or fishing parties I have in. With Cook's abilities there is always plenty of fresh and cured meat and fish for all. But what Victoria and I cannot work out is how we get all this meat. Enough for us, Victoria, Springer, as well as all the other labourer families on the estate. Yet I cut but a few animals from my own herds. I have barely any bills coming in for fresh meat or fish, let alone all the smoked and cured produce that we eat so regularly, as well as being able to sell the excess.

'I know I don't have a smoke house on my land, so where does it all come from? In fact, if we are reading the numbers right in the ledgers, I am selling more than I produce, even after we have deducted for all of us who live on the estate.'

Springer is starting to laugh louder and louder. 'Ah, yes, well, er, ummm, your land is not the only land with game and fish on it. And if they don't look aft—'

'Oh no, you're not poaching from my friends on the nearby estates, are you? Please tell me that you're not training a secret army of poachers with my farmhands, ghillies, woodsmen and poor Ivan?'

'Well, no, but you wanted me to train them to understand the ways a poacher works, and to do that they have to learn how it is done. Only then can they know what to look for,' replies Dan in a calming voice.

George takes a seat, mopping the sweat from his brow with a white handkerchief, as he thinks about what to do with this man. 'Please assure me there is no way these people can trace their losses back to me.'

Dan smiles. 'Guvnor, there is no way that anyone will notice. It's spread out over several areas and does not affect our neighbours at all.'

'Several,' comments George as he mops his brow faster. 'How big is this network of yours?'

Dan gives him an assured look. 'None of your neighbours are being poached, guv. In fact, much the opposite. For they be some of your better customers, taking all the excess we be having lately. The only people targeted are Lord Fitzgerald and friends of his, with most of the game coming from his very estate right here. Why do you think we know about this cabin and one or two others like it?'

George thinks for a bit. 'Springer! You led me here, so you knew he was poaching Lord Fitzgerald's land!'

'Aye, better to take from the devil who be deserving of Dan's attention than to have Dan working your own land. That there man of ours be needin' to keep his skills sharp. Besides we have

Cook, and when you have Cook you control Dan. Keep Cook happy and Dan will see thee right.'

Dan raises his pipe and tilts his head in agreement.

'Remind me to give Cook a raise when we get back, Springer, for I want her very happy and this man extra contained,' replies George as the other two men laugh at his discomfort.

Dan walks over to the fire, adds two more shovelfuls of coke and pushes it around to mix up the new pieces with the glowing embers.

'Well, it will be three or four hours before we can get the ball rolling, so we might as well get warm and toasty for it is cold and damp in the woods early in the morning.' He returns to his chair by the window and sits down, watching the woods in the foreground and rocking slowly backwards and forwards as he looks for any signs of movement.

Springer takes to the small bed and chucks a spare blanket towards George to wrap round him as he sits in the other chair. 'Get thee some rest, my friend, for it be a long day ahead.'

* * *

Springer wakes George by the shaking of his shoulder. The room is just beginning to fill with daylight as his eyes open and he looks around. 'Here, George, the last of the tea.' He passes George a cup of his favourite brew and then walks over to the window.

'Dan's been gone near an hour now. He will soon be setting the cat amongst the pigeons and putting all in motion.' He turns to George. 'Are ye sure thee wants in on this? Thee can stay here until the doing be done. I will think not the least bit less of you, my friend.'

George drinks deeply from his cup before answering. 'I know time is catching up with me and I am not as strong as I once was. I also know that you have great affection for me as well as a need to avenge what they have done to the children and Victoria's siblings. But I also think of my brother, his wife and my nephews. I need this, my friend. God willing, with you by my side, I will have the strength to endure and satisfaction enough to walk away content that I could do no more.'

Springer puts his hands on George's shoulders. 'There be not a man alive I have more respect for than thee. The kindness and help you done served Victoria and me when we be needin' it the most is more than I could repay in many a lifetime. Thee's been a father to me when I had none and a friend when all around would have nowt to do with us. I would have done this for you, and you alone. But add in the fate of them there youngerns, Oliver and Edward, and the condition we found Jennie in, along with all those that have suffered for the greed of just a few men. I must put right the wrongs they have done to everybody; it is just my way.' His eyes lower as he thinks for a moment, takes a breath and looks back at his friend. 'I will live with what I be about to do, for once done is done I will fight no more and turn my back on these wicked ways to see my children grow and live better lives than me. But hear me well, George, should I fall or my strength fail me, promise to look after my kin and Victoria, for they will need you more than ever.'

George stands up and puts his cup down. 'My boy, three years ago my world was coming to a close. Life had so little to offer me, and what was available had little appeal. Then, out of the blue, a pregnant woman and her man stood in my yard with but a bag between them. Now I feel there is another ten or more years in me, and that is all because of you and Victoria. Let's finish this and go home for I still have plans that are not yet done, and you're the one who needs to do them with me.'

Springer looks at him perplexed, wondering what he wants him to do next. George heads to the door, opens it and storms off across the open ground. As he reaches the far side of the clearing, he hears Springer quietly calling to him.

'This be the way, you daft bugger,' he says, pointing at a small path. 'Thee be movin' in the wrong direction. That there be the way back home, you stubborn old coot.'

George marches back across the open ground, looking at Springer as he walks past. 'I was just stretching my legs. I know this is the way to go, young man. Now follow me,' he says as he marches off along the path.

Springer closes the cabin door with a smile and a shake of his head. He slips on his jacket before jogging to catch up with the briskly walking George.

* * *

A mile away, on the edge of Pippinsford village, Dan is watching the Hare and Hound tavern. He observes several people walking by, some entering or exiting the building and others just walking past. He pays them no mind as he waits patiently for his intended target. Finally, a tall, thin weaselly man scurries across the road and into the tavern. It is the person Dan has been waiting for all morning. He gives it five minutes or so before heading over and entering the building. Walking straight through the reception, he stops at the entrance to the bar and looks around.

He can see his old friend Arthur loading a fresh barrel onto a stand behind the bar and at the end of the counter is the man he watched walk into the building. Already drinking from a tankard of ale, he has his jacket collar up to hide his face from all but the people facing him.

Walking straight up to Arthur, Dan coughs politely to get his attention. 'A tankard of your finest Burtons ale, my friend. For I have missed its taste for a long time now,' he says as he places a coin on the counter.

'Yes, sir. Just as soon as I have moved this empty barrel out of the way,' Arthur says before looking up. As he sees Dan's face before him, a huge smile appears. 'By God, you're a sight for sore eyes!' he cries, pours his drink and places it in front of him. 'Where have you been? For nobody has seen you in an age.'

'Well, you know how it is in my line of work – you need to follow the game and the stock around. But I heard that the salmon are now running well up on old Fitz's stretch and holding up in the mill pool by bluebell spinney, waiting for a rise in water level to take them onwards.'

Arthur is trying desperately to point out the man at the end of the bar, using his eyes and some head nods, but Dan just keeps talking away. 'I think I will finish this fine drink of yours first, then spend the rest of the day filling a sack or two with a few of them fine specimens as I have people waiting for delivery of said plunder.'

The man at the end of the bar has been listening to every word, barely moving his tankard from his lips as he tries to stay anonymous. He lowers his drink to the counter, quietly slips off his chair and slides round the side of the bar into an adjacent room. As the door closes, Dan looks round with a smirk on his face.

'Dan, for the love of God!' says Arthur. 'Do you not remember that man? It's one of Brannigan's snitches, Snivelling Ives. By now he will be halfway out of the window and off looking for Brannigan or Sykes.'

'I know. I can picture him now, scurrying everywhere looking for them.' Dan takes a deep drink from his tankard and speaks again. 'Things are about to get a mite exciting around here, Arthur. I feel a change for the better is not far away.' He finishes his ale then looks up at his friend. 'Time I was gone. I hope to see you again soon, my friend. I really do.' He pauses and looks around the room to ensure nobody is looking at him. 'Oh, I nearly forgot! I have something for you.' He leans forward and so does Arthur, expecting Dan to whisper something in his ear as he tilts his head.

Dan hesitates for a minute. 'I cannot believe I'm doing this,' he says before quickly kissing Arthur on the cheek. 'That is from Cook. She sends her love.' He turns and runs towards the door, wiping his lips with his sleeve as he goes.

'You old bugger, have at yer,' shouts Arthur as he throws the near-empty tankard after him. By the time the tankard bounces off the wall, Dan is long gone, leaving Arthur shaking his head and laughing at the sheer cheek of the man. He's also relieved to know Cook is alive and well after all this time.

Dan is swift to leave the village, and in no time at all, he has made his way through the built-up areas and is moving cross-country on ground he knows only too well. The old tracks he used to use are still there, just a little more overgrown than he remembers. But that is no problem as it means there is more cover to move around in.

Within the hour, he is within sight of the mill pool by bluebell spinney. He checks the lie of the land down to the river and all the connecting ditches, paths and ways out of the area. Finally, he follows the gully to a sharp bend before the pool on the river where he always used to put his lines or gill nets to catch the fish in the shallows before they shoal up in the deeper pool.

He moves back from the water's edge a few yards and starts to look along the undergrowth. After a few minutes, he finds what he is looking for – a thick square of old oak covered in layers of rope sacking with moss and grass growing through it. To most it looks like part of the ground, but when lifted, it exposes a hole with the sides and bottom lined with trimmed pieces of seasoned oak. In the centre of this hole is a sack containing one of Dan's poaching nets and a smaller bag inside the sack containing a sheet. Tipping the contents out of the sack, he starts to inspect the fine netting. It seems to have withstood the ravages of time rather well. But then again, Dan always looks after the tools of his trade and this net was always dried, then soaked in linseed oil before storage to prevent it rotting.

Unwrapping the net fully, he pegs it to the edge of the riverbank just below the waterline. He then throws a weight attached to a string to the far bank. Removing his trousers and shoes, he wades across the river and pulls the net across, securing it just under the waterline with pieces of folded and twisted hazel pegs. Once happy with the net's position, he wades back across the river, pushing a few more pegs in the bottom of the net to hold it tight to the riverbed, and returns to the hole with the oak board.

He dries himself off with the sheet and dresses again, then sits with his legs in the hole and the oak board angled up on his side with a few cut pieces of branch to support this weighty piece of wood and hold it in place. From a distance, it's just possible to make out the top of Dan's head above the foliage, but it would take a keen eye and someone who knew he was in the area to spot him amongst the natural cover.

Back at the village, as expected, Snivelling Ives had slipped through the window of the tavern and has been hunting high and low, looking for Brannigan or Sykes to inform them of the return of Dan-the-poacher, and to collect a reward for his information.

Running out of places to look, he is just about to head to the park when he spots Crossy and Sykes exiting the house of a few ladies that provide a special after-dark service. One of the women watches from the balcony window above, smoking a long thin clay pipe full of tobacco. She puffs and blows rings in the air as the men walk down the street towards the tavern. She yells out to them, 'Come back soon, you hear?'

Sykes sighs and shakes his head. 'We have got to find us a better place. The women are looking ugly even when I am drunk and I'm beginning to feel married to that old dog, such is the time I spend round there.'

Just when things could not be getting worse, he looks up to see Ives scurrying towards him, waving his arm in the air. 'Oh shit, what does he want?' he mutters. 'I swear he is like a cockroach, appearing out of nowhere to find me.' They watch as the man swiftly crosses the road to intercept them.

'Mr Sykes, Mr Sykes,' he calls as he runs up to them. 'I have good information for them that want to know.' He nods at the two men.

'Well, what is it this time, you little worm? Out with it,' barks Sykes. As the man pauses to catch his breath, Sykes speaks again. 'I've not got all day, so speak up or be on your way.'

Ives looks at him and rubs his hands together. 'Was in the tavern a little time back when who should walk in but Dan-the-poacher? Sat right beside me he did, bold as brass, talking he was.'

Sykes looks at Crossy then back at Ives. 'You have my attention, so get on with it.'

Ives sniggers. 'Well, it would seem that he is back in the area plying his trade again and will be here for a day or so.'

Sykes clenches his fists and grinds his teeth. 'I want that man so bad. Him and that whore of a wife of his, Cook. They stitched us up right proper last time. I swore then that I would get that man if it was the last thing I ever did. Now tell me, did you hear any more?'

'Well, I might have heard a little more, but that depends on you.' He puts out his hand and rubs his thumb over his fingers.

Sykes grabs Ives with both hands and pins him up against the wall beside them. 'Why, you money grabbing little sh—'

Ives screams out, 'It's how I make a living,' as he tries to push the big man off him. 'So, if you want to know where he be, I want payment. And if you don't want to pay, there will be others who will pay me for what I know. Don't you forget, I know what the bounty is on his head from Lord Fitzgerald. So do we have an accord?'

Reluctantly, Sykes dips into his pocket and gives him some coins. 'There, that's all I have for now. But if you are correct with your information, I will ensure you get your share of what is coming.'

Ives looks at the coins in his hand. It's not as much as he would like, but as the expression goes, it is better than a poke in the eye with a sharp stick. With luck there will be an additional share to come, and he divulges the rest of what he knows. 'Dan was talking about going fishing for the salmon at the mill pool by bluebell spinney.'

Sykes lets go of the man and turns to Crossy. 'Go to Lord Fitzgerald's estate and let Brannigan know where Dan be poaching. Ives and I are going to see if we can spot him down on the river.'

'Me?' cries Ives. 'Why me? I don't want to go down to the river.'

'You want more money, don't you? Well, if I find where he is, you can go back and tell the others exactly where to find him, can't you?'

Ives thinks about it for a minute then nods in agreement.

The three men part ways, with Crossy heading for his master's estate on the far side of the village.

Sykes and Ives go to find Dan-the-poacher plying his trade. Leaving the main road outside Pippinsford, they follow a footpath through the undergrowth and across the meadow. Sykes has taken out his pistol and charged it ready for firing as they slowly make their way towards the river.

Nearing their destination, they both crouch low and move quietly along the river's edge towards the mill pool. Peering downstream, they catch the faintest glimpse of a man, just as he is leaving the water's edge with something in his hand. They creep along the uneven riverbank, getting closer and closer with every step. They can see the back of a man bent over, working on something. Ives steps on a dry twig, and it cracks. The man quickly straightens up and looks around nervously. Sykes and Ives are quick to lower themselves into the undergrowth and take cover, holding still until the man returns to what he was doing.

They watch him intently, observing every move as he turns and seems to sit on the ground behind a thicket of grass with just the top of his cap showing. Sykes takes his chance and points his pistol at where the man's body should be and pulls the trigger.

There is a loud bang, a plume of smoke and a thud as the bullet makes contact with its target and the cap drops down and disappears.

Sykes is up like a shot. 'I've got the bastard!' he yells as he rushes over to claim his prize. As he approaches, he can see a man lying on his side next to a small campfire that is burning charcoal. A pot of simmering water hangs over the fire and at its side a pair of socks on sticks are drying in the heat.

Sykes approaches and rolls the man over onto his back. 'Who the hell is this?' he asks as George opens his eyes and gives them both a shock. He sits up, holding his side, and looks at the pistol in Sykes's hand.

'So, it was you who fired at me for no reason.' George takes his hand from his side and looks at his blood-stained clothes. 'I do not think the magistrates will be too happy with you shooting a member of the public like this!'

Sykes thinks on his options. Shooting at an innocent man would not go down well with his employer, but if it were a poacher he shot dead, Sykes would be a hero. However, to get away with that, George would need to be dead and set up.

Sykes starts to load his gun with powder. George attempts to get to his feet, but he pushes him back down to the floor to bide more time while he reloads his pistol. Just as he is ramming the ball down the barrel, the gun is swiped away from him and tossed into a bush. He looks across and is shocked to see Springer glaring down at him. 'Be a small world, eh? Reckon I be not what thee be expectin' to see.'

Sykes's reaction is to swing at Springer wildly with several swipes of his fists. But being a pugilist, Springer dips under and leans away from the blows before coming back with a couple of left jabs of his own followed by a heavy right to the jaw. *Crack* goes Sykes's jaw as it shatters with the impact of the blow.

'That be for young Oliver,' Springer says as he steps back to deliver a left and right to the head, then two uppercuts to the stomach. Sykes buckles from the impact and Springer brings up a knee to his face. The blow knocks him upwards and back while also twisting his body as he is launched through the air.

'That there be for Edward,' he yells as Sykes hits the ground with a thud, blood flowing profusely from his nose and mouth.

Ives has seen enough. For a while, he was frozen with fear, but now he has regained some of his senses and realises that there will be only one winner here. He turns to run but feels a sharp pain in his chest. Looking down, he can see the handle of a knife sticking out in front of his heart. He slowly starts to bring his hands up to the knife, looking at the man standing before him.

'For all them lives that you've had a hand in taking and families left without fathers, at least they will have peace now,' says Dan, who watches as Ives slowly pulls out the blade. The blood from the now open wound pumps into his clothing, spreading with every beat of his cold, black heart. The knife falls from his hands as he drops first to his knees and then face down onto the ground.

Dan picks up the blade and wipes it on the coat of his victim before folding it back up and placing it inside his hip pocket. He then makes his way over to Springer, who is now playing with Sykes like a cat does with a mouse, jabbing and punching him at will before inflicting some heavier blows.

Soon, Sykes is down on his knees again. This time as he stands back up, he pulls a large knife from his boot and holds it out before him. 'Them boys had it coming to them. And just so you know, when I stuffed that kid into the sack, I'm sure he was still alive.

Come to think of it, when I dragged him all the way to them furnaces and swung that sack into the flames, I'm sure I heard him call out for his brother one last time.' He sniggers as he speaks, in an attempt to put Springer off his guard and force a mistake.

But Springer shows no emotion. Inside, he is raging and full of hate for the man, but his self-control and discipline holds firm as he concentrates on the task at hand. Sykes steps in with his blade, striking left and right as he tries to cut the body of his opponent. Springer twists and moves to avoid each lunge of the knife. Finally, at the right moment, he grabs the outstretched hand and twists it up Sykes's back, then hits his elbow up with the palm of his hand until Sykes's shoulder pops out of its socket.

'Aaaahhhhh,' Sykes yells out, his arm now hanging limp down at his side. Springer flicks the knife back in his direction with his foot and allows his opponent to pick it up with his good arm.

Sykes obliges and wildly lunges with the blade until again Springer steps in, grabs his wrist and twists the knife away from his grasp. This time, he plunges it into the side of his thigh and leaves it for him to pull out. Sykes hobbles backwards as he pulls at the knife, grimacing with pain as it leaves his body, and he turns to face Springer with the bloodied blade.

It is at this moment that Sykes understands Springer is going to take him apart piece by piece. He raises the knife and hobbles forward, slashing at the air in the vain hope of catching Springer with one of his lunges. As he overextends, Springer steps in and disarms the man again. This time, he thrusts the knife into Sykes's groin, right up to the hilt. He screams as the blade finds its mark and carves into his manhood with devastating effect. As Sykes hits the ground and struggles to pull out the heavily imbedded knife, Springer speaks again.

'That be for the little girl, Jennie.' He grabs the knife and twists it deeper, and Sykes screams even louder. 'That there be for the rest of them that can speak no more but suffered at the hands of thee.'

Springer moves round behind Sykes and takes his neck in his forearm, gripping the back of his head with the other hand. Slowly, he tightens and begins to twist.

Sykes tries to grab at the forearm around his neck with his one good hand, but it is a futile attempt. The vice-like grip does its job, slowly choking the life from his opponent as Springer whispers in his ear. 'This be from my Victoria.' He tightens and twists more and more until he can hear the popping of the bones in Sykes's neck. He releases Sykes and watches him fall to the ground.

'Let that be an end to this man's evil.'

Dan is wrapping the other body in a cotton sheet; he has already tied his feet together and his arms to his torso. Now, he ties the sheet tightly, ready to transport.

George looks at Springer. 'Are you OK, my boy?'

Springer nods in his direction and then looks at his bloody side. 'That there looks to be needin' a healer's hand, George,' he says with concern in his voice.

George pats his side. 'Fish blood, my good man. Supplied by Dan.'

Springer looks confused. 'But that there shot I be hearing; it was aimed right at thee, struck you with a thud.'

He smiles and taps down on the oak panel with his cane. 'Dan said it were strong and I would be safe, and strong it was. I was hiding behind it all the time.'

Springer looks up at Dan, who tilts his cap back at him. 'Thee be an annoyance at times, Dan. For I be sure George was downed by that there pistol shot. Had me right worried it did for a time.'

Dan throws another sheet and some string towards Springer. 'Best you wrap and bind that body tight. Once done, you two big men carry the bodies up the hill by that rock wall. I will create a screen of branches to cover them until the wagon comes to pick them up. But be fast, for if my timing is right, others will be here soon to see what has gone down.'

There is no more encouragement needed, and the campfire is kicked into the river. Springer collects Sykes's pistol, and the bodies are carried up the hill to the stone wall where Dan is waiting to hide their work. He positions the bodies in a shallow dip in the ground and covers them with branches, long grass and a sprinkling of fallen leaves. Once he is satisfied, they move further up the hill to observe what happens next.

They do not have to wait long before the sound of horses echoes through the woods and across the fields. Minutes later, they start to appear on both sides of the river, spreading out and looking for signs of Dan and their friends. Lord Fitzgerald leads the way with around ten riders on the near bank while Brannigan and Crossy lead the same number of riders on the far side of the river.

It does not take them long to find the area where the fighting took place, and several people have dismounted their rides to investigate and read the signs. They begin to point at the ground, no doubt able to see all the blood on the grass and bushes. But as the bodies were wrapped and carefully moved without leaving a trail, it will only be speculation as to what happened by the river and to whom the blood belongs.

'So, what is next, my boy?' George asks.

'Well, to start with, best we watch these for a while and see when they leave and what direction they go in,' says Dan.

Springer thinks for a while as they observe Lord Fitzgerald's men beating through the bushes in the hope of flushing somebody out. 'Dan, you be watching them there men and keep an eye for us up on the edge of yonder wood.' He points at a line of trees far up the river. 'They be here for some time now, expanding the search as they find nowt to go on. George and I will take to paying their magistrate a visit and have words on what be recorded in Edward's diary. Watch for us to signal at thee with the waving of George's cap then lead them towards us. For I be setting a trap to catch a fool.'

As George and Springer stand up to leave, Springer swipes Dan's cap off his head. 'That be needed, Dan, so thank thee kindly.'

The two men are swift to move along the hillside, leaving Dan to watch intently while filling his pipe with tobacco. Then lighting it with a freshly struck match, he takes a few draws on the end and leans against the dry-stone wall as he watches the men below hunt for him.

Springer and George reach the outskirts of Pippinsford village on the half-hour mark. Springer has Dan's cap on, and a large full-length coat wrapped around him to hide himself as much as possible as he walks through the village. George splits off to make some purchases in one of the shops they pass.

It's still early morning and the villagers are not out in any great number yet, allowing Springer to move swiftly onwards. It does not take him long to arrive at his destination. Pausing to take one last look around to ensure nobody is near or watching him, he walks up the steps and enters the large stone building. Inside, there is one smartly dressed man in his uniform sitting at a desk and writing a report in a ledger.

Upon hearing someone enter the building, without looking up he says, 'Take a seat and I will get to you soon enough.' Then he hears a *click-click* as Springer pulls the pistol hammer back, locking it into a firing position. The man looks up and stares down the barrel of a gun pointing directly at his head. Fear is written all over his face as he stops writing, puts down the quill pen and raises his hands. Springer takes off his cap and the man recognises him instantly. He begins to sweat and tremble as his fears worsen at the sight of Springer.

'Yes, you be knowing who I be. Hunted by you and them there others, turning a blind eye to helping those that need salvation for coin in your pocket. Ye be no better than your master.'

Springer just flicks the end of the barrel to get the man up, and then flicks it again to get the man to move towards the magistrate's office. As they approach the door, Springer pushes the pistol to the back of his head.

'You get this wrong and more's the pity for what beholds your fate.'

The man knocks on the door and waits for a response from inside. With no reply, Springer pushes the gun forward, touching the officer's head and encouraging him to knock again, this time a little harder.

'What do you want? I'm busy,' comes the response from somebody inside.

With more encouragement from Springer, the man opens the door and enters the room, tightly followed by Springer behind him. The chief magistrate catches sight of him and freezes.

He is sitting on his huge chair, being fed pieces of food by a scantily clad girl straddled over his huge belly. But the sight of Springer has brought that to a halt, as she stops and lowers her head. On the far side of the room sits another girl who looks identical, her clothes messed up, a bruise on her cheek and a cut lip. Instantly, both girls try to cover up their modesty as best they can.

Springer recognises them as the twins who used to play with Rebecca. They are just a little older than when he last saw them but look no different in how they style their hair. He thinks for a minute. 'Jessica and Prudence, I remember thee,' he says as the names finally come back to him.

Both girls look at him, then down to the floor in shame. 'We prefer to be called Jess and Prue.'

'What be you doing here with that fat old man? He be old enough to be thy father and belly enough for two of him.'

There is a quiet pause before Jess speaks up. 'We were leaving the village a few days back in our wagon as we cannot afford to live here anymore. He and his men stopped us on the road passing the factory and Mama and Papa were arrested and taken away. To see them again, we have to do things for him.'

George has just arrived in the room. He has heard the girl speaking from the doorway and walks straight over to her, gently escorting her away from the man. 'Put your clothes on, my dear, and wait with your sister. That's a good girl.'

The chief magistrate speaks. 'Do you know who I am? I have ten men in this station, fifty more people around the village.' George turns and punches the chief magistrate in the face, knocking him over the back of his chair. As he staggers to get his wallowing body back up, George throws him against the desk.

'Your men seem to be out looking for Dan, while you corrupt and violate little girls just so they can see their parents. You disgust me beyond words.'

To Springer's surprise, George has the bit between his teeth. The treatment of these girls is too much like the abuse given to Jennie, and it has hit a nerve with George, making him not only angry but vengeful. 'Where are their parents?' he asks the man.

With no response, George hits him with the first thing he grabs off the desk – the small bronze of a horse – which cuts deep into the man's head.

'Owww!' he screams as the blood starts to flow. 'You hit me!'

'I will do far worse if you do not answer me. Now, I said, where are the girls' parents being held?' The man whimpers and jibbers but says nothing. Staggering back to his feet, he holds on to his large marble desk for support. George slams the bronze down on the man's outstretched hand and the base plate smashes three of his fingers to pieces against the hard surface. He yells out again in agony and tucks his crushed fingers into his chest. 'The mine. We sent them to the mine two days ago!' he bellows as he sits back down at his desk.

George turns to the two girls, who are now holding each other and crying. 'Fear not, for I promise I will help you find your parents. But for now, you need to trust me and come with us.' Jess is the stronger of the two and she looks at George and nods, while Prue just holds on to her sister tightly.

Springer looks round the room and notices a huge ornate and well-decorated safe in the corner. He nods at George and then back at the safe. 'Well, well, look what we have here! Let's take a look inside, shall we?'

George drags the magistrate over to the safe and throws him at it. 'Open it,' he demands.

The magistrate looks at him from the floor. 'He will kill me if I do.' Springer turns and points the pistol at him, but it is George who speaks first.

'What makes you think Springer will not kill you where you grovel right now? Or me for what happened to my brother? Because if my friend does not pull the trigger, I surely will.'

The man fumbles with his one good hand at the chain round his neck, pulling it out from inside his clothes. He grabs the key at the end of it and inserts it into the safe, twists it left then right then left again, and the mechanism clicks. He spins the wheel on the front and then pulls the door open and moves out of the way.

George steps forward and looks inside. It is full, from top to bottom, with rolled up, wax-sealed documents. He takes one at random and views it, then breaks the wax seal, undoes the ribbon and unrolls the parchment. Taking his spectacles from his top pocket, he places them on his nose and begins to read the document. He then takes two more of the documents and sits at the table to read them in greater depth.

He looks up at Springer and at the other men. 'If they move, do not hesitate to wound them, my friend. Just do not kill them, for I think that would be a more desirable way out after reading this.'

The three men look at each other, all now curious to know what George has found. As he finishes reading the documents, he sighs and takes off his spectacles, placing them back in his chest pocket, then puts the three sheets of paper back in the safe.

At the bottom of the safe is a small white cotton sack which George pulls out and opens. 'Oh my,' he says as he sees what is inside, then closes it back up and places it on the top of the safe.

From the next compartment, he pulls out another bag, but this one is quite a lot heavier. He opens it and peers inside. 'Well, it would seem you have been busy.'

George places the heavier bag inside the lighter one and passes it to the girls. 'Would you be a dear and hold on to this?' he asks. 'I feel your parents and many others will find it useful later.' He then turns to Springer and the two men.

'That Lord Fitzgerald has most certainly been keeping an ace in the hole for himself. For every person who works for him, or to whom he sold a property, has signed a working contract. That contract has in the small print an acknowledgement that this deed supersedes the contract stating they own their property. All the deeds in that safe state the same clause, that once the occupiers leave Lord Fitzgerald's services, the house becomes his again. If they try and sell it, they would be breaking the law as they do not own it outright to begin with.'

The two officers look at each other, then at George as he chuckles at the shocked expressions on their faces. 'Well, it would seem there is no honour amongst thieves. As all you are really doing is keeping your homes warm for him, for he can repossess them whenever he wants with these deeds.'

The two men again look at each other, not knowing what to say or think. George moves away from the girls and walks around the room, collecting three of the oil lamps from their wall hangings, then continues to speak. 'If these were to be lost or destroyed, the only person to lose out would be Lord Fitzgerald. As he would have lost his hold over all the buildings in question.' George pauses for a moment. 'Well, him and, of course, the people who lost his deeds to all those houses, for they might not be in his good books anymore.

'I would estimate there must be documents and deeds for around two hundred properties. No doubt ranging from the new factory to workers' cottages, shops, farms, not to mention the large estates and new townhouses he has been building around the village. They must be worth a pretty penny, no doubt.'

Both men watch in horror as George opens each lamp and pours the contents over the papers in the safe, then strikes a match. But as he goes to light the documents, he pauses, looks back at the two girls and blows out the flame. 'Would one of you like to do the honours and take revenge on the man who has hurt you and your family?'

The girls look at each other and after a slight pause Prue stands up and walks over to the chief magistrate. She bends down, puts her hand in his pocket and pulls out her father's vesta case. Looking him in the eyes, she says, 'Pig.' Then she slaps him as hard as she can across his face before making her way to the safe. She kneels down, her eyes never breaking contact with the chief magistrate as she removes a match.

Still staring at him, she strikes it on the side of the case. 'This is for Mama and Papa and what you did to Jess and me.' She drops the match in the safe and turns to watch the flame swiftly take hold and spread, engulfing the entire contents in fire.

'I think it is time we be gone,' says Springer, ushering the two men towards the door. The younger man takes his chance and goes for Springer's gun. It's a very brief struggle, with one headbutt from the big man knocking him back and the pistol whipped across his head rendering the man unconscious.

Springer passes George the pistol. 'Wait outside in the courtyard. I be along once this here problem be attended to,' he comments while picking up the man and dropping him by the safe. He looks around to ensure the girls have gone before grabbing the man by the neck and twisting it until it breaks. Then, taking another lamp from the wall, Springer pours the oil over the body and flicks the last of the liquid towards the safe. The flames soon run along the trail and over the body, engulfing all in a vicious fire. With one last look back, Springer leaves the room and heads outside to the courtyard. Unable to see the others, he puts on Dan's cap, lifts up his coat collar and walks along the road. Twenty yards on, one of the girls peers out from a side street and beckons him towards her.

On arrival, George passes Springer the pistol. 'Watch him,' he says, gesturing at the magistrate, 'while I now take care of some business.' He then takes something from the bag that Jess is holding. 'Wait five minutes, dear boy, and be ready to move when we get back.' George hurries off down the street, leaving Springer confused and wondering what he is up to.

It takes George a few minutes to find his objective – the stagecoach that had brought him here once before. He saw it pass as they turned up the side road and had an idea that may be of benefit to them. 'Yes,' he says to himself as he spots the man he was hoping to see talking to the coach driver.

Swiftly George walks up to the two men. 'Good morning, gentlemen. Has it been a busy day for you so far?'

They look round at him and the driver replies, 'Busy with them people arriving here for that man Lord Fitzgerald and his birthday celebrations. But they are not the nicest people to transport, always moaning and telling us to go faster.'

The smaller of the two men rubs his chin, then clicks his fingers. 'I know you, don't I? Yes, I do, but from where?'

George helps him along. 'Not from where, but when. You delivered me to the Hare and Hound tavern and wisely advised me not to get food from a certain bakery.'

'George,' the man replies. 'But what are you doing here? There was a devil of a scandal when you were here last, and a lot of

Fitzgerald's men were looking for you for days.'

'I thought for a moment you would not remember me, Ernie.'

'Oh, I never forget a face, sir. Names maybe, but not a face. Now tell me, sir, are you really Steven Todd's brother like some were saying?'

'That I am, Ernie. And from what you have just said, I take it you're not a fan of that man Lord Fitzgerald?'

'Lost many a good friend from the village to his expansions, as he calls them. Never seen them again once they have gone from the village. But I have a family to feed, so I still need to work, even if some of it involves him.'

George weighs up the risk before he next speaks. 'I am Steven's brother, and like your friends, I never saw him, his wife or sons again.' He pauses for a second. 'Supposing me and a few other people – that you would know for sure – were here to right a few wrongs and make a few less desirable people disappear, would you be willing to give them just one trip on the coach and not remember it?'

The men look at each other. 'The risk would be dangerous. Could even put us in harm's way,' replies the driver.

'I would say probably fatal for those who have harmed other people, but rewarding for those who are willing to help.' George opens his hand to reveal twenty gold coins.

The men look at his hand and then at each other. 'If it removes some of Fitzgerald's enforcers, I will do it for free,' says the driver.

George puts ten coins in the driver's hand and ten in Ernie's. 'Help us and take the coin anyway. I'm sure you can put it to better use than those who had it before. But we must hurry, as I have friends waiting and we are in a rush to get to the lane above the river at the mill pool. We need to follow the road to the wood beyond and be let out there.'

'Give us five minutes to prepare the horses and turn the coach around and we will do it,' replies Ernie.

Moments later, George is shuffling down the side lane to join Springer and the others. 'Get ready to move,' he says, checking to see if anyone is watching. Barely has he spoken the words than he hears horses' hooves clicking on the cobblestone road. 'Let's be gone from here,' he says, leading the group to the coach. The door swings open and Ernie beckons them inside. 'Quickly,' he says. 'Get in before anybody sees you.'

The driver watches intently to see who enters the coach. Fortunately for all, there are no bystanders in the vicinity, but he does notice smoke rising from the magistrates building. Then, looking back down the side of the coach, he sees Springer, a man he knows only too well from days of old, pushing the chief magistrate into his coach.

A smile appears on his face, and he shakes his head. For he knows now that if Springer is back, all hell is going to break loose and them that deserve retribution are going to find it coming at them hard.

There is a tap on the roof from inside the coach and the driver flicks the reins and lets loose the horses. They make good time and are soon through the village and off onto the back roads. Within ten minutes, the vehicle is nearing the mill pool. Twice, the driver must slow down as groups of horsemen gallop past at pace from the opposite direction. A short time later, his team of horses have reached the beginnings of the woods. With one final look round to ensure the coast is clear, the driver pulls up.

Ernie jumps down and flings open the door and the people inside file out and head to the cover deeper in the woods. The last one out is George. As he steps onto the ground, he turns to the two men. 'Thank you, my friends. We appreciate what you have done for us, and the risk you have taken.'

The driver tilts his cap at him. 'We will drive to the next village before returning, to look like we were carrying a passenger, so will be back this way in an hour. If you need a lift, wave us down. If not, I wish you the very best of luck with your endeavours.' Slamming the door shut, the carriage moves off with Ernie waving goodbye from the window.

George turns and chases after the others. He soon catches them up as they make their way to the front of the wood overlooking the river, valley and all the land in between. On both sides of the river, they can just about make out figures on horseback still searching the area, looking for Dan.

In the far distance, they can see a thin plume of smoke rising into the sky from the direction of the village. 'I think that be your building on fire, magistrate. More's the pity I could not leave thee there to feel the heat, for you deserve it no less than that there man of yours we left behind,' comments Springer.

'My men will hunt you down and capture you all for this, you mark my words. And when they do, I will personally reside over the case myself and ensure you all hang. That is if my cousin permits it to get that far, as I know he wishes to feed you to his dogs for sport.'

Springer shows him the back of his hand, knocking him to the floor with the force of the blow. 'That there be where thee belong, you fat little pig. Face down in the dirt. For I be not forgetting what thee has done to so many hereabouts.'

George has moved out into the open scrub in front of the wood and is waving his cap around above his head. After a few minutes he turns to Springer. 'How long should I do this for?'

Springer smiles. 'Thee only needed to wave a few times, George. Dan would have spotted thee with the first wave.'

Suddenly, from the bushes beside them, a voice speaks. 'You took your sweet time getting here, Springer.' Dan is smiling and puffing away on his lion's-head pipe. 'I had to move this way a bit sharpish as they were getting a little close to me.' He looks at the group and notices the two girls. 'And who might these two young ladies be, then?'

'This is Jessica and Prudence. Sorry, my dears. Jess and Prue, as they like to be called,' says George as the girls both politely smile and nod in Dan's direction.

Dan nods back. 'Katharine and Peter Wilson's twin daughters. Growed thee have since I last saw you. I know your parents well. How are they both doing? It has been a while since I last saw them.'

The girls both look in the direction of the chief magistrate. 'They were arrested when we were leaving the village a few days ago,' says Prue.

'It would seem that as of a few days ago, their parents are guests of Lord Fitzgerald. Our chief magistrate here has been forcing these girls to satisfy his own amusement as payment for them being able to see their parents.'

The pipe drops from Dan's mouth and hits the floor as his expression turns to anger. 'My Cook is their godmother, George. She will not be happy with this.' He walks up to the man and kicks him firmly in the groin.

'Aaaahhh,' he yells as he falls to the ground.

'Touched my Cook's goddaughters, did you? You are no better than an animal,' he says as the magistrate rolls around the floor moaning, while holding his balls in his hands. Both girls look at the downed man with satisfaction and smiles on their faces.

Springer takes Dan to one side and explains what happened at the magistrates building, the fate of the man inside and the documents they destroyed in the safe. After that, he explains in detail what he needs Dan to do next.

While he listens to every word Springer says, Dan does not take his eyes off the magistrate. Anger has built up inside him that is not usual to his nature. He nods at all that Springer says and reaches out to take the pistol from his hand. 'It's mine and George's turn to up the heat and get the next part done, my friend. Take the girls to the willow cabin on the far side of the wood and get a fire going. I organised some supplies to be put in there with a friend this morning. We will be along shortly.'

George looks at them both. 'Should I not take the girls, as you are better at this kind of thing than me?'

Dan looks at Springer and they both chuckle. 'And what, may I ask, is so funny?' asks George.

'George, great that thee be, but your sense of direction is, at best, very bad and, at worst… well, thee be lost looking for that there pocket watch if it was not held in place by a chain.'

He takes offence to his directional abilities being questioned, grabs the chain and pulls on it to get his watch from his pocket, only to find the watch is missing from the end. 'What the…? Where the…?' He looks around to see if it has landed on the floor near him.

Dan steps forward. 'Use this one until you find your own,' he says as he passes George a pocket watch.

George looks at it and opens up the front cover. 'Wait a minute! This IS my watch! How did it come to be in your possession?' He looks up at Dan and then across to Springer. 'Are you sure that man is on our side, Springer? Because I am beginning to have my doubts.'

Springer and the girls laugh as they move deeper into the woods, while Dan just looks at them and shrugs his shoulders. He wears his innocent 'butter would not melt in my mouth' expression, as if protesting his innocence without saying a word.

With a swift move of his hand, he takes his cap back from Springer's head as he passes, then picks up his lion's-head pipe from the floor, taps out the spent tobacco on the heel of his boot and pops it in his chest pocket.

George walks over to the ailing chief magistrate and helps him back to his feet. 'Sure is not your day today, is it, guvnor?' he says as he drags him to the edge of the woods. Dan heads out into the open area in front of the trees and starts to make his way towards the riders looking for him.

After walking around for some time while waving his arms around and calling out, Dan is finally spotted by one of the mounted men. 'Over there! I see him over there, heading for the woods,' he yells as he turns his horse and charges towards him. The rest of the riders are all some distance behind, allowing Dan plenty of time to amble back to the edge of the woods.

Just inside the treeline, George is tying the magistrate's hands behind his back, pulling off his white horsehair wig and replacing it with a long dark brown example he bought from the hat shop in the village. He wraps a piece of cord round his mouth two or three times, knots it at the back of his head and stands him behind the last thick tree trunk before the open area of meadow and scrub.

Dan has nearly reached them as the first rider approaches at full gallop. He turns, raises his pistol and aims at the man. Seeing the weapon being pointed at him, the rider pulls back on his reins to stop his horse. The horse locks up its legs and skids to a halt, rolling up grass as it does. Dan fires and clips the man's arm, knocking him to the ground. Then he turns and runs towards the trees as the other riders some two hundred yards away come bearing down on his position with pistols and rifles now drawn.

He reaches the cover of the wood and swiftly places his cap on the magistrate, takes off his coat and wraps it around the man, holding it in place with a leather strip tied around his waist. Then he cocks the empty pistol and points it at him.

At this point, the magistrate does not know that the pistol is not loaded. 'Let's kill him now, before the riders are on us, and be done with it,' yells Dan.

'No, Springer wants him to hang for crimes he has committed,' replies George, who grabs for the gun and fights with Dan over its possession. The magistrate sees them fighting and takes his chance to escape, running out from the wood into the path of the oncoming Brannigan and Lord Fitzgerald, along with the rest of their men. He gets a good twenty or so yards from the treeline before the first shot is fired. At that moment, it dawns on him that he has been set up. Fearing for his life, the magistrate turns and runs to find safety in the woods.

He is only ten yards from the trees when the next round of shots is fired by the riders that are now only a few yards from him. Several of them hit their mark and the magistrate staggers forward a few paces before more shots hit him in the back, knocking him to the ground. The riders slow to a walk as they approach the fallen man, allowing the horses to encircle him.

'Finally, we got the bastard!' shouts Brannigan as he dismounts and goes to look at the body. As he rolls him over, the cap and wig fall off, exposing the magistrate for all to see.

'What the hell…?' he says as Lord Fitzgerald closes his eyes and sighs deeply, realising that spread out dead on the floor in front of him is one of the few relations of his that he actually liked. At the same time another rider arrives from the village to advise of the fire in the magistrates building. He explains that they have contained it to the chief magistrate's office, but everything in the room is burned to nothing and one man has been found dead.

Lord Fitzgerald looks up at the sky. 'God's teeth! How can one man cause such damage? It does not seem possible.'

He turns to Brannigan. 'I don't know what I pay you for, because I sure as hell do not seem to get a good return on my investment. Now, you and Crossy come with me to see the damage for ourselves. Then I want you to find out who is behind all of this. For somebody out there knows something. And I need you to find them, damn your eyes.' He looks round at the other riders. 'A thousand guineas to the man who brings me back that bastard poacher tonight. He must be somewhere in this wood. Now find him, or by God don't come back at all, as I will replace the lot of you come the morning.'

Lord Fitzgerald turns to the rider that delivered the news on the fire. 'Go to the undertakers and organise for this body to be collected and cleaned up, then taken to my private chapel.'

The rider turns his horse and trots off, followed by Lord Fitzgerald, Brannigan and Crossy as they make their way to the village. The rest of the men head into the woods to look for Dan-the-poacher.

Deep in the thick of the forest, George is swiftly following Dan along a narrow track. They drop into a deep ditch with running water at the bottom and follow it for about twenty to thirty yards. As they push on, the sides get higher and higher until only their heads are above the natural height of the ditch. Finally, they are confronted with a mat of roots from a large old willow tree above the ditch.

Dan carefully pushes apart the roots that hang down into the water below to reveal a tunnel cut into the bank behind. They follow this for a while and come across another round poacher's hut. The bank surrounding the building is raised above the roof and covered in bramble bushes, hawthorn and blackthorn, making an impenetrable wall of natural defences.

Dan opens the door and exposes another well-maintained dwelling with a fireplace in the middle, surrounded by wooden chairs, benches and shelves against the walls. The cabin even has a stone sink with a water pump attached to it, providing fresh water from a stone-lined well dug into the ground below. Two lamps on the walls bring light to the cosy little space.

The smokeless charcoal fire has not long been lit, but the coals are already starting to glow, and its heat is noticeable by all in the room. The girls, being farmer's daughters, are busy cutting up vegetables and throwing them in a pot of water that is hanging over the fire and already contains what looks like diced venison.

George struggles to understand how these kinds of places exist. They are quite homely and positioned in areas where people are constantly looking for poachers. Yet, if you did not know the entrance, you would never find them. 'Are there many of these places round here?' he asks Dan. 'Bearing in mind I have already frequented two such buildings today.'

'Five or six on Lord Fitzgerald's land, and two on the outskirts, but not all are like this one. Some are more like a small cave in the rocks, just enough for a shelter and somewhere to store your tools of the trade.'

Springer instantly starts to chuckle as he knows where this is going before it is even mentioned.

'Do you have any such places on my estate?' George asks with a frown.

Dan looks at him with a shocked expression. 'On your land? No, guvnor, nothing like this.'

George modifies the question. 'Do you have any places like this around my land, but not actually on it?'

Dan pauses before answering. 'Um, no.'

Springer's shoulders are bouncing as his chuckle turns into a hearty laugh. He cannot help but smile at how naive George is when it comes to the ways of a wily poacher like Dan.

Again, George changes the question slightly. 'Dan, if I was to go around my land, tenant farmers' properties and check everywhere, would I find any type of poacher's cabin, smoking shed or charcoal burner hidden on my estate?'

Dan looks at George as he strikes a match to light his pipe before answering. 'No.'

'No!'

'No, m'lord. If you were to find your way around your own land without getting lost in the process, you would not be able to find any poaching or smoking sheds anywhere.'

George thinks about what Dan has just said. But before he can respond, Springer speaks. 'Best we be working out a new plan, George. For we have them there lasses to consider, as well as the woods being full of men that be keen on shining like a shilling up a sweep's arse in the eyes of that there Lord Fitzgerald. For I be in no doubt that there be a princely sum on Dan's head an' all that be seen with such a man.'

The men talk for a while and plot what to do next as the day is now getting on. They still intend to be finished here tonight and on their way back home tomorrow with all finished once and for all. But the way things have unfolded has already caused several changes to their initial plans. A rethink of what they are going to do, and in what order, is essential to keep things on track.

CHAPTER 10

Price of Betrayal

Back in the village, Lord Fitzgerald is reviewing the damage. They have entered the smouldering building and are making their way through to the chief magistrate's office. The damage to the establishment is limited to a small area as the floor, walls and most of the features are made of stone or marble or metal. The fire was mainly confined to the wood, paper and fabric.

One of the magistrate's men is escorting Lord Fitzgerald around the building. 'The body has now been removed, but it was here.' He points to a burned patch on the stone floor in front of the safe. 'The door to the safe was half open, with the contents as you see it now. We thought it best not to touch anything until you had seen it first.'

Lord Fitzgerald looks at the pile of ash from the burned documents that now fills the bottom half inch of the safe, along with a thinner layer on the two shelves above. He bangs the top of the unit with his fist several times before yelling out in a fit of rage. 'I don't care about the dead man on the floor. His job was to protect this safe and its contents at all costs and he failed. I had the safe and its documents moved here for its protection in the first place. This fortress of a building along with the magistrate and his army of constables was supposed to be the most secure place in the area. Pray tell me how a building filled with and surrounded by guards and even my own bloody family failed in such a simple task. Because here we are, with a pile of ashes that used to be worth a king's ransom.' He turns and looks at Brannigan. 'I want the people responsible for this found. Not tomorrow, not the day after, but now! I want them alive and brought before me at my party tonight, so I can look them in the eyes when I snatch the life from their bodies.'

He stares at the bottom of the safe in a trance as he thinks of the amount of money he has just lost, and all the scheming and bribing that went into getting all those documents together. Shaking his head and slapping his thigh with his riding crop again and again, the sheer disappointment of the situation sinks in.

There is no way he can recover all these signed documents from the people he sold the properties to without raising suspicion. But it does not stop him thinking of ways he could approach the problem and get at least some of them re-done.

'Get all my benefactors and law-givers from London down here for the day after tomorrow, along with my personal advisers. Let's see what they suggest. I pay them enough, so perhaps they can earn their keep for once and find a way to get at least some of these documents re-written and signed.'

As the two of them leave the room, Lord Fitzgerald is thinking about the party tonight and the possibility that the people who have just burned out his strong box and the arrival of Dan-the-poacher might be connected and not a coincidence.

'Speak to Lord Fenner for me. He has some new men with him that he uses for personal protection. Ask him to send them with the others for tonight's security, as I would like more enforcers at the party this evening just in case we have some uninvited guests.'

Brannigan tilts his hat at his master and walks away. He knows better than to argue with Lord Fitzgerald when he is in this kind of mood. Anyway, it gives him a chance to get a drink and find out from his men how the search for Dan is getting on.

* * *

Back at the poacher's hut, several hours have passed. They have all eaten well and a new plan for the evening has been drawn up. As with anything they do as a team, there is a plan B and even a backup plan to just leave the village if all goes wrong. But for now, the men still want to try and finish the job tonight and end the nightmare of looking over their shoulders for those that would hunt them down. While also taking revenge for what has been done to them, their families and friends in the past.

They have heard voices and horses pass the poacher's hut several times since they have arrived. And have even listened to people saying they can smell food in the air and what they will be doing tonight when they get home. But as the cabin is so well hidden, low to the ground and access so difficult to find, they have had no worries about ever being located.

Now that the evening is drawing in and the wood has been combed many times, Lord Fitzgerald's men have widened the search to a larger area, convinced that Dan has slipped the net and moved away from the river and surrounding woods. This suits the group fine as they can start to activate the next part of the strategy. With the twins now insisting on helping George and Springer out, it frees up Dan to help with a more daring manoeuvre needed to pull off their next objective. For even the chief magistrate's body still has a part to play in this audacious and bold scheme.

As the girls know the area very well, they will now meet with Robert and the wagon he is bringing, leading him to where the bodies have been stashed by the wall.

Dan is first out of the cabin and away through the undergrowth. He is on a scouting mission and will catch up with the others later once he has found out a few more pieces of information.

George and Springer wait another half hour before making their way towards Lord Fitzgerald's estate with a minor detour on the way. Only the twins remain, needing to wait a few more hours before leaving to intercept Robert on a small lane on the southern side of the village.

Springer and George make their way cross-country to Victoria's family home. As they move along the hedgerows and narrow paths, George speaks out. 'I have to ask you, Springer, do you think Dan has places like that cabin on my estate back home?'

Springer looks at him and chuckles with a shake of his head.

'Still be up on your mind, eh? Well, if the truth be told, I know not. But while Cook be on your stove and happy with her cottage, that there Dan will not dare to raise her wrath. Besides, the books show a better than fair profit, and thee's estate be running well. Why be fretting over Dan? He will always be Dan-the-poacher. Just be glad that there be one on your side and not against.'

George sighs heavily as he lowers his head. 'It's just that now I realise for several years, some staff on my estate took advantage of me. If it was not for you and Victoria, I fear all I own would be gone by now, along with me.' George pats Springer on the shoulder. 'Forgive an old fool, but with all now going so well, I do not want to lose it all again. Especially with several families now dependent on the farm for work and a place to live. I am just a little more careful as I do not want to let them down.'

Springer stops and turns to George. 'It may have slipped thy mind, George, but we be back in hostile territory again. We have blood on our hands and be pickin' a fight with nowt but the meanest of men. All this while looking to get done what others cannot. That be not what I call bein' careful. Come the morrow, I pray the only fighting I will ever do again will be with a goose for the table.'

They continue their journey, cautiously moving until they see the estate run by Victoria's father. As they get closer, Springer can see the place has barely changed in the past few years. The trees may be a little larger and one or two of the outbuildings have been repainted in the yard, but no significant changes or new structures can be seen.

They look through the windows for signs of Victoria's sister, Rebecca, but to no avail. Cautiously, they move around the building, checking the gardens, but still there is no sign of her. They watch as a carriage leaves the yard and pulls up in front of the house. Moments later, Henry and his wife leave the house and enter the carriage. They are well dressed for the evening – Henry in a fine evening suit and top hat and his wife in a light green ball gown with matching green hat and parasol. As the vehicle pulls away, Springer turns to George. 'Well, we tried. Let's be on our way, for she be not here anymore.'

George looks at him with a puzzled expression. 'How do you know?'

'The carriage, it be going to Lord Fitzgerald's for the celebrations. If Rebecca be here, she would have been dressed in all her fineries and joined her parents for the night. Now let's get the going while the going be good.'

George takes the lead as they head round the outskirts of the park and make their way to Lord Fitzgerald's estate on the far side. With so many people heading to the same destination by all manners of transport, it takes some time to get there safely without being seen.

Finally, from the top of the hillside, they can see their objective spread out in front of them, glowing with many hundreds of lanterns lit over the entire grounds and building. 'Well, this be more than I remember,' says Springer. 'That there man has gone and made himself a fortress.' The place looks like a palace and has a dozen or so tall marble pillars spread along its front. A wide arc of stone steps lined with a lattice of railings leads up to the main entrance. Various-sized towers and extensions have been added to the sides and back of the building, enhancing its grandeur. The roof has also changed with the use of slate, stone and clay tiles in various areas along with different patterns of design to improve the look. Several new tall and ornate chimney stacks reach for the skyline, all bellowing out thin plumes of smoke. On the highest tower, a huge weathervane in the shape of a dragon is showing the direction of the wind, while below the points of the compass are marked with the letters N, E, S and W in elaborate scrollwork.

At the front of the establishment and either side of the main driveway are symmetrical flowerbeds, box hedging and borders with several fountains being fed from a central rectangular pool of water. There is a huge gatehouse at the start of a long driveway, and an ironwork arch above it has the name 'Fitzgerald' woven into its elaborate design.

Each side of the gatehouse stand two large turrets and from the turrets an enormous stone wall stands a good twelve feet tall. The wall is far from completed around the whole of the estate, but it is well over seventy per cent there and groundworks and wooden scaffolding can be seen on the areas that are not yet finished.

At various distances along this wall are pairs of turrets and between them smaller entrances to the grounds within. These smaller archways allow additional roads to join the main driveway as well as side and rear entrances, creating a small network of routes in and out of the estate that horse-drawn carriages are now travelling along.

On the main road leading up to the front of the building, several carriages are lined up, ready to drop off their passengers. George and Springer continue to watch as once the people have disembarked from the carriages, the drivers move their teams of horses down one of the side roads and around the back of the building towards the stable yards.

'In all my days, I have never seen such a sight. The scale of this gathering is almost beyond imagination,' George says in wonder.

'For us, my friend, this be good news. With so many new faces, footmen, drivers and servants, getting in be not a problem for the canny likes of us, providing we be dressed right proper and come for the right area.'

After watching a little longer, he speaks again. 'Come, let's be moving down towards the house.' They make their way round to one of the side roads and follow along the hedgerow.

'Men being what men are, some of these drivers will not be waiting in a yard all evening. The call of a jug or two while them there masters be full of pomp and show will be too much.' They move to a spot around a hundred yards from one of the open gates. Inside the archway, two men, presumably enforcers, are ensuring that no undesirables enter the estate. They are both walking around the entrance, then sitting by a small metal-framed fire rubbing their hands together to keep warm. The purpose of the fire is no doubt to shed light around the entrance as the daylight is beginning to fade fast.

Over the next ten minutes, George and Springer wait and watch, until finally their patience is rewarded with two coaches trotting down the road. The first one is more like a buggy and not fit for the purpose they require. But the second is a coach with a driver and a footman on the back.

'That there be the one we be needing,' says Springer. They watch and then hide as the buggy gets checked at the gate then moves on past. The second one stops for longer and the men on the coach strike up a conversation with the guards.

'Horses are restless. I just need to stretch out their legs a little and wear them down a bit,' yells the driver.

'Yeh, yeh, have heard that several times tonight already. The village is that way, about two miles. And yes, it does have a tavern, but it will cost you a bottle to get back in this way,' replies the guard. The driver raises his hand as he moves on, out of the estate grounds and down the road with his team of four horses at a fair trot.

As it passes, George goes to move on it. But at the last moment Springer holds him back. 'Wait, there be someone inside that there carriage. Let's be following them to the village, for we know where they be going and can check out the coach at the tavern.'

Being aware of the coach's destination makes it easy for them to follow at a safe distance and take their time. They arrive at the village a little after dark. The light has all but gone from the sky and the odd streetlamp helps light the way. They can just about make out the carriage parked down a side road adjacent to the Hare and Hound tavern, with the horses facing away from them. With little in the way of lighting on this side road, Springer and George walk towards the coach with no fear of being recognised. Just lifting their jacket collars and pulling down the front of their caps is more than enough to mask their identities.

The two of them split up at the coach, with one of them taking to the left and the other to the right. They can see each other through the open windows of the carriage, confirming that it is now empty. As they make their way forward, they see the driver and footman standing with the horses, passing a bottle between them.

They are talking about someone as they reach them. 'Big scary man, isn't he? I would not want to come across his like in a dark alley,' says one of the men.

'You're not wrong there,' the other replies. 'Where do you think he is from?'

'Damned if I know, damned if I care. One thing is for sure, he is not from around here.' The man passes the bottle back, but it is another hand that takes it from him. As the driver looks up, a huge fist hits him in the face, knocking him backwards through the hedge. The other man barely has a chance to move before Springer picks him up and drags him through the bushes as well. There are a few more blows thrown and yelps of pain before all goes quiet.

Within minutes, a new driver and footman appear from the bushes. Wearing white horsehair wigs and with hats in place, they look passable at a distance. But with George just about squeezing into the skinny footman's uniform, and Springer too tall for his clothes, it will be touch and go if a close inspection is done. Springer takes his place at the front of the carriage as he can at least drive a coach with four horses, whereas George waits by the coach door. It is not long before a man shrouded in a large black cloak appears from the tavern and walks straight for the carriage. He carries a long leather bag and is wearing a large triangular hat.

George opens the door just in time as the man steps up and climbs into the waiting coach, which tilts heavily to one side with his first step. It soon levels itself as the cloaked man sits down inside and bangs the roof.

'Let's get going. Back to where we came from and stop outside the servants' entrance on the east side,' he requests as he sits back in his seat. George rushes to the back of the coach and steps up into position, holding on to the two handrail grips as Springer turns the horses and moves off along a side road. Before long, he is turning down a lane and back onto the main village street, moving the horses along at a steady walk until reaching the edge of the village, where he flicks the reins and puts them into a brisk trot.

As they arrive at the gate entrance, the two men standing guard slow the carriage down by waving their arms. Springer leans forward and passes them the half-full bottle and nods. The gift is gratefully received by the guards. 'That's what we have been waiting for,' the man says, pulling out the stopper and taking a deep drink as he waves them on.

Springer has been to Lord Fitzgerald's house before and knows several of the entrances, so he knows of the required destination and heads round to the side delivery doors away from the guests. He brings them to a stop at the servants' entrance, or the 'boot room' as it is known.

George steps off the back and runs around to open the carriage door. The man inside is already up and soon stepping down out of the vehicle. He looks at George closely from under his large hat before turning to the building and making his way to the stairs to the entrance below the balcony above.

He pauses for a minute. 'Driver, wait here for instructions,' he says before going down the steps and entering the building through a doorway below the stone and marble double stairs.

The main stairway curves up from the staff entrance, first outwards then inwards to a small patio with a stone balcony. From this vantage point, guests can walk in and out of the side reception room to view the gardens from the comfort of the seated viewing area. The boot room below is obscured from anyone positioned above and only more senior staff use this entrance point before and after their shifts, along with deliveries specific to that area of the house. With the estate being so vast, there are several such delivery points to cope with the sheer volume of supplies needed and the distances involved in getting them to where they are needed.

It is not long before three servant men appear from this lower boot room doorway, walk up the stairs and across the path towards the carriage. 'You two follow me,' one of them says to Springer and George. 'These two men will look after the horses and park the carriage while you are inside.'

George and Springer look at each other before dismounting the coach and following the man back down the stairs. They cross a narrow hallway and up to a door that he opens and, with a sweeping curve of the arm, indicates the men should enter the room. The door is closed behind them, and they hear the man's footsteps fade as he walks away.

They look around the room. Most of the walls are covered in shelving and stores of linen, crockery and washroom materials. On the far side, they see the cloaked man with his back to them, standing over a table and looking at something.

'Well, gentlemen, as I know you two are not the driver and footman I left with, who are you?' He turns to face them as he clicks down on a pair of fine engraved pistols, one in each hand.

Springer and George raise their hands as they look at each other before Springer speaks. 'We be not here for you, but them there others that have been doing wrong to our kin, families and the youngerns.'

'The loss of our loved ones for the greed of one man must stop,' George adds. 'Even if it costs us our lives. So, if you have a mind to shoot, then get on with it, boy, for I will see justice served this day or die trying.'

'You are confident, I will give you that. Shall I take a guess then and presume that you two are part of the reason I have been summoned to work here for Lord Fitzgerald? To watch his back and protect him from undesirables at large in the area?' he asks as he walks towards them. 'What to do with you, I wonder. I cannot have you interfere with my own plans and needs. For at the moment, you are a hinderance.'

'I beg to differ. For I now be sure that if it was not for Dan, George and I, you would not be where thee needs to be to get the doing done.' Springer turns to George. 'It took me a bit of thinking time, but if I be right in my way of working, we be in the presence of another Fitzgerald, one by the name of James.'

The man steps forward and raises his pistols in readiness to fire. 'How do you come by this kind of information? For it is about to cost you your lives.'

Springer pulls the hat and wig from his head and throws them down on the floor. 'I be Springer, a man hunted with his family for near on three years, and this here be George Todd, the brother of a good man, Steven Todd, who once owned most of where you now stand, along with all of them there others who lost their homes, lives and kin to that there murderer and his dogs. Now if it means that much to your way of thinking, pull them there triggers, but be sure to end me well for I am not easy to kill. Nor am I the forgiving type should I still be standing and able to fight.'

The cloaked man steps even closer, squeezing down gently on the triggers as he moves. 'We be warned there might be another man here with vengeance on his mind, be set to do the same as George and me. This warning be coming from old Bob and Emily. But if them names mean nowt to you, be damned and get to using them pistols or step to one side for I have no time to waste. We done three of them there dogs so far today and I will run no more. My family will not grow up hiding in the shadows.'

The cloaked man pauses and thinks for a minute or two before pushing the hammers gently forward on his pistols and lowering them to his sides. He turns and places them on the table, removes his hat and cloak and lays them down on top of his pistols.

It is only now they see the real size of the man in front of them. His arms, chest and neck are huge with thickset muscles and the tattoos Emily had talked about are there to be seen in full glory. He is indeed an intimidating sight for any opponent.

'I am James, the only surviving brother of Lord Fitzgerald, and I now have a younger sister I found a few years back in Paris. She is still recovering from her ordeal but doing well at the château where she now lives. I have started over in France and have a wife and two daughters, with a third child on the way. But no matter what I do, the nightmares of my past still haunt me. Like you I cannot get my brother's betrayal of our family out of my head, nor his treatment of others like Emily's father. On hearing that my brother was celebrating his birthday from people invited over from France, I could take it no more. I decided it was time to right a few wrongs and pay him a visit and deliver the kind of suffering he has put on so many others.'

'Does he know you live?' asks George.

'Yes, he knows one of his brothers is alive, as I visited and exacted some revenge on the ship captains who slew my four brothers. I left them with permanent reminders of what they did to four innocent men. But I am not sure if he knows which one as nobody recognised me and not all the captains contacted him.

'I was young when he sent me to sea and the changes in my appearance and physique make it difficult to all but my closest friends like Bob and Emily to know who I once was.'

'Them two friends of ours have more than enough reason to see your brother dead by their own hands. But they say you want more than just death for him,' says Springer.

'I have stood in the room with him twice today already, and several times in the last week since I have been here. He has stared hard at me but not recognised his own brother. Given the chance tonight I will infect him with a blade covered in toxins that I have added to in the years since it was given to me by a tribal elder. The sickness and fever it will deliver shall be lifelong and never fully heal, but if others were to get to him first, I would not feel cheated. He has many enemies and no doubt all of them have reason enough to want him dead.'

'So where do we go from here?' asks George.

'Well, you will not get far, looking like you do. For a start the clothes do not fit, and secondly all the service staff are in gold uniforms. So, you need to get service uniforms or clothes to blend in with the guests. That's it, blend in with the guests. The housekeeper was explaining the set-up earlier in the week. I know that the first floor is where HE chooses to have his rooms to live and sleep, as the main room opens onto the great stair balcony overlooking the entrance hall. Second floor is for important guests and associates and above that the lesser people. The staff live in the attic and at the tops of the turrets, out of the way.

'I need to leave and be back with his party in the main hall very soon as he feels I intimidate people and the man likes to always have the edge over all around him. You need to get to the second floor and find some suitable clothes or you will not get any further in this building. If you want to help, create a distraction or remove some of the enforcers. Anything that will get him away from his guests for a while and allow me time to get close to him.'

James picks up his coat, hat and pistols and heads towards the door, turning only to say, 'I wish you good hunting. With luck, at least one of us might get to him tonight,' before opening the door and leaving the room.

George lets out a sigh of relief. 'That man is enormous!' They also make their way out of the room and begin to look for a way up to the second floor.

'I know! Even I be thinkin' 'ard about tangling with that there man myself. Seems the only thing I've seen bigger is your old bull Winston, and that be by not much.' Cautiously, they move around the inside of the building checking all the rooms until they finally find some stairs that take them up to the next level. Stepping out into the room is like stepping into a museum of antiques and oddities.

'This be Lord Fitzgerald's military area,' says Springer. 'For I recognise that there suit of samurai armour. It was once owned by Victoria's father.'

Each room is full of works of art, statues, paintings and decorative ornaments from all around the world. As they move through yet another room of fine items, they hear a voice from behind call out.

'You, what are you doing here? This area is not for the likes of you!' The two men stop, frozen to the spot for a moment before they slowly turn around and face the person calling out to them. Standing before them is a beautiful young woman dressed in a royal-blue evening gown, holding a glass of wine.

'Well? I'm waiting for an answer. Who are you? And what are you doing here? Be quick before I shout for assistance.'

Springer stares at her for a minute. He recognises something in her. Could it be? 'Rebecca? Be that you?' he asks.

'My name is Rebecca. Rebecca Fitzgerald. And what is it to you, a mere servant of somebody? Now tell me what you are doing here before I have my husband flog you from our house.'

'Surely it cannot be. For the young lass I be knowing would not say such words,' replies Springer.

She walks up to him. 'I recognise you! You're the man who killed my sister and my brothers. You're that murderer, Springer!' She slaps him hard around the face. 'Murderer,' she spits. 'Have you come to kill me as well?' She hits him again, this time drawing blood from his mouth and nose with the jewellery on her fingers before George steps in and pulls her away from him. She kicks and fights like a wild animal and George is forced to put his hand over her mouth to stop her screaming out while Springer stares at the floor in shock and disbelief.

Finally, he looks up at her and speaks. 'Is that what thee believes? That I did kill my beloved Victoria and her, no, YOUR brothers, Oliver and Edward?'

George has backed onto a bench seat and has sat down, holding the fiery woman between his legs. His arms are wrapped round her, and he is covering her mouth with his hand.

She is breathing heavily and staring hard at Springer but is now not fighting like she was, just trying to get some words out. 'Let the lass speak, George,' Springer says.

'Mother told me all what you did to Victoria and that you killed my brothers when they tried to stop you raping her, before running away, dragging her body with you. You are nothing more than an animal. I hope they hang you for what you did.'

It takes a while for Springer to collect his thoughts and get over the shock of what he is accused of before answering the accusations. 'Your sister Victoria is well. She be at home, looking after our youngerns Edward and Molly with Cook. You be not forgetting Cook now, surely?'

Rebecca just stares at him. 'You lie. She is dead! Murdered by you! And Cook was killed by Dan-the-poacher when she confronted him. My husband told me how Dan was the one terrorising the village, and they hunted him down like a dog and left his body to rot somewhere in the woods for the animals to feed on.'

'What Springer tells you is the truth, my dear,' says George. 'For Cook and I are godparents to your niece and nephew along with Cook's husband, Dan-the-poacher. And Victoria is doing well and runs the books on my estate. For she is a very clever woman and has taught me a great deal when it comes to finances and commerce,' says George as Rebecca turns her head to stare at him.

'You lie! Dan is not Cook's husband. My mother would have

told me so if it were true. You are just trying to save your worthless skins, that is all.'

Springer walks towards Rebecca and George. 'Your mother be telling you a lot, but I be afraid to say that most of it be a far way from the truth, young Rebecca. For a start, Victoria left here with me as she was being matched to Lord Fitzgerald by your mother against her wishes. We both have been hunted by that man since the day we took to our heels and made good our escape from this place.

'I be only too glad to tell thee of your sister's plight, but for now I be needin' to ask thee things that be on my mind as this makes little to no sense to me. Like how be it that you have become Lord Fitzgerald's wife? For you are nowt but half the years of him.'

She straightens her back so she is sitting upright and pushes out her chest. 'Mother said I was the one Lord Fitzgerald desired all along and that marrying him would make me a powerful woman in society. She was right. Here I am in this huge house with dozens of staff at my beck and call. I want for nothing, and Lord Fitzgerald loves me very much. He told me so just the other day.'

'So why be you not by his side with all that be present to celebrate his birthday then?' asks Springer.

'His birthday? You are mistaken. He has some design engineers here from the factory to review productivity and expansion plans.'

George shakes his head. 'My dear, there are many people here from all over the country and even some from abroad, for such is the size of the event, all here to celebrate his birthday. They number in their hundreds in the rooms and halls below your very feet.' He pauses to allow his words to sink in before continuing. 'When was the last time you left these rooms and went outside?'

'Outside? A lady of my position does not need to go outside. I have everything I need delivered to these rooms. All I need to do is pull a cord or yell out and people come running. But if you must know, I was in the gardens with my mother two or three weeks ago discussing when I would be having my first child.'

Springer takes a deep breath and looks up at the ceiling. 'Pray tell me thee be not with child, youngern.'

'Not yet, but it is only a matter of time. He just has a little problem at the moment. You see, he is always under such pressure, that is all.'

'Ye be not far wrong there, lass. Ten years of living in the Paris brothels would cause most men to have a problem or two, 1 be sure of that.'

Rebecca does not respond to Springer's words. She just gives out a huff and folds her arms in discontent. 'You have not told me why you are here. Surely it was not to find me, for you did not know I was even here.'

'Thee be right there, though I did pass by your father's house to look see if thee be home as a favour to my Victoria, but once we see Henry and your mother leave on that there carriage, we knew thee be not at home anymore.'

Rebecca perks up. 'Mother and Father? I wonder where they could be going at this time of night?' She pauses for a minute, as a great sadness looms over her. 'Oh, they are here, aren't they? With Lord Fitzgerald.'

Springer nods. 'I be right sorry, lass. It be not nice the things they have done and said to thee.'

Rebecca is quiet again. 'You still have not told me why you are here and what you want in this house.'

George speaks up. 'A week back, a girl arrived in our local village looking for me. Well, it was Victoria and Springer she was looking for, but my name was given to her as someone who could help find them.

'Poor child, both her hands were dislocated, and she was starving and gravely ill. Her body was terribly bruised and beaten and had been abused by the men that had held her prisoner. The girl had travelled for some time in that awful state to find us and lucky she did, as she would not have lasted much longer. Apart from her clothes that were more like dirty rags, the only things she carried with her and protected with her life was a little blue diary, a marble and a story we could not ignore.'

Rebecca says with excitement, 'Edward used to keep a little blue diary. Funny how I remember it now.'

Springer speaks up. 'Lass, that there diary… it be Edward's. And thee knows the girl well, for she once be a friend of yours from times passed. Her name be Jennie, Jennie Meadows.'

Rebecca looks at Springer. Her expression is more alert as George continues the story. 'She was one of a group of children who had carried on what Edward and Oliver had started, trying to save their friends who were in mortal peril. But it was to no avail. Eventually they were all caught, and their fates sealed by the enforcers. Jennie was the last of them. With no options left, and her family abandoning her to the authorities, she took on Edward's last request and lit out to find your sister and Springer. She had been captured on the way to them but had escaped Brannigan and the others at a great cost to herself. She had been beaten, violated by Sykes, and sustained awful injuries, but never gave up. It took her six weeks or so to find us and deliver the diary. By then, you would not have recognised her for she had suffered so badly.

'The diary she carried explained a lot more to us than what we knew before, including the true fate of Oliver and Edward and who had imposed it upon them. For they succumbed to such a sad and terrible end that for many of us, our tolerance has now been exceeded and action needs to be taken.'

Tears are now rolling down Rebecca's cheeks. She looks blankly across the room as she speaks. 'Some nights in the weeks before Oliver disappeared, he would climb into bed with me after he had one of his nightmares. Shaking and sweating with fear and dread, he would make me promise not to tell Edward in case he stopped him going out with him on the nights they would raid the village.

'He would murmur about terrible things, such terrible things, and I thought they were just bad dreams or the fantasies of a child. But they were not dreams, were they? That little boy was living in constant fear and still trying to make things right for others. And worst of all, Mother and Father knew all about what was going on.'

George lets go of Rebecca. There is no need to hold on to her anymore. What they have spoken about has hit a nerve. 'Are you here to put things right?' she asks Springer.

'Young lass, we have already begun putting things to right. By the morrow, we will be finished and long gone from this here place of ill repute, with a fare thee well and never to return.'

Rebecca thinks for a moment. 'You might think me naive and still a child, but do you have one thing on you that would help me believe all that has been spoken? Just one thing to ease my mind that this be the truth of it?'

Springer looks at George as he pats his clothing. 'I have nowt that would… wait!' He dips into his pocket and pulls out the miniature drawing Victoria gave him and passes it to Rebecca.

Victoria is instantly recognisable. Rebecca's hand rises to her mouth and cups her lips. 'That there be your sister, Victoria, your niece and nephew.'

She turns it over and reads the back, then shudders as tears start to flow again. 'I would know her writing anywhere. Her calligraphy is perfect and the way she writes her name with the V curved is not like anyone I know.'

She looks at the drawing again. 'Edward… and who is the younger one?' she asks.

George is quickest to respond. 'Molly. The girl is called Molly after my late wife, God bless her soul.'

Rebecca passes the picture back to Springer. 'With so many false truths, my life has been thrown from one place to another, so tell me why you are really here?'

Springer picks her up off the bench. 'The people who done harm to all of them there youngerns and village folk are due a reckoning and we be here to do the collecting. Three have felt the wrath of righteousness, with three left to feel the sting of comeuppance for their evil actions.'

'I must ask, is my father one of these men?' Rebecca says with apprehension.

Springer shakes his head. 'Your father be easily led and poor in judgement. He will suffer enough when reflecting on all the kin and family he has lost. As for your mother, I'm sorry, but she be cold and bitter twisted. I now know of her past and she will sell all to stake her claim to a seat on the top table.'

Rebecca steps into Springer's arms for a comforting embrace, something she has not had in a long time. 'All I loved in this world has been taken from me. Even my oldest sister, Edith, refuses to visit, having left with her husband as he serves his military service on distant shores. I now understand why. She knew something was wrong here, had dropped hints that I chose to ignore through ignorance. But it would now seem that this is to be my lot and I must live with it,' she says with such sadness in her eyes.

'My dear Rebecca, your sister Victoria, she be right smart and wise to such things. If the night goes in our favour, perhaps she may be of help to thee, for I know she be thinking of you.'

Rebecca grips him tight before releasing him. She wipes the tears from her face, straightens her dress and composes herself like a lady does before setting to a new task. 'What do you need to end this night? For I will help all I can.'

'We need to get to the next floor to get clothes, so we look like guests at the party,' says George.

Rebecca thinks for a minute. 'Follow me. For I know a few ways that you can move between the floors unseen.' She leads the men through two of the large rooms and into a small area cut back from the hallway. Moving up to a statue of Lord Fitzgerald recessed in a scallop of the wall, she pushes down on part of his belt and a click can be heard. As she pushes on the statue, it glides back and the whole scallop rotates effortlessly into the wall, revealing a secret path and a spiralling stairwell.

'These stairs lead to a room below and the hallway to the guest suites above. He uses them to move between floors without being seen.'

Hearing footsteps tapping on the floor behind her, she ushers the men inside. 'Now go, before you are seen with me,' she says while looking over her shoulder. As the men enter the narrow path, Rebecca pulls forward the statue so that it locks back into position, leaving no trace that it had ever moved. She turns and walks several paces before being confronted by one of Lord Fitzgerald's manservants.

'Are you alright, my lady? I thought I heard voices,' he says, looking over her shoulder to the area behind her.

'That would be me. I am bored, and if I cannot speak to my husband, then I will do the next best thing and speak to his statue. At least it does not disappear on me all the time.' She walks at the man, making him move swiftly to one side to avoid contact.

'I am sure his affairs will not keep him much longer, my lady, but you must understand that the expansion of the factory is very important for business. He has had a lot of people to attend to tonight to ensure all his plans are correctly carried out.'

Rebecca walks on without taking any notice, leaving the man to his own devices as she heads for the lounge and a seat by the fire.

* * *

Downstairs in the main hall, Lord Fitzgerald is doing his best to look enthusiastic about the party. He greets his guests one after the other while smiling and delivering a few choice words. Between audiences, he is ripping into Brannigan and Crossy over the fire and loss of his documents, along with the arrival of Dan-the-poacher in the village and their inability to apprehend the rogue.

'I want that man's bollocks on a plate and served to me tonight, you hear me? Tonight.' He stops and smiles at another group of guests and exchanges a formal greeting before turning back to his men.

'And where in God's name is Sykes? I have yet to see him here tonight and I want all my best men close at hand.'

'I'm sure he is chasing up some leads on the poacher, sir. You know how he hates that man with a vengeance. With him being reported back, Sykes will move mountains to get at him,' answers Brannigan as he tries to calm Lord Fitzgerald down.

While the debate between the two men has been going on, James arrives back on the scene. He takes his position a few feet behind Lord Fitzgerald as the other man moves to one side.

'Well, take off the shirt and jacket, man. I want everybody to look at you and all your markings and be intimidated. Otherwise, what is the point of looking like a savage? I want people to be afraid to step near me, for that is what you are here for, yes?' James says nothing, just takes off his jacket, waistcoat and shirt and throws them towards one of the servants nearby. The man catches them, folds them neatly and walks off towards the cloakroom. James stretches back and shrugs his shoulders, showing a huge torso and arms like tree trunks full of tattoos. The effect is instant, as many of the guests around the room stop and stare in his direction. Some are more composed than others, but it creates a frenzy of conversation within many of the groups in the great hall.

After another greeting of guests, Lord Fitzgerald turns to Crossy, flicking his fingers to beckon him forward. 'Check on the wife and ensure she is in the rooms upstairs. Let her know I will be with her in an hour or so. Then see if Sykes is around here somewhere. I do not like it at all that he has not been seen for a few hours. It's just not like him, not like him at all.'

Crossy dips his head. 'Right you are, sir.' He turns and leaves Lord Fitzgerald to acknowledge another guest who has just approached him.

* * *

Back up on the second floor, George and Springer have been going through some of the guest rooms looking for suitable clothing so they can scout out the rest of the building without creating suspicion.

In a wardrobe in one of the bedrooms, George is first to find suitable attire that fits, along with a stylish cane and hat, while Springer has moved on to another room to find clothes in his height.

George is soon back with him. 'I cannot get this shirt and cravat to fit right. Could you help me, Springer?' He tries not to laugh at his attempt to dress in a fine shirt and waistband.

'I be not able to help in these matters. You will have to go back to young Rebecca, for she be a woman and knows these things. I be along shortly once I find what be needed for me.'

George storms off out of the bedroom, cursing and moaning at what he is attempting to wear, while Springer looks at a jacket that may just do the trick. Within minutes, George is back where they left Rebecca. He closes the statue behind him and quietly searches the rooms, finally coming across the young lady in the drawing room writing a letter.

She looks up at George and tries not to laugh at the fit of his clothes, then looks round as she realises the danger this could bring. 'Quick, follow me,' she says as she leads him into the nearest fitting room. 'Let's be making a bit more of a gentleman of you, shall we?' She closes the door and gets to work on his dress attire.

It's nearly ten minutes before the door reopens and Rebecca leads the way out. She turns to watch as George steps out in his splendour, tapping his cane on the floor and prancing with a real elegance. He smiles at Rebecca as he walks around the room. 'You look positively charming, George,' she says as she admires her handiwork.

George smiles and dandily steps forward a few paces before stopping in his tracks. Rebecca notices the smile drop from his face as he looks past her. A faint *click-click* echoes in the room, followed by, 'Oh dear, this does not look good, does it now?'

Rebecca turns round and is shocked to see Crossy pointing a small defence pistol directly at George. With just moments to compose herself and act, she speaks. 'And what do you think you are doing, pointing a pistol at my husband's friend?'

Crossy is taken aback. 'His friend? Coming out of that room with you? That don't make sense to me.' He looks at Rebecca, who is trembling a little. 'Still, your husband will be here within the hour, and you can explain this man to him yourself.'

He then looks back at George. 'I seem to recognise you from somewhere.' He pauses for a few seconds. 'Yes, that's it, you came looking for information. Information on your brother. That's right, Todd was his name. Steven Todd. I remember him and his family. They caused us many a problem afore we got that farm of his.'

The smile starts to return to George's face. 'That's right, my boy. The family you and the others put down in the mines to slowly die.'

Crossy chuckles. 'Well, it looks like you might be going to visit the same place yourself now, don't it? That's if HE doesn't feed you to the dogs first.'

George shakes his head. 'No, I don't think so. Not this time.'

'Oh! You don't think so? What makes you think this will not land you down there then? For I know many people have been looking for you for some time now. There is even a sizeable reward for your apprehension, something I am only too willing to collect on.'

'Because I have something that you do not have, and that will make it a little difficult for you to collect your prize.'

'And what's that then, a miracle?'

George points behind Crossy. 'Better than that. Him.'

'Really? Is that the best you can come up with? The "there's somebody behind me" old chestnut? Don't make me laugh, old man. I was not born yesterday.'

With that, a hand closes over the top of the pistol, holding the hammer in place, while another grabs Crossy by the throat and pulls him back. 'Well I be blowed, fancy meeting thee here, Crossy. A man I be wanting words with for many an age now,' says Springer gruffly.

George steps forward and takes the gun from Crossy's hand while Springer grabs Crossy's shoulder with his now free hand and rotates him up and around, pinning him against the wall by his throat.

Crossy can now see his face. 'You!' he gurgles out.

'Aye, it be me thee see before you. Not long back a girl by chance made it to us, a girl called Jennie.'

Crossy's eyes light up. 'She lives?'

'Yes, violated and beaten by thee and that there friend of yours, Sykes. But she made it to where the lass be now safe with friends.' He pauses for breath. 'In a diary she be carrying, the last few entries be the final words of a boy stripped of life, words that tell of the fate of his younger brother, Oliver, amongst others.'

Crossy starts to chuckle. 'I think the girl liked it rough, from what I hear. She put up a better fight than them two brothers did.'

Springer grits his teeth as he throws the man across the room by his throat. He bounces off a high backed chaise longue, catapulting him over the writing slate Rebecca was using earlier and into some porcelain figurines on the display cabinet. They shatter into pieces across the floor as Crossy staggers about before getting up on his feet, coughing and spluttering.

George stands in the large doorway with Rebecca by his side, tucked into his arm watching as Crossy pulls a huge, thick-bladed knife from his waist and points it at Springer. 'Been waiting for the chance to kill you, Springer. Put an end to the legend that you are unstoppable.' The two of them start to move around the room, vying for the best position to attack from.

In the hallway, the noise has not gone unnoticed by the man tasked with watching over Rebecca. He has come running out of the servants' area and down the corridor towards the group.

George hears the footsteps and has two options open to him: use the pistol and make all aware of their presence, or option two. He pushes the walking cane up into the air and catches it near the tip and, with good timing, swings it hard round the corner of the room. The heavy silver ball connects hard with the man's head, knocking him to the ground. Then, leaving Rebecca for a second, he steps over the man, swings the cane and delivers another blow to the stunned man's temple. This time, the cane snaps on impact, but it has had the desired effect as he is knocked senseless. With the man now out of commission, George steps back to protect Rebecca. He knows better than to get in the way of Springer, for he wants revenge for what they have done to the children.

The blade lunges through the air again and again as Crossy tries to cut Springer. But after almost every swipe, Springer hits back with a stiff jab to the face. It does not take long for blood to start flowing freely from Crossy's nose and mouth as the frustrated man rages and over-lunges with the next swipe. This allows Springer two vicious hits hard to the ribs, the second of which cracks at least one of them, if not more.

'Aahhhh,' Crossy yells in pain as he swipes back with the knife, only for Springer to catch his wrist, twist him round and push down hard on his shoulder with his other hand. The pressure forces him to release the knife and it drops to the floor, where Springer swiftly picks it up and plunges it deep into his thigh. 'Aaarrrrr,' he yells as he staggers backwards and holds on to a chair to prevent himself falling to the ground.

'That be for all of them there youngerns,' says Springer as he watches Crossy fumble with pulling out the knife. Blood is running from the wound as he slowly draws the knife back through his leg, moaning with pain as he does so. Finally, he gets the knife out with a sigh of relief and points it back at Springer, slashing wildly through the air and leaving a trail of blood spatter from the blade that hits Springer, the wall, George and even Rebecca, who lets out a squeak as droplets hit her face.

He stands himself back up by pushing off the chair, with his blood-soaked hands staining everything they touch with red smears. Staggering forwards he roars in defiance as he lunges for his opponent. This time, Springer catches his wrist with both hands and turns the hand back, facing the blade towards Crossy's body. Both men are exerting great pressure. Springer is twisting the blade towards Crossy, while Crossy is trying to push back with all his might. There is only going to be one winner here and as the blade continues to slowly rotate and get closer and closer to Crossy, he yells, 'No, no, no, please.' The blade reaches below his ribs, pointing upwards, firstly cutting into his clothes and then into his flesh beneath, the tip ever moving inwards as the pressure intensifies. Crossy panics, pure terror written all over his face as he realises that the end is coming no matter what he tries to do. Springer momentarily lets go with his right hand, then punches up hard with his palm on the hilt of the knife, driving it into Crossy's body. A second shove pushes the blade all the way up into the bottom of his heart, piercing the organ's wall and releasing a torrent of pulsing blood.

Crossy lets out a last blood-curdling gasp as Springer just stares into his eyes and watches as the signs of life ebb slowly away. 'There be no mercy for the likes of you from me, you murderer and violator of women, for you deserve no less.' He releases the man, who slowly falls to the floor.

George turns to Rebecca, who is still tucked into his arm, now looking away from the dying man. 'My dear, he was not a good man and has hurt many people in his time, including your brothers and Jennie.'

She nods in acknowledgement but is still a little shocked and is not yet ready to let go of George. He holds her in a gentle embrace and waits until she is ready to step away on her own terms. Springer rips a curtain from the window. He lays it out on the floor, drags Crossy's body onto the edge and rolls him up in the fabric, using the sash cords to tie the legs and arms tight inside. He then throws the body over his shoulder and heads towards the turret stairs, taking it down and across to the boot room stores and dropping him in a corner. He then covers the man with linen from the shelves above. Once he is satisfied that it is well covered, he returns to the others, stopping off at one of the rest rooms on the way to clean up and remove as much blood as he can from his clothes and hands and face.

CHAPTER 11

Hello, Brother

On the far side of the village, along a narrow wood-lined road, two horses pull a heavy wagon at a steady pace. The driver has a lit lamp beside him, shining through a raised slot to light up a square area ahead of him on this darkest of nights. The air is almost completely still, and with barely a sliver of moon in the sky, patchy clouds covering the glare from the stars, there is very little in the way of natural light to see his way forward.

The man continues for around half a mile before calling out to his horses. 'Woooah,' he utters as he pulls back on the reins, applies the wooden wheel brake and waits. Sliding out a satchel from under his seat, he pulls a cloth-wrapped package from within, carefully opens it up and starts to eat the pieces of roasted chicken.

'Do you have any more?' comes a voice from the darkness. Robert nearly jumps out of his skin, such is the shock. He slowly rotates the lantern until it picks up the two faces of the girls, Jessica and Prudence, smiling directly at him from the side of his wagon.

'And who might you be to startle a man in the dark like you did?' he asks.

'Who we are is not important, but we know you are Robert, and we are aware of why you are here,' says Jess, while Prue climbs aboard the wagon and sits beside him. She turns the light to face forward before helping herself to a piece of chicken from the cloth wrap on his lap. 'We are here to direct you to some special packages,' she says as Jess mounts up and sits on the other side of him. 'Now let's go while it is still dark and take the next left for about a mile.'

Robert does not know what to say. The two girls have taken him completely by surprise and left him speechless. But with them knowing his name and where to go, he releases the brake and flicks the reins to get the horses moving again.

The girls share his meal between them, and stare at Robert as they ride along. Smiling and giggling to each other, they eat the food that they have now claimed for themselves. The constant attention makes Robert feel uneasy. Finally, he can take no more and looks at Jess. 'What do you find so amusing that you two must keep having to look at me so?'

They giggle as only girls can. 'Well, George and Springer both said you were kind of a rugged handsome young man, but we think you are more in the line of cute and baby-faced, rather than rugged,' says Prue.

'I am not cute. Only my mother would ever call me cute,' he snaps while concentrating on where he is going on the narrow road. 'I would consider myself as rugged and hard-working, much like my pa,' he says with a half-smile.

The girls go quiet for a minute and look at his face from both sides before Jess speaks again. 'No, definitely cute and baby-faced,' she declares with a smile of her own.

Robert sighs and shakes his head. 'My father was right when he said all women are nothing but a pain and make no sense.'

The girls both look at him. 'Is that so?' comments Prue.

'Yes. He said that when God made the world in seven days, he created night and day, the land, sea and air, all the animals and fish. Then he made man in his own image and stopped to watch his creation develop and grow in the world. Everything got on well with each other, all were happy and content, and life was complete harmony. As a reward for such perfection, God felt that man deserved a partner to share in the happiness, so he made the female of each and every species of life to reward man for all that was good in life.' He stops speaking and continues to drive the team, while the girls wait for him to finish, but he says nothing.

Finally, Jess speaks up. 'And what happened next?'

'Oh, that's when it all went downhill. The constant nagging, moaning, demanding, forever wanting more. Man's life from that moment on was shattered and nothing but misery and suffering was to follow.'

The girls start to rip into him while he tries to keep a straight face. After several minutes of abuse, Jess finally asks him, 'What did your mother say about this?'

Robert turns to look at her. 'Nothing.'

'What do you mean, nothing?'

'She said nothing. She just picked up a broom and started hitting him round the head and said that if that was the case, he won't be getting any for a month.' The girls start to laugh instantly, while Robert just smiles and concentrates on the path ahead.

Another twenty yards down the track, he suddenly gets a smell of something. 'Quiet,' he says as he stops the horses and looks round. The girls instantly go silent as he sniffs the air again, slowly reaching down the side of his boot for his knife.

A man steps out from beside a tree to the left of the wagon. As he does so, he pulls a pipe away from his mouth. 'Ease up there, young Robert. It's only Dan.' Robert breathes a sigh of relief and pushes the knife back down the side of his boot.

'You had me right worried there, Dan.'

'Follow on behind me. It is just a few yards up here. By the way, I am glad to see you are alert to your surroundings. Several people be passing this way in the past hour or so and you are the first to notice me.'

Robert smiles. 'It was not that hard; you and Father smoke the same type of tobacco – Old Hobb. It is a smell I can usually notice when he is up the fields having a puff when mother is around. For she does not like him partaking in the habit, so he usually sneaks one while rounding up the stock.'

'Right, stop the horses here and give me a hand, lad,' Dan says as he walks round to the back of the wagon.

Robert pulls up the wheel brake and dismounts past Jess. The two men grab the first of the wrapped bodies and slide it on the back of the wagon, closely followed by the second. They then cover the bodies with sacking to reduce suspicion among those that may be a bit curious. 'We will ride with you to the outskirts of the village, then wait while you go to the physician and pick up the magistrate's body,' says Dan. 'We cannot afford to be recognised, but you are not known round here. Just say you are here to take the body to Lord Fitzgerald's private chapel, for it be what they would expect.'

Robert climbs back up on the front and grabs the reins from Prue while Dan is happy to plant himself on the bodies in the back. Soon, Robert is flicking the reins and moving the horses towards the village.

It is a short ride to the outskirts, where Dan hops off the back as Robert slows the horses to a stop. Both the girls climb down and stand by Dan, who is now speaking to Robert.

'It's down the main street and on the left.'

'Yes, I know, I took father here once when he opened his hand on a blade while shearing sheep,' replies Robert.

'When you leave, go down the road further and take the next left and keep going. We will find you along the road somewhere in a safe area and mount back up.'

Robert nods and flicks the horses on. He makes his way into the village and continues until he reaches the house of the physician. Driving into the small courtyard, he heads towards the house and raps the large brass horse-head knocker on the door three times. It takes a while, but finally he sees first a light and then a shadow as someone comes to the door and opens it.

'Yes, what can we do for you at this time of the evening?' asks the elderly butler at the door.

'I'm here to pick up the body of the chief magistrate and take him to Lord Fitzgerald's private chapel.'

The old man thinks for a while. 'Oh. The master thought you would be picking it up tomorrow, due to Lord Fitzgerald's birthday celebrations. He has already left to attend the party with his wife and enjoy the festivities. You will have to come back tomorrow, I'm afraid.' He starts to close the door and Robert is forced to think on his feet.

'Well, if that's your decision, I will go back to Lord Fitzgerald and let him know. I'm sure, knowing his ways, he will go into a frightful rage and throw your master out of the party. But that will not be my problem, though it might be yours when he returns. Then again, that will not be for me to worry about as you are the one making the call.'

The door had almost closed when it stops and, after a few seconds, reopens and the butler stands in the doorway. He points to a building on the other side of the courtyard. 'Knock on that red door. The body cleaner, Hibbot, will help you load the magistrate onto the wagon. Now good day to you, sir.' The door closes and Robert walks over to the next building and raps on the glass. With no response, he raps again, louder than before.

'Coming, coming, coming,' shouts a man from inside. Three catches can be heard to unlock before the door opens and standing before Robert is a grubby bald man holding a bottle in his hand. 'What do you want this time of the night?' the man asks. He smells of a mixture of mothballs and damp musty paper. That and the smell of cheap alcohol on his breath makes him barely tolerable to face head-on. Robert looks at him sideways so he does not have to smell his foul breath any more than he must.

'I'm here to pick up the body of the magistrate and deliver it to Lord Fitzgerald's private chapel.'

'Oh, are you, by God.' The man swings around and points back in the direction he just came from. 'Well, that is the way we need to go then. Follow me.' He staggers his way into a large open room with four raised stone slabs in a line. On one of them is the cloth-wrapped body of a man stretched out on a wooden frame.

As they approach, the man points at a bowl on the edge of the table. 'Take a look. Go on, it won't bite.' Robert peers into the bowl to see several blood-stained balls of lead resting in the bottom of the container.

'Eleven, I say again, eleven musket and pistol balls I pulled from that man.' He takes a swig from the bottle before continuing. 'I've done three before, even done four, but never eleven. They must really have wanted the magistrate dead, whoever they were.'

He takes another swig from the bottle before placing it down on an empty slab. 'You pick up the handles on the front and I will pick up the ones on the back, for I have a better chance of getting there if I follow you.'

The two men pick up the stretcher holding the body and walk towards the door. Robert quickly realises that the faster he moves, the less wobbling goes on behind and he quickly ups the pace to the back of the wagon, half towing the drunken man behind. Once there he places the front of the handles on the back of the wagon and climbs up to lift the stretcher over the top of the other bodies. With him pulling and Hibbot pushing, they soon have the body loaded in place and slide him off the stretcher.

'I see you have two already.'

Robert looks at the man. 'It's been a busy night.'

'Ah, I see. As I have not been asked to clean them up, they must be destined for the factory furnaces. Better I do not ask who they were then, for they once might have been known to me.' He taps his nose with his finger as best he can in such a drunken state then staggers back to the doorway, dragging the body board behind. He enters the building, closing and locking the door behind him without saying another word.

Robert mounts the wagon and skilfully turns the horses in the tight space. He heads back out of the courtyard, turns left, takes the next left and follows the road onwards. As he goes through the village, he lifts the cover on his lantern, strikes a match and lights the wick, then positions it ready for use when he is away from the streetlamps and lit houses of the village.

In a short time, the houses start to thin out and the way darkens. The lane starts to take a more countryside feel with hedgerows, barns and trees replacing the cottages and new large built houses. Robert opens the hatch on the front of the lamp to see where he is going. Further on, he sees the three ghostly shadows of his accomplices moving around on the side of the road. He slows the horses down to a stop, allowing the girls to climb aboard the front, one each side of him just like before.

'Now you are to drive over to Lord Fitzgerald's estate,' says Dan. 'Tell them at the entrance that you are taking the magistrate's body to the chapel as requested by Lord Fitzgerald himself. If you can, park up on the far side of the building away from the main house and all the lights so most will not even know you are there.'

Dan reaches into his pocket and pulls out two black shawls and passes one each to the girls. 'Put these on when you get near his estate and just look down and cry a little. They will think you are mourners and will pay you no mind.'

He looks back at Robert. 'If you are able, just wait without unloading the body. If people ask what you are doing, just say that you are waiting for Lord Fitzgerald to attend with his associates. What you are really waiting for is George and Springer to arrive. They should get to you before midnight and let you know the next part of the plan as it is still a little up in the air at the moment.'

Dan looks round and checks for signs of anyone else, then turns back to Robert. 'I need to get on with other things now. I will see you all later tonight.' With that, he slips off into the darkness, disappearing in seconds and leaving Robert with nothing more to do than flick the reins and get the horses moving again.

The girls place the shawls over their heads and giggle and laugh as they practise their fake attempts to cry. They heckle Robert about his looks and direct him to Lord Fitzgerald's estate, even though he knows the way. Within a mile, they join another larger road and have several coaches passing them by at speed as the three of them amble on down the road at a steady pedestrian pace.

As they reach Lord Fitzgerald's estate, Robert can see several coaches at the main gateway ahead waiting to enter. He turns off on a side track, choosing to use one of the smaller entrances away from the crowds. As he approaches the gate, the girls start to snivel and cry. He hears footsteps coming from one of the turrets, then a voice. 'And what can we do for you then?' calls out one of the guards now standing at the side of the large wooden door.

'I have the body of the chief magistrate to drop off to the chapel. Thought it better to use a side entrance so as not to disturb the guests of Lord Fitzgerald.'

Three men walk up to the wagon and see the three bodies. 'By Christ, I did not know there were three of him,' says one while the other two laugh and walk back round to Robert.

'What's with the other two?' one of them asks.

Robert remembers what Hibbot had said earlier and replies, 'Two for the factory furnaces. Got asked to drop them off as they were starting to go bad, hence they are rolled up in extra sheets.'

'Who do you think they are?' one of the men asks the others.

'Do you think we should take a look?' The girls snivel louder as they hear the man speak.

Robert's heart sinks at the thought of the men viewing the others in the back, as they might know them. 'Be damned, man, don't look at what you're not supposed to here or you'll end up joining the dead yourself,' another man says. He points to Robert. 'Move on, follow this road for a while, take the first right and follow it around the back of the estate so his guests do not see the bodies. You will see the building on the far side of the estate. Cannot miss it with its huge spire and a cross on the archway over the entrance.'

Robert raises his hand in acknowledgement and flicks at his team of horses, the girls still weeping loudly, keeping the act up until further down the road. As they move out of earshot, the girls start to giggle. Robert is close to having a heart attack. 'Quiet, please, they still might be able to hear you,' he says to the girls. His heart is still pounding as if to burst out of his chest at any second.

The two girls lean forward and look at each other. 'I think he needs something to brave him up a bit,' says Jess to Prue. As Robert concentrates on the road ahead, both girls turn and look at him and with a quiet countdown they move forward and kiss him on his cheeks at the same time.

'You're our hero,' Prue says.

Robert does not know whether to shout at them or be flattered. It is certainly not something that has happened to this country boy before. He just keeps his eyes on the road and follows it around the immense grounds. Finally, in the distance he can see his destination and it is huge. Nearly the size of Pippinsford village church but much more ornate.

As he gets closer, he can see it is surrounded by a wide gravel track. Over the far side of the church, furthest from the estate house, it is shaded and in near darkness. He manoeuvres his wagon through the arched entrance with the sign of the cross above it and pulls to a halt on the far side tight to the wall of the church. They are now virtually out of sight from the well-lit stately house on the other side of the building. Robert lets out a huge sigh of relief as he sits back and takes stock of what he has just done.

Both girls lock onto an arm on each side. 'What are we supposed to do now?' Prue whispers.

Robert looks at one girl then the other, then closes the front of the lantern to shut out the light. 'I do not know about you, but I am going to try and get some sleep. I have been driving almost nonstop for nearly a day and a half now and I have another night to go.'

With that, he picks up a wide cloth hat from behind him, puts it over his face and leans back to take a well-earned rest. The girls look at each other then tuck into Robert's sides, shuffling and wriggling around to get comfortable as they both snuggle into his shoulders.

* * *

Inside the main building, Springer has returned to join George and Rebecca in the room they'd fought in. He has three different-sized samurai swords in his hands, a wooden club-like weapon with bits of metal studding poked into the bulge at the end, and a spiked glove.

'Well, George, time we be deciding. Do we get the going and look for them there men that we came for, or do we wait for them to come here? For we be knowing now that within the hour he be paying this here youngern a visit.'

George thinks on it for a moment. 'I think it better to take them on here where we can prepare our ground, than to search around an unfamiliar building in the hope of finding them.'

Rebecca also has a choice to make. Does she stand by these two men or by the one she is married to, now knowing all that she does about him and her parents and the lies she has been living with.

She thinks on what she can expect her life to be going forward, or what life could be like if she were to leave the safety of this estate. For one of the first times in her life, she thinks like her sister Victoria did and concludes it would be better for her to get away from this place. A decision they may all yet live to regret in an hour's time if George and Springer fail in their attempt to end Lord Fitzgerald's reign.

Rebecca speaks up. 'I am not a brave woman, not by a long way, and I am used to the finer things in life. But I would like to find happiness like my sisters Edith and Victoria. If I were to stay here, I would have power, wealth, position in society and a tomb to live it in, as I would also have loneliness, isolation and a life placed before me with no freedom or choices of my own.'

Looking at both men, then staring down at the floor in front of her, she continues. 'You would think if you had wealth, you could buy happiness or use it to be happy, but wealth is what I have lived in for over a year now. It surrounds me. I eat, sleep and breathe in it. I can ask for anything and it would arrive. If I requested something, it would be instant and of the highest quality. But this wealth is not in my pocket. If I was allowed out and walked past a stall and wanted to purchase a toy for a child or offer a cripple a coin for food, I could not. For I have never seen money in all my time here. I would not even know where to get money from, in what is supposed to be my own home.'

Rebecca sighs heavily and visibly trembles as she speaks. 'This may be to my regret, but for once I will make a decision of my own choosing. Come with me, gentlemen, if you please.' She leads the men to a reception lounge two rooms along the corridor. 'If he chooses to leave an appointment without being seen, he will leave via the study downstairs and come out from a secret passageway, which is in the middle part of this display case. It will slide forward and around to the right. Usually, on big occasions he will have three or four people escorting him, so he will not be alone when he comes out.'

George and Springer both look at Rebecca. 'You sure that you want to be doing this, my dear?' George asks. 'He will know it was you who told us of the passageway.'

Rebecca cautiously nods while trying to keep her composure intact. They both see there is great fear in her eyes when she speaks and trembling in her hands as she leans back onto a bureau for support. 'I am not one for a fight, being neither brave nor heroic, so I will take my leave in the room over there and wait. And yes, I am aware that whatever the outcome of this affray, my life is about to change as I will not stay here any longer that I must.'

'Thee be far braver than thee realise, young Rebecca, for this be not for the faint of heart. If the going be in our favour, ye be more than welcome to stay with Victoria and meet our youngerns. For they be family to thee, being their aunt and all.'

Swiftly, the two men move furniture and objects around, clearing an open space in the middle for the altercation to come. Then they block up all the doorways leading out of the room, to ensure they know where the fight will come from and prevent any from escaping or calling for support. This leaves just the entrance to a small study for Rebecca to remain safely inside. What weapons they have are spread out at convenient locations around the periphery of the room, ready for grabbing when needed. Within twenty minutes everything is set and they are as ready as they will ever be. Springer turns to George and speaks. 'This will be short and swift, my friend. Dare not hesitate for it will be your last. Thee must strike first and strike fast. Don't stop until the doing is done. If one of us should fall, keep going until you have given your all. Even then, I fear much may depend on James and the way he decides to act, as he be a size to himself.'

* * *

In the reception hall below, Lord Fitzgerald is getting bored of greeting people he does not care about. With a gap in the people arriving and him noticing a man he really does not want to see heading his way, he excuses himself from the people around him and swiftly makes his way to an adjacent room. As always, Brannigan is by his side with two other enforcers. James follows him with another guard a few yards behind, ensuring protection from all sides. James turns and closes the door behind the last man. 'Hold this closed,' he says to him as Brannigan activates the passageway entrance.

Lord Fitzgerald speaks. 'Oh, how utterly distasteful it is to have such commoners in my house, touching and looking at the things I possess.' He looks at Brannigan. 'Do be sure to get everything cleaned in the morning. Hopefully that will get rid of the odious smell of them all faster.' He sighs heavily. 'I suppose I had best try again to sire this child with this wife of mine. If only the woman was more fruitful. I'm sure she must have a problem inside, you know. For it should not be taking this long. My father had many offspring with several wives, and I am from his loins. If it does not happen this time, I will have her checked out by the physician to ensure all is working correctly.'

Lord Fitzgerald follows Brannigan and the others into the passageway. As James goes to follow, a noise makes him stop and look back. He can see the door to the study being pushed hard and the man on the inside is struggling to keep it closed. 'I know he went in here. I saw him,' a voice yells out from the other side of the door. 'Lord Fitzgerald, Lord Fitzgerald, I know you're in here. I need to speak to you about a matter most urgent,' the voice hollers out.

James closes the passageway entrance, turns back and tells the man to let him in. The door is released from its catch and bursts open as a man on the other side barges in followed by three more people. 'Where is that cad?' he asks as he looks round the room. The man is clearly puzzled by Lord Fitzgerald not being present.

'I saw him enter the room. I know I did,' he says to the others as he scratches his head then turns to James. 'Did you see Lord Fitzgerald enter this room?'

James is careful with how he answers. 'Afraid I cannot see him in here, sir,' he replies as he looks around the room with the man.

With nobody there to vent his frustrations out on, he starts to speak to James. 'Do you know what that man did?' he asks.

James shakes his head.

'Because I would not sell him my lumber yards, he has put down a new county law to stop the cutting down of all the trees over six inches in diameter. Six inches! I cannot even cut down my own trees in my own forests,' he says in frustration. 'How am I supposed to keep my workers fed when I cannot get any wood to the yard? You tell me.'

James feels for the man, but at this moment in time, there is nothing he can do to help. With other things on his mind, he wants this man out of the way quickly, so he can complete his own agenda. 'Last I saw he was heading to the ballroom. Perhaps you can intercept him there and ask him yourself?'

'The ballroom!' he yells out. The man and his companions need no second hint of a lead. They are out of the room in a flash and storming off towards the ballroom in earnest. As the last man leaves, James closes the door and heads back to the secret doorway. 'Stay by that door and let nobody in,' he tells the other guard as he opens the passageway and heads off inside to catch up with the others.

Some way up the hidden route, Lord Fitzgerald is taking his jacket and plumed hat off to hide the fact he has been entertaining at a party away from Rebecca. He places the items on one of the pegs on the wall and ruffles his shirt to look a touch more casual but still smart. Brannigan's men have now reached the secret doorway and one of them activates the lever, opening the entrance and allowing the men to step through into the room followed by Lord Fitzgerald.

They file through as a group, not noticing anything until Springer pounces on the first guard. The large wooden and metal club strikes the man round the head and the second swing across his back and shoulder shatters both the stem of the club and the man as he hits the ground, lifeless and broken.

George lunges forward onto the second man from behind the open door, who has managed to pull his pistol from his waistcoat pocket. But as he straightens his arm to aim at Springer, George strikes down with the samurai sword, cutting deep into his wrist and nearly severing his hand before swinging the sword around his head and into the man's side, imbedding the blade deep into the waist of his victim just below his ribs.

The way George has wielded the sword is not how this type of blade was designed to be used, leaving it wedged in the side of the man's body as he falls and twists against the door, pulling the blade from George's hand and at the same time pushing the secret door back against the wall, closing off their escape route.

Lord Fitzgerald panics and steps back against the far wall. He recognises Springer instantly and realises the danger he is in. He looks around for a way to escape, but the doorways have been blocked off with furniture and statues and the way back down the tunnel has been covered by the downed man pushed back against the door. For the moment, he is trapped and can only watch as the fight unfolds before his eyes.

Brannigan has pulled out his large knife and his trusted weighted cosh and has no option but to take on Springer, who is now standing right in front of him. With his typical wild eyes and snarling manner, Brannigan thrashes and strikes through the air with both his weapons. George turns his attentions to the fourth man, who is raising his pistol at Springer to take a shot. Rushing towards him and grabbing at his gun arm and body while twisting him round, he takes them both to the ground as they fight over the control of the weapon. They roll across the floor, pulling and pushing as they swing punches and kick wildly at each other, tussling for supremacy of the gun as well as each other.

Over with Springer and Brannigan, the standoff intensifies as Brannigan swings with first his knife and then his weighted cosh in the hope of making contact with his opponent. While they have been focusing on each other, Lord Fitzgerald has positioned himself behind Springer and jumps on his back, grabbing him round the neck and pulling him backwards, while Brannigan moves in and slashes his blade across Springer's front, cutting a shallow slice through his shirt and across his chest, then follows it up with a strike across the side of his face with his cosh.

It stuns Springer as he staggers, but he is still aware of his surroundings and starts to accelerate backwards, hitting the solid wall behind him with as much force as he can. The impact knocks the wind out of Lord Fitzgerald as well as banging the back of his head on the wall, and he releases his grip immediately, falling to the floor, dazed and gasping for air.

Brannigan lunges forward again, and Springer is forced to take the impact of the cosh, first across his forearms as he defends his head and then over his shoulder as he turns away from the swinging blade of the knife.

On the floor, the fight is intensifying as they roll to the edge of the room. George is losing his grip on the gun and in a last-ditch attempt to salvage the situation, he releases the gun and reaches for the small samurai blade on the shelf. He grabs the knife and plunges it deep into the side of the man at the same time the pistol fires. Both men react simultaneously to the pain they've inflicted on each other. As the enforcer tries to get to his feet, he falls back down onto George's chest. With the man now on top of him, it is hard to move or know the damage the pistol shot has done to him.

Slowly the man on top of George stirs and begins to lift himself up again. He gets to his knees and with great effort pulls the knife out of his body. He looks at the red-stained blade in his hand before dropping it to the floor.

George has placed the blade well, more by luck than judgement, as it has pierced the man's lungs and other important veins and arteries. He holds his position for a while before slowly falling backwards to the ground, the life having left his body forever. George, on the other hand, is still breathing. He has taken a bullet to the left shoulder and is bleeding heavily. He may be out of the fight but is still alive and starts to turn himself around and sits up against a wall. Taking his handkerchief from his pocket, he plugs up the hole in his shoulder, wincing with the pain as he does so.

Springer and Brannigan are still in the fight, moving around the room as they toy with each other. Brannigan lunges forward and swings with his blade and Springer steps to one side, placing his right hand into one of the units. When he pulls it back out, he has the spiked metal glove attached to his hand.

Brannigan strikes down with his cosh and Springer punches it with the glove, sticking the cosh onto the spikes and then twisting it out of his hand. As he flicks it to the ground, the contents of sand and lead droplets spill across the floor for all to see. He then thrusts the knife towards Springer, who twists his body to allow the blade to travel past his face within inches of making contact. Springer brings a right uppercut to Brannigan's stomach, setting the spikes deep into his body.

'Huh.' Brannigan lets out a ghastly moan as Springer grabs his right shoulder with his left hand and pulls the glove back out of his stomach.

'Ye know not how long I be waiting to do this,' whispers Springer in Brannigan's ear as he rams the glove back into his stomach again with a vicious uppercut. The spikes puncture everything inside him and as Brannigan slowly drops to his knees, he looks at Springer knowing that this fight is now all but over.

'There be so many who would wish to put to you this final blow. Most be not of this world now. So, I be right proud to do the deed in their stead,' says Springer as he pulls out the glove and steps to one side. Brannigan slowly leans forward, holding his stomach as Springer delivers a final blow to the back of his head, releasing the imbedded glove and watching Brannigan drop to the ground, his evil on this earth finished forever.

While the fight continued, nobody noticed Lord Fitzgerald moving round the room. Having picked up the unfired pistol in his left hand and in his right the last medium-sized samurai sword from a side table, he now stands over George with the blade point resting on his chest. He glances up at the exhausted Springer, watching as the secret door slowly gets forced open behind him.

'Ah, better late than never, right?' says Lord Fitzgerald as he sees James force his way through the passageway door, then look around at all the bodies strewn across the room.

Springer is exhausted and just stares at Lord Fitzgerald. He does not realise that James is now behind him. 'Get done with the doing,' says Springer as Lord Fitzgerald slowly raises the pistol towards him.

James sees what is about to happen and reacts with lightning speed. He grabs the large blue-and-white porcelain vase and smashes it over the back of Springer's head, knocking him to the ground. Then he walks towards Lord Fitzgerald, reaching into a pouch on his side as he steps over one and around another body lying on the ground.

'Really?' says Lord Fitzgerald. 'That vase cost me a fortune, you know.' He looks at the pistol in his hand. 'A piece of lead costs virtually nothing.' He shrugs and lets out a sigh. 'You just cannot get the staff these days. Oh well, never mind,' he says as he places the pistol on the side and raises the sword with both hands above his head in preparation to finish off George.

Suddenly, a slice across his hand forces Lord Fitzgerald to drop the sword. 'What the…? Ouch.' Another swipe cuts up his cheek, then a thin cut through his shirt and down his chest, followed by one across his stomach. 'Aaahhh,' he yells as he turns away. He feels the sting across his back and then both buttocks. He turns back round only to feel the stings across his thigh and leg, up the back of his arm and across his shoulder. The pain and sting from each cut builds and intensifies by the second. 'For the love of God, man, stop,' he screams.

A hand grabs him by the throat and pins him to the wall. 'Hello, my brother. It's been a long time,' says James.

Lord Fitzgerald looks at him, perplexed. 'Who are you?' he asks.

'Until now, you never thought to even ask my name, brother. Seven years at sea, years living in France… I even found the last of our sisters in Paris still alive when I killed your whore of a friend, Madam Kelly.'

'That was you!'

'Yes, that was me,' he says as he raises the slime-dripping blade and handle and pushes the oozing liquid into the cut on his brother's cheek and across his chest.

'Aahhhh, that stings,' Lord Fitzgerald yells as he stares into the man's eyes. Suddenly, he spots the small white scar on his chin.

'James! Is that you?'

'Finally, you remember who I am.'

Lord Fitzgerald starts to stutter. 'P... P... Please let me explain. I had to do it. Father, he was so unreasonable. He was going to send me to sea for a year. I would never have survived.'

'For the death of our parents, the murder of our brothers and sisters, the killing of our friends and strangers alike, whatever time you have left, I sentence you to a time of suffering and everlasting pain.' James rams the blade into his side and twists it, shattering it into pieces.

'Aaahhh,' screams Lord Fitzgerald as James crushes the handle in his hand and pushes what he can into the wound with his thumb before throwing him across the room to crawl into a corner, cowering and snivelling.

Springer is now back up on his feet and has watched the last few minutes unfold. 'That hurt, that did.'

James looks at him. 'That vase was as thin as paper and weighs nothing. Besides, I had to do something to save your life,' he says, washing his hand in a vase of flowers to remove all the slime and poisons from his skin.

Rebecca has come in from the other room and is tending George as best she can, while Springer picks up the pistol and walks over to snivelling Lord Fitzgerald. As he raises it to fire, James says, 'If you shoot him, he will die for sure. But what I have just done to him with the cuts will leave him to suffer in pain for years. And without his enforcers to protect him, others like him will tear down his empire, bit by bit. I know because I have seen it done before. The best way to make a man like that suffer is to make him watch as everything he owns slowly gets taken away. Oh, he will fight to hold on to it as best he can, but like in a wolf pack, once the dominant male is weakened, the fall to licking the leftover scraps is inevitable as the stronger and more aggressive members take over.'

Springer stares down at the whimpering Lord Fitzgerald, who now looks at him and puts out a hand in submission. He turns to look at James as he lowers his pistol, then back at the snivelling man on his knees. A quick flick of the pistol to his head knocks him down to the floor. 'I be needin' something,' he says as he turns and walks up to James. 'If in a year he be not dead or sickly, I finish what thee started.'

James nods. 'Seems fair to me.'

'Time we be leaving. If thee have a mind to help with the bodies, it would be right kindly of you, James, as we have a place to hide them all from those that might take an interest.'

James nods as they both watch George stagger back to his feet, helped by Rebecca.

'That there old boy be as hard as any a man half his age, I swear,' says Springer.

'Less of the old, my young Springer. Yet again I am shot at and this time hit and wounded on one of your adventures. It seems that from the day I first met you, I have been constantly putting my life at risk to save yours.'

James and Springer laugh at his comments. 'I would not laugh if I were you, young Springer. Wait until Cook, Bebe and your good lady Victoria find out I got shot and injured defending you again.'

Springer's chuckling stops instantly as this thought sinks in. 'He be right about that. When them their women find out, I be sleeping in that there barn for months.'

James laughs louder. 'Then don't tell them. Make something up.'

George, Springer and even Rebecca look hard at James. 'You do not know our Cook, for I swear down now that she be already in the knowing of what has passed here today and be plotting my fate,' replies Springer.

As Springer and James wrap the bodies in sheets and take them down to the boot room ready for disposal, George and Rebecca make their way over to Lord Fitzgerald in the corner of the room. He has not moved from the spot, just continues to blubber and sway backwards and forwards as the toxins start to set in and weaken his body. They stand over him, looking down at this pitiful man as he slowly looks up at them.

George is the first to speak. 'For what you have done to my brother and all the others, I so wished you dead by my hand. But now looking at you, a snivelling, grovelling excuse of a man in front of me, I realise that a far worse fate will soon be upon you.'

Lord Fitzgerald looks up at them both, drooling from his mouth as he reaches out with his hand towards Rebecca. 'Help me, my dear.'

Rebecca pushes his hand away. 'I can only picture that my little brothers reached out in the same way when you had them taken away. For that and all the lies you and my own parents made up to make me feel that you were the victim, may God forgive you and my mother, for I will not.'

James moves in to tie his brother up. He says nothing as he finishes off the bindings, just picks him up and slumps him into a large chair. Staring down at the man, he finally says his last words to him. 'If by some small chance you do recover and I hear of you again, Springer or myself will be back to finish what was started here.'

In the other room, Springer speaks with Rebecca. 'Your sister will be right pleased to see you. As will Cook, for they talk about you often.'

Rebecca nods at him. 'I know, but I do not feel as if I am ready to see her yet. I have been quite nasty in my opinions and ways of late and need to find myself again. I do know I cannot stay here anymore, for Lord Fitzgerald would take out what has happened here on me.'

She thinks for a moment. 'If it is alright, I will grab a bag of what I can carry and leave with you. I am not sure what I will do yet, but it will give me some time to decide my future.'

'When Victoria and I made our way from this place right fast like,' says Springer, 'we had but the clothes we be walking in, a large case, big bag, and a small pouch with all the wealth we had in the world. Within weeks we had but just a bag and our wealth. All else be too much to carry while looking back at them that be wanting to do us harm. Pack just what be of value to sell – jewellery, coin and small precious pieces. Once sold later, there be enough to buy the clothes that thee be needing to travel on.'

Rebecca nods as she understands his advice and disappears to collect what belongings she will need while Springer carries the last body down the stairs to the boot room.

CHAPTER 12

Live With Your Choices

Over at the chapel, it has been some time, and Robert and the girls are feeling a bit on edge. In two hours of waiting, they have seen nobody. So, when a team of horses pulling a carriage is seen heading towards them, Robert, Jess and Prue are on full alert, wondering if it is their friends or somebody else.

It enters through the archway and goes around the back of the church to the dark side of the building, pulling up beside Robert.

As Springer leans forward and tips his hat at them, they have their answer. 'Ye be a sight for sore eyes, young Robert,' says Springer as the coach door opens and James steps out. 'Now let's be putting these bodies on the back of that there wagon. Jess and Prue, kindly step thee down and be ready to enter the coach,' continues Springer.

As Springer and James start to take the bodies from the floor of the coach and chuck them into the back of the wagon, Robert stares at James in awe. 'So you be James, the friend Ma and Pa talk about. I never knew a man could grow so big in this world.'

James smiles at him. 'Well, I know who you are, young Robert, for you have your mother's eyes.' The switch is done in minutes and the girls enter the coach and take their seats beside Rebecca and George, introducing themselves to each other as they do.

Robert, James and Springer are standing together between the coaches as Springer speaks. 'Robert, as we leave this here estate, start making your way home right quick like. Take James here for his work be done now. I will catch thee up once the doing is done for the girls' family and all the others who are trapped.'

James puts his hand on Springer's shoulder. 'You're not coming with us?'

'No, not yet. Them there young girls' – he points at the coach – 'their parents be held down in sewers for work in Fitzgerald's mines. I be a fixing to free them and such people as want to go. For that be where many a child and families alike spent the last of their days when your brother be wanting the homes they once be living in.'

James is taken aback. 'Is that where Rebecca's younger brothers met their fate?'

Springer nods. 'Oliver and Edward be not alone in the number of youngerns that tried to make a difference. Dammed near a dozen or more gave their lives getting people trapped below food and clothes to keep the reaper from their door. George's brother, along with many from the village, fell foul to Lord Fitzgerald's plans to grow his empire. Them there children be amongst the bravest I ever knowed, for to fight back when so many an adult looked the other way or worse, pretended it be not happening, shows a courage that I must at least match, if not better.'

James lowers his head before raising it again and speaking. 'Then I will join you, my friend. For I am no less ashamed for what my brother has done here than you.' He enters the carriage and closes the door behind him while Springer continues to speak to Robert. 'Remember to follow us right tight out of the gate before going your own way. If we be stopped, stay on the wagon for I will deal with problems if required.'

Both men mount their transports and prepare to leave. Robert follows Springer out of the chapel entrance and down the narrow track. They travel round the estate to the side entrance they have both used before and slow down as they reach the gate. A guard waves them down with a lit lamp and approaches the coach driven by Springer.

At the same time, James leans out the window and speaks. 'We are heading to the factory on instructions from Lord Fitzgerald. The wagon behind has material for the furnaces and is under my escort to the site.'

The man looks at James. 'I will be the judge of that,' says the man in a drunken slur as he walks around to the wagon and raises a torch, exposing all the wrapped bodies in the back.

James opens the door and steps out of the carriage. With his full size on display, he speaks again. 'You speak to me in that disrespectful tone again and you will join them. Do you understand, insolent buffoon?'

The man is taken aback, but before he can speak, the two other men standing by the warming fire rush over. One holds on to his friend and marches him away while the other speaks to James.

'I am sorry about that, sir. He is a little worse for wear. I apologise. Please be on your way.'

James considers his options then speaks. 'If that man is here on guard when I get back, I will deal with the three of you personally and start to fill that cart again. Do you understand?' The guard tilts his hat at James as he climbs back into the carriage and shuts the door. He hits the ceiling of the coach on the inside and Springer flicks the reins and moves off, closely followed by Robert in the wagon behind.

They follow each other for around half a mile before Springer turns off towards the village and Robert continues his way down the lane. Now not following the coach, he opens the hatch on his lamp light at the front to see where he is going and within minutes has disappeared into the darkness.

Inside the coach, James is inspecting George's wound. He moves the blood-soaked handkerchief and looks at the hole, ripping at his clothing to get a better look at the damage. The shot itself has not penetrated too deeply, as it was largely stopped by the thick material. But it has pulled a lot of the threads into the wound. He closes the area back up and covers it with his own handkerchief, then opens the carriage door to speak to Springer. 'I need access to medical tools for your friend George. We need to work on him sooner rather than later or we may have a problem with infection.'

Springer looks back at James and raises his hand in acknowledgement. As they enter the village, he turns the horses towards the physician's house on the main street and they pull up in the courtyard.

The coach doors open, and James helps George out of the carriage, closely followed by Rebecca. As Springer also assists James with George, Rebecca is banging on the doorknocker. It takes a while for the butler to get to the door and a minute to open it. As he does so, Rebecca pushes it wide open and speaks. 'Yes, I know your master is out at my house, for I am Lady Fitzgerald. I need access to his room for an injured man.' She walks straight past the old man and through into the patient room, followed by Springer and James helping George on his way.

The butler does not say a word; he just watches events unfold from a distance. For whatever he would say would make no difference. George is placed in the large reclining chair while James goes through the cabinets for surgical tools in the way of probe sticks and grippers to grab the lead ball.

'I need alcohol and bandages to wipe the area,' James says to Rebecca as he starts to cut the clothing around the wound.

Rebecca is struggling to find the alcohol. She looks in several cupboards and on many shelves to no avail. Then, out of the blue, a hand reaches out to her with the bottle of alcohol they require.

It is the butler. 'Well, I might as well serve somebody tonight for I'm not going to get much sleep the way things are going,' he says as she takes the bottle with a smile and passes it to James.

White sheets and bandages soon follow with the butler helping Rebecca to find all the required items. James wipes clean the area around the bullet hole with alcohol. Soon he is pushing a metal probe into the hole in George's shoulder to find the bullet. George is in a lot of pain, but barely shows it to the others.

Finally, after several attempts the probe taps the edge of the bullet deep inside the shoulder muscle. James switches to an extractor, washes it with alcohol, then slides it down the path left by the bullet. As the curved set of tongs reaches the same distance inside the cavity, he opens the tool and slides over the musket ball and clamps down. Then slowly he pulls the tongs back out of the wound, picking out the lengths of clothing fibres that were pushed into the wound as they reveal themselves.

As the ball comes out, James checks the end of it. Material from George's waistcoat and shirt is lifted from the projectile and James smiles at the success of the operation.

'Well, George, we got all the material out. All we have to do is cauterise the wound and you will be good as new in a month or so.' James heats up a brass rod with a diamond-shaped tip in a flame until it glows orange. He wipes around the wound again, cleaning every part of the entrance hole and surrounding surface. He then picks up the hot iron and says, 'On the count of three, I will press. Ready? One!' James presses down instantly and moves the flat sides around the wound as Springer holds him down. George lets out a fierce groan and twists with the pain.

Once James is satisfied that he has done enough to seal the wound, he removes the hot iron, much to George's appreciation as his body relaxes and he lets out a huge sigh of relief. He continues to wipe, bandage and wrap his patient in clean linen as Rebecca speaks.

'You seem to know your way around a wounded man, James. Are you also a physician?'

He smiles at her. 'No, nothing of the sort. But necessity taught me about wounds and healing a long time ago. On the whaling ships, if you could not stitch or cauterise a wound, you would surely die, as most would be from shark bites and open cut injuries. Bleeding out got most of them that died, so you learned to clean and seal a wound as fast as you could so you had a better chance of survival. Again, when in Paris, the time we rescued my sister, one of us came away missing his hand. We had a tough week controlling the fever in him, but the man who tended his wounds was a great physician and watching him work taught me a great deal.'

After pausing for a minute, James speaks again. 'What we need to do is make sure this man does not go into shock by keeping him talking and ensuring he is understanding us and replies. For what I have done can take it out of a young person and this man is no spring chicken.'

George's eyes open. 'I heard that, young man. If it was not for this hole, I would show you what an older man can do to the likes of you, so help me.'

The group cannot help but laugh at George, as he just never gives up. He's always ready for whatever is required, just like tonight. But unfortunately, he always seems to be the one to get the worst of it.

He stubbornly sits up and slowly gets to his feet. 'We need to get going if we are to help the girls get their parents back. For I gave my word I would do just that.' Rebecca helps him back to the coach as Springer and James start to clear up the mess.

'Well, Mr Springer,' says the butler. 'If you are back in town, I would say Lord Fitzgerald has not been having a good time tonight with his birthday celebrations!'

Springer turns to look at him. 'You know who I am?'

'Yes, sir, that I do. Won money on you in the big fight and have seen you in town may times in days gone past. It is good to see you back as it means that his men will not have it all their own way for a while.'

Springer smiles, but it is James who speaks next. 'Why are you not at the celebrations with the others from the village?'

'You would not see any of the old villagers at his party, sir. For a start, not many would be invited. And secondly, nobody would want to go. He is not popular here. Only the new money people from around these parts would be invited or attend such a high-profile gathering.'

James thinks for a minute. 'So, most in this village tonight would not miss him or his enforcers if they were no longer around?'

The man starts to get a little nervous at the questions but has gone too far to stop now. 'Most have lost or are missing friends and family to them evil men, so no, they do not like any of them.'

'What if I were to say that many of the missing people were about to find their way back to the village. Would you be able to pass the word round to people that they would be needing help?'

The butler thinks for a minute. 'The enforcers would round them all up again, along with anybody that they found helping them. Then they would also disappear, sir. So, I do not think they would help as they would be too afraid.'

Springer steps in as he now understands where James is going with this and decides to risk everything on his next few words. 'Brannigan, Sykes, Crossy, the magistrate and all Lord Fitzgerald's bodyguards be not of this world anymore. We have seen to that. Lord Fitzgerald himself be sick with ailments that be pushing the reaper to his door, eager for his soul given the chance. Now we be soon set to rescue those below ground, but we can only get them out, for there may be too many for us to take and keep safe.'

The old butler looks at them both. 'I want to believe you, so help me I do. I know the magistrate is dead as I have seen his body. But the risk is great for the people here. Why, less than a week ago the Wilsons were taken when leaving the village and they had such lovely daughters.'

Springer thinks for a second. 'Would they be Jessica and Prudence, by any chance?'

'Why yes! But how would you know their names?' the butler asks.

'Please come with us,' Springer asks as he leads the man outside to the carriage and opens the door. He leans in and says a few words before stepping back and holding the door open. The butler cannot believe his eyes when the two girls come down the steps, for he knows them well and gets a hug from them both.

'Mr Jenkins, it is so good to see you again,' says Jess.

'It be a promise made by that there man you be keen to help with the bullet wound. He gave his word to the girls that we would get them their parents back, as well as all the others we be finding down there. It would ease my mind if more be willing to take a hand with the caring of those we find, as many may require more help than we be able to give.'

The old butler has tears in his eyes as he hugs the girls, then steps back and wipes his face. 'I will get my coat and knock on every door I know. They may be afraid to go looking for people for fear of getting caught, but if you were to send them here, we would help all we can, for most will have friends or family in the village.'

As the butler walks back towards the house, James shouts after him. 'Get them to light up the village so people can see it glow in the sky. That way they will know what way to go in the dark.' Mr Jenkins raises his hand as he enters the house and reaches for his jacket and hat. Returning swiftly wearing said items and with a cane in his hand, he walks past them and on into the village.

James helps George climb back up into the coach with the girls, while Springer takes his position at the front controlling the horses. Just like Robert, he has the skills to turn the team of four horses around in a very tight area and get back onto the road.

With a flick of the reins, they head to a location he has had little experience of finding. He slowly moves down the back streets and towards the quarry where the old forge used to be. In the darkness he can see the outline of an old building wedged against the rock face. As he gets closer, it becomes clear that it is the disused building and forge written about in Edward's diary. He pulls up the horses as the recognisable face of Dan appears from inside the forge and walks up to the coach carrying a large cloth bag in his hand.

'I thought you were not coming. Such has been the time you have taken getting here,' he says.

'You don't knows the half of it, but here we be now,' says Springer as he ties off the reins before dismounting the coach. The carriage door opens and James steps down to the ground.

'By heck, he be big! Near twice the size of me,' Dan says as James stretches out his arms, takes off his overcoat and hat and places them inside the coach.

'Dan, that there man be James, brother of Lord Fitzgerald. Returned as Bob and Emily said he would to right a wrong and take his brother to task, and that be surely what he has done. For we be right grateful he threw down with us and not against, for the outcome would not have been good if he had not.'

Dan tilts his cap in James's direction. 'Grateful for the help,' he says as he drops the cloth bag inside the coach door and says hello to the girls. He looks at the injured George, who is now asleep, then back at Springer. 'That be what George asked me to bring. But what happened to him?'

James is first to respond. 'Took a pistol shot to the shoulder. We have removed the ball and cleaned and sealed the wound. But it is a lot for an old man in his later years to take.'

'Less of the old, young James,' murmurs a semi-conscious

George from inside the carriage.

Dan laughs and shakes his head. 'He can still hear well enough then,' he says before turning back to Springer and continuing. 'The tools you requested are inside the fireplace near the entrance. The back opens and moves round just as the book described and I have lit the first few candles going down into the tunnel, but no further as I don't like caves. So, I will wait with the others for your return.' He passes them both a vesta of matches and watches as the big men set off.

Springer and James waste no time in getting into the wrecked building. Picking up a sledgehammer and a pickaxe each from the fireplace, they head through the opening and make their way down the stairs and pathways.

'Those brave children did this just to get food down to those trapped below ground,' says James.

'That they did on many occasions. The accounts in the diary would make most men ashamed that it be youngerns who saw the truth and be helping them that had been taken.'

There is not much more in the way of talking as they make their way along the narrow rocky route, lighting the well-used candles and the odd lamp as they go. They move into the brickwork drains and continue as the children had done many times before and follow the disc marks and arrows left by them on the walls and floor. The construction of the area has changed a little from what Springer had read, but not enough to hide the route he must take. They rip away some of the sheeting that hides the final length of tunnel and move on until they reach the large room with brick pillars and metal bars round the outside.

As their eyes become acclimatised to the poor lighting, they start to make out the shadows of people in different areas. Some are standing but most are sitting or lying down. It is difficult to count the number of people, but many are present. Unlike the children before who were sneaking around while trying not to be caught, these men are here with a purpose. As the prisoners see the two men, they begin to crowd around the bars near them, asking questions and requesting help.

'Stand thee back and we will soon have thee all out of here,' says Springer as he looks at the pillars between the iron bars.

'So, we take out the pillars and not the bars then,' James says as he moves to the next pillar along.

'I be thinking that them there brick pillars be damp and soft down here. If they be shattered, the bars should push over.'

'Please stand back all of you and cover your eyes,' hollers James as they prepare to strike the bricks with sledgehammers. *Thud, thud, thud.* The first few hits just dent the damp bricks and do not make much of an impact. But after ten or so hits, large chunks of brickwork start to crack and split off. The pillars break apart with the heavy impacts from these powerful men. Within minutes, they shatter and collapse from the relentless strikes and the bars break free of the brickwork.

With the set of bars now free on both sides from the pillars, the only thing holding them up is where they are imbedded at the bottom into a two-foot wall topped with a line of mortar. The two men soon smash this down and push the bars back to break them over. As they fall forward there is a huge crash as they hit the floor, bouncing and vibrating as the metal frames settle on the ground.

'The guards are coming. I can hear their boots on the ground,' shouts one of the prisoners as he points in the direction they will come from. James and Springer both grab their pickaxes, along with the hammers they are already holding, and step through the open gap to take on the men. They can hear the hobnail boots thumping on the ground as they run towards them. The two men cover the ground swiftly and as they hear the key turn in the lock and the door open, they are in position. A guard steps through with a club in his hand and moves towards the prisoners. James steps out, clasping the pickaxe in both hands, raises it over his head and behind him before throwing it forward. It rotates through the air several times before striking the man, impaling his chest and sending him backwards to the floor. A second man running forward comes to a similar fate as Springer swings his pickaxe and drives it into his stomach, leaving him screaming in pain as he also hits the ground.

James steps forward, swinging the sledgehammer around his shoulders and contacting a man's head, ripping it apart on impact and covering the others around him with a spray of blood, brains and bone matter that shocks the advancing guards to a standstill.

They look down at their fallen comrades. The sight of such horrific injuries and the blood on their faces and bodies have the last three men shocked and terrified. 'Be damned with this. I'm getting out of here,' one yells as they turn around and start running back to the doorway.

Springer has not finished with them yet. He is building up a rage and winds up his hammer by swinging it around three times before releasing it towards the fleeing men. The last one out the door takes the full impact of the hammer in the centre of his back, crushing his spine and catapulting him through the entrance and into the backs of the others, knocking them all to the floor.

As he shudders and shakes on the floor, the others stagger to their feet while looking at their fallen friend. They do not go back to help him, just turn to run. Unfortunately for them, James has covered the ground swiftly. He grabs both men by the clothing around their necks, slinging one backwards towards Springer while pinning the other up against the wall. He punches the man repeatably in the face, before releasing him to drop to the floor. Springer has caught the other man by the throat and with a vice-like grip of his huge hand, he squeezes tighter and tighter, crushing the life and air from his body before slinging him across the room, barely alive and gasping for breath.

James and Springer look at each other then turn and take stock of the people they have come to save. They are greeted with muffled cheers and people grabbing and hugging them, patting them on the shoulders and back. Tears fill their eyes as they finally begin to realise they are really being rescued from this awful place. It is quite an emotional experience for the big men as well, as they look at the faces of so many desperate and terrified people.

Before long, James speaks. 'Listen, everybody. Please follow Springer and he will lead you out of here to waiting friends and family. Help those who are struggling, and I will follow up from the rear. Now let's get going for I am sure there must be more guards around.'

Springer swiftly steps over the broken bars and leads the first of the people along the path towards the surface. The others follow behind, some holding on to each other to aid them on their way. It's slow going as many are ill, sick or just too weak to go any faster. But move the group does, ever onwards and at a speed all can keep pace with.

Within half an hour the first of the people are coming out of the building and are greeted by Dan, George – who is now out of the coach – and the two girls. Pointing to the light in the night sky, they encourage all the people to continue towards the glow in the village as friends will be waiting. People with lit lanterns are also heading from the village towards the rescued prisoners. They are keen to help and hope to find loved ones they have not seen in a while. Shouts and screams of joy are let out as many are reunited with lost friends. For the first time in a long while, the villagers have something to celebrate.

Jess and Prue look at every person coming out in the hope of spotting their parents amongst the people rescued. They go through everyone without finding them. In the distance, James arrives with the final group. The girls are swiftly with them and find their old neighbours, the Saddlers, amongst the group. As they start to speak to them and ask about their parents, their heads drop. 'I'm sorry, my dears,' says Roberta Saddler, 'but your parents perished when the new tunnel collapsed while they were removing blast rubble. I know because we helped pull them out. They were arm in arm when we found them.'

The girls look at each other and start to cry. George has heard the conversation and is swift to hold both the girls as best he can with his wound. They both grip on to him, tears now flowing down their cheeks.

Roberta rummages in her pockets and says to the girls, 'It may seem cold to you that don't understand, but we took these from them. We were going to use them to barter extra food from the guards when we were at our weakest, but they should belong to you now.' She holds out her fist and drops two rings into Prue's hand before turning away. Taking a few steps, she looks back and says, 'I'm sorry for your loss.' Roberta is ashamed of what they have been forced to do to survive, but now understands the circumstances that drive people to scavenge from the dead to keep on living.

Jess and Prue look at the rings. They are their parents' wedding bands, and it is only now that it really hits home that they are gone forever. They take a ring each as they hug each other in comfort and cry for the loss of their parents.

George calls out to the Saddlers. 'Please wait a minute. I have something that may be of help.' They stop and turn around as George makes his way to the coach and grabs the cloth bag. He takes out a pouch and puts it in his pocket, then walks over to them. 'Thank you for giving the girls the rings. I'm sure that was not an easy thing to confess to doing. I understand what it takes to survive in adversity, and I am sure the girls do too. It is just a lot for them to take in. This we took from the magistrate's office safe when we paid him a visit. It would seem they stored quite a bit of money in it. Would you see to it that it is split between the people who came out of the tunnel as it might help to get them where they need to go or help them to start again. For after tonight, I do not think any of you will be in danger again, as most of them that were corrupt have now been taken to task.'

Roberta takes the bag, hugs him and kisses him on the cheek. 'Thank you,' she says before turning and making her way towards the village with her husband. For the Saddlers, like so many others, this has been a traumatic time. It will take a while to come to terms with what has happened and a lot longer to put it behind them.

Springer has gone back to the derelict building. Making his way to the entrance to the cave system, he closes the granite doorway to the passage. He is joined by James as he looks at the marks on the wall left by the children and the crosses through them as they perished in their attempts to save their friends.

Turning to James, who is also seeing the marks for the first time, he speaks. 'Them there youngerns be the best of us all. Each mark be a loss.' He punches the copper skirting, distorting it out of shape. 'I be sad and ashamed not to have been here and done what be needed doing sooner.' He goes to punch the wall, but James sees what he is going to do and pulls him back.

'No, my friend, it will not help. But what you have done here today will make a big difference to a lot of people. The truth has come out and them that were once lost are here to tell their side of the story. There are too many freed people to discredit what has been going on for sure, and not enough of the enforcers and criminals left to take them prisoner. Nobody will ever go missing again and you have helped the children find peace. It is the parents who will now need to live with what they have done to their own families. For all will now know what they did to secure a better life for themselves. Come, let us go. We have a long way to travel and friends waiting on our return.' James leads Springer out of the building and back to the coach.

As they arrive, they come across George, Dan and Rebecca with the girls Jess and Prue, who are beside themselves at the loss of their parents and all that has happened. It takes a while, but eventually they convince the girls to come with them to Bob's farm. For there, they will be safe and can decide what they want to do next. Getting them away from Pippinsford will only be the first step in their journey.

With the girls finally calmed, the group board the coach with James and Springer sitting up front. They enjoy each other's company and have many things in common, not to mention a few good confrontations thrown in, and are keen to continue their conversation. With a short debate over who is going to drive the team of horses, Springer takes the reins from James and once he hears the door on the side of the carriage close, he flicks them and gets the horses moving. A few of the people from the village and those who were saved are still nearby and wave them off, but most have already departed to tend to their loved ones.

The coach heads off along the road with Springer asking James a question. 'So, whose carriage be this that has served us well this very night?'

James looks at him and shrugs. 'I don't know. It just happened to be there when I needed one and sort of just stayed around most of the night.'

'Well I'll be. It seems to me that ye be the type that likes to take what not belongs to thee without so much as a by your leave.' James smiles at Springer before they both start to laugh.

As dawn breaks and the sun begins to rise above the treeline and the coach finally arrives at Bull Farm, they have made good time and are just four hours behind Robert. As they pull up in the yard, Emily is straight out of the farmhouse to welcome them. She first rushes over to hug Springer and James, then helps the others down from the carriage. The smell of bacon and sausages frying in the pan fills the air and she hastily ushers all of them into the house. As they file in, they can see she has moved everything around to accommodate everybody with a place to sit and plenty of food on the table.

Robert has only just started to eat and stands up to greet all the others as they sit down. 'Where be Bob and Jethrow?' asks Springer as he looks around the room and notices their absence.

'Oh, they are up in the field with the wagon. They started early to deal with the foundations on the new pigsty,' Emily says with a smile as she begins to pour George a cup of tea from the last of his own stock.

'Seems like the right thing to do now we have the material, and the men have been waiting all night to get going. Anyway, I see we have some new faces amongst us.' She turns to Jess, Prue and Rebecca.

Introductions are soon underway and the events of the night are talked about over breakfast. The conversation is fast and furious, but after a short time it becomes clear that the night's events have taken their toll as one by one they start to nod and doze off.

'I think we had better get you to your beds as I don't think I can carry you all on my own,' says Emily.

She escorts the two sisters and Rebecca to her own bedroom and the large and small bed she has made up for returning people. George and Dan go into the two beds made up in Robert's room and Robert is in the hallway on a makeshift bench.

As for James and Springer, they have fallen asleep where they sit and are both snoring away, making some sort of harmonious grunting sound. Both are far too big for Emily to move, so they will just have to stay where they are for now.

Emily stands and watches the two men for a while, thinking of what they have both been through in their lives and yet they have both remained such gentlemen. You could not have found two people more different in upbringing and social standing and yet here they sit after fighting a common cause without complaint, when they could be at home with their families and loved ones.

'God bless you both, my boys,' she says, 'and I hope after this you have the closure and peace that you deserve,' and she leaves to tend to the horses outside in the yard.

* * *

It is late afternoon when Springer finally opens his eyes. Looking around, he is now on a bed, and opposite him, James is still asleep on his side. He cannot work out how he got here, but he feels good for the rest he has had. Sitting up, he stretches out and yawns loudly. As he stands up, James has started to stir as well. He looks around, just like Springer.

'I know not how they got us here either.'

James chuckles. Within a few minutes they are up and heading to the kitchen for a wash in the sink to clear their heads, each one pumping the water for the other. They can hear talking and laughing outside, and it is only then they realise the kitchen seems empty and more spacious. It soon dawns on them that the big table and all the chairs have been removed. With laughter and banter coming from outside, curiosity has them heading towards the sound of voices around the corner of the house.

'Well I be,' says Springer as they come across the table set outside with all the chairs around it. A fire is roaring beside it with a whole pig roasting to one side of the flames and a large black pot is simmering on the coals. Robert seems to have taken charge of roasting the beast while Dan sits to one side lighting his pipe and taking a few deep puffs. Rebecca, Emily and the twins are busying themselves at the table positioning plates, cutlery and other items.

Emily sees the men approaching. 'Well, it's about time you woke. We thought you would never come round, the way you both snored and grumbled in your sleep.' The sisters giggle as they stop and watch as James and Springer draw closer. Dan raises his pipe in acknowledgement of the two men before turning to Robert to give him advice on basting the roasting carcass.

'Well, what be all this then? Who be worth all this trouble and effort?' asks Springer.

'Why this is for you two. For after today I do not know when we will see you again and I wanted to thank you both for all what you have done,' says Emily as she walks up to the pair of them and gives them a hug and a kiss on the cheek.

'My Victoria might be a little jealous if she be seeing you do this,' says Springer with a grin. 'Where be Bob, George and Jethrow?' he asks.

'We be right behind you,' replies a voice from behind them. 'And I would appreciate it if you two young men would stop that tomfoolery and handling my wife like that, for you have had more from her than I have had in many a month,' yells Bob.

'Huh, and that's all you will be getting, you dirty old man. By God, you would think women were put on this earth just to satisfy men by the way he talks.' Her comments are met with a roar of laughter from all around, but Bob is not deterred by her answer. He walks straight up to her and lifts her off the ground in a huge embrace and spins her around.

'Put me down, you animal,' she squeals as she wriggles out of his grasp and clips him round the head before turning and walking back towards the table with a smile on her face.

George has one arm strapped up in a sling, but it has not stopped him helping the others as best he can. 'Well, while you slept all day, us real farmers finished the footings. Spread out a good foot or more of the hardcore in the way of tile and brick pieces and screened a layer of lime mortar down on the new pigsty floor. And what a grand job it looks as well, even if I do say it myself.'

Jethrow chuckles. 'More like Bob, Dan and myself did the work with George giving instructions.'

George huffs. 'I am a wounded man, bloodied in battle, but I still did what I could,' he says to all who will listen.

Everyone is laughing as Springer speaks. 'From what I be remembering, it be more like thee fell on that there poor man and your portly size crushed him to death. The gun fired under the sheer wei—'

George swiftly steps in. 'I beg to differ, young man. I was like a man possessed. You were lucky to have such a finely tuned instrument of a man with you in that room. In fact, if you had not got in my way, I would have dealt with them all.'

Springer smiles and shakes his head. 'Sure as eggs are eggs, there be not another like you, George. For the world be not of a size to have more than one.'

With all the banter, they do not see Robert and Dan lifting down the roast from its cooking position and placing it on a wooden tray in the middle of the table. It is only when Robert whispers into his mother's ear and she turns round to see the joint ready that she pipes up for all to hear. 'Well, everybody, would you please take your places around the table as our pork has arrived, and I am starving.'

She positions everyone at the correct place at the table while Jess and Prue pour the drinks for all, then take their seats amongst the group. 'Before we start, I would like to say a prayer. It is not usually done in this household, but I feel just for today it is a requirement that is needed under the circumstances,' says Emily as all the party look down at the table.

'Dear Lord, I thank you for bringing all our men home safe, for the addition of new friends and closure to years of turmoil and misery. I thank you for the justice that has finally come to those in need of it and I pray in time you can deliver comfort and peace to those who have suffered loss and pain. For the friends and family we have lost, I hope you have it in your good graces to guide them into your loving arms and show them your kingdom in all its glory. While for those left behind, give them the strength and courage to endure and move on without prejudice, to find happiness once more. Amen.'

The whole group responds, 'Amen.' The prayer makes for a slow start to the meal, especially for Jess, Prue and Rebecca, but with the encouragement of Emily and Bob and all the others, they tuck into the food before them, and the conversation starts up again. As they talk, it is not long before the banter between George and Springer returns and laughter can be heard once more.

Nearly an hour has passed, and all are fit to burst with all they have eaten. James has taken Rebecca for a walk around the farmyard and is now on his way back while Robert is sitting back in his chair eyeing up a piece of crackling he would so dearly like to eat, but has no room to fit it in.

Bob taps the glass in front of him. 'I think this is as good a time as any for a small announcement.' He looks round and waits for Rebecca and James to return to the group. 'My good wife, Emily, has offered Jess and Prue a place to stay until they are ready to move on should they choose to do so, or remain if they so desire. And I am pleased to say they have accepted our offer.' He looks round at his son. 'If that meets with your approval, boy.'

Robert sits up in his chair. There is no doubt that the girls, especially Jess, have set a pulse in his heart. 'Well, yes, if they want to, it would be great, well, should I say, fine with me.'

The girls look at each other and then the rest of the people before Jess speaks. 'It is difficult for us, for we have just lost our parents and at present just seem to feel numb and in disbelief. It is kind of Emily and Bob to offer us sanctuary, at least for a while as we come to terms with our situation. I do not wish to think what would have happened to us if it were not for Springer and George arriving when they did. But we are grateful. Grateful to you all for such kindness.'

There are several nods and taps of the table in acknowledgement of Jess's words but not a lot of noise, as it does not seem appropriate.

Emily, who is sitting between the girls, places her palms on each of the girl's hands and speaks. 'It would be nice to outnumber the men in this house for once and there will always be plenty to do round here, pushing the men to get the work done.'

George taps the table. 'A wise move by such young ladies and what a kind offer by Bob and Emily. As for young Robert, I think he will have his hands full with these two fine fillies putting him to task.'

Jess turns to Robert. 'Are you good with having us around?' she asks with a cheeky smile.

Robert blushes red as he answers. 'Well, yes, I can see no problem with that as long as it is good with you.'

Rebecca is next to speak up. 'While we are talking about the future, James has just offered me a place to stay with his sister and another girl on a vineyard in France for a while.' She turns to Springer. 'I know Victoria would be desperate to see me and I her and your children, my niece and nephew. But I feel perhaps now is not the time. You see, I have been naive and taken for a fool by those I thought had my best interests at heart. I have also taken a bit much for granted, been selfish and spiteful in my ways. Become to some extent what I despise most in a person. Before I visit my sister, I need to find myself and get back to being me again. I am sure, however, that I will return soon and visit her, perhaps even come back here and stay for a day or so, if it would be good with you, Emily.'

'My dear, you are welcome here anytime.'

George coughs loudly to break in on the conversation. 'Well, if that is the case, it is time for me to add my words.' He places his hand inside his sling and pulls out three identical pouches. 'Dan was kind enough to make these out of a piece of leather. I know not where he found the material, but I have learned over time not to ask what I do not really want to hear the answer to.' The group chuckles as he continues. 'But I took this from the safe at the magistrates. I gave most to the families and people we pulled from the mines to help them start over but kept a little back for all you young ladies.'

He passes each one of the girls a pouch. 'A few years back, a couple came to me with less than this. But it was all they had to get their hands on a plot of land for themselves. To me it was more than a king's ransom as it was everything they owned. From that they built themselves a new life and around them a new community of friends and family. I hope that this helps to start you three off on a path in the same way it has done for my closest friends. For they deserve all the happiness this world has to offer for what they do for other people around them.' George pauses for a moment. 'As for me, I also now have closure for my brother and his family. The people who took them from me are now dead or suffering. I feel I can turn a new page and can now look to the future with new friends and family.' He stands up and raises his cup. 'I offer a toast to all here. To absent friends and family, a future of our own making and a long life to live it in.'

The whole group respond by raising a glass or mug. 'To absent friends,' they call out as they take a drink and look around at each other.

The conversation continues for another hour or so with James talking about living in France, his whaling exploits, the trip to Paris to find his lost sister, his family and wonderful wife Emma and the café they run in a small fishing port. It would seem from the way he talks that this will be the last time he will ever visit England. With all his anger and rage now released, the man seems to be finally at peace with all in his life. After all, he was only ever here to deal with a long overdue visit with his brother and take him to task for the things he had said and done to the ones he loved.

Later that afternoon, George, Jethrow, Dan and Springer are tacking up their horses ready for the ride home. They still have a job to do, and with luck, they can collect the stock they have hopefully got to take back to George's estate.

Bob and Emily have said goodbye to everyone at least three times already and are now standing by the entrance to their farm waiting for everyone to pass by. Jess and Prue have finished helping Robert assemble the team of horses on the front of the carriage, have said their goodbyes to both Rebecca and James and are now making a fuss of George – their wounded hero, as they call him – along with the other three riders.

Springer walks over to James and shakes his hand firmly. 'It be a right honour to have met thee, my friend. Take good care of young Rebecca for me and have a safe journey back to your family.'

James smiles at Springer. 'Likewise. It has been an eventful two days and it seems as if I have known you far longer. It would be good to part hoping we would meet up again one day and talk some more in my wife's café while drinking and eating. So, I will not say goodbye but see you soon.' He turns and mounts the front of the coach, watched by Springer until he is in position and holding the reins.

Springer walks over to Rebecca, who is already in the coach and leaning out of the window. 'Fare thee well, lass. I will tell Victoria that ye be a fine woman now, but she will be sad not to see you for herself.'

Rebecca wipes the tears from her eyes. 'Tell her I will visit her soon and that I love her most dear. But for now, I need to be away from here like you both did years ago, find myself again and forget the horrors of this terrible place.'

Springer steps forward and gives her a kiss on the cheek. At the same time, he passes the picture of her sister and their children into her hand. 'She be wanting you to have this, I think. Be sure to use it as a reminder not to be forgetting her.'

She clasps the gift, knowing full well what it is from the feel of its shape. 'Thank you. I might not have seen it before, but she is a lucky woman to have found such a man as you, Springer.'

Springer steps back and watches as James calls to the horses and the coach starts moving off. Rebecca looks at the picture a while before looking back at everyone and waving as she passes them all. Moving their way up the path to the road above, the carriage is soon on the road and making towards the coast and its final journey with James. Within minutes they are out of sight and the sound of the horses' shoes drumming on the ground fades until they also can be heard no more.

It is the turn of the men to leave next. As Springer mounts his horse, the group start to move off. As they pass their friends, they call out their goodbyes and farewells, waving and talking as they go. George may be in pain and strapped up on one side, but he still insists on carrying a special cargo. For wrapped in a blanket and sitting across his saddle is the black-and-white collie, Oscar. His head poking out of the blanket, he is alert and watching all that is going on around him.

For George, this is a big thing. For it is the start of a new breeding line with a dog not of the area. And he cannot wait to see how he will perform out in the fields.

Bob and his wife along with their son and two guests watch until the four riders are out of sight, then turn and head off towards the farmhouse. As they are walking, Bob says to Robert, 'Have you shown Jess and Prue the whole farm yet, son?'

Robert looks at him curiously. 'Well, not the far meadows and high ground to the west, Pa.'

Bob goes quiet for a moment. 'Well, don't you think you should show them all the areas of the farm while Mother and I sort out the house?' He looks at Emily with a wry smile.

'Oh, hell no,' Emily says as she hooks her arms with both girls. 'Let's get in the house, quick,' she cries, as they march swiftly across the yard and step through the doorway. She slams shut the lower half of the door and stares back at Bob and Robert. 'We need more wood for the fire and the animals need feeding, so get on with it, you dirty old man.'

The girls and Robert cannot help but laugh as the dejected Bob turns and heads off to start feeding the animals. 'No respect for me in my own home anymore,' he mutters as he walks across the yard with his collies walking by his side.

CHAPTER 13

The Price We Pay

The four horsemen have now been riding hard for over two days to get back to George's estate and home for all. George has finally passed his dog to Dan to carry as the pain from his wound makes him ache and feel weak. Brandy has been taking the edge off the injury, but it will take a good month to heal before he can begin to use his shoulder and arm with any real purpose. Even then, this type of wound on an elderly farmer will take its toll and will cause him ongoing discomfort.

His arm may be causing him problems, but George's mind is at work ten to the dozen. 'I think when I get home I will start to ride my lands and woods a bit more, pay more attention to all I have acquired in my lifetime,' he says to all that will listen.

Dan rolls his eyes as he strokes the head of the young collie he is now holding while Springer and Jethrow laugh out.

George looks at each one of them in turn. 'What? I am only thinking that it would be a good idea to take a closer interest in the estate, that's all.'

Springer shakes his head before speaking. 'Ye be affected by the drink, George. It be making thee think on things that be not there. Your lands be as safe as any that I have ever known.'

George looks at Springer. 'Oh no, I have been drinking just enough to take away the pain, nothing more. My mind is still as sharp as ever.'

The three men are still chuckling and looking at one another as Springer speaks again. 'George, thee be somewhat of a mind that all over that there land of yours be poaching huts hidden in plain view. Much like the ones you have seen in the past few days. Dan has already said there be none on your land. Let that be the end to it.'

George wants to say a few more words on the matter but thinks better of it. He shuts up and continues riding beside Springer for a while before speaking again.

'Don't be thinking Oscar is yours, Dan. You are only holding him because my arm aches a little and I want him to know the smell of you.' Dan lets out a huge sigh as Springer and Jethrow burst into laughter again. They have pushed hard over the past few days and are now but a few miles from where they were to meet up with their friends and bring home the new livestock.

Springer is starting to get nervous and fidgety. 'Dan, do you think my Vic—'

'Yes, she will know. As Cook can work her ways on me, Victoria would have got it out of Cook, probably within hours of us leaving the farm,' Dan says without even turning round. 'But what should concern you more is when them women see that George has been injured. For I am certain Cook will want to check it out and she will know a pistol hole when she sees it.'

Springer thinks for a minute. 'Why be that there a fear for me to worry on?' he asks curiously. Dan shakes his head and speaks. 'All of them women fuss over George like he's a father figure… and Bebe, well, she will want answers as to why you had George in harm's way and did not protect him well enough. Then there is Victoria, misled by you to start with, and now George returns shot while in your company. I'm telling you now, this will not end well for you.'

'Oh, I not be thinking of that, but then again, this was all his idea. Was it not George who planned the switch to get the going in the first place?'

In the background Jethrow is chuckling to himself. 'You sure be in a pickle, Springer,' he says between bouts of laughter. 'For I would not be in your shoes for all the sheep on the hills.'

Springer looks round at Jethrow. 'I was in as much danger as George! That there fight was as brutal as it gets. Taking on Brannigan, I took many a blow and have the bruises to prove it.'

'Yes, you did, my boy, and what a fine display it was,' says George. 'But as usual, it was I who had to save you from being shot, twice. Not once, but twice, wrestling that man to the ground and taking the hit to protect you.'

'Thee be squeezing him right flat to the floor alright – that part is true. That there man could not point a gun, least of all fire it with thee's hefty figure bearing down on him, for there be no air left in his lungs to breathe. I be thinking now that maybe that there shot be self-inflicted to make me look bad and you to gain favour with the women folk.'

George looks down at his chest and stomach. 'It took me years to get this fine figure,' he says, then looks back at Springer. 'Let's just leave it for Victoria and the little ones to come to their own conclusions on what happened to their poor godfather George. Let them decide the fate of the big nasty Springer.'

Springer just shakes his head while Jethrow and Dan grin at the pair of them.

The conversation stops abruptly as the four men look up the road and stop their horses. For in the middle of the road stands the largest, most fearsome-looking brown-and-white bull they have ever seen. Its back is nearly the same height as their horses, and the horns have almost six feet of width between the two forward-pointing prongs.

Jethrow is first to speak. 'By Christ, what a beast! Do you think that he is friendly?' Just as he finishes his sentence, the bull lets out a huge bellow that unnerves the horses, sending out vibrations the men can feel through their bodies, as it stamps the ground with a front hoof and snorts loudly.

'George, that thing makes your bull Winston look like a goat in comparison,' Jethrow whispers without moving a limb.

As the four men are looking around for options, wondering which way to head off should the beast charge at them, there is a rustling in the bushes beside the bull. 'Here he is, Pa. I've found him on the road!' A young man steps out beside the bull and pats him on the side of his neck before putting a collar round his head and slipping the rope through the ring on his nose.

'We've been looking for you for nearly an hour, Percy, you daft animal,' he says as he rubs the animal's forehead and scratches round his ears. The huge bull rubs his head on the young man, pushing him backwards with the force of each roll of his enormous frame.

George and the others are speechless. They just stare in disbelief as the young man turns the huge bull and walks it up the road as if it was a puppy. Out of the corner of his eye, he sees the men on horses and turns back. A huge smile appears on his face as he recognises them all. 'Well, blow me, we had just about given you up for dead,' says Rob, one of the Underwood brothers. 'Pa! It looks like George and the others are back,' he yells out as he walks the bull towards the four men on horseback. Moments later, Rob's brother steps out from the bushes followed by their father, Ernie.

'By God, we were beginning to lose hope that you would make it back in time, George,' he says.

George slides off his horse and walks up to the bull. He has a love of cattle that goes back years and to see a specimen like this is a real treat. 'My God, man! What is it?' he asks as he strokes the side of the bull's head.

'He be one hell of a sight, eh, George? One to even cast a shadow on your mighty bull,' replies Ernie.

'He must be part English Longhorn.'

'Yes, that he is, George. Crossed with a South Devon for size and gentleness. He should bring some size to the cattle we have round here, that's for sure.'

George looks at Ernie. 'I don't suppose you got this bull for me?'

Ernie looks at George and shakes his head. 'I'm sorry, George. This one is for me. He is a little softer natured. The one I got you is his brother. That bugger is near half a foot bigger at the shoulder and a little feistier.' George's face lights up like a child in a sweet shop, while his companions all look at each other in shock.

'I tell thee all now, I be not going in a paddock with that there's brother. Not for all the game you've ever poached, Dan,' Springer says with true concern in his voice.

Jethrow is just staring at the beast as it turns around again and walks down the road with Rob leading the way and Ernie, Bill and George – who is now leading his horse as he walks beside them asking questions on the breeding of the animals.

'Its balls are bigger than my head. I reckon he will be able to get at every cow in the field without moving from the spot,' says Jethrow.

Springer and Dan laugh. 'I don't think them there cows are going to like what is in store for them,' says Springer.

'How much does that thing eat?'

'I don't know, but I reckon it will need plenty of room when it comes out the other end.' Dan laughs.

The three horsemen follow the walking group into a field about half a mile away, where they meet the rest of the men from George's estate and find a fine selection of quality pigs, cattle, crates of chickens, geese and turkey, some sheep and two goats.

However, the main conversation is reserved for what happened with Lord Fitzgerald and his enforcers. Brannigan, the magistrate, Crossy, Sykes and all the others are spoken about in detail. How they met their end at the hands of Springer, George and Dan. The encounter with the big man James and who he was. Not to mention Victoria's sister Rebecca and the release of the people from the tunnels below ground in the mine. As the facts and demise of each person are discussed in full detail, there are cheers and laughter from the group of labourers who used to work in Pippinsford and were so badly treated.

They hold back on the whereabouts of the bodies and the involvement of Bob, Emily and their son Robert. As they do not want to discuss people who are at risk of being found should the wrong people hear about it. The only disappointment the men have is knowing that Lord Fitzgerald is still alive, and nobody knows the true impact of the injuries inflicted by his brother on that evil man. That is something that will be found out in the months ahead by some of the labourers and their families as they visit friends and family still living in the village.

For now, it is time to head home and face the wrath of the women they know are waiting to administer their justice on the wayward men. As they prepare the wagons and separate the stock for different people, Springer is apprehensive – more so than at any time in the last week – as he will have to confront Victoria with the truth about where he has been and what he has done. The worry of her reaction is heavy on his mind as he has never lied to her before.

They start the wagons and herds moving in the direction of George's estate. Ernie leads the way with his new cattle, bullock and other supplies with his two sons up front with Percy as they will be the first to split off from the group and head off down a fork in the road. The other two tenant farmers head towards their smallholdings with their new stock a mile or so away from Ernie, greatly appreciative and happy with their animals.

George has relinquished his horse to Ivan and can lead his new bull back to the farm himself. He is so proud of this huge animal that he cannot stop looking at it. His new dog, Oscar, is doing his best to help by moving the sheep along. But his enthusiasm and lack of skill have forced him to be put back on a lead.

Being quite a sizeable convoy – with the rumble of the wagon wheels on the road and the animals making such a racket – they are seen some distance away by several people working on the farm. With them yelling and calling to all around who can hear them, others soon join them standing at the entrance, excited to see their loved ones returning.

As the line of animals, wagon, horses and people enter the yard through the gate, everybody stares in awe at the huge bull that has been named 'James' for obvious reasons known only to those returning.

George passes the rope to one of the waiting men, who leads the bull and the cattle to the large barn that has been readied in anticipation of their arrival. All the animals have places waiting for them, as everything was planned in advance. They will all be inspected and watched for a while before being moved around the estate to join the other livestock.

As the wagon passes into the yard, the kitchen door opens, and first out is Fern. She bounds over to George, jumping and bouncing with such excitement at seeing her master. Jennie and Cook follow, with Victoria holding Edward in her arms. Bebe is last out but the first to reach her man as she hugs and kisses George.

Oscar has slipped his rope and joined Fern jumping around George and Bebe. The two dogs stop, stare at each other and crouch, move slowly towards each other as if moving sheep, before tearing off across the yard and into one of the fields, barely more than a foot between them as they zigzag this way and that across the field and back, coming to a halt by George's feet. After a brief pause, they crouch, staring at each other, then tear off again back out into the field and across to the far side of the yard.

George winces in pain from Bebe's hug, a sight that is noticed by both Bebe and Cook, who walks over and inspects the area around the wound. She looks up at him. 'I will take a closer look at this tomorrow, George. For tonight I wish to see my husband and spend time with him. Bebe and Jennie can serve your food as it is already prepared and waiting in the kitchen.'

Cook moves across to Dan, gives him a kiss and a hug then speaks. 'Is it all over with?'

Dan nods. 'Yes, dear. It be over.' She holds his arm as they turn and head towards their cottage on the river.

George walks back towards the house with Bebe. They meet Jennie halfway and he puts his good arm around her shoulders. 'Come, my dear, the three of us have a lot to talk about and I for one am starving.' As they reach the house, Fern and Oscar bolt between their legs through the open door, and both jump into Fern's blanket-covered wicker basket facing George.

'Or should I say the five of us have things to talk about!' says George as the others laugh at the cheek of the two dogs. He stands in the doorway and looks back at Springer. 'I think we can do without you around here for a few days, my friend. Spend time with Victoria and the little ones, for you have earned it by God.' He does not wait for an answer, just disappears inside, closing the door behind him.

Jethrow has already left the yard and walked off into the distance after seeing his wife running down the track from his cottage. This leaves Springer staring at Victoria and Edward. He takes Edward from her arms and places him on his shoulders, puts his arm around his beloved and starts to walk back to their cottage.

'We be one short,' he says.

'No, she is in the house asleep. I was dropping a dress off for Jennie and was on my way out the door when you arrived.' Victoria hugs him tightly and looks at the bruises on his face and neck.

'Did you get done all that was needed on your trip?'

'That we did, lass, that we did.' He looks at her with the saddest eyes, but as he goes to speak, she gets her words in first.

'It took me two days to get it out of Cook, longer than ever before. Will you tell me all what really went on, or do you want me to go after Cook again for the answers?'

'If thee wish, for it seems like you have a time to work on me with your womanly ways.' He smiles at her and holds her a little tighter.

'But what I will give up for free is that a young Rebecca be sending you her love and said she may well visit in the near future.'

Victoria looks at her man. A smile appears on her face before she turns and looks forward. 'You, my man, have no idea how much my womanly ways are going to open you up, for in a week you will not have a secret left that I will not know about.' The couple walk on along the track and through the spinney to their cottage overlooking the valley. It would seem that for now, at long last, a level of harmony and peace has entered their lives.

As they enter their cottage, the need to look over their shoulder to see if anyone is watching them has finally gone. Though it might take some time to get used to that kind of normality.

* * *

Back in Pippinsford, a week on from the chaos left by Springer, James and the others, Lord Fitzgerald's world is collapsing like a deck of cards. His enforcers are all but gone, some missing or absconded while others he knows are dead. His hold on the village has diminished as the people have grown in confidence and taken back control of their lives. The fear and intimidation from Brannigan, Sykes, Crossy and others is now gone. The corrupt magistrate is dead, and his men are on the run from those seeking retribution for the cruelty they imposed.

With so many people released back into the village and surrounding area after Springer and James freed them from below ground, stories of what they have been through spread like wildfire. People who had been thought missing or moved to better parts of the country now speak out about their abduction and forced labour. They tell all who will listen about their experiences, from the moment they were taken through to where they had been held and by whom. The news spreads through the local villages and towns, filtering out further and further until even the king and parliament hear about the events at Pippinsford and send officials to investigate the claims that the king's subjects have been mistreated on a grand scale. Most of the people released are still afraid, surround themselves with family and friends for protection and begin to rebuild the lives they once had.

All the wealthy people of influence, nobility, politicians and such like are severing their ties and associations with Lord Fitzgerald in a bid to save their own skins from the scandal that now ensues. They now refuse any dealings with the man, his factories or any produce that he provides in an attempt to distance themselves from the investigations.

With the cash flow from these sources virtually stopping overnight, other areas of his business empire begin to suffer as well. Supporters and investors that once flocked to his side now disappear to avoid the witch hunt for anyone connected to him. The factory he was once so proud of closes then burns to the ground as people take revenge for the atrocities carried out behind its walls. The mine is sealed shut, with the entrance dynamited to ensure it is never used again. His many fruit farms fall into disarray as the farmhand's rebel and fight back. Those who lost their farms to him and still live return to claim what was once theirs.

Lord Fitzgerald himself is bedridden. Just like James predicted, a fever burns inside him like nothing any of the physicians around him have seen before. Temperature, sweats, shakes take their toll on the man's body as they fight to keep him alive. But the thin, deep razor cuts that were stitched up within hours of being inflicted continue to swell. The stitches either rip through the skin or are cut away to relieve the pressure. Each time the cuts are re-stitched, they react and tear open, again and again. The wounds themselves are festering and weeping pus, and the smell of the dying and rotting tissue fills the air around him. Every wound across his body seems to be ulcerating in the same way, festering out of control, scarring and disfiguring his body.

Those so-called learned men of the medical profession who surround him daily try leeches, bleeding, potions and remedies stretching back to a bygone era, but nothing seems to quell the fever or infection that rages and eats into the man's organs. Lord Fitzgerald suffers in continued pain while these men try ever more obscure methods to heal his wounds. What none of them realises is that this kind of infection will come and go for the rest of his life. The wounds will reopen and ulcerate periodically, even after they look fully healed. The infection will ultimately eat into his bones and joints and continue to cause pain and suffering until the day he dies. Such is the potency of the necrotic properties of stingray venom, in combination with all the additions James had loaded onto the blade.

From the moment these cuts were inflicted by his vengeful brother, Lord Fitzgerald was doomed to enter a world that would scar and slowly disfigure his body and curse him with a never-ending state of ailments.

As time passes, Lord Fitzgerald becomes more incoherent and unable to function at any level for days on end. The juniors in his ranks along with his benefactors try to keep his affairs in order, looking to buck themselves up in his favour as he recovers. But without his constant input and the enforcers to force his will, they have little chance of holding back others like him from taking what they want from his empire.

Just as predicted, when the alpha male shows weakness, others will try and take his place. And in the case of Lord Fitzgerald, having held a party for nearly four hundred of the most powerful and influential people in the land, all are now fully aware of what happened to him and his men that night. Now, many of them seek to grab any and all opportunities that may present themselves. As the weeks go on, many of his so-called friends take to breaking down his estate, taking all they can get. A building here, a farm there. Payments and bribes to accountants and benefactors to release another lucrative property or factory.

Fitzgerald's life is now one of survival, dictated by how well he can fight for his existence in this world. Wealth, status and his position in social standings diminish by the day as his rivals cut chunks from his once mighty empire. Over the next six months, he spirals down the ladder of society, losing his businesses, estates, and any wealth he had squirrelled away to pay his crippling debts and buy off people to keep him out of jail. The loss of all his deeds and papers he once used to control those he needed has allowed many to break away without fear of reprisal. Many return to the great city, their adventures in country life now satisfied and a return to the capital a more desirable option.

When he finally has nothing left and nobody to turn to for assistance or aid, Lord Fitzgerald is cast out onto the streets he once ruled with nothing more than the clothes on his back. He quickly descends into another world where just staying alive becomes a challenge all of its own. As his health deteriorates, he becomes what he most hated in the world – a beggar, scrounging and stealing whatever he can to stay alive. He ends his life as a disfigured tramp living in the shadows of society. Moving from one village to another, selling wild stories in the local taverns of a once wealthy lord, in return for scraps and the odd drink from them that feel sorry for this poor lost soul.

The last ever sighting of him was over a year later by a group of farm labourers telling him not to travel across the peat bog they were cutting fuel bricks on. They warned him that some of the ground had very deep pools of water below the thin crust of matted vegetation and as the night was closing in, he should stick to the safety of the nearby pathways. They did not know who the man was, just that he was desperate, down on his luck and walking in an area that was treacherous and full of danger. They showed caring and compassion for his safety, even offering him some food to take on his way.

But to these concerned men, as he did to so many others in those last few days, he just cursed at them, throwing sticks and rocks in their general direction before scurrying off into the darkness and the unknown beyond. This time though, it was across an ancient bog he did not know and a fate known only to him.

From that day forth, he was seen no more. The legend of Lord Fitzgerald and his once great empire was now but a memory of times gone by.

* * *

As one man's empire falls from its towering heights to oblivion, the rest of Europe is in turmoil as countries feud over land, sea and the unknown rest of the world. The diplomatic war between France and England has escalated, and France aligns with Spain in the hope of breaking the stranglehold the English navy has over the oceans. Napoleon Bonaparte is moving through Europe, cutting a swathe of victories with his huge armies and famed old guard. Ever on his mind are plans to invade England and rule his enemies so no more can they hound his every move.

Far away in the Pacific, this war has now arrived as the great nations attempt to colonise the islands for control of its resources and strategic location, allowing trade to flow home and fund the war effort along with great riches and wealth for their monarchies and emperors.

On this front, the Spanish and French have stolen an advantage over the English, having already conscripted mercenaries and tribesmen allied to their cause with promises of treaties and a percentage of the prize. They clear the islands of all the native people, killing the old and most of the men and keeping only the fittest for manual work building the stockades and warehouses in preparation for invasion. They enslave the women to service and care for their armies by using their own children to control them.

As with any great plan, it is only as good as the information used to form its objectives. In the case of the village of Boranui on the island of Nuku Hiva, they strike when most of the men of the village are either away at sea in a fleet of fishing canoes or trading inland with the forest people. But far worse than not killing all the men from this village is not knowing who they are. For this is no savage tribe of simple natives. It is run by tribal elders with a vision to prepare its people for the oncoming of civilisation. They welcomed foreign people to settle amongst them, provided they abided by the elders' rules and assisted in the education of their people. Many of the men here were once whalers, soldiers or sailors, serving on ships around the islands. Remaining after service, they now have wives and families and know they would not be able to adapt to living in western society. The events that now follow such an unprovoked attack will rock these so-called civilised nations and their invading armies to the very core.